"A suspenseful plot . . . and surprises galore."
—*The San Diego Union-Tribune*

"A thrilling story."

—*Pittsburgh Post-Gazette*

AND PRAISE FOR HER SUSPENSE-CHARGED NOVELS
FEATURING NEWS REPORTER
IRENE KELLY

"Jan Burke's Irene Kelly stories [feature] tense and thoughtful plots, writing that manages to be sharp and sardonic without calling attention to itself, [and] a Southern California setting that skips all the clichés. . . . [An] excellent series."

—*Chicago Tribune*

"A skilled writer. . . . Jan Burke is on the fast track."
—*USA Today*

"Gripping . . . compelling . . . Jan Burke doesn't come up for air until every detail is nailed down."

—*Michael Connelly*

"Spine-tingling, nerve-fraying, breath-suppressing suspense . . . in the mystery pantheon with Patricia Cornwell, Sue Grafton, Robert B. Parker, and John Sandford."

—*The Tennessean*

"Fans of Patricia Cornwell will appreciate her plot-driven tales."

—*Alfred Hitchcock's Mystery Magazine*

"Jan Burke raise[s] the emotional ante with each succeeding book . . . a witty and resourceful writer."

—*Los Angeles Times*

Books by Jan Burke

JAN BURKE

EIGHTEEN

Introduction by Edward D. Hoch

POCKET BOOKS

New York London Toronto Sydney

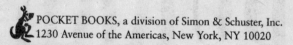 POCKET BOOKS, a division of Simon & Schuster, Inc.
1230 Avenue of the Americas, New York, NY 10020

Copyright © 2002 by Jan Burke
Introduction copyright © 2002 by Edward D. Hoch

ISBN: 0-7434-8051-1

First Pocket Books printing January 2004

10 9 8 7 6 5 4 3 2 1

POCKET and colophon are registered trademarks of Simon & Schuster, Inc.

Cover design by Ray Lundgren

Manufactured in the United States of America

For information regarding special discounts for bulk purchases, please contact Simon & Schuster Special Sales at 1-800-456-6798 or business@simonandschuster.com

"Sub rosa" ("The Loveseat") Spannen Gebundeld 1993, Dutch language suspense anthology published by Bruna/Meulenhoff. Reprinted in Duivelse fantasieën, Meulenhoff, 1999.

"Why Tonight?" *Alfred Hitchcock's Mystery Magazine,* Mid-December 1993. Reprinted as "Warum heute?" in Im Strandkorb: Das grosse Sommerlesebuch, Goldmann, 1999. E-published by MightyWords.com.

"The Mouse" 1993, 2001. First published in this collection by A.S.A.P. Publishing.

"Revised Endings" Viva (Dutch language magazine) 1994. English language version in *Murderous Intent* Mystery Magazine, Summer/Fall 1998.

"Ghost of a Chance" *Red Herring Mystery Magazine,* Summer 1994.

"Unharmed" *Ellery Queen Mystery Magazine,* Mid-December 1994. Reprinted in special limited edition with introduction by Wendy Hornsby and illustrations by Phil Parks. A.S.A.P. Publishing, 1996. Reprinted as "Ongedeerd" in Spannen Gebundeld, Bruna/Meulenhoff, 1996. Reprinted as "Ongedeerd" in Duivelse fantasieën, Meulenhoff, 1999.

"The Muse" *Alfred Hitchcock's Mystery Magazine,* February 1995.

"White Trash" *Alfred Hitchcock's Mystery Magazine,* October 1996.

"Mea Culpa" *Malice Domestic 6 Short Story Anthology,* edited by Elizabeth Foxwell and presented by Anne Perry. Pocket Books, 1997. ISBN: 0-671-89633-4. Read by Reed Diamond on audio edition of *Malice Domestic 6,* Dove Audio, 1999. ISBN: 0-7871-1719-6

"A Fine Set of Teeth" Signed special limited edition, bound and illustrated, with introduction by Michael Connelly. Also, an audio version with music by Tim Burke and reading by Jan Burke. A.S.A.P. Publishing, October 1997. Reprinted in *Alfred Hitchcock's Mystery Magazine,* October 1998. Reprinted in *Women of Mystery III,* edited by Kathleen Halligan, an anthology of short stories from *Alfred Hitchcock's Mystery Magazine* and *Ellery Queen Mystery Magazine.* Carroll & Graf, 1999. ISBN: 0-7867-0570-1

"Two Bits" *Ellery Queen Mystery Magazine*, May 1998.

"A Man of My Stature" In *Crime Through Time II: Historical Mystery Short Stories*, an anthology edited by Miriam Grace Monfredo and Sharan Newman, presented by Lady Antonia Fraser. Berkley Crime Prime Mystery, 1998. ISBN: 0-425-16410-1

"Miscalculation" In *Death Cruise: Crime Stories on the Open Seas*, an anthology edited by Lawrence Block. Cumberland House Publishing, 1999. ISBN: 1-58182-007-0

"An Unsuspected Condition of the Heart" In *Irreconcilable Differences*, an anthology edited by Lia Matera. Hardcover edition by HarperCollins, 1999. ISBN: 0-06-019225-9. Paperback edition by William Morrow & Co., April 2001. ISBN: 0-06-109733-0

"The Man in the Civil Suit" In *Malice Domestic 9*, introduced by Joan Hess. Avon, 2000. ISBN: 0-380-80483-2

"The Haunting of Carrick Hollow" written with Paul Sledzik. In *Crime Through Time III: Historical Mystery Short Stories*, an anthology edited by Sharan Newman and Miriam Grace Monfredo. Berkley, July 2000. ISBN: 0-42517-509-X

"The Abbey Ghosts" *Alfred Hitchcock's Mystery Magazine*, January 2001.

"Devotion" 2001. First published in this collection by A.S.A.P. Publishing.

CONTENTS

INTRODUCTION

Let me tell you about Jan Burke.

I remember thinking sometime during the early 1990s that the baby boom had finally hit the mystery field. Each month brought a crop of new young writers to publishers' lists, people I'd never heard of and probably would never read. When Jan Burke's first novel about reporter Irene Kelly, *Goodnight, Irene*, appeared in 1993 it caused barely a ripple on my consciousness. Even when it was nominated for both the Agatha and Anthony Awards that year I didn't feel the need to read it. There were too many other books and too little time for them all.

My opinion began to change the following year when *Ellery Queen Mystery Magazine* published her small gem of a story called "Unharmed," which promptly won that magazine's annual Readers Award. While publishing a new Irene Kelly novel each year, Jan was also turning up with increasing frequency in magazines, anthologies and limited editions. One story, "A

Fine Set of Teeth," was unique in having an audio version read by the author with music by her husband Tim Burke. It was the first Irene Kelly short story and I found it a delightful mixture of music and mystery, with some very funny musician jokes along the way.

Though I'd seen Jan at various writers' gatherings over the years, the first time we had a real conversation was at the 2000 Left Coast Crime gathering in Tucson. We were sharing a table in the signing room after our panels, autographing books and magazines for fans, when a member of the organizing committee came along, urging us to attend the 2001 Left Coast Crime in Anchorage the following year. The event included a plan to fly some writers in small planes to remote communities that had rarely if ever been visited by an author. Inviting someone from cold and snowy Rochester to visit cold and snowy Alaska in February was an exercise in futility and I quickly declined. However I was more than a little surprised when Jan seemed interested in the trip. It occurred to me then that she was a rare writer indeed, one interested not just in promoting her own books but in publicizing all mysteries, all reading, to those who might never have been touched by the pleasures the written word can bring.

Two months later at the Mystery Writers of America awards dinner in New York, Jan Burke won the Edgar for *Bones,* judged the best novel of 1999. It was the first of her novels I'd read, but certainly not the last. In February of 2001 Jan did indeed go to Alaska, and in May of that year she won the Agatha Award for her story "The Man in the Civil Suit," published within *Malice Domestic 9.*

Jan has played an active role in writers' organizations, chairing several promotional programs for Sisters in Crime and most recently serving as president of MWA's Southern California chapter. But it is her short stories that interest us here. Those readers who know her only through the Irene Kelly novels will be surprised at the wide range of style and subject matter in these eighteen stories, two of them published here for the first time.

Certainly Irene is here, and one new story, "Devotion," brings back some familiar characters from *Bones*. But you'll also find unusual historical mysteries like "Miscalculation," "An Unexpected Condition of the Heart," "A Man of My Stature," and "The Haunting of Carrick Hollow," all showing remarkable degrees of research. There are stories of kidnapping and murder, stories for dog-lovers and Hitchcock-lovers, and one new story, "The Mouse," that has no crime in it at all. You'll even find a couple of ghost stories lurking here. One of them, "The Abbey Ghosts," is a fine tale already included in an anthology of the year's best mysteries.

Read them, enjoy them! Jan Burke is the real thing.

Edward D. Hoch
Rochester, New York

NOTES ON THE STORIES

This collection includes my first short stories and my most recent. I haven't been at this all that long, but I hope you'll enjoy the mixture of tales within. Here's a little background on the stories you will find here.

"Devotion" and "A Fine Set of Teeth" feature characters created in my novels. "Devotion" is a new story written especially for this collection, and several of its characters are from *Bones*.

Ben Sheridan plays a major role in "Devotion," and as always, I enjoyed writing about him. Judging from my mail, readers like him too. Like other amputees, he is who he is—not defined by this one difference. If he helps to dispel some myths about amputees along the way, that's thanks to the many people who helped me create him by openly talking to me about their own lives after limb loss.

The dogs are also back. In addition to what I learned about SAR dog work from dog handlers who helped me with *Bones* and *Flight*, bloodhound handler Milica Wilson of Colorado gave me information that was invaluable for this story.

"A Fine Set of Teeth" is the first Irene Kelly short story, and was first published by A.S.A.P. Publishing. My husband, Tim Burke, is a musician, and some of Irene's experiences in this story are drawn from life. Our friends had a field day contributing the musician jokes.

In addition to "Devotion," two other stories will be new to most of my readers. "The Mouse" is published here for the first time. It isn't a mystery story, but it's close to the bone. "The Loveseat" was my first published work, but until now, it has never been published in English. Although I had sold *Goodnight, Irene* before I wrote "The Loveseat," the book was not published until almost a year after this story appeared in a suspense anthology in the Netherlands. Meulenhoff, which publishes my novels in Dutch, will always hold a place in my heart because my editor there recognized the story's dark humor.

"Why Tonight?" was the first of my stories to be published in the U.S. I sold it to *Alfred Hitchcock's Mystery Magazine* not long before *Goodnight, Irene* was released. I was thrilled to make it into this magazine, which I had read for many years. After several years, I still have an attachment to this story, although I'm not exactly sure why—perhaps it's the Kansas setting.

"Unharmed" debuted in *Ellery Queen Mystery Magazine*—another magazine stacked in piles next to my bed. On the way home from work one night, Tim heard a news story on the radio. He thought I might be able to do something with it if I wrote it from a certain perspective. He had no sooner finished telling me about it, than I excused myself, ran into my office, and wrote "Unharmed" in one sitting. Tim had to finish making dinner that evening, but he didn't seem to mind.

Many of these stories reflect my love of history. I'm especially grateful to Sharan Newman, who heard me complaining about a character—a medieval knight in my imagination who really wouldn't leave me alone. She offered me the chance to write an historical short story. She didn't get the story about the knight (he still pesters me from time to time), but she did give me a home for "A Man of My Stature"—it's inspired by a true crime which took place in the U.S. in the late nineteenth-century. I took the basic idea behind the crime and came up with a different set of problems for the narrator than the ones which led to the capture of his real-life counterpart.

Others inspired by true stories are "The Haunting of Carrick Hollow," "Two Bits" and "Miscalculation."

"The Haunting of Carrick Hollow" was the result of my first and (so far) only attempt to work with a writing partner. I doubt anyone else could have made it as painless as Paul Sledzik did. Paul's a good friend who works as a forensic anthropologist, has been the Curator of Anatomical Collections at the National Museum of Health and Medicine, and (among other areas of expertise) is known for his ability to recognize tuberculosis in skeletal remains. He came up with the question that became the center of this story, and wrote some of the most difficult scenes. My hope is that he'll continue to try his hand at fiction, because I found his work on this one to be exceptional. The story is set in late nineteenth-century New England.

"Two Bits" was inspired by a famous kidnapping case of the nineteenth century—I read about it while researching *Hocus*. I married this true story to some observations made by a searcher concerning a much more contemporary kidnapping. The outcome and the family portrayed in the story are entirely fictional, a blend of all these elements with lots of "what if?"

"Miscalculation" is set aboard the *Queen Mary* and based on a little known fact about the ship's wartime service. I read a single sentence in a large book about the ship, and that sentence so disturbed me, I decided I needed to explore the *Queen Mary*'s history for more information. As it turns out, it's not easy to get anyone to talk about this particular tragedy, and I appreciate the help given to me by those who confirmed my early research into the matter.

Two stories are set in Regency England: "An Unsuspected Condition of the Heart" and "The Abbey Ghosts." I became attached to the Regency through the works of Jane Austen and Georgette Heyer. Terry Baker of the Mystery Annex bookstore knew I loved Austen's works, and introduced me to those of Heyer. Heyer's wit, insight, and knowledge of that period helped me to escape the grim images that were left dancing in my head while I researched *Bones*. When I read her books at night, I'd be magically transported to the world of the *haut ton* before I fell asleep. "An Unsuspected Condition of the Heart" is an homage to Ms. Heyer, but no one should take that to mean that I think I've captured her style or come close to her achievements—she was one of a kind. I enjoyed writing it, but I have never done so much research for so few pages in my life. I have a fondness for this narrator, so he may return.

"The Abbey Ghosts" is a different style of story, although also set in Regency England. Audrey Moore of the bookstore Mysteries to Die For, in Thousand Oaks, California, asked me to write a Christmas story. To my surprise, it also ended up being a ghost story. Cathleen Jordan kindly chose to publish it in *Alfred Hitchcock's Mystery Magazine*.

"The Man in the Civil Suit" is a humorous story written for the *Malice Domestic 9 Anthology*. The anthology was a tribute to Agatha Christie, and contributors were asked to include some reference to a Christie title or work somewhere in the story. *The Man in the Brown Suit* has always been a favorite of mine.

Writing short stories allows me to venture beyond the world of Las Piernas, the contemporary beach city in the Irene Kelly books. "Mea Culpa" is set in the 1950s, and allowed me to explore writing from the point of view of a young boy. "White Trash" and "Revised Endings" allowed me to play "what if" in situations where one might feel frustrated enough to do violence. "The Muse" allowed me to write a story interwoven with references to the films of Alfred Hitchcock.

Some years ago, I'd been reading ghost stories in preparation for a Halloween event at Beth Caswell's Sherlock's Home mystery bookstore when I decided to try my hand at one that might be a little different. "Ghost of a Chance" was first heard by Beth's customers.

To all the mystery writers, past and present, whose

short stories have delighted me, my thanks for giving me a love of this form. My thanks to Jim Seels, Cathleen Jordan, Janet Hutchings, Martin Greenberg, Sharan Newman, Miriam Grace Monfredo, Elizabeth Foxwell, Lia Matera, and the many others who've worked so hard to bring mystery short stories to readers. And most of all, my thanks to you who read our stories, who keep the fine tradition of the mystery short story alive. I hope you'll enjoy this collection.

Jan Burke
Southern California

EIGHTEEN

THE LOVESEAT

THE SHOVEL HALF-RANG like a muted bell as it struck the metal. Leila Anderson sighed and stopped digging, wiping the back of her leather glove across her forehead. She was hot and tired, but determined to finish planting this last section of her garden.

She turned from the corner where she had been working and looked across the big backyard. It should have been *our* garden, *our* yard, *our* house, she thought to herself. Sam should be here with me.

But he wasn't. Samuel Barrington had left her for a girl of twenty-two, a girl who made mooning cow's eyes at the silly man. Before Cow Eyes—Marietta Hinchley—came into the picture, Leila had known exactly how things were going to be. She knew that after four years of being engaged, she and Sam would finally marry; knew that they would move out of the apartment they had shared and into a lovely house;

knew that she would keep getting promotions at the investment firm she worked for; knew that Sam would continue to be able to pursue his doctorate in mathematics, because she, Leila, would support them, just as she always had. And most certainly, back in those golden days, Leila had known what was expected of her. Her ability to predict and her own predictability. That was Leila's life.

But Sam had surprised her. She hadn't ever been fond of surprises, and this one did nothing to endear them to her. "You're so reasonable, Leila," Sam had said that day. "I know you'll understand." Leila would always be his friend, Sam had told her, but in Marietta, he had found passion.

Passion! Didn't he know she, Leila, was capable of passion? Of course she had always been controlled around him. She had eschewed the sentimental, been the "reasonable" woman he had come to rely on. As logical as his beloved mathematics. The habit of it was ingrained in her so deeply, that even as he was telling her of his unfaithfulness, she had reacted just as she had known Sam would want her to react, exactly in the way he had come to depend on her to react: reasoned, calm, controlled. But that was on the outside. Inside, she raged. Raged passionately.

So used to pleasing Sam, though, she was determined not to let him know how wounded her pride was. She reasoned that at that particular moment, the only psychological weapon she had to defend herself with was her dignity, and she used it like a knife.

She had met Marietta the next day. Sam, oblivious to the tension between the two women, had begun his "let's all be friends" campaign without delay. A beautiful, slim, athletic, young woman, Marietta had tried hard to upset Leila's equanimity. She made allusions to Leila's age, which was not more than eight years above her own; she hinted that Leila was out of shape, which was untrue. Leila was not the athlete that Marietta was, but she was no slouch. Sam had seemed a little displeased with Marietta's lack of grace. And Leila knew that while Sam had been relieved and grateful that she had not fallen apart, Marietta had been hoping for a tantrum, a scene. Marietta, Leila had seen in a moment, was a bitch. Leila had smiled, certain that Sam would more than do his penance.

He would do his penance, but at that moment he was too smitten with Marietta to realize what he had let himself in for. He saw Marietta as a lonely child, dependent on him for guidance. He later tried to apologize to Leila for Marietta's bad behavior, saying that Marietta was alone in the world, without family to guide her. Sam thought himself capable of teaching her manners. Leila thought it was the biggest joke Sam had ever played on himself, but said nothing.

Hoping that living well was indeed the best revenge, she went on with her life. She had chosen this house on her own and bought it. The house had been built in the 1920s, and she loved its polished wooden floors and arched windows and tall ceilings. The day after her furniture was moved in, she went to work on the garden with all of the passion she had leftover from the end of her relationship with Sam. She dug up old, neglected flower beds and planted them with bright, beautiful blossoms: impatiens and fuchsia and pansies and geraniums; a wild, unpredictable mix of anything that would give her eye a moment's pleasure.

She planted pink jasmine and roses along the high stone fence that surrounded the big yard. She was glad of the privacy that fence gave her yard, her little oasis of color and fragrance.

She had saved this corner for last. A week ago, while pruning back the poorly tended honeysuckle that had overgrown this corner, she discovered something that had made her cry. Beneath the vines she had found something made of stone, broken in two parts. When she had realized it was a loveseat, it had suddenly come to symbolize her broken romance with Sam, and for the first time since the day he had told her of Marietta, she had cried. Four months of bottled pain and humiliation burst from her like champagne from an uncorked bottle, and cold, predictable, passionless Leila wept in her garden.

The relief of it had been great. Later she called her old friend, Arnie, who was a landscape contractor. Arnie, who had benefitted more than once from Leila's ability to chose investments, was happy to make arrangements to have the broken loveseat hauled off. The day after it was gone, Leila went back to work in the garden.

On this warm June day, she had dug up about two feet of soil in the area of the corner, preparing to plant a last trio of rosebushes, when the shovel had rung out. She knelt down on all fours, picking up a small hand spade, and tried to clear away the soil that covered the metal object that was thwarting her progress. Thinking of Sam and Marietta, she dug with furious movements, showering dirt everywhere, some of it landing in her hair and on her clothes. Before long, the spade struck the object as well. She scraped aside enough of the soil to reveal a dark, rusty piece of metal. Curious, she continued to dig at the soil surrounding it. It was flat and smooth. She reached a curving edge and burrowed with her hands to grasp the edge of object. She tugged and pulled, and suddenly it came free, causing her to fall back on her rump. Dirt flew everywhere, and she laughed as she looked at the heavy object on her lap. A frying pan.

"Why would anyone bury a cast iron skillet upside down in the corner of a garden?" she wondered aloud. It was heavy and large, but there were no special markings on it. She set it on the brick walkway which curved past the area she was working on. She brushed herself off and looked into the hole from which she had pulled the skillet. A shiny object caught her eye, and once again she used the hand spade to clear the soil away. She soon had freed enough of the soil to see that it was the lid of a jar, and could tell that the jar was still attached.

Feeling a certain mild excitement, as if she were a backyard archeologist, she carefully worked around the jar, finally freeing it. She brushed it off with a gloved hand and held it up. A Mason jar, filled with old-fashioned buttons. The glass of the jar was thick, and she wondered how old it was. She set the jar next to the skillet, trying to make sense of them, and of their burial.

Unable to succeed in solving that puzzle, she stood up and went back to work with the shovel. But she had not been digging very long, when once again the shovel struck an object. She knelt again and went to work with the hand spade. This time, she found a small, crude wooden box, about the size of a shoe box. The blow from the shovel had splintered the lid, and inside the box was a small canvas bag filled with old marbles. She continued to use the hand spade.

An hour later, she had an odd collection on the walkway: to the skillet, the button jar and the marbles, she had added an old pocket watch, a wedding band wrapped in a linen handkerchief, a fragment of stained glass. The handkerchief bore pretty embroidery, and the initials "CG"; the inside of the ring was inscribed, "*Chloe and Jonathan, 2-22-41.*" There was no inscription on the watch, but the crystal was cracked and the hands stopped at 6:10. Again she wondered why this particular group of objects had been buried here. A child might bury marbles, maybe even buttons, but a skillet? A wedding ring or a pocket watch? Why hide such objects? It was unsettling.

Leila continued to dig, and the next discovery brought her up short. The toe of a rubber boot. She was afraid to touch it, afraid the boot would still be attached to the owner. She stared at it, wondered if she should call the police, then smiled to herself over this unexpected nervousness. Still, when she reached down to move the soil away from it, her hand trembled. *The toe of the boot felt as if it had something in it.*

Timidly, she used the small spade, afraid to reach down into the soil with her hands. But as she made her way through the layer surrounding it, she saw no bones or rotting flesh. She pulled it free and held it upside down, spilling most of its contents on the walk. The boot held a woman's black leather shoe, and nothing but more soil. She pulled the shoe out. Further digging led to no new revelations.

Leila gathered the collection of objects and took them back to the house, where she cleaned them off as best she could. She poured a glass of red wine and sipped it thoughtfully while she took a long, hot bubble bath in her claw-foot bathtub. She climbed out when the water began to chill, and made her decision.

"I appreciate your coming by on such short notice," Leila said to her guest, as they reached the back patio.

Alice Grayson smiled as she looked across the backyard, then back at the young woman who had invited her here. "You've done wonders with it."

"Thank you."

"As for the notice, I am no different than most old ladies; I have more time than opportunities. And I must admit your invitation intrigued me. Buried treasure in the backyard of the house you bought from me?"

"Have a seat, please," Leila said, gesturing to a rattan patio chair that was next to a low table. The table, covered with a lumpy cloth, held what Alice Grayson assumed was the "treasure."

Leila took a seat on the other side of the table and poured a glass of wine for each of them. "How long ago did you live here, Mrs. Grayson?"

"Alice. No need for formality. And it's Miss Grayson. I never married. And I never lived here."

She laughed at Leila's look of surprise.

"This house belonged to my uncle, and then to my brother. I inherited it from him."

"Jonathan?"

It was Alice Grayson's turn to look surprised. "How on earth did you learn his name?"

"I believe I found his wedding ring, along with a rather strange assortment of other objects." Leila lifted the cover.

"Good Lord," Alice said, and her blue eyes grew watery.

Leila watched her in silence, amazed at how discomposed the older woman seemed. She had met Alice Grayson only once before, when the escrow had closed, but had taken an immediate liking to her. Alice had told her that she was in her seventies, but Leila thought she seemed more lively and energetic than Leila did at thirty. Alice seemed to have liked her too, giving her a phone number to call should she have any questions about the house. Leila knew that she couldn't have expected the questions which actually did arise.

"I'll be happy to give all of these things to you," Leila said. "They seem to mean something to you. But please, can you tell me why this particular set of objects was buried here?"

Alice dabbed at her eyes. "Forgive me. I'm sorry to be so emotional. After all these years, you wouldn't think that I could react so strongly. Yes, certainly." She sighed. "Where to begin?"

She reached over and picked up the gold band. "This was Jonathan's wedding ring; his wedding ring from his first marriage, to Chloe Manning. Chloe was a lovely young girl. They were both young; she was nineteen years old, he was about twenty-one, I believe. It was just before the war."

"In February of 1941? That's the date on the ring."

"Yes. That April, our uncle died after a long illness and left this house and his store to Jonathan, who had worked for him. Jonathan and Chloe were very much in love. She was pretty, and full of life and laughter, and she spoiled him rotten. She was an excellent seamstress.

"He thought her the perfect wife in all but one regard. She was a terrible cook. But Jonathan didn't want to hurt her feelings so he always ate the meals she made for him with a smile. I lived just down the street then, and he'd come over to visit me after dinner, and groan and down bottles of antacid. She caught on, and one day gave him a large, heavy box with a big bow on it. There was a big, cast iron skillet in it. She laughed and told him she would help him run the store if he would help her cook."

"Do you think this is that same skillet? Why would he bury it?"

"I would be surprised to learn it was not that skillet. As for why, well, perhaps it is best if I continue to tell you their story.

"In December of 1941, they had a little boy, William, named after my uncle. He was born two days before Pearl Harbor. Jonathan was drafted. They were very brave about it, as were most people then. Chloe and I ran the store, and Little Billy kept us too busy to feel sorry for ourselves."

She paused and took a sip of wine.

"She was staying with me then; she had rented her place out to a group of women who worked at a war plant. One rainy night, after we closed up the store, Chloe told me she was going to stop by our little church on the way home. It was the winter of 1944. Jonathan had been wounded and was being sent back home. Chloe had been worried about Jonathan; said she hadn't been able to sleep much, and wanted to pray for his safe return. Billy cried when she tried to get him to leave with me when we reached the steps of the church, so she took him with her. I still remember them standing under their umbrella on the steps, giving me a little wave."

She stopped again, her eyes filling with tears.

"Please, I didn't know this would be so painful for you," Leila said. "Perhaps you'd rather tell me another time."

"No, no, I'll be all right. All of this happened almost fifty years ago. You'd think I'd be able to talk about it."

"Time might heal our wounds, but that doesn't mean we forget how much they hurt in the first place."

Alice smiled. "Something tells me you know something about being wounded, Leila. Well, you may be right. Still, I owe you an explanation for my brother's odd behavior.

"So, on that night, I went home alone in the rain. It had been raining hard for a couple of days. I waited, but they didn't come back. Finally, I put on my raingear and walked back to the church. There were firemen and emergency vehicles blocking the street. The roof on the church had collapsed. It had been a flat roof. The scuppers on the drains from the roof had been plugged by leaves, and the water built up on it until it just gave way. Chloe and Billy were killed."

"I'm sorry."

Alice shook her head. "I identified their bodies. They took them away. I sat there, next to the place they had been killed, unable to move, getting drenched by rain. I kept wondering how I could possibly tell Jonathan about what had happened. A policeman tried to get me to go home. I saw one of Chloe's boots; I guess it had come off of her when they pulled her body out. I picked it up, and a piece of stained glass that lay next to it. Don't ask me why. I didn't know then, and I don't know now. The policeman walked me home. On the porch step, he handed me Jonathan's pocket watch and little bag of marbles. Billy had been carrying them."

After a moment, Leila said, "And Jonathan? What became of him?"

"He was devastated, of course. I worried for a while that I would lose him, too. He wasn't quite recovered when he returned, and with Chloe and Billy gone, he just didn't seem to have the will to live. He pulled through, though. The war workers who lived here were laid off and moved on, and he moved back into the house. He went back to the store and went on with his life. He began to talk to me more about Chloe and his son, seemed able to cherish their memory instead being beaten down by it."

"You said Chloe was his first wife. Did he marry again?"

"Yes. Not right away, mind you. About fifteen years later, he met another woman. Monica."

She said the name with obvious distaste.

"You didn't like her."

"Not in the least. She was an Amazon of a woman, and bossy to boot. But Jonathan was lonely, and had been for years. And I think she appealed to him on some—hmm, *basic* level, we'll say. He was turning forty, and she made him feel, well, virile.

"Just before Jonathan and Monica were married, Jonathan told me that he was going hide all of his reminders of Chloe and Billy from his new wife. He said Monica was insanely jealous of their memory, which he couldn't understand."

"Can you?"

"Of course. Monica could see for herself that Jonathan's heart still belonged to his first wife. How could she compete with a memory?"

"But Jonathan was aware of her jealousy?"

"Yes, even Jonathan could see that. He told me she had destroyed his favorite photo of Chloe. He decided he wanted to keep his reminders where Monica couldn't harm them. Now, thirty years later, you've found the place where he hid them. Where were they?"

"Beneath the loveseat."

Alice looked back to the corner of the garden where the loveseat had been. "I should have guessed. You've had the pieces taken away?"

"Yes, I'm sorry if it was special to you in some way."

"No, not to me. But it was to Jonathan. He used to sit there with Chloe. An extravagance for newlyweds, but the house had come to him furnished by my uncle, so that loveseat helped them to make the place their own. In much the way you have, with this garden. Jonathan would have loved this garden."

"How was the loveseat broken?"

Alice laughed. "That was the time Monica went too far. They weren't married for more than a year or two when they started having problems. She'd throw tantrums, and he just withdrew more and more from her. He'd come out to the garden.

"One day, Jonathan was sitting on the loveseat, doubtless remembering happier times. Monica came striding across the yard, carrying a sledgehammer."

"What?"

"Yes, a big old sledgehammer. She lifted it up over her head and brought it down with all her might. Jonathan barely got out of the way in time. Busted the loveseat in half."

"Was she trying to kill him?"

"Jonathan told me he didn't believe she meant to harm him, but I don't think he was certain of that. In any case, they separated, and she went off to live with a sister in some other state. He divorced her. He was disappointed, but he didn't seem overly bitter. Said that maybe he'd caused it by hanging on to his memories of Chloe. He lived here by himself until he died, about a year ago now. I miss him."

Alice looked away for a moment, then turned back to Leila.

"In the last ten years he was pretty much crippled up by arthritis, and he couldn't take care of this yard. You've made it beautiful again, you've brought it back to life. As I've said, it would make Jonathan proud."

"Thank you. It sounds strange, but I'm sorry I didn't get to know him."

"You would have liked him. I think he would be quite happy that you are the one who came to live here. I think Chloe and Billy would be, too."

They chatted for a while, and then Leila brought out a small box and loaded Jonathan's mementos into it.

"After all your hard work, you should keep something for yourself," Alice said. "I know they're rather silly little treasures, but are you sure there's nothing here you'd like to have?"

"They aren't so silly after all, are they? And they've been buried together for all these years. I wouldn't want to separate them."

"So, you *are* sentimental after all." Alice smiled. "Don't look so surprised, Leila. When you bought this old house, I wondered about you. You seemed so business-like, so self-possessed, so emotionless. But why, I asked myself, would such a modern person want such an old house? I don't know who made you believe that feelings don't matter, but they were very wrong."

Leila looked out across the yard. "You know, Alice, until I moved here and worked on this garden, I don't think I would have been able to understand that." And before she knew it, Leila had told Alice the story of Sam and Marietta.

Alice listened patiently. "This Marietta sounds a lot like Monica. A perfectly dreadful girl. But I'm not sure Sam has forgotten you any more than Jonathan forgot Chloe. I think Sam just needs to wake up and realize that you're a person with feelings. It sounds as if you've been more like a mother, or perhaps another male friend, than a partner to him. The next time you see him, don't be afraid to let him know you have feelings. And if he can't respond to them, find a man who can."

Leila laughed and thanked her.

Alice gave her a hug, and carrying the box of treasures, took her leave.

Leila made a big bowl of soup for dinner, went to bed and slept soundly.

*   *   *

The next day was a work day. She noticed that for some reason, men in the office were paying attention to her. She wondered if they had paid attention before, without her being aware of it, or if something about her had changed.

Later that evening, in line at the grocery store, a good-looking man stood just ahead of her. He smiled at her. When she smiled back, he spoke to her, laughing with her about an article featured on the cover of a tabloid. Suddenly, she heard a familiar voice calling her name.

"Leila?"

She turned to see Sam and Marietta at the next checkout stand. She waved, and turned back to talk to the man who had been flirting with her. "Friend of yours?" he asked.

"Former boyfriend," she whispered, as the checker handed the man his change.

The man looked back at Sam and Marietta and shook his head. "He's crazy," he whispered back, and to her shock, leaned over and kissed her cheek. "Goodbye, Leila," he said loudly, "Don't forget our date!" He winked and smiled as he walked out with his groceries.

Leila blushed deeply, but then smiled to herself. The checker had to announce the amount she owed twice before Leila returned her attention to matters at hand. As she pushed her cart from the store, Sam came up beside her.

"Who was that?" he demanded.

"Who?"

"The man with whom you just made a spectacle of

yourself. The one who kissed you in the store. Or are there so many men kissing you in public that it is no longer a memorable experience?"

"Really, Sam, I don't think it's any of your concern."

Before he could answer, they heard Marietta from behind them. "Sam!" she wailed as she tried to catch up to them with her own cart. "Sam, get over here and help me."

"Your master's voice," Leila said, and started to load her groceries into her car.

"What's that supposed to mean?" he said angrily.

"Leila, is this fellow bothering you?"

She turned to see the man from the store. He had pulled up next to them and rolled down his window.

Sam looked so dismayed, it was all she could do not to laugh out loud. "No, he's an old friend," she said to the man. "He was just going back to his car to help his girlfriend."

They all turned to see Marietta stomp her foot in impatience.

"Girlfriend?" the man said. "I only see his daughter."

"Oh, no," Leila said, unable to stop the laugh. "That's his girlfriend."

"Now see here—" Sam began, but fell silent as the man opened his car door and stood next to it. He was at least six inches taller than Sam.

He extended a hand. "David Kerr," he said amiably.

Sam shook the hand awkwardly. "Sam Barrington," he mumbled. To Leila, he said, "I'll call you later," and excused himself.

"Thanks for the rescue," Leila said to David, when Sam had left.

"A pleasure. As your knight in shining armor, do I deserve to know your last name, Leila?"

"Leila Anderson," she said. "It was going to be Leila Barrington before that sweet young thing happened along."

"You're hopelessly stuck on him, aren't you?" he asked.

"I'm afraid so."

"Well, we're two peas in a pod. My ex-wife shops here with a fellow I call 'Junior' on Tuesdays. If you want to return the favor, I'll meet you here tomorrow night at six."

Leila laughed and agreed to see him there the next evening. She said goodnight and whistled as she drove home.

On Thursday night, Leila invited Alice Grayson to dinner. They giggled like schoolgirls over Leila's recounting of the last three days. Tuesday night, David's ex-wife had ignored the young man she was dating, nearly pushed Leila aside and said flat out that she missed David and would like to see him for dinner sometime soon.

David had thanked Leila, and they promised to keep one another posted on their progress.

On Wednesday, Sam had stopped by her office to ask her to go to lunch, an unprecedented event.

"I'm worried about you, Leila," he had said.

"Why?"

"How well do you know this David Kerr?"

"Not well at all."

"That's what I mean! And you kissed him in the store!"

"I believe he kissed me."

"You're mincing words and you know it. Okay, so you were kissed, but you allowed it. Right in front of everybody! That's so unlike you!"

"Maybe I've changed, Sam."

He sulked in silence for a moment, then said, "I'm not sure I like the change. I liked you the way you were before."

"You dumped me the way I was before."

"Leila! That's an unkind way of putting things."

"It was an unkind way of doing things."

He had the good grace to look guilty, but said nothing.

"It's true, Sam. You all but said I was passionless. And I can see why you thought so. It's my fault, really. I hope Marietta gives you all the passion you can bear."

"There's more to life than passion."

"Really? Such as what?"

"Stability, reliability, companionship."

"Don't forget faithfulness."

He turned red and looked away. After a moment he said quietly, "I really hurt you, didn't I?"

"Yes."

"I'm sorry."

"Don't be, Sam. Thanks to you, I have a whole new life."

"With David?"

"No, probably not with David."

He seemed about to say something, but he hesitated. She decided not to wait for him to make up his mind to tell her what it was. "I'd better get back to work, Sam."

"Yes, I suppose so," he answered distractedly.

As they stood outside the door to her office building, he suddenly hugged her, nearly throwing her off balance. "Listen, I'm really quite fond of you, Leila. We are friends, aren't we?"

"Of course," she said, freeing herself from his embrace. "Goodbye, Sam."

"Excellent!" Alice exclaimed. "Although I'll warn you, Leila. Watch out for Marietta. From what you've told me, she won't take any of this very lightly."

Leila invited Alice to come over on Saturday afternoon. "I'll be planting the roses in the back corner. I called my friend, Arnie, and ordered another loveseat. He's going to try to find one similar to the old one. He thinks he can have one here by Monday, so I need to get the roses in place."

On Friday, Sam came by her office at lunch time again. Leila had already agreed to have lunch with some of her coworkers, and summoning all of her willpower, she told Sam she would not be able to join him. "Let me take you to dinner, then," he said.

She hesitated. "What about Marietta?"

"She's got an aerobics class until ten. She has aerobics every night," he added glumly.

"All right, I'll meet you for dinner. Where?"

"Café Camillia at eight?"

She smiled. The restaurant was a favorite of hers, and Sam knew it. "Fine."

That evening, she put on a rather daring dress, one she had bought on impulse. *Impulse,* she thought, liking what she saw in the mirror. What a heady new feeling this occasional obedience to impulse had given her!

When she arrived at the restaurant, Sam was already there, nervously wringing his hands. When he saw her, he looked as if someone had just sent enough electricity through him to light Manhattan.

"Leila?"

"Yes, Sam, what's the matter?"

"You—you look lovely."

"Why, thank you."

But throughout dinner, Sam hardly spoke a word. He looked unhappy. She began to think that the whole evening was a miserable failure. Maybe he was wishing he hadn't invited her to dinner.

"Sam?"

He looked up at her, startled.

"Sam, are you regretting this?"

"Oh. No, not at all."

"You don't seem very happy."

"I'm not."

"Why? Have I done something wrong?"

"No, I have."

"What do you mean?"

He shook his head. "Forgive me, Leila. I haven't been good company this evening. I've got some thinking to do." He glanced at his watch. "Marietta will be home soon. I'd better go." He motioned for the waiter and paid the check.

He walked her to her car. Suddenly, he said, "Leila, do you still care for me?"

"Yes, Sam. You're still my friend."

"I don't mean as a friend. I mean, do you think you could still care for me?"

She smiled at the anxiousness in his voice. "I think you already know I do."

"What do you see in me, Leila? I've cheated on you, broken our engagement, been a cad. I didn't want to admit it before, but I have been."

"I agree. But I think it has been for the best. We each had things to learn, didn't we?"

"I'm just afraid the tuition may have cost me too much."

"Talk to Marietta. I admit I don't like her much, but she deserves to know how you really feel. Then come and tell me how you feel about me. But not until then, all right?"

He nodded, then watched as she drove off.

Leila had just finished mixing a huge bag of mulch into the garden soil when she heard the sound of the gate opening. At first, she thought it was Alice Grayson, but she turned to see an odd vision of Marietta, taller than usual, gliding toward her. Then she realized Marietta was on skates. Of course, Leila thought, the latest fitness craze. They were a fancy, in-line pair, with fluorescent pink wheels. As Marietta drew closer, Leila saw that her face was a hard mask of fury, and she was flying toward Leila like a Valkyrie on Rollerblades.

"You bitch! You miserable old bitch!" she shouted, and tried to grab on to Leila.

Frightened, Leila dropped the shovel and started to run toward the house, but the skating Marietta was faster. Leila was amazed at the other woman's agility. Marietta caught hold of Leila's hair and yanked hard. Leila came to a halt and Marietta slammed into her. Leila toppled to the ground, landing facedown in the dirt. Marietta fell on top of her. In no time flat, she had her hands around Leila's throat, choking her.

"Sam is mine! I won't let you have him!"

Leila couldn't breathe. Her head pounded as she tried to pry Marietta's fingers from her throat. But Marietta was strong, and her fingers didn't budge.

"Let her go," Leila heard a voice say, but everything around her was swimming out of focus.

"No! I'm younger, I'm prettier, I'm stronger—"

"You're dead," the voice said, and Leila heard the shovel ring out once again. She fell into darkness.

Sam and Leila were sitting on the loveseat. Two rosebushes grew on one side, a third on the other.

"Marietta still hasn't come back," Sam said. "I think she's left me for good."

"I wouldn't be surprised if you never see her again," Leila said.

"I suppose you're right. She went absolutely insane when I told her that I had decided to beg you to take me back. The language she used! Called me things I never imagined anyone would ever call me. And when Miss Grayson called that evening to tell me that Marietta had come by to attack you like that—"He looked at the bruises on her throat and winced. "I'm so sorry, Leila. You should have called me sooner."

"I didn't want to worry you. I'm fine now, really."

"Anyway, I'm glad Miss Grayson called me. I guess it was while I was over here with you that Marietta cleared all of her things out of our old apartment."

"Alice was a great help that day," Leila said, thinking of the apartment key that was now in a jar of buttons. She leaned back against Sam, who put his arms around her. "I'm glad you came over to see me."

"Of course! You needed me."

They sat in silence for a while, Sam holding Leila close, amazed by how strongly he had felt about her lately. Oh, he had thought of her often during the few months he had spent with Marietta, but somehow, something had changed in Leila since she had lived in this old house. He looked at the riot of colors around him. Amazing, he thought. And this loveseat. That seemed so sentimental, so unlike the old Leila.

"You planted this garden yourself?" he asked in wonder.

"Yes, all except this corner. Alice Grayson helped me with this one."

"Ah, that explains the loveseat."

Leila merely smiled.

It seemed to Sam that he had never desired her more.

WHY TONIGHT?

W**HY TONIGHT?**
As she lay staring up at the lazily circling blades of the ceiling fan, Kaylie asked herself the question again and again. She wasn't sure what caused her to ask herself that question more than any other, especially as there were certainly other matters she should be addressing before the sheriff arrived. But through the numbness that surrounded nearly every other line of thinking, one question occurred to her repeatedly, refused evasion by tricks of distraction: Why tonight?

Was it because of the heat? It was hot tonight. But then, it wasn't the first hot summer night in Kansas. Even her grandmother used to say that the devil couldn't be found in Kansas in August; in August he went back to hell, where he could cool off. No, the heat had not decided this night would be the night that Joseph Darren died.

She had met the man whose body hung from a rope tied to the rafters of the garage on another, long-ago August night, when she had gone down to the small, man-made lake on the edge of town, hoping it would be cool there.

She had talked Tommy Macon into driving her down there that night. She smiled, thinking of Tommy. Tommy who used to have a crush on her. Tommy, taking her out to drag Main in his big old Chrysler. Kaylie calling 'Hey!' to Sue Halloran, just to rub it in. Sue calling back, half-heartedly, like a beaten pup.

Willowy. That's what Joseph called her that night. If his eyes had moved over her just a little more slowly, it would have been insulting. He had taken in her skinny frame, a body she dismissed with the word 'awkward' up to that moment, that moment when Joseph asked, "Who's the willowy blonde, Tommy?"

When he introduced them, Tommy, who would never be a Thomas, whispered to her, "Don't never call him 'Joe'." He needn't have bothered with the warning. She knew from that first moment that Joseph would be extraordinary. He would never be "an average Joe." Tommy was sweet and clumsy, but she was too stupid in those days to see the advantages of being with a sweet and clumsy man.

She sighed, closing her eyes. Too late to mourn the loss of Tommy, still married to Sue, and five kids and fifty pounds later would stay married to her. Kaylie couldn't even bring herself to contemplate the idea of mourning Joe. She tried it. Not mourning him— calling him Joe.

Joe. Joe. Joe. She said it like a curse. *Joe you.* It suited him now, she decided.

He was a poet, he had told her, when he was Joseph. A poet. Tommy confirmed it. Tommy, naively bragging on a man he hadn't even realized was already his rival. Joseph's poetry had been in every issue of the *Butler County College Literary Magazine* every semester he had been there. Tommy didn't claim to understand it all, but he thought it was pretty interesting that Joseph used all small letters, like that Ogden Nash—no, hell, no, that e.e. cummings fellow. That, and did Kaylie know that Joseph could recite all of the words to "American Pie" and tell her exactly what they all meant?

Joseph never did recite "American Pie" for her or unravel its meaning. Too late now.

Kaylie shifted to her side, looking out the top half of the bedroom window. The busted air conditioner sat in the bottom half. It made her mad just to see that air conditioner, so she forced herself to look up over the top of it.

The refinery was still burning. Flames, in the distance, reflected odd colors off the clouds of smoke that billowed and rolled into the night sky. Even with the wind blowing most of it away from town, the air was filled with the stench of burning oil and gas, and doubtless would be for some hours.

Maybe it was the fire. Was that why Joseph had died this night, and not some other night? Had the stinking, burning oil made the sky so different tonight, so different that things had come to this?

She turned away from the window, restless, unwilling to watch it, knowing neighbors had died there tonight. No time to think of that, not now.

Damn, it was hot.

She wondered if Joseph's students would miss him. He had always managed to have a coterie of A.Y.M.s around him. That was one of Kaylie's secrets, calling them that. An A.Y.M. was an Adoring Young Miss, and many of them had fastened their hungry, barely-lost-my-innocence gazes on Professor Joseph Darren.

And why not? He could have been a Made-for-TV English Professor. He taught poetry, was a *published* poet (mostly through a small local press owned by a childhood friend). All those A.Y.M.s thought he was *so sensitive.* (Their own boyfriends were sweet but clumsy, and *so immature,* i.e., not twenty years their senior like Professor Darren.) He was handsome and tall and distinguished looking, with an air of vulnerability about him. Slender but not gaunt. Big, dark, brooding eyes. Long legs. Long lashes. Long, beautiful fingers.

His fingers. Only one of Joseph's poems had been published in the *American Poetry Review,* and it was Kaylie's favorite. For some years now, it had been the only one she could stand to read. It was a poem about something that had really happened. It was a poem about the time he righted a fallen chair, the chair beneath his mother's dangling feet, and stood upon it, then reached up and placed the fingers of one hand gently around her ribs, and pulled her to him, holding her until he could use the fingers of the other hand to free the rope from her neck.

He had shown the poem to Kaylie not long after they met, and told her that his mother had committed suicide one hot summer day. Kaylie could see at once that he was a troubled man who needed her love to overcome this tragedy. Thinking of that poem now, she held her own strong hands out before her. Had she taken him that seriously then? Well yes, at eighteen, the world was a very serious place. At forty, it was serious again.

But the poem had genuinely moved her, and after they were married, she had sent it off to the *Review*. Joseph had been unhappy with her for sending it in, told her she had no business doing so without his permission, and he was probably right. But in the end, it had been that poem in the *Review* that got him the teaching job.

Joseph's talk of his travels around the world had pulled at her imagination. He had travelled a great deal after his mother died. His father had passed away the summer before, and there was an inheritance from that side of the family that he came into upon his mother's death. Joseph told her of places he had been, of Europe and Northern Africa and India. She had pictured the two of them travelling everywhere: riding camels on the way to the Pyramids, backpacking to Machu Pichu.

But after they married, he didn't want to go anywhere. He had satisfied his wanderlust, it seemed. When she complained about it, he gave her a long lecture about how immature it was of her to want to trot all over the globe, to be the Ugly American *Turista*. Those other people didn't want us in their countries, he told her. Besides, he couldn't travel: he had to get through graduate school.

So she washed his clothes and darned his socks and typed his papers instead of riding camels. One of her friends was almost a feminist and told her she shouldn't do things like that for him. But her almost-feminist friend was divorced not long after that, and, as Joseph asked Kaylie when he heard of it, *didn't that tell her something?* Soon she stopped having anything to do with the woman, because Joseph told Kaylie that the woman had been coming on to him. Now, she wondered if it was true.

There had been years of small deceptions, she knew. He had seemed so honest in the beginning. She had misunderstood the difference between baldly stating facts and being honest. On the night he told her about his mother, he also told her about his daughter, Lillian. He said he loved Lilly, but he didn't marry Lilly's mother exactly because she had tried to trick him into marrying her by getting pregnant. He might as well have said, *"Let that be a lesson to you."*

When he finished graduate school, Joseph told Kaylie that he had decided against having any more children. He had a vasectomy not long after he made that announcement. She was twenty-one then, and didn't object very strongly; it was a disappointment, but she could understand Joseph's point of view. She told herself that they would have more time to do the things they wanted to do. And even every other weekend, Lilly was a handful.

But somewhere around thirty-five, it became more than a disappointment. It was a bruise that wouldn't heal. Every time her mind touched upon it, it hurt.

By then, their isolation was nearly complete. They were estranged from her family and most of the people she knew before her marriage. Their few friends were his friends; their hobbies, his hobbies; their goals, his goals. He reserved certain pleasures for his own enjoyment. Infidelity was one of them.

Her own private pleasures were far less complicated. Four years ago, she had planted a garden, perhaps needing to give life to *something*. Joseph never
liked what she chose to plant there, but otherwise, he
ignored it.

Jim Lawrence, on the other hand, had liked the garden. One day when he was driving his patrol car past
the house, he had seen her trying to lug a big bag of
fertilizer to the backyard. He had stopped the car and
helped her. When he saw the garden, he smiled and
said, "Well, Kaylie, I see Professor Darren hasn't
taken all of the farmer out of you yet." He spent time
talking with her about what she had planted, compli-
menting her without flattery.

For a while, after he had left that afternoon, she felt
a sense of loss. But as she continued to work in the
garden, that passed, and she began to mentally replay
those few moments with Jim Lawrence again and
again. She began to think of them as a sort of infidelity. She took pleasure in that notion.

That brief, never repeated encounter made the garden all the more valuable to her. She had spent a long
time in the garden late this afternoon, watering it, trying to protect it from the heat. She had gone out to it
again in the early evening, after supper but before the
summer sun was down, letting its colors and fra-
grances ease her mind, cutting flowers for her table.

Jim Lawrence parked the patrol car next to the curb in
front of the Darren house, allowing himself the luxury
of a sigh as he pocketed the keys. This had been one
helluva night, the worst he had faced since becoming a
sheriff's deputy, and it was far from over. He had been

glad to let the high muckety-mucks take over at the refinery. He had no desire to try to juggle the demands of firefighters, OSHA, oil company men and every kind of law enforcement yahoo between here and God's forgiveness. Let the sheriff handle it himself.

The task he had been given that night was bad enough. He had spent the last four hours getting in touch with families who lived outside of town, out on farms, and bringing someone from each family to the temporary morgue at the junior high school. Mothers, fathers, wives, husbands—brought them into town to help identify the bodies ("No, Mrs. Reardon, he wasn't fighting anybody. His fists are up because . . . well, that's just what happens to the muscles in a fire." How could you say *that* gently?) For some, all they could do was give some needed information ("Who was his dentist, Mr. Abbot?") to the harried coroners.

Emma, the woman who worked dispatch, did her best, but she was fairly new on the job and ill-prepared for a disaster of this magnitude. In the midst of the chaos that came with the refinery fire, she had managed to log a call from Kaylie Darren, asking Jim to come by, no matter how late, whenever he had a minute. It was important that he come by, but it could wait.

Emma hadn't managed to find out what Mrs. Darren had wanted. He tried to guess, figured she must be having problems with her neighbors. Maybe the Hanson's teenage sons had been causing her some trouble. They had been knocking over mailboxes, setting off firecrackers and making general nuisances of themselves this summer. Hormones and heat. Bad combination.

Still, Kaylie wasn't the type to complain about such things. He had known her back before she was Mrs. Darren. Kaylie Lindstrom. They went to high school together. She was blond, blue-eyed, skinny. Just started to fill out some when Joseph Darren had nabbed her. Have to give the son of a bitch that much—he had foresight then.

Jim mused over all he knew of Joseph Darren. Mother was a suicide. He had lived in Wichita for a while, got a girl pregnant. He gave his daughter his name, but never married her mother. Had the daughter with them every other weekend. Of course, that was when she was little. Daughter was grown by now. Hell, she must be—what, twenty-two? Older than most of the students Joseph Darren was rumored to be sleeping with. Jim remembered hearing that the daughter was married not long ago. Maybe she did better for herself than Kaylie did.

He thought of the day Kaylie had shown him the garden. He thought she had seemed starved for attention, and he had meant to come by again sometime. But maybe *because* she seemed starved for attention, he had hesitated to do so.

He got out of the patrol car and walked wearily toward the house, wondering if Kaylie knew her garage light was on.

She met him at the door, opened it and beckoned him inside before he could knock. Must have been watching for the patrol car. He stood in the front hallway, studying her for a moment. She looked good, slender and fit, but she was tense and talking too fast. Asked him to come in, thanked him for coming over, said she knew that he probably had his hands full what with the fire and all and . . . and trailed off, apparently not able to say whatever it was she had to say. His weariness left him then. He realized that something very serious was going on; she hadn't called to complain about the Hanson kids or anything like that. He already knew he wasn't going to like it.

He had seen this before, when a person had something they wanted to tell him, but couldn't lay his or her hands on the starting thread of the story. He would make the first tug, so that she could begin the unravelling.

"Emma was a little flustered tonight, Kaylie. She didn't tell me what it was you needed to see me about."

"No, I—I guess I forgot to tell her."

Tug or wait? He waited. She was looking up at him now, searching his face. Goddamn, it was hot in this house. What was she looking for?

"Kaylie?"

"Joseph's dead."

Wait. Keep waiting, he told himself.

"He's in the garage."

"Why don't you show me, Kaylie?"

She nodded. He followed her into the kitchen, to the door leading to the garage. When she opened it, there was another blast of heat, and as he entered the garage he realized that the clothes dryer was on. But that distracted him only for a moment.

Jim saw the feet first. The shoes, black leather shoes; dark gray socks; sharply-creased gray pants, stained; fingers curving, hands limp at his sides; long-sleeved white shirt (stray thought: must have been hot, wearing that thing on a day like today); red tie, collar, rope; head bent forward, eyes open and staring down; rope continuing to rafters. One straight, still line of lifelessness. Ladder not far away. All baldly illuminated from overhead by a single light bulb in a white ceramic socket.

Behind him, Jim heard the rhythmic hum and whisper of the dryer.

In front of him, Kaylie swayed a little, and he caught her to him, letting her bury her face on his shoulder. She didn't cry, she didn't even put her arms around him, just leaned into him. He held on to her.

Joseph Darren's lifeless eyes continued to stare down. Jim stared back.

You son of a bitch. Just like your mother. Wasn't that enough to teach you what this would be like for Kaylie, coming in here to find you like this?

"Let's go back into the house," he said.

She looked up at him. Didn't say anything, didn't move. Kept watching his eyes. What was she looking for?

"Shouldn't we cut him down?" she asked.

"No, I'm sorry, we can't. With this fire, well, I'm afraid we'll have to wait a while before I can get a crime scene team out here."

"A crime team?"

"An investigator, a criminalist, whoever else they want to call in. And a coroner. A suicide is a reportable death. I'm sorry, Kaylie; it's the way I have to handle it. Let's go inside."

She let him lead her back into the kitchen. He closed the door to the garage and felt her relax a little as it clicked shut. The kitchen was bright and gleaming, its white-tiled counters scrubbed, the white linoleum shining. The second hand on a round, plain-faced, battery-operated clock ticked away the time with small, jerking movements. On a dish drainer below it, two plain, white dishes, a wine glass and two sets of silverware were drying. On the kitchen table, a red vase held a wild assortment of summer blossoms, mostly roses.

"From your garden?" he asked.

"Yes, I brought them in today. Can I get you something cold to drink?"

"Thanks, that would be nice. I'll be back in a minute."

"You're leaving?"

Looking at her troubled face, he felt another surge of anger toward the man in the garage. Hell, and he hadn't done so well by her himself; left her waiting around with her husband's corpse for several hours.

"Just for a minute. I'm just going to go out to the car; I'll be right back. You'll be all right?"

"Yes. Yes, of course."

Hot as it was outside, it was actually cooler than in the house. The stench from the fire was all that kept him from asking Kaylie to talk to him on the porch. He called in on his radio; Emma, who was feeling guilty about not taking a better message from Kaylie, called him back and told him that she had tried to get the county people to cooperate, but it would at least an hour before they could get anyone out to him. He gathered up his clipboard and forms.

On his way back to the house, he noticed the air conditioner in the bedroom window. He wondered why she wasn't using it.

They sat at the table, drinking lemonade, both silent for a time. He decided that he would get the business end of all of this over and done with, so that he could spend the rest of the time he waited with her as a friend, not an officer of the law.

"I need to ask you a few questions, Kaylie."

She nodded. "Go ahead. It's all right, Jim."

She was tense again, he could see. He didn't want to make this any harder on her than it already was. Slowly, he told himself. Take it slow and easy. "Did your husband go to work out at the college today?"

"Yes. He was at the college most of the day. He has a full schedule for summer session. I'm not sure exactly when he got home—I was working in the garden this afternoon. But I heard the phone ring and came in to answer it; Joseph had already picked it up. That was at about five o'clock, and it looked like he had just walked in not too long before that."

"He was dressed like he is now?"

"Yes, that's what he had on. I think Lillian called before he had a chance to change."

"Lillian? His daughter?"

"Yes. He talked to her. I—I know there's never any one reason for these things, but the call seemed to upset him."

"Why?"

She looked away. "I shouldn't have said that. It's my fault, not Lillian's. I don't think I ever made him very happy."

"Kaylie."

She looked back at him.

"Don't do that to yourself. Please."

She said nothing for a moment, then sighed. "You're right, of course."

"Tell me about the phone call."

"Lillian called to say she was pregnant."

"That upset him?"

"I know it sounds foolish, but you have to understand Joseph. He was so afraid of growing old. That's why he had those affairs with his students."

He looked at her in surprise.

"Yes, I knew about them. It's a small town, Jim. I got 'Dear Abby' clippings in the mail whenever she ran a column on cheating husbands. Or some anonymous 'friend' would call me and tell me that she had seen Joseph going into a motel outside of town."

"Good Lord."

"It doesn't matter now."

"Maybe. Maybe not."

"It doesn't. I don't think he saw himself as being much older than his students. Working at the college—well, all I'm saying is, the news that he was going to be a grandfather really shook him up."

"Did he say anything to you about it?"

"No, not much. But he didn't change his clothes or go on with his usual routine. He started drinking wine, so I hurried and made dinner, trying to get him to put some food in his stomach. But he kept drinking throughout dinner. I should have known something was wrong then. But when I hinted that he should stop drinking, he became quite foul-tempered. I didn't feel like putting up with it, not in this heat. So I went back out to the garden. I spent quite a while out there—maybe if I had stayed with him . . ."

"Kaylie, don't. None of this is your fault."

She was silent for a time, then said, "I'm sorry. You must have other questions."

"Not too many more. Had he been depressed or anxious lately, other than tonight?"

She reached toward the vase and absently touched a petal on a yellow rose. "I guess it doesn't do any harm to talk about this now."

He waited.

She plucked the petal and held it to her nose, then let it fall to the table. "He didn't talk to me much, Jim. Not about anything. But recently he had started taking Valium. I don't even know the doctor who gave him the prescription."

"Do you know when he last took any?"

She shook her head. "The bottle is in the bathroom. Do you want me to get it for you?"

"No, that's okay, I'll take a look at it in a minute. Did you see him again after you came in from the garden?"

"No—I mean, not alive." She reached up and took another petal from the rose. "This is the part I feel the worst about," she said softly. She looked over at him, studying him.

What is she looking for?

She dropped the petal, reached for another one. "I didn't know he was out there. I was out in the garden, then cutting flowers and arranging them in this vase. I thought he had gone out, or that he might have gone to bed early. Then I heard the explosion over at the refinery, and I stood out on the porch and watched the flames for a little while. I turned on the radio and listened to the news about it, listened while I washed dishes, cleaned the counters and mopped the floor. Then I went into the bedroom, where it was cooler. I can't say I was especially surprised that Joseph wasn't there. I go to bed alone quite often. Sometimes he comes in late."

Jim found himself staring at the door to the garage.

"I didn't go out there until much later," she rushed on. "I had some laundry to do. That's when I found him. I came back inside and called you—I mean, called the sheriff's office."

Emma had logged the call in at about nine, when things were still hopping from the fire. "So the last time you saw him was about when?"

"I guess it would have been about six-thirty."

"And do you know what time it was you came in from the garden?"

"A little before sundown; before eight, I suppose."

He looked at his watch. It was just after one o'clock in the morning; the refinery had been burning since eight-thirty. The man could have been out there in the garage for a long time. In this heat, even the coroner might find it difficult to set a time of death very accurately. He did as much of the paperwork as he could, then asked if she would mind if he looked around.

She didn't object, but asked him if it would be all right if she waited back in the bedroom. "It's cooler in there," she explained.

Remembering the air conditioner, he understood.

He looked over the living room and the professor's study. If Joseph Darren left a suicide note, it was not on any of the clean and tidy surfaces of either room. There was, in fact, nothing very personal in them. Next he looked through the bathroom. Towels and washclothes neatly folded on the rack; chrome on the fixtures shining, toothbrushes in a holder, toothpaste tube rolled from the bottom. No thumbprint on the bottom edge of medicine cabinet, like you'd see in his own house.

All the contents were in well-ordered rows. The medications were lined up, labels facing out. Non-prescription on one side, prescription on another. The Valium bottle was there, half-empty even though it was recently refilled. Maybe the professor had considered pills before he decided to stick with family traditions.

The other prescriptions were mostly leftover antibiotics; none past their expiration dates. There was only one made out to Kaylie. Premarin.

Premarin. Where had he heard of that before? He stretched and yawned. Premarin. Oh, sure—his mom had taken it. Estrogen, for menopause.

Menopause? Kaylie? Maybe she needed it for some other reason. She was only forty, for godsakes. Some women went through it that early, he knew. But Kaylie?

Well, if she was going through it, she was. It didn't really bother him. No children, but at forty, maybe she didn't want to start a family. Hell, she was going to be a grandmother. Step-grandmother.

He felt a familiar sensation. Tugging at a mental thread.

Something had bothered him, earlier. In the garage. The light being on? No, he could understand that. She wouldn't turn it off, not with him in there. She walked in, saw him hanging there, probably was so shaken she ran back out and didn't venture back in.

But she *had* ventured back in. He knew then what it was that had bothered him. The dryer. Lord Almighty.

He leaned against the sink, suddenly feeling a little sick to his stomach. What kind of woman washed a load of laundry in the same room where her husband was hanging from the rafters?

Slow down. Slow down, he told himself. It was weird, no doubt about it. But not necessarily meaningful. Maybe she cleans when she gets upset. The house was so immaculate, it was almost like being in a museum.

He would just ask her about it. He walked to the bedroom door and knocked.

"Come in," she called.

He opened the door. This room, unlike the others, was slightly in disorder. The bed was rumpled, although made. An old-fashioned walnut dressing table held a silver mirror and brush and comb, a few lipsticks and other make-up items, a couple of small bottles of perfume and a small cluster of earrings, as if she had been sorting through them, choosing which pair she would wear. Photographs of a couple he recognized as her parents, long dead now, took up most of the rest of the space on it.

Two walnut nightstands, apparently part of the same set as the dressing table, stood at either side of a white, wrought-iron bedstead. The one nearest him was bare of anything but an alarm clock. The one on the other side, nearest Kaylie, held a skewed pile of women's magazines. On top of the magazines was a familiar-looking volume. Their high school yearbook.

She was sitting on the edge of the bed, her hands folded in her lap, looking out the window. She hadn't turned toward him, and now, looking at her profile, he saw not Kaylie Darren but Kaylie Lindstrom, the girl he had known in high school. She wore no make-up, no earrings, no perfume. This room was more her room than any other, and the fact that she had shared the bed she sat on with a man as cold and empty as that other nightstand seemed grossly unfair to Jim Lawrence.

She turned toward him, looked at him and smiled a quick little smile and said, "Am I in your way? Did you need to look around in here?"

He couldn't make himself ask her what he needed to ask her, at least not yet. So instead he said, "Why don't you use the air conditioner?"

"It's broken," she said with resignation.

"Let me take a look at it," he said, striding toward the window.

"It's broken," she said again.

"Broken things can be fixed," he said firmly. He bent down to take a look at it, pushing the switches and buttons on the side panel. Nothing.

"Can they?" she was saying. "Surely not all of them. That thing has been broken for years."

He turned back to her, inexplicably irritated by her lack of faith.

"Did Professor Joseph Darren ever even *try* to fix this thing?"

Her eyes widened a little, and she smiled again. "No, he just went out and paid someone to put in this ceiling fan. He thought the air conditioner was too noisy anyway."

"That ceiling fan doesn't do much to cool it off in here," he said, reaching into his pocket for his Swiss Army Knife.

"No, it doesn't. But it was cool enough for Joseph," she replied, watching him open the knife to a screwdriver implement and start to remove the panel.

I'll just bet it was cool enough for him. The professor apparently had ice in his veins. But was it cool enough for you, Kaylie? His thoughts were brought up short when he pulled the panel away. The problem with the air conditioner wasn't difficult to find. The power cord had been disconnected from the on/off switch terminals. Deliberately.

That son of a bitch.

"Jim?"

He was too angry to reply. He followed the cord back toward the bed.

"What are you doing?"

He looked at her, hearing the alarm in her voice. He must have frightened her somehow. He realized he was scowling and headed right toward her. Did Joseph Darren stalk toward her like this in anger, hurt her? He took a breath.

"I'm just going to unplug it. Your—" He stopped himself. He needed to get a grip. He had just been about to tell her of Joseph Darren's deception, and here she was, not a widow for one full night yet. "—your air conditioner is going to be easy to fix. I'll need for you to get up for a moment and let me move the bed away from the wall. The outlet is behind the bedstead."

She was looking up at him again, in that way she had looked at him several times this evening. *What are you looking for, Kaylie? Tell me.* Her lips parted, almost as if she had heard him, and she clutched at the sheets beneath her.

He waited.

"Jim—" she said, but then looked down, away from his eyes. She stood up and walked away from the bed.

"Kaylie?"

She shook her head, still not looking at him.

He shrugged and reached for the bedstead, and heaved it away from the wall. He bent to unplug the air conditioner, and stopped short. There were footprints on the wall behind the bed.

Two footprints, to be exact. From the soles of a woman's athletic shoes. A little garden dirt, perhaps. Two feet, toes pointing up, slightly apart.

He looked at Kaylie, then back at the footprints. He bent down. While the wooden floor under her side of the bed was dusty, something had slid along the floor under his side. He looked more closely, and saw white paint chips missing off one slightly bent rung of the bedstead. The paint chips were on the floor, in the area between and beneath the footprints. He gripped the top of the bedstead, thinking of the single wineglass, picturing her beneath the bed, bracing her feet against the wall, straightening her legs as she pulled . . . the way the direction of the rope marks on the neck would match up with a suicide-by-hanging. He closed his eyes for a moment. When he opened them again, it was all still there before him. He slowly straightened.

"He came home one day about twenty years ago and announced that he was going to get a vasectomy," he heard Kaylie say behind him. He couldn't bring himself to look at her. He bent down again and unplugged the air conditioner cord, then walked back to the window.

"He had decided that I wasn't going to have any children. He had his child. Lillian. Did you know that child hated me? Not so much anymore, but it was awful when she was growing up. I don't think she would have hated me so much if Joseph hadn't told her that I was the reason he didn't marry her mother. He lied. To me and to Lillian and to God knows how many other women. He lied all the time."

"Yes, I know he did," Jim said wearily, and knelt to begin replacing the wiring Joseph Darren had undone.

"Today he told Lillian that she should get rid of the baby."

The screwdriver stopped for a moment, then went on.

He finished replacing the panel and got to his feet, looking out the window at the smoke, which had turned the moon blood red.

Without looking back at her, he knew she hadn't moved. She stood there, silent now.

"Kaylie, I'm an officer of the law." For the first time, his chest felt tight as he said that.

"Yes," he heard her say.

He walked over to the outlet, plugged the air conditioner in, listened as it hummed to life, giving off a dusty smell of disuse.

"You fixed it!"

He looked over at her, at the way her face was lit up in approval and admiration.

"Yes," he said, and moved the bed back against the wall.

He walked back to the air conditioner, adjusted its settings. He closed his eyes and bent his face to it, letting the cool air blow against him; felt it flattening his eyelashes and buffeting his hot skin.

"Kaylie."

"Yes?"

"Go turn the clothes dryer off."

She hesitated, but then he heard her leave the room, heard her going out into the garage. He looked out the window and saw the headlights of other cars coming toward the house. He stood up straight, lifting his fingers to his badge, feeling the now-chilled metal beneath them.

Fifteen years as a deputy sheriff, only to come to this.

Why tonight, he wondered.

THE MOUSE

AT ONE TIME OR ANOTHER, everyone has carried a dead mouse around in his or her pocket. I didn't know that when I was in the fifth grade, or even in the seventh grade. I didn't know it until fairly recently, when I confessed one of the greater shames of my childhood to Peggy, a friend at work.

Peggy and I are friends who work together; we don't socialize outside of work very often. I don't know why she was the one I confessed to, except that maybe sometimes when you're around someone for eight hours a day and you're comfortable with them, you start to tell them things about yourself, find yourself blurting out stuff that might end up making it impossible for them to be comfortable with you again. That was how big that mouse was by then.

I told Peggy that I'm not sure now whose fault it was that the mouse died. Maybe it was my fault, and

49

not remembering is just a way of fleeing some of the guilt I felt when it died. I was ten years old, and so much was going wrong when I was ten, the death of the mouse seemed almost like a sign from God. Looking back, perhaps it was.

I was in fifth grade, and my mother had cancer. It was a word then, not something I really understood, just knew adults were very afraid of that word. I also knew that my mother was in the hospital a lot and I heard words murmured here and there about breasts being removed, and she was sad and tired and holding on to me more. I knew that my long hair had been cut for the first time in my life, cut because other people had convinced her that cutting it was something that needed to be done, something to make her life easier. But I think my hair was just something else she lost that year. Those were the things I knew, even in fifth grade.

The mouse was a classroom pet. It was brown and white and Mrs. Hobbs had allowed us to have it. It would sleep most of the time, but now and then it would run in its exercise wheel. Doreen Summers, who was my best friend, had brought it to school. Mrs. Hobbs said that if Doreen and I shared the responsibility of taking care of it, we could keep the mouse at school.

No sweat. Doreen and I were what they used to call "good citizens" in school. We were Girl Scouts in the same troop. We were two good Catholic girls who went to catechism class together. Of course, we also kept each other updated on any new cusswords and phrases we had learned. (Our favorite at the start of fifth grade: "A dirty devil's behind in hell." Her brother taught us that one.)

We were each ornery in our own way, and got into our share of trouble, but we knew how to take care of a mouse. We had each had hamsters as pets, and taking care of the mouse was not too much different. Every day, you put in fresh water and some food. Once a week, you cleaned the cage. Doreen couldn't stand that job, but allergies had long inhibited my sense of smell, so I didn't mind as much. Still, she didn't shirk her duties. Doreen would take care of the mouse one week, I would take care of the mouse the next week. With a typical children's sense of fairness, we decided that if one of us was absent on her mouse-caring day, she would have to make up a day for it at the beginning of the next week.

In October, a new girl came to school. Her name was Lindy and she was pretty and smart. Mrs. Hobbs liked Lindy so much, sometimes she hired Lindy to babysit her children. Only later would I wonder about the judgment of a woman who would leave several young children in the care of a ten-year-old. At the time, it just made Lindy seem all the more superior.

Lindy hated me. I have figured out the part about the dead mouse in everybody's pocket, but I still haven't figured out exactly what made Lindy single me out as the object of her hatred. Maybe it was because I looked like a target: unsure of myself with my short haircut; noticing that Doreen wasn't exactly flat-chested anymore; worrying about what it meant to have my best friend grow breasts and my mother lose hers; wondering why adults shook their heads and looked at me with pitying faces when the cancer word was whispered. Or maybe I sparked some silly set of insecurities in Lindy.

Whatever her reasons, Lindy ridiculed me at every turn.

Gradually, she even wooed Doreen away from me. Soon, taking care of the mouse was the only connection Doreen and I had to one another. She dropped out of Scouts, which Lindy had declared was something for "kids." Doreen's mother still made her go to catechism, but we stopped walking over to church together.

I started going home for lunch more often, choosing to lose a few minutes to the walk home over sitting in the school cafeteria, watching Lindy snicker with Doreen as they looked over at me. I took long walks around the schoolyard by myself at recess. For the first time, I dreaded going school. When the flu went around that year, I caught it twice. I was glad to be sick with it. Throwing up was better than school.

One cold Monday morning, Mrs. Hobbs opened the classroom door, and let us in. The students who sat near the corner where the mouse cage was kept immediately complained of a smell. The mouse was dead.

Mrs. Hobbs was furious, angrily demanding that Doreen and I come over to the cage. "The mouse has starved to death," she shouted, even though we were right next to her. "Which one of you was supposed to be feeding it?"

I looked at the cage in horror. No food. No water. I envisioned the little mouse, trapped, unable to do anything but starve. I started crying.

Doreen said with certainty that it was my turn to feed the mouse, I stammered that I thought it was Doreen's. I was trying to figure out if that was true, even as I said it. I counted back on my fingers, confused, because each of us had been out for parts of the previous two weeks with the flu. Lindy proclaimed it was my turn. That settled it as far as Mrs. Hobbs was concerned. After all, I had been showing an amazing lack of attention to everything connected to school lately.

"Get rid of it. Get rid of it right now," she said. "Take the cage out to the trash bin behind the cafeteria." It was clear to everyone in the classroom who she was giving the assignment to. Doreen went back to her seat.

I picked up the mouse cage with the dead mouse in it and walked out of the classroom. I hadn't had time to take my coat off yet, so I didn't have to go back to my desk or do anything else to prolong my time in the hated classroom. My nose was running and I could hardly see for my tears, but I walked out to the big metal trash bin. I set the cage down on the ground near the bin, took out some tissue and blew my nose. I tried to calm myself. I opened the little wire door on the cage and took the mouse out.

His body was cold and stiff, but his fur was still soft and he seemed very small in my own small hand. I dropped the cage into the dumpster, but I didn't put the mouse in with it.

I stood there, crying, wishing I was the one who was dead. I asked the mouse to forgive me for killing it, and asked God to please forgive me, too. I knew that Mrs. Hobbs had told me do something and that probably I should put the mouse in there and go back to class, to accept whatever happened as my penance for killing the mouse, even if I wasn't the one who had killed it. It was at least a venial sin, I figured, to not have checked on the mouse on Friday.

The biggest problem for me at that point wasn't facing Lindy or Doreen or Mrs. Hobbs or the class. It was ignominiously putting the mouse in the Dumpster without a Christian burial. All of my dearly departed hamsters were interred in a shady spot in my backyard. The class mouse, I decided, should rate at least as much consideration.

I wavered for a while, then went into the girls' bathroom. I carefully pulled off two paper towels and made a makeshift shroud of them. I gently tucked the dead mouse into my coat pocket. I wouldn't go back to class, I decided. I would just walk home. I washed my swollen, reddened face and scrubbed my hands, and left the bathroom.

The janitor was standing in the hallway outside.

"What are you doing out of class so long?" he asked.

"Our mouse died," I said, "Mrs. Hobbs asked me to get rid of it." Not a lie, really, but I couldn't bring myself to tell him that I hadn't finished my assignment.

"Better not have plugged up the toilet," he growled, then seeing my face, gently added, "Sorry about the mouse. They don't live very long anyway. Go on back to class now, it'll be okay."

I couldn't talk, let alone tell him that I was just about to ditch school for the first time in my life. Under his watchful gaze, I walked back to the classroom. I decided I would go home for lunch, and bury the mouse then.

Mrs. Hobbs might have felt bad about yelling,

because she didn't say anything when I came back into the class. She didn't call on me, or even ask why I was still wearing my coat. Maybe she didn't even look at me; I couldn't say for sure, because I was just staring at the top of my desk, not saying anything to anyone, just wishing for two things: that it would be lunch time and that my hair would miraculously grow longer again so that I could hide behind the curtain of it.

But I hadn't been back in the class for an hour before the kid sitting next to me complained that something smelled bad. I knew what he was smelling, even though I couldn't smell it myself.

Mrs. Hobbs demanded an explanation. When I started to tell her that I wanted to take the mouse home and give it a funeral, she looked like she wished corporal punishment would be immediately reinstated. I looked helplessly to Doreen, who had officiated at some of the backyard ceremonies. She was silent. Mrs. Hobbs wasn't. Apparently, pets in Mrs. Hobbs's household were not given funerals. She told me to go back out, and this time, do as I was told.

I left the classroom hearing laughter. It seemed to start near where Lindy was sitting.

I didn't go to the trash bin. I went home.

My mother was sleeping. She had been awake earlier, but I knew that since she had gone to the hospital, she slept whenever she could manage an hour or two away from me and my younger siblings. I took a big spoon out of a kitchen drawer, gathered up a box of toothpicks, a rosary, a St. Francis holy card and some sewing thread. I quietly went out to the backyard cemetery and buried the mouse between the bodies of a hamster and a sparrow I had found not long before. I gave him the traditional gravemarker: a cross made with two toothpicks, on which the crossbeam is held in place by wrapping the thread around the intersection of the toothpicks. I put the rosary around my neck, recited the Prayer of St. Francis, and moved my right hand in benediction over the grave.

I could hear a bell tolling; the telephone. I ran inside. I wanted to catch the phone before it woke my mother. But I was too late; she stood in her robe in the kitchen, looking at me as I stood with dirt caked on me, spoon in hand, rosary around my neck. She had the phone to her ear, but I don't think she was listening too closely.

She knew.

She knew I had been caught with a dead mouse in my pocket. But her face wasn't angry like Mrs. Hobbs's.

"Yes, she's here," I heard her say. There was a long pause, then she said, "No. I think I'll keep her home today."

She hung up the phone. I thought she might be angry about my ditching school, but she just told me that maybe I should get out of my priest's clothes and wash up, maybe put on some pajamas instead. I nodded, then hurriedly followed her advice. By the time I was in my pajamas, she was lying down again. I tip-toed into her room, thinking she might have fallen back to sleep, but she was awake. She patted the bed next to her, and I crawled in beside her. She held me as if I were much smaller, close to where she had once had breasts. I had not ever been allowed to see her chest after the surgery, a radical double mastectomy, but I imagined that day that I could hear her heart better.

"Did you say the Prayer of St. Francis for the mouse?" she asked.

"Yes."

"Then he had a very nice funeral," she said, and fell asleep.

Eventually, I went back to school. I don't remember now how long I stayed out; it seems to me I might have been allowed an extra day at home with my mother. No one mentioned the mouse to me. Doreen asked me if I wanted to walk to catechism with her. I said yes. We didn't talk on the way there or the way home, though, and we never did anything together again after that. But she stopped hanging around Lindy.

The cancer moved to my mother's liver. I said the Prayer of St. Francis one hundred times, but God didn't accept it as a trade. She died the summer I turned twelve.

I started seventh grade the next fall at a new school, a junior high. All the kids from my school went to it, but kids from two other schools went there, too. I was making new friends and was feeling pretty good about the fact that I hadn't cried at school, not even when other girls complained about their mothers.

One day, one of the new friends, Barbara, stopped me in the hall outside of geography class. She seemed uneasy about something, and asked me to walk away from the other kids who were waiting for the teacher to arrive. We moved a few feet away, closer to the lockers. "I have to ask you something," she said. "Lindy has been going around saying that you used to walk around school with dead mice in your pockets. Is it true?"

"No," I said quietly. "It's not true." I hesitated, wondering if anyone would believe the truth if I told it. Was every other kid from Mrs. Hobbs' class saying the same thing?

But before I could make up my mind about what I would reveal, a locker closed behind us. I turned to see Doreen. She must have heard every word.

Doreen had changed a lot since fifth grade; we had even less in common. She had grown much taller and had really big breasts now, and I was still short and flat as a griddle. Doreen had beautiful long hair, and was popular. My hair was cut even shorter after my mother died, and my circle of friends was much smaller than Doreen's.

She looked from me to Barbara, then her face set in a frown. I was expecting the worst. "Barbara," she said, shaking her head. "Use your brain."

She walked off. Barbara smiled at me and said, "Yeah, now that I think about it, that was a pretty stupid story Lindy was telling."

But every now and then, throughout the school year, I was asked about dead mice.

I moved to a neighboring town the next year, when my father remarried. I grew my hair long again and, after a couple of years, I even got breasts and grew taller. No one at my new school knew about what happened when I was in fifth grade, or even that my father's new wife was not my birth mother. By then, I knew how to keep a secret. And my stepmother defied the fairy tale image, loving her stepchildren so well that I decided God had not, after all, abandoned us.

Until the day before my college graduation, I never saw anyone from elementary school. That day, I had gone into a department store to buy some new underwear. As I approached the counter, I recognized the saleswoman. Lindy.

My first impulse was to run from her, my second to think up something cruel to say. Or maybe something snotty. ("Lindy, I'm giving the commencement address tomorrow. Why don't you come on down and heckle me—you know, mention the mouse thing from fifth grade.")

Instead, I just bought underwear. She didn't seem to recognize or remember me.

In the car in the shopping mall parking lot, I held on to the steering wheel and screamed behind my teeth. As much as I wanted to, I knew I would never forget Lindy, or fail to recognize her.

To my surprise, Peggy cried when I told her the story of the dead mouse in my pocket. It dawned on me, as I finished telling it, that just about all of us have these memories of some moment of humiliation, have secrets that weigh down our pockets, but are really no larger than a mouse. The things that we think will bring our lives to a halt, don't. And no one remembers our shame as well as we do.

The next day, Peggy told me that she had gone home and told the story to her mother and to her elementary-school-aged daughters. Her mother cried, too.

Her daughters wanted to know if it was really true that I used to carry dead mice around in my pockets.

"Tell them yes," I said, "it's really true."

REVISED ENDINGS

H ARRIET READ THE LETTER AGAIN. She wasn't sure why; each re-reading upset her as much if not more than the first.

"Once again, I must tell you that the ending of this story positively reeks," Kitty Craig had written. "I can't imagine any reader believing Lord Harold Wiggins would choose this method of killing off his enemy, nor would any reader believe he could manage to mask the taste of antimony by mixing it into the braunschweiger. Rewrite."

Harriet Bently had been writing the popular Lord Harold Wiggins series for ten years now. She knew exactly what dearest Harry (as only Harriet had liberty to call him) would choose to do in *any* given situation, even if her editor did not. After all, Harry had moved into Harriet's life—lock, stock and barrel. No, she didn't invite him to tea like a child's imaginary friend; but she thought of him constantly, and had grown comfortable with his presence in her life. Like any series character and his author, they had become quite attached to each other.

It was more than Kitty Craig's rude tone that upset her. Kitty was notorious in the publishing industry for her biting, sarcastic remarks; Harriet told herself (not entirely successfully) that she shouldn't take Kitty's insults personally. What upset Harriet was Kitty's disregard for Lord Harold Wiggins's intelligence. His trademark was to effect justice without costing the English taxpayers a farthing for an imprisonment or a trial; once Lord Wiggins knew who the guilty party was, he cleverly killed the villain. In this book, Lord Wiggins made sure the poisoner Monroe would never age another day by slipping him a lethal dose of antimony. Monroe was a villain of the first water, and certainly deserved the punishment Lord Wiggins meted out. Harriet couldn't help but feel proud of her protagonist.

Her previous editor, Linda Lucerne, had loved Lord Harold almost as much as she did. Linda never changed much more than a punctuation mark; Kitty used industrial strength black markers to X through pages of manuscript at a time. Pages that had taken hours of research, planning, writing, and rewriting before they were ever mailed to Shoehorn, Dunstreet and Matthews (known affectionately as SDM), the esteemed publishers of the Lord Harold Wiggins series.

Yes, Linda Lucerne had loved Harriet's style, and said so from the moment she accepted the first novel, *Lord Wiggins Makes Hay While the Sun Shines*. And make hay he did. Linda's faith was proved justified, and the success of *Makes Hay* was repeated in *Lord Wiggins Beards the Lion in His Den* and the next seven Lord Harold Wiggins books. Alas, Linda had suffered a heart attack just after the tenth book, *Lord Wiggins Throws Pearls Before Swine,* had been mailed off to SDM. Upon her recovery, she had opted for retirement from the publishing industry.

Harriet tried hard to remember a sin she might have committed that would have justified so mean a punishment as having Kitty Craig become her new editor.

She had known other writers who had suffered under Kitty's abuses. Upon learning that Kitty would be her editor, Harriet had complained long and loud to her agent. But Wendall had pointed out that Kitty had been personally chosen for Harriet by Mr. William Shoehorn III. He had also mentioned that unless she was willing to come up with a new main character, they had no hope of moving to another publishing house. SDM owned Lord Harold. Wendall urged her to be open-minded.

Harriet loved Lord Wiggins too much to forsake him, and so she had tried to follow Wendall's advice. Tried, that is, until she received her first editorial letter from Kitty Craig. A long list of changes were demanded, each demand phrased in abusive language. The one that bothered Harriet the most was the demand to change the ending:

"How absolutely boring! Monroe dies when he swallows lemonade laced with strychnine. Strychnine! That old saw? Is your imagination so limited? Formula writer though you are, I would hope you could come up with something a tad more original."

Old saw indeed! Strychnine was a classic poison, she lamented, famous throughout detective fiction. But Kitty would hear none of it.

Harriet decided to be big about it; after all, she didn't want a reputation as the sort of writer who simply couldn't let go of a word she'd written. She was no rank amateur. She could bear the burden of criticism; being showered with the unwanted opinions of others was inevitable in her profession. And so she set herself to the painful task of revising the ending of *Pearls Before Swine*. That in turn meant that she had to revise a number of passages in the story, but she did not complain.

In fact, by the time she mailed off her new version, she was quite pleased with it. This time, Lord Wiggins offered Monroe a piece of chocolate cake chock-full of Catapres. It had been a bit tricky for dear Harry to obtain the drug, but she had managed it. Monroe had suffered heart failure thirty minutes after eating his dessert, allowing Lord Harold all the time in the world to leave the scene. It was certainly not as popular in fiction as strychnine, so Harriet thought Kitty might be contented.

Kitty hated it.

"You are going to have to do better than this. Catapres? Could you possibly devise anything more obscure? No reader is going to recognize this as a poison. Crimeny, it sounds like a resort that would appeal to people from the Bronx."

Not being from New York, Harriet couldn't guess what Kitty meant by her last remark. She steamed and stewed for a while and then went back to work. Now it was a challenge.

In version three, Lord Harold arranged for Monroe to be bitten repeatedly by a Gila monster.

"What utter nonsense!" Kitty wrote. "How the heck does an English lord happen to have a twenty-inch Arizona desert lizard hanging about?"

Even Harriet had to admit that the Gila monster wasn't her best effort. She spent a little more time on version four. There might not be many Gila monsters roaming about the English countryside, but she knew that rhododendrons weren't so rare. And so it was that Lord Harold made tea from the deadly leaves, and served it with scones to the unsuspecting Monroe.

"Harriet, please. You are trying my patience. This is so unimaginative. If you want this to sell anywhere outside of the East Lansing Lawn and Garden Club, rewrite."

Harriet wasn't even sure how she found the nerve to try a fifth time. She needed to publish annually to maintain the lifestyle to which she had become accustomed, and Kitty's demands were delaying the publication date of *Pearls Before Swine*. She had arranged to attend the annual Mystery World Awards Banquet, the Whodundunits. Her flight from Los Angeles to New York was booked, the hotel arrangements made. But now she wasn't sure she could face the inquires of her fellow authors; they were bound to notice that the next Lord Harold Wiggins book had not arrived on schedule.

She had grown more bitter about this trial by rewrite as each day passed. But once more she devised an ending, this time with antimony, arranging elaborate plot devices to allow Lord Harold Wiggins access to an industrial poison. And still Kitty wasn't satisfied.

As she held Kitty's fifth nasty letter, something snapped inside Harriet. She began to see Kitty as the root of all evil in her life. Before Kitty, she had been happy. Nothing much had disturbed the world dear Harry had shared with her; he had paid her way, she had kept him alive. It seemed to Harriet that Kitty wanted to kill them both. Well, Harriet decided, we'll see who kills whom.

The idea began to comfort her. She would attend the Whodundunits, slip a little something into Kitty's wine and sit back and enjoy her evening, knowing that her troubles would soon be over. In a room full of people who were constantly dreaming up ways for other people to die, the death of a woman who was almost universally despised by them would present a monumental problem for New York's Finest.

Harriet became quite delighted at the prospect. She did not doubt that she would be able to kill. After all, she had already murdered over thirty characters. (Three was Harriet's lucky number, and so she made it the average body count in her books.) Among those thirty characters were a great many individuals she liked better than Kitty Craig.

For her first real life murder, she would need something special. For weeks, she consulted her reference works on poison. She searched the pages of *A Panorama of Poisonous Plants, Powders, and Potions.* She studied the listings in *Lyle's Lethal Liquids,* even considered *Conroy's Compendium of Caustics.* But her most promising candidates were found in *Everyday Toxic Substances: Our Dangerous Friends.*

She made a long list of factors to consider. Reaction

time. What would dear Harry say? Quick, she decided. Very quick and highly toxic. Kitty in prolonged, relentless pain was a tempting picture, but she concluded that having Ms. Craig dead before the salads were served was preferable; attention-getting though agonizing death throes are, it might put a bit of a damper on the evening's festivities.

The poison would need to be something that could be transported easily; if discovered among her belongings, it could not seem out of place. Her final prerequisite was that it be something she could obtain without raising suspicions.

After hours of concentrated effort, she finally had the means in hand and the logistics of delivering it well planned.

She hummed a happy little tune as she latched her suitcase closed and carried it to the front door. She sat in the entry, lovingly caressing the corners of her carry-on bag. Harriet was far too careful to have her plans spoiled by the possibility of lost luggage. She could hardly contain her excitement when the taxicab pulled up in her driveway and tooted its horn.

She was pleased to learn that she was not the type to get the pre-homicidal jitters. Dear Harry would be thrilled to find his creator so calm, so poised, so at ease with this new role. Indeed, both flight attendants and Mr. Johnson, the gentleman seated next to her in first class, found her a charming traveling companion.

Harriet couldn't remember the last time she had really noticed or been noticed by a man, and she gloried in the handsome Mr. Johnson's attentions. At first she wondered if deadly intentions might somehow serve as an aphrodisiac. But then Mr. Johnson confessed himself to be a great fan of Lord Harold Wiggins, and said he recognized Harriet from her cover photo. This was sheer flattery, she was certain, as she hadn't updated that photo in ten years.

In New York, he accompanied her to baggage claim, and helped her to retrieve her suitcase. As he carried it for her, she learned that he was staying at the same hotel. Harriet was sure at that moment that this was her lucky day.

It was as they stood waiting for a taxi that Harriet saw the young woman. Ticket jacket in hand, no doubt late for a plane, she ran across the opposite sidewalk. Looking directly at Harriet, she took two quick steps off the curb; Harriet screamed a warning in her mind that never reached her lips—the driver had even less of a chance to stop the car in time. The car struck the young woman and hurled her several yards down the street.

Harriet experienced the moments of intense awareness that come to those who are caught as unwilling spectators to such events: with absolute clarity she heard the grating screech of the car's brakes, saw the disbelief on the woman's face at the moment of impact, heard the dull thud as it launched her into an unnatural and graceless flight, watched the awful landing.

Harriet rushed toward the woman and stood frozen above her. There could be no doubt that the woman was dead. Heads and necks are not configured in the same way on the living. Harriet had never before stood so close to the dead.

In contrast to the clarity of those few moments was the enveloping confusion which followed. Somehow, she ended up back inside the terminal, sitting on a plastic chair next to Mr. Johnson, who held her as she cried.

He didn't question Harriet's purchase of an immediate return flight; he took the same one back to Los Angeles. She left her carry-on bag on the plane.

Mrs. Johnson opened the envelope from Shoehorn, Dunstreet and Matthews without the sense of dread she had come to expect.

> *Dear Harriet,*
>
> *You are no doubt as saddened as we are about the unfortunate incident at the Whodundunits. Why no one who knew the Heimlich manuever could have been there at the moment Ms. Craig choked on that chicken bone is beyond me. We're all brushing up on our CPR here at SDM.*
>
> *I look forward to serving as your new editor. I've browsed through several of the drafts you sent to Ms. Craig, and I hope you won't mind my saying that I believe your first effort was the best. Will you be too angry with me if I send it along as is?*
>
>

Lord Harold's Biggest Fan,
Lana Dunstreet
>
>
> *P.S. Best wishes on your recent marriage. I hope Mr. Johnson realizes how lucky he is.*

GHOST OF A CHANCE

I T WASN'T HARD for the ghost to awaken me.

It was the second night after David died, and my grief was still so great as to thin my sleep to gossamer. Just about anything would cause me to wake up suddenly, reach for his side of the bed, feel the emptiness there, and then the emptiness within myself; next would come a tightness in my chest, the pressing weight of the sudden loss of my husband.

Some might believe I saw the ghost because I so wanted David to be alive, I imagined he had come back to me. The only problem with that theory is, it wasn't my husband's ghost.

I had awakened from my fitful sleep that night because the room felt cold; I opened my eyes to see a man standing at the foot of the bed. Until I was fully awake, I almost thought it was David. Like David, he was about six feet tall, with dark brown hair and big, brown eyes. He was handsome, but I discovered that even handsome men who suddenly show up uninvited at the foot of my bed can scare me. This one did. I opened my mouth to scream, and he vanished.

I was more than a little upset, but I convinced myself that I had dreamed the whole thing, and fell back into a restless slumber, full of dreams of David dying. The next morning I felt grumpy and ill-at-ease. It was the day of David's funeral, and there wasn't anything on earth that was going to make me feel good about that day. As I looked in the mirror, I became even more certain of that. I looked like a blouse someone had left to wrinkle in the dryer. My blond hair framed a colorless face and I had dark shadows under my blue eyes.

"You'll be just fine, Anna," I said to myself. At forty-two, I wasn't in bad shape. The lines that had appeared on my face weren't etched too deeply. Gave it character, my father said. I was getting more character every year, but I'm not the type to fret over it. At least, I hadn't been until *she* came along.

I wondered if she would have the nerve to show up at the funeral. I wouldn't know her if she did. When he made his confession, David never told me her name, and I never asked for it. As far as I was concerned, it was important not to know the name of the woman David had met at the St. George Hotel every Wednesday for fifteen weeks. For fifteen weeks, on the night I taught a class in—of all things—ethics, Ms. X had taught David that he could still lure a woman to bed. I wondered if they had laughed about that. He wasn't laughing when it ended. "A temporary madness," he had told me, weeping as he did. "Forgive me," he pleaded.

To this day, I'm not able to be very precise about

why I did forgive him. At the time I was outraged, hurt, angry, humiliated. The pain of betrayal remained; whatever trust was between us had taken a torpedo broadside. But the ship didn't sink, it just listed.

Maybe the reason I stayed with him wasn't really so complex. David and I had been together for twenty years; and in that twenty years I had come to love him more than anyone else on earth. He was a habit I couldn't break. Fate broke it for me.

David had made his confession six months ago, and strove to be the ideal husband in the time since. Together we tried to renew our marriage, and somehow, we were making it. On the morning of the day he died, he told me that he was working on something that would really make me proud of him. I had no idea what it was. "I'm proud of you all the same, David," I said to the haggard reflection in the mirror. Ten minutes later I was still sitting on the bathroom floor, sobbing.

I pulled myself together, hoping I wouldn't shame myself at his funeral. As I put on a plain black dress that David had always liked, I held on to the anger I felt toward his killer. David had come to the college to pick me up that night. I was on my way to the car when I heard the shots. The college is in a part of town that has become rougher over the years, and I didn't think much about hearing gunfire. It wasn't an everyday occurrence, but it wasn't that rare. When I saw the crumpled form on the steps that lead up from the parking lot, I didn't know it was David until I was only a few feet from him. He was unconscious, and bleeding to death. Nothing, not even a ghost in my bedroom, will ever terrify me the way those moments did, when I held David as he died.

No one saw the actual shooting, but several witnesses saw a blue Chevy speeding away from the scene. No one knew anything else. No model, no license plate, no description of the driver, no mention of how many people were in the car. No motive, just someone who got their kicks by driving around firing guns at people. There was some speculation that David had been hit by gunfire aimed at someone else, since other bullets were found lodged in a nearby tree, a wall, another car. "Random violence" seemed to be the theory of the newspapers.

I was one of the believers in the theory. No one would want to kill David Blackburn. The man had cheated on me, and I didn't want to kill him. I didn't know anyone with a stronger motive.

The funeral was well-attended, with or without David's former lover. The priest didn't know David, but did the best he could to say generically comforting words. My family tried to brace me up, and succeeded in large degree. David's parents were long dead, but his sister sent a wreath; she had wanted to come to the funeral but couldn't manage the airfare from Maine to California, and refused my offer to buy the ticket.

There were neighbors and old friends, and a large contingent from Emery & Walden. David was the Vice President of Human Resources for Emery & Walden, a local manufacturing firm that employed about twenty-five hundred people. Many of the employees had contact with him, and trusted him as someone who would treat them fairly, as someone who had concern for their well-being. He often acted as a buffer between them and Mr. Winslow Emery III, the self-involved young man who was now at the helm of the company.

Today Winslow Emery looked tired and worn. It was understandable—he had attended a lot of funerals lately. Five days earlier, an acid tank at Emery & Walden had ruptured, causing the deaths of three workers. OSHA was investigating. David had been troubled by the deaths, as he was by the suicide of the plant manager, who apparently blamed himself for not responding to worker complaints about the tank.

I thought about David championing that troubled soul. His name, if I recalled, was Devereaux. I watched Emery walk away from David's grave with the gait of a man twice his age. A good-looking blonde walked next to him. She had introduced herself to me as Mr. Emery's secretary, Louise. Emery didn't seem to notice her.

I noticed her, as I did two other women, Lucy Osborne and Annette Mayes, who lingered longer than most of the others. Both were at least fifteen years younger than I, and gorgeous. Lucy was a brunette, Annette a redhead. I wondered if David had stayed with my type or looked for something different when he chose a lover. Something in the way Annette looked at me made me decide he had tried something different. Oddly, I didn't feel the animosity I thought I would feel towards her. I really didn't care. David had come back to me. Fifteen weeks was not twenty-one years.

I sat next to the open grave longer than my sister, Lisa, thought I should, but I refused to be steered away. My father told her to let me be and then gave me a hug and said they'd be waiting for me at the car, to take my time.

"I guess this is goodbye, David," I said aloud, and

was startled to feel a warm hand on my shoulder. I looked up into the eyes of the ghost.

This time, I was angry. This was my private moment with David, and I didn't want living or dead intruding on it. At the time, the man seemed to be among the living. I couldn't see through him and his hand was warm. "Can't a person have a moment's peace?" I said, trying to remove his hand, but only touching my own shoulder. That frightened me.

He shook his head sadly and removed his hand.

"I don't believe in ghosts," I said.

He shrugged.

"Are you David?" I asked, thinking maybe I was seeing him transformed somehow.

But the ghost shook his head.

"Could I please have a little time to say goodbye to my husband? Would that be too much to ask?"

He gave a little bow and vanished.

I was shaking. "David," I said, when I had calmed down, "Why isn't it you? If I'm going to go crazy and see ghosts, why isn't it your ghost? Show up, David. Materialize, or whatever it is you do. I want you back."

I waited. Nothing.

"Goodbye, David," I said, giving up. "I'll miss you. I don't know what I'm going to do without you. Be very sad for a very long time, I suppose."

I looked up and saw a man walking toward me. I knew this one was among the living. There was nothing extraordinary about Detective Russo's appearance. He was a plain-faced man, neither handsome nor ugly. He was of medium height, had mouse-brown hair that was cut short. His eyes, his voice, and his face usually reflected very little of what he was thinking or feeling. If you talked to him for a while, there was no mistaking his intelligence, but he didn't walk around with his IQ embroidered on his sleeve. An ocean of calm, he seemed to me. I could use it.

"Hello, Detective Russo," I said as he approached.

"Hello, Dr. Blackburn," he said quietly. "I'm sorry if I interrupted you. Just wanted to make sure you were all right. I'll leave—"

"No," I said, standing up. "Don't worry about it. I need to walk to the car; I'm keeping everyone waiting."

He surprised me by offering me his arm, but I took it and we walked in silence toward the limo. When we reached it, I invited him to join us at the house, but he politely declined.

"Were you watching me the whole time I sat there?" I asked.

"Yes, ma'am, I was," he said, not seeming in the least embarrassed about it.

"Did you see anyone else?"

"While you sat there?"

"Yes."

"No, ma'am, I didn't. Why?"

"Nothing, really. Nothing at all. I don't suppose you've learned anything more about what happened?"

"No, I'm sorry, Dr. Blackburn. But we're still working on it."

"It's why you're here, isn't it?" I said.

"Yes, ma'am."

I got into the car and let Lisa's chatter roll over me as my father held my hand.

Back at the house, the ghost became rather nervy. I would see him standing among groups of people, watching me. Everyone excused my vacant stares as widow's grief, which was fine with me. I wasn't in the mood to be entertaining.

The gathering thinned out quickly. Lisa left only after I reassured her for the fifty-third time that I wanted to be by myself. Only I knew I wasn't going to be able to be by myself. The ghost was growing as eager as I was to have her leave.

"Okay," I said, after I saw her drive off. "Let's talk."

He looked even sadder than before.

"What? Did I say something?"

He didn't reply.

I decided that even if he was a figment of my imagination, I needed to play this out. Avoiding him obviously wouldn't work. "Let's sit down," I said.

He followed me into the living room, and we sat on opposite ends of the couch.

"Who are you?" I asked.

No answer, just gestures that I couldn't make anything out of.

"Can't you talk?"

He shook his head, pointing at his mouth.

"If I gave you a pen and paper could you write a note?"

He shook his head again.

"I thought ghosts were supposed to be cold. When you touched me today you were warm."

He shrugged.

"Perhaps you haven't been dead long?"

He nodded, and held up four fingers.

"Four days?"

He nodded again.

"Most people would be cold."

He waited.

"Why me?" I asked.

He walked over to the mantel over the fireplace and pointed to a photograph.

"Because of David?"

He nodded.

"Is something wrong with him?" It immediately seemed like a stupid question. The man was dead. Things don't go too much more wrong, unless—"He's not in some sort of eternal torment is he? I don't believe it. That can't be true."

The ghost made a frantic gesture to get me to stop talking, then looked up.

"Are you looking in the direction David traveled?"

He nodded.

"Thank you," I said. I found myself crying. I had felt in my heart that David, for all his weaknesses, was a good man, but it was nice to have confirmation. I suddenly felt a sense of relief. I decided I owed the ghost a favor.

"What can I do for you?"

He got up and paced, tried to gesture, couldn't get through to me.

"Wait, settle down."

He sat down again.

"You know David, right?"

He nodded.

"You are a ghost?"

Yes again.

I thought about everything I had heard about ghosts. "Are you trying to haunt me? Did I do something wrong to David?"

No.

"Are you trying to right some wrong done to you?"

Yes.

I figured he probably couldn't explain the details just yet, so I tried to question my way to it. "Did you know David before you became a ghost?"

Another yes.

"But I never met you?"

He shook his head.

"Did you know him a long time ago?"

No.

"You knew him recently?"

Yes.

There weren't many possibilities. "You knew him from work?"

Yes again. He seemed anxious, as if this would give me the answer.

"You're one of the workers who died when the tank ruptured!"

He looked stricken, but shook his head. He held up the four fingers again.

"Oh, that's right. That was five days ago. You said you died four days ago. But the only person who died four days ago was the . . ."

He could see the understanding dawning on me.

"You're the plant manager."

He nodded sadly.

"Mr. Devereaux?"

Yes, he nodded.

"You killed yourself."

He stood up, shaking his head side to side, mouthing the word 'No!'

"You didn't kill yourself?"

Again, just as firmly, no.

"Someone killed you?"

Yes.

"Who?"

He pointed to his ring finger on his left hand. There was no wedding band, but I could guess.

"Your wife?"

Yes.

"Your wife killed you?"

I tried to remember the stories. I couldn't. Everything had been blurred by the events of three days ago. I went over to a stack of newspapers that I had been meaning to take out to the recycling bin. I put the two unopened ones—which I knew had stories of David's murder in them—aside, and reached for the one from the day David was killed. That was the day after Devereaux's suicide. The suicide was front page news.

"Will it bother you if I read this to you?"

No.

" 'Mr. Chance Devereaux . . .' Chance? Your first name is Chance?"

He nodded.

" 'Mr. Chance Devereaux, plant manager of Emery & Walden, died of an apparently self-inflicted gun-shot wound yesterday evening. His wife, Louise, who is also employed at Emery & Walden, discovered her husband's body when she returned home late from work. She said her husband had grown despondent following the deaths of three workers Tuesday in an industrial accident caused by a ruptured acid tank. Mr. Devereaux had received complaints from the workers about the tank, but failed to repair it . . .' "

I looked up to see him angrily indicating his disagreement.

"We'll get to your side of the story in a moment," I said. "Where was I? Oh yes, '. . . failed to repair it in time to prevent the deaths.' " I read on in silence. The rest of the article was simply a rehash of the previous reports on the accident.

"My name is Anna. May I call you Chance?"

Yes.

"Is your wife Emery's secretary?"

Yes.

"And you didn't kill yourself?"

No. He pointed to the ring finger again.

"Your wife killed you."

Yes.

"How?"

He pointed to his mouth again, only this time I saw what I had missed before: he wasn't pointing, he was imitating the firing of a gun into his mouth.

"She shot you in the mouth?"

He nodded.

I shuddered. "How did she manage that? I've seen your wife. She's not a very large woman."

He pantomimed holding a glass, pouring something into the glass, then adding something to it. Then he pantomimed sleep.

"She drugged your drink?"

He nodded.

"That should come out in the autopsy."

He made a helpless gesture.

"It didn't?"

He shrugged.

"You don't know if it did or it didn't, but they declared it a suicide?"

He nodded again.

"Have you . . ." I tried, but couldn't think of a more polite way to phrase it. "Have you been buried?"

He nodded, looking very unhappy.

"You don't like where you're buried?"

He looked into my face and made the Sign of the Cross.

"You're Catholic."

Yes.

"And you aren't buried in consecrated ground?"

No.

"Is that why you're haunting me?"

He gave me a look that said he was disgusted with me and disappeared.

The moment he was gone, the house felt very empty. "Come back," I said.

Nothing.

"Chance, please come back. I apologize. This is a very difficult time for me. I didn't mean to offend you by calling it 'haunting.' If you come back, I'll try to help you."

He reappeared.

"How do you do that?"

He shrugged.

"Let me know if you figure out more about this ghost business."

He nodded.

"What does this have to do with David?"

He studied me for a moment, then pointed to David's picture and then his head.

"David shot you, too?" I said in disbelief.

No! He might as well have been able to shout it.

"Wait, wait. I'm beginning to understand. David

told me he didn't believe the things that were said about you. Is that what you mean?"

Yes. He kept gesturing to his head.

"David didn't just *believe*, he *knew* they weren't true."

Emphatic nod.

"He had proof?"

Yes.

We continued to piece a conversation together with questions, nods and pantomime. From what I could make out from Chance's gestures, David had proof that Chance had tried to act on replacing the acid tank long ago, but Emery refused, citing costs. David had told him where he hid the papers that would show Chance was not to blame.

"Was David killed because of this?" I asked.

He nodded slowly. He placed a hand over his chest, eyes downcast, as if to say, "I'm sorry."

"Not your fault," I said, but I was lost for a while. When I had managed to regain my composure, I said, "I've got to contact Detective Russo."

Chance wasn't happy with this idea, but I ignored his gestures until he got frustrated and vanished. This time, I didn't mind so much. I needed some time to absorb what he had told me.

I dialed police headquarters and asked for Russo. He wasn't in, but the man who took my call said he would page him. I was grateful he wasn't there; it occurred to me that it would be difficult to tell him that I had been talking to Chance Devereaux's ghost. Only about fifteen minutes had passed when he called me back, but I was better prepared.

"Anything wrong, Dr. Blackburn?" he asked.

"No," I said. "In fact, I think I may have some more information for you about my husband's case, and perhaps another case as well. But first I need to ask you a few questions."

There was silence on the other end of the line.

"Detective Russo?"

"I'm here Dr. Blackburn. Just what is this all about?"

"Maybe this would be easier to explain if we spoke face-to-face."

"I'll be right over."

When he arrived, I could tell he wasn't exactly pleased with me. I was surprised to see him betraying any emotion, and found it a nice change; somehow it made his face more interesting. He politely declined my offer of coffee and we went into the living room.

"You said you had some questions for me?" he asked when we were seated on the couch, just as Chance and I had been seated earlier.

"Yes. I was wondering if you were familiar with the case of Chance Devereaux?"

He didn't answer at once, and while I waited for him to reply, Chance reappeared. I tried not to look at him, but Detective Russo caught me glancing away. "What's bothering you?"

"Nothing," I said.

"Just now, something upset you."

"I'm generally upset right now. You didn't answer my question."

"Yes, I'm familiar with the Devereaux case."

"Do you believe he killed himself?"

Chance was gesturing to me to follow him. I wondered if he could use telepathy. I kept looking at Detective Russo, trying to tell Chance with my mind that he needed to be patient. It didn't work. Chance walked over to the bookcase, and began pacing.

"I don't believe I should discuss that with anyone outside the department," Detective Russo said curtly.

"All right, if you can't discuss it, you can't. I'll just tell you that I don't believe he did."

At that moment a book fell from the case with a thump that made me jump half out of my skin.

"You seem very nervous, Dr. Blackburn. Why don't you tell me what's going on?"

I got up and picked up the book. Irving Stone's *Men to Match My Mountains*. I looked up at Chance as I replaced it on the shelf. I finally understood what he was trying to say.

"I remembered that David had been very concerned about the allegations that were being made. He told me he had proof that Chance Devereaux had wanted to replace the acid tank, but that Mr. Emery refused."

He didn't seem to believe me. "That's a very serious allegation. Mr. Emery could be subject to criminal prosecution if what your husband told you is true."

"I'm almost certain of it."

"And you think your husband was killed to keep him silent?"

"Yes."

He eyed me skeptically. "Why didn't you mention this before?"

"As you've noticed, Detective Russo, I've been very upset. David's death was a horrible shock." I didn't have to fake my response there. Just thinking about it made the color drain from my face.

"I'm sorry, Dr. Blackburn," he said.

"No, please. And please call me Anna—only my students call me Dr. Blackburn. All I'm asking is that you help me search the place where I believe David hid the papers."

"And where would that be?"

"Our mountain cabin," I said, daring to peek over at Chance, who was nodding and urging me to get going.

"Is that why your husband took off work on Wednesday afternoon?"

"What?"

He pulled out a notebook and flipped through it. Finding the page he was looking for, he said, "Your husband left work at about eleven o'clock Wednesday morning. He didn't return all day. Said he wasn't feeling well. A woman in the office—an Annette Mayes?—said she thought he left because he was so disturbed by the deaths of the three workers the day before."

I had nothing to say. Chance distracted me, making motions that seemed to mean, "Stand up, let's go!"

"Look, Detective Russo, could we talk about this on the way to the cabin?"

"Lady, before we take off on a two-hour drive, why don't you tell me what's really going on?"

For three or four seconds, I actually considered doing it. But whatever sense I still had allowed me to remain silent. "I thought I could depend on your help. Obviously, I was wrong. I'm leaving for the cabin and I'm leaving now."

"All right, all right," Russo said in a peeved tone. "Let me call in."

He made the call while I got my coat and keys and

purse. Chance disappeared for a while. I looked at Detective Russo, and realized he probably didn't have more than his suitcoat to keep him warm. I hesitated only for a moment before going into David's closet. "I know you don't mind, David," I said as I took a winter coat out, "but it bothers me." Chance suddenly appeared next to me, motioning me to hurry. "I am hurrying!" I said.

"Anna? Who are you talking to?" Detective Russo asked. He was standing at the bedroom door.

"Oh . . . just talking to myself. I was getting one of my husband's coats for you. I thought you might be cold up in the mountains. There's snow up there now. He's a little—he was a little taller than you, so it might be too big. But it will be better than nothing."

"Thank you," he said, taking it from me. "Are you sure it won't bother you to see me wear it?"

I looked away from him and shook my head. "Let's go."

Chance vanished. I figured he had his own means of transportation.

Detective Russo and I didn't say anything to each other for about the first twenty minutes of the trip. Chance suddenly appeared as a reflection in the rearview mirror. I jumped a little, but fortunately, Russo didn't see my reaction; he was looking out the passenger window.

He turned to me. "It was your husband, wasn't it?"

"What?" I asked, puzzled.

"When I came into the bedroom, you were talking to your husband, asking him if you could loan me the coat."

I colored, but didn't answer.

"Don't be embarrassed. I talked to my wife after she died."

"I'm sorry," I said. "I didn't know you had lost your wife."

"About four years ago now. But at first, I used to talk to her all the time. I learned to be careful—almost got a stress leave imposed on me when my lieutenant overheard me one day."

"Did your wife ever answer you?"

He looked out the window, and for moment, I didn't think he was going to reply. When he spoke, his voice was so low I had to strain to hear it. "In her own way, yes, she did," he said.

He laughed then, suddenly self-conscious. "You probably think the department sent you out with a nutcase."

"No, not at all. Until recently, if you had told me you talked to the dead, I might have questioned your sanity. But not now, Detective Russo."

"If you're generous enough to loan me this coat, I suppose you might be willing to call me John," he said.

"Okay, John. Anyway, I doubt anything you could tell me about conversing with your wife would surprise me. These last few days . . ." I stopped, needing to steady myself.

"Do you want me to drive?" he asked.

I glanced in the rearview mirror. Chance was nodding.

"If you wouldn't mind, I'd appreciate it," I said, and pulled off the freeway. "I'm a little shaky."

"I understand," he said. "You've held up really well so far, all things considered."

I stopped the car and turned to look at him. "No, I haven't. I just try not to make a public production out of it. It would seem to—I don't know, cheapen his memory."

He didn't say anything, just traded places with me, and we got back on the freeway. I positioned myself on the seat so that I could look at Chance without being too obvious. "Do you know Mrs. Devereaux?" Russo asked.

"I met her for the first time at David's funeral," I said, looking back at Chance, who wore an angry expression.

"At least the two of you will both benefit nicely from Emery & Walden's employee life insurance program."

"We would have, but not now. I haven't had a chance to get the details, but David told me that Mr. Emery was changing to a less expensive insurance, one that wouldn't pay as much. But we've been in fairly good financial shape anyway, with no children and two incomes."

"The insurance hasn't changed yet," he said.

"What?"

He glanced over at me. "It doesn't change until the end of the month."

"I didn't know."

"The interesting thing is, the current insurance not only pays higher than the new one, it also covers death for any reason."

"You mean, including suicide?"

"Including suicide."

Chance was clenching his fists.

"It wasn't suicide," I said, and both Chance and John Russo looked at me at once.

"What's your interest in Devereaux?"

"I told you. David was concerned about him. He knew Chance Devereaux didn't ignore the complaints about the tank. Devereaux felt bad about what happened, but he didn't blame himself. He was a practicing Catholic. He wouldn't have committed suicide."

"How do you know about his being Catholic?"

I looked away. "David and I are Catholics. You know that from being at the funeral today if you didn't know it before. David must have mentioned that Devereaux was Catholic, too."

He was silent for a while, and I thought he might not believe me. I was right. But I didn't know how right until he spoke up again.

"I don't think you're being honest with me," he said. "I kept hoping you'd just tell me. I'm a cop, Dr. Blackburn. I've seen all kinds of things. It wouldn't have surprised me."

I didn't understand his harsh tone, nor did I believe for a moment that the police were accustomed to having people say they had received information from ghosts. Not sane people. I gave him directions to the turnoff for the cabin, then asked, "Just exactly what did you mean by that last remark?"

He sighed. "I meant that a woman answering your description was seen keeping a regular weekly appointment with Mr. Devereaux. We got a tip from a clerk at the St. George Hotel. Said you registered as Mr. & Mrs. Devereaux, but he had been in the business long enough to know hanky-panky when he saw it. You were having an affair with Chance Devereaux, weren't you?"

I couldn't help but look back at Chance. He was shaking his head, pointing to his ring finger again, then at me. "Mr. Devereaux and I were each married," I said.

Chance shook his head while I heard John Russo say, "To other people, yes. But you wouldn't be the first married people on earth to look for greener pastures. Every Wednesday. What broke it off, Dr. Blackburn?"

His words, combined with Chance's gestures, brought it home to me. "Oh my God. My husband and your wife."

"Leave my wife out of this!" John Russo said angrily.

"No, no, that's not what I meant," I said, a numbness coming over me. I gave a questioning look at Chance, who nodded, then pointed at me and made the signs for 'See no evil, hear no evil, and speak no evil.' His flippancy angered me, but I understood what he meant. I had avoided learning the details of David's infidelity, shut myself off from it. Now both Chance and I might pay for it.

I looked back at Russo. I took a deep breath. "That wasn't me and it wasn't Chance Devereaux, either. That was Louise Devereaux and my husband. Six months ago, David told me he was having an affair. He told me he met the woman every Wednesday night at the St. George Hotel. I taught a class that night. You can check that with the college. I never knew who it was. But Chance Devereaux and my husband look something alike, and Louise Devereaux and I both have blond hair and blue eyes. They must have used her name. I imagine if you look a little further, you'll find that, like me, Chance Devereaux had some standing appointment on Wednesday nights, some business or other engagement that allowed his wife to meet my husband without causing Mr. Devereaux to be suspicious."

Chance nodded in painful agreement, and made his "sorry" gesture again, as if feeling guilty for his earlier routine. The discovery of the details of the affair was too much for me. It was as if I were back in time, once again experiencing that moment when David admitted to the affair. The hurt and anger and humiliation started all over again, and now the police were privy to the whole awful business. I started crying again, wishing to God I could have kept my composure.

"I'm sorry," John said.

"That doesn't help a damn bit," I answered, and kept crying.

By then we had reached the cabin. Although it hadn't snowed since Thursday, there was still plenty of it on the ground and the roof of the cabin. The snow was dirty by then. What must have been a pristine blanket two days before was now sullied and rumpled. The snowplows had been by, building up large drifts along the way. We parked on the roadside; the entrance to the drive was blocked by the snowdrift. Any other weekend, David would have cleared the drive while I went to work putting away groceries and building a fire . . . who'll clear the driveway, now, David? I guessed it would be me.

Russo held off getting out of the car. He reached over and took my hand. "I truly am sorry, Anna. I feel like an ass. I should have checked it out. I only got the information from the clerk today, and not ten minutes later, you were calling, asking about Devereaux. I jumped to a conclusion, and I had no right to do that. I did a lousy job of asking you about it anyway. I wouldn't blame you if you wanted to scratch my eyes out."

I couldn't answer.

"Please forgive me."

"It seems like men have been asking me to do that a lot lately," I said.

He let go of my hand and waited.

I managed to pull myself together, somehow. "I'm sorry, John. I'm having a perfectly horrible day and I can't seem to keep my balance. Just when I feel as if I'm steady on my feet, something knocks them out from under me. You're not to blame for it."

"I don't know about that, but like I said, I'm sorry. Feel up to going inside and looking for those documents?"

"Why not? What more could go wrong today?"

We got out of the car and started up the drive. John donned David's coat, which was only a little too big for him. As we walked, I was fascinated by the fact that Chance, who walked next to me with a comforting arm around my shoulder, left no footprints. I was musing over the fact that his touch was as warm as any living person's, when suddenly John stopped me from walking any farther. "Hold it. It snowed up here Thursday, right?"

"Right," I said. "David and I were looking forward to—never mind, that doesn't do any good."

Chance gave my shoulder a little squeeze, as if to help me find my courage. Russo watched me for a moment, then asked, "Had you made any arrangements with anyone to come up here? Any other guests or a caretaker?"

"No, no one."

I followed his gaze to where two pairs of footprints entered and left the cabin. Whoever had been to the cabin had cut across the woods, as if to avoid being seen.

"Would you mind staying here for a moment?"

I shook my head.

"Why don't you give me the key to the front door? I'll just make sure it's safe."

He walked to the cabin, careful not to disturb the prints. It gave me an opportunity to talk to Chance.

"You knew someone was here, didn't you?"

Yes. He made the gesture for his wife.

"Louise and who else?"

He seemed stumped by this question, but then pantomimed filing his nails.

"Emery?"

He actually smiled, the first time I had seen him smile.

"I don't think Russo believes you killed yourself."

He patted me on the back.

"No, I think he doubted it before I said anything."

He patted me again.

"Well, thanks. Did they find what they were looking for when they came here?"

He shook his head, smiling again, then suddenly laid a finger to his lips. I turned to see Russo coming out of the cabin. He was upset.

"Someone has been here and ransacked the place. I called the sheriff; they'll be out as soon as they can, but it may be a little while. I don't know if you'll want to go in there. They did a very thorough job of it, and I doubt they missed anything."

"I have a feeling they did," I said. "I'll be okay. Let's take a look."

"Try not to touch anything if you can help it."

After everything else I had been through that day, seeing the cabin a complete wreck was only mildly unsettling. Russo was right; no piece of furniture was left in place, every drawer had been pulled out and dumped on the floor, pictures had been removed from their frames. I almost reached out and touched one of David and me, but Russo stopped me.

"You'll be able to fix it after they dust for prints," he said.

"I know who did this," I said. "Louise Devereaux and Winslow Emery."

"How do you know?"

"First, who else has any reason to search this cabin? Secondly, I'll bet those footprints are those of a man and a woman. I can't tell you the other reason."

"Your husband's ghost tipped you off?"

"Something like that." I thought of David, having an affair with someone who was vicious enough to place a gun in her husband's mouth and pull the trigger. It dawned on me then that she might have killed David as well. I shuddered. "Poor David."

"Maybe you'd trust me more if I told you something." He paused. "I don't tell many people about this." Even Chance seemed curious.

"It's about my wife, Susan," Russo said. "I told you she died. I didn't tell you how."

I waited. He walked over to the empty fireplace and stared down into its charred hearth. "She was killed. Shot to death, like your husband. Only she was in another man's arms when it happened. His wife caught on to what was happening before I did. She was waiting for them, I guess. Killed them both, then turned the gun on herself."

"John—"

"Let me finish. I hated Susan for it at first. But I missed her, too. And I hated missing her. Then I started blaming myself. Homicide detective gets called out in the middle of the night all the time, doesn't make for much of a home life.

"Anyway, one night, she came back. Her ghost, I suppose. You think I'm crazy?"

"Not at all," I said.

"Well, I don't scare easy, but that scared the living hell out me. She asked me to forgive her."

"She could talk?"

"Yes, can't your husband talk?"

"It's not my husband, John." I turned to Chance. "Can I tell him?"

Chance nodded.

"He's here, now?" Russo asked, startled.

"Yes, he's here. It's Chance Devereaux. He started visiting me the night before the funeral. He wants to be buried in a Catholic cemetery, but as a suicide, they wouldn't allow it."

"He told you it wasn't suicide?"

"Yes. He can't talk; I think it has something to do with the way he died. But he isn't so hard to understand once you get used to it. He made it clear that Louise drugged his drink, then shot him while he slept."

"We've suspected something like that," John said. "He had enough barbiturates in his system to make it seem unlikely that he would have shot himself; but it was right on the borderline, nothing solid enough to convict. Still, I wondered why he would take sleeping pills if he planned on shooting himself that same night. What would the point be? Between that and the insurance, she wasn't completely in the clear."

I watched Chance walk over to the fireplace. John followed my gaze.

"He walked over here?" he asked, taking a step back.

"Yes. He wants us to look inside it, under the metal plate in the hearth. The one over the hole where you clean out the ashes."

Russo got down on all fours and lifted the plate. I wasn't too surprised when he pulled out a sheaf of papers. Chance touched me on the shoulder, then disappeared.

The papers proved that Chance had warned Emery about the tank eight months before the disaster. One of Emery's fingerprints had been left at the cabin, on the door to a storage shed. Facing prosecution in the deaths of the workers as well, Emery later broke down and confessed to helping Louise kill David, and told police that Louise had killed Chance. He had been having an affair with Louise Devereaux for the past six months. They met on Wednesdays. They were both convicted of murder.

I saw Chance one other time; when I signed the forms saying I would pay to have his body moved to the Catholic cemetery. He met me near his old grave, and hugged me. He was still warm.

John Russo and I married a year later. When the going gets rough, we tell one another ghost stories.

UNHARMED

PACING MY SMALL CELL, trying not to listen to the racket around me.

They've just brought a meal to me, and I'm going to settle down to enjoy it. In the two days since Cindy's death, I haven't been able to get enough to eat. The authorities don't know what to make of my appetite.

They've been by to see me a couple of times now; can't make up their minds. I've watched them eyeing me, trying to figure out what went wrong, why I didn't save her. Wondering if I killed her, or if it was an accident. They aren't convinced of my innocence, but they're equally unsure of my guilt.

I'll tell you what I couldn't begin to try to explain to them. Decide for yourself.

The last time I lost my appetite, I was with Cindy. We were together that evening, as we were every evening . . .

*　　　*　　　*

She set the meal before me with a small flourish. I stared at it, only half-listening to her prattle mindlessly as she fumbled around in the kitchen, dishing up her own dinner. She insisted on this, this "eating in" every evening. And believe me, she was no gourmet cook. I could barely force myself to eat the unappetizing lumps in gravy that were supposed to resemble beef stew. Not that I know the first thing about cooking, but I wouldn't have minded going out once in a while, nabbing a bite on my own. Fat chance. Cindy wouldn't let me out of her sight.

Out of her sight. Poor choice of words, Alex.

Cindy was blind. That sense of duty I felt toward her, that protectiveness that is a part of my nature, welled up in me and made me feel ashamed. As penance, I finished off the last of the tasteless gruel.

Don't let me mislead you. I didn't stay with Cindy out of guilt or pity. I knew she was blind when I met her. I thought, at the time, that I was fully prepared to live with that fact. Being with her gave me a sense of purpose unlike any I had known before. I thought I loved her. I had even thought she loved me.

From the moment we met, though, Cindy had taken over my life. I admit that I allowed her to do so. In the beginning, I had an illusion of power. I was piloting her through the obstacles of life. What I failed to understand at the time was that I was also becoming completely dependent on her, not just for material things, but for companionship and a sense of being needed.

I was shuffled around a lot as a kid; I confess that I wouldn't know my own mother if I met her on the street. Cindy offered stability, a chance to stay in one place. You don't know how much I longed for that as a kid. But even the chance to have a place called home doesn't explain how much I needed her. The praise and affection she lavished on me in the beginning became all-important to me; I would have done anything for her. But these days, she doled out her praise and affection in a miserly fashion.

Some might say I was ungrateful. After all, I was better off than a great many others. I wasn't homeless, begging for a handout. Many in my position, with my background and limited education, would never live so well.

To our friends, we still appeared to be devoted to one another. Few of them realized that my devotion was a chore or knew how hard I had to work at it. Even the ones who knew how demanding Cindy could be still idealized our relationship.

I wondered at that, scratching my head in puzzlement. She heard the sound, of course. "Alex! Will you quit that scratching!" she snapped. I silently sulked off to my favorite chair. I didn't like admitting she was right. Lately I had gotten into the nervous habit of scratching my head, and it annoyed the heck out of her. I'm sure it bothered her as much as her whistling between her teeth bothered me. Our nervous habits had started grating on each other.

Face it, Alex, I thought with a sigh, *everything about her is grating on you.*

Perhaps you think I was unnecessarily harsh in my evaluation, especially considering her physical challenges. Not so. Through my association with her, I met other blind people, and have found that they are as varied in personality as the sighted. I can honestly say that I would have been happy to be a friend or even more than a friend to a great many of them. Cindy would have driven me crazy even if she'd had 20/20 vision.

But I was stuck with her. My dependency on her for my livelihood was never far from her mind. Or mine. At night, I often dreamed of running away, living on my own. So vivid were these dreams that I would often startle myself awake. "What were you dreaming, Alex?" Cindy would ask sleepily. "You've been running in your sleep."

I've been running away from you, I wanted to say, but it was no use. She always fell right back to sleep after asking the question. What did she really care about my dreams?

I heard her whistling to herself as she finished cleaning up the dishes. That damned whistling was the worst of it. I tried in every way I could think of to let her know it annoyed me, but to no avail. She didn't understand me at all.

Sure, the age-old complaint.

By the time she suggested an evening walk, I was more than willing to get some fresh air. I anticipated a stroll through the nearby park; maybe a chance to run into a friendly neighbor. But as I made the turn outside the door of our building, Cindy tugged at me so hard I nearly lost my balance.

"Oh no you don't, Alex. I know what you're up to. Well, we're not going to the park. Not this evening."

Well, okay, I admit it—there was a good-looking gal who often took a run through the park about that time of day, and she and I had exchanged some tender looks of longing. But it never went any further—how could it, with Cindy never more than two feet away from me?

I guess Cindy picked up on even my most momentary lack of attention to her and her needs.

I was soon distracted from all thought of the park. Cindy was, as usual, directing me in rude and abrupt tones. "Left, Alex." "Right, Alex." It was humiliating, being treated more as an errant child than as her partner.

I suddenly realized that this was what she envisioned every day of our life to be like. She would never trust me completely. She would depend on me, but not as a trustworthy companion. Not someone to really love. Knowing that I wasn't trained for anything that would allow me to live as well as I did with her, she meant to use me shamelessly. She would rely on me to guide her from corner to corner, to keep her from bumping into things, to listen to her, to sleep beside her. But my own needs—to be treated with dignity, to be loved—those were of no consequence to her. She was in control.

"Slow down, Alex!"

All of these commands! I thought angrily. *Couldn't you think of some gentler way to let me know what you want?*

She started whistling again. If it had been real whistling, real honest-to-God whistling, I think I could have lived with it. But there we were, walking toward the intersection, and she was doing it, whistling through her teeth. A tuneless, maddening sucking in and out of breath. I wanted to howl from the irritation of it.

It was just at that moment that she insisted on crossing the street. There was a van coming. I saw it, knew she was unaware of it. Knew without a doubt that the young driver was too intent on beating the light to pay attention to anything but the color of the signal.

Cindy tugged at me.

I stopped to scratch.

She lost her balance, losing her grip on me as she stumbled off the curb.

I let her go.

It's going to be hard to find work again. Maybe you can explain to them that I won't fail next time. Tell them, if you would be so kind, one other thing: please don't give me a whistler.

News Item:

BLIND WOMAN KILLED

A young blind woman was killed by a hit-and-run driver yesterday evening at the corner of Madison and Oak. Police report that Cynthia Farnsworth, 24, was struck by a blue van driven by a white male youth.

Farnsworth, who had a guide dog with her, stepped off the curb just as the light was changing. James and Lois Church, who witnessed the accident, said the dog refused to cross the street, but did not attempt to prevent Farnsworth from doing so. One other witness, who asked that her name be withheld, claimed Farnsworth was thrown off balance and into the path of the van when the dog stopped to scratch his ear.

Guide dog trainers refused to speculate about the dog's behavior, saying only that the dog's training and fitness will be evaluated.

The dog was unharmed.

THE MUSE

THE JET BLACK PANTYHOSE were calling to him. The feet of the pantyhose, to be precise. He knew he shouldn't look. Knew it would only encourage her. But he folded the edge of the newspaper down, giving in that much.

"Bee-yoll." Her voice was childlike, crooning. Her puppeteer voice.

"I'm not in the mood for this, Ellie," Bill said.

"Oh, Beeeeee-yoll."

Her hands were all he could see of her, and not really much of her hands. The makeshift pantyhose puppets were "looking" at each other.

"He's very angry with you," the right hand admonished the left.

"No, he's not," the left answered, then they both looked at Bill.

"I'm not angry," Bill said to the hands, giving in a

little more. Addressing the puppets now. "Not really angry. Just tired."

"Quit distracting him. He's on an important deadline, and he has writer's block," the right said.

"He never has writer's block," the left replied. "He's upset about Mir."

"The prospect of a visit from Miriam is an unpleasant one," he agreed.

Ellie's head emerged above the edge of the breakfast table. He saw that she had cut the crotch out of the pantyhose, and was wearing them over her head.

"You are the strangest woman I know," he said, causing her to smile. Ellie considered this a grand endearment. Bill knew that.

Her head tilted a little to one side, as if studying him for a portrait. "It's fine now. Not even my evil twin can stop you."

"She is your younger sister, not your twin," he said, but she was leaving the table, pulling the pantyhose off.

Ellie was right, as always. Not about the twin business, of course, but about the novel he was working on. He got up from the table feeling invigorated, and went straight to the computer. He had a new slant on a passage he had considered unworkable until a moment ago. This was the effect she had on him. Ellie was his Muse.

He had known she would be from the moment he first saw her. Seven years ago, well past three o'clock in the morning on a hot summer's night, at a gas station on Westwood Boulevard. Bill supposed he would forget his own name before he forgot that night.

He had been uneasy, at loose ends. It wasn't insomnia: it's only insomnia when you're trying to sleep. He had been trying to write. It was his best kept secret then, his writing. None of his professors at UCLA, who knew him as a recent graduate in mechanical engineering, would have ever guessed it. Well-written papers and a flair for creative problem-solving didn't make him stand out as more than a good student. His friends, although from varied backgrounds and majors, held the same prejudices as the few women he had dated: they assumed that engineers were unlikely to read novels, let alone write them. His father, who expected him to come to work for the family company in September, was also unaware of Bill's literary aspirations.

In those days, Bill thought that was for the best. If he was going to fail, he preferred not to advertise it. And while he had faith in the basic idea for his novel, he had to admit it wasn't working out. Frustrated when he stalled in that place in the manuscript where he had stalled no fewer than ten times before—where the boy ought to get the girl back again—he stood up and stretched. He needed some fresh air, he decided. At least, the freshest he could find in L.A.

And so he had restlessly made his way down to Westwood Boulevard, head down, his hands shoved down into his pockets, his long-legged gait taking him quickly past record stores and restaurants. He glanced up just to keep from running into parking meters and lampposts, glancing at but not really seeing the boutiques and movie theaters closed for night. The gas station was closed, too, but the sight that greeted him there made him slow his stride.

A lithe young woman was tugging on one of the water hoses most people would use for filling radiators. She was using it to wash a gold Rolls-Royce.

He came to a halt on the wide sidewalk, fascinated. She looked up over the hood, used the back of her hand to move her bowl-cut, thick, dark hair away from her eyes. Big brown eyes.

"Want to go for a ride?" she asked him.

He nodded, but didn't move forward.

"You'll have to give up hesitating if you're going to ride with me," she said, opening the driver's door. But Bill was distracted from this edict when he saw an elderly man sleeping on the front seat.

"Wake up, Harry," she said, gently nudging the old man, who came awake with a start. "We're taking . . ." She looked over her shoulder. "I'm Ellie. What's your name?"

"William. William Gray."

She turned back to the old man. "We're taking Bill here for a ride on Mulholland Drive. You can sleep in the back."

The old man reached for a cap, rubbed a gnarled hand over his face and quickly transformed himself into a dignified chauffeur, moving to hold the passenger door open for Bill, waiting patiently as Bill finally moved toward the car. Harry gave a questioning look to Ellie, now behind the wheel.

"No, you need your rest."

Harry nodded and climbed into the back, asleep again before Ellie had started the car.

They had traveled Mulholland and beyond that night, climbing canyon roads that twisted and turned.

She was a good driver; calm and assured, not crazy

on the winding roads. At first, he was afraid, wondering if he had made the biggest—and perhaps the final—mistake of his life. He started envisioning bold headlines: "Missing UCLA Student Found Dead," or "Still No Suspects in Topanga Canyon Torture-Murder Case." Perhaps he wouldn't be missed much. Maybe he would only rate a small article on a back page, near a department store ad: "Boy Scout Troop Makes Grisly Discovery in Canyon."

"Either you just had a big fight with your girlfriend or you're a writer," she said, not taking her eyes off the road. "I'm betting you're a writer."

He hesitated, then said, "I'm a writer. Or I want to be one. How did you guess?"

"The time of day, the way you were walking. You looked frustrated, I suppose."

"Anyone can be frustrated. Why would you think I'm a writer?"

She shrugged, then smiled a little. He waited, hoping she would answer, but she startled him by saying, "You're also a bit of a romantic."

He laughed nervously. "That's an odd thing to say."

"I am odd. But there's nothing odd about knowing a romantic when you see one. At three—" She glanced at the clock on the dash. "At approximately three-twenty-five in the morning, you agreed to get into a Rolls-Royce with a sleeping old man and a woman you had never met before."

"Perhaps I just needed an adventure."

"Perhaps. Perhaps both. So, what's your favorite movie of all time?"

"*Rear Window,*" he said without hesitation.

"Wonderful!" she said, laughing but still not taking her eyes from the road. "Whose work in it do you admire, Hitchcock's or Woolrich's?"

He smiled. Many people knew that Hitchcock directed *Rear Window*. Fewer knew that it was written by Cornell Woolrich. "Both, really," he answered. "I'm a fan of both. I've seen every Hitchcock film, with the exception of a few of the very early British ones."

Soon they were discussing Hitchcock and Woolrich, and Bill forgot all about Boy Scouts and headlines. She had seen most of the films he had seen, read more Woolrich.

He eased back into the passenger seat, studying her. She didn't make a move toward him, didn't reach across the seat, didn't even look at him much. Every so often, finding a vista she liked, Ellie would stop the car. The first time she stopped, Bill expected her to turn her attention to him. But she didn't do more than glance at him. "Just look at it," she said, gesturing to the carpet of city lights below. Soon he realized that was all she would ask of him—just to look at it.

At one of these turnouts, she kicked off her shoes and rolled down a window, resting her bare feet on the sill. She drove barefooted the rest of the night.

She asked him questions. He talked more that night than he had ever talked in his life. About his writing, his family, his childhood, his love of Woolrich stories and Hitchcock films and chocolate and on and on, even describing the furniture in his apartment.

"And you?" he asked. "Where do you live?"

"Somewhere in these hills. Perhaps I'll take you there someday."

As many questions as she asked, and as few as she answered, somehow she still managed to make him feel that he was of vital interest to her, not in the way some questioners might—as scientist studying an insect—but as if she cared about him from before the time she had met him. He was wondering at the trust he had placed in this stranger just as the sun was coming up over the hills. She had parked the car on a ridge. Harry was snoring softly.

"I'll take you home," she said.

"I'm not sure I want to go home," Bill answered, then quickly added, "Sorry, I don't mean to be pushy. You've been a great listener. You're probably tired and—"

She reached over then, and laid a finger to his lips. She shook her head, and he stopped talking, unsure of what she was saying 'no' to.

She took him back to his apartment, leaving Harry asleep in the car.

"Do you want to come in?" he asked on his doorstep.

She shook her head, an impish smile on her lips. "I know exactly what it looks like—I'm sure you've described it perfectly. Besides, you're very busy. You've got to get a little sleep, and then you'll wake up and write your book. It's going to be terrific, but no one will ever find that out until you write it."

She turned and skipped back to the car.

"Will I see you again?" he called out.

"Stop worrying," she called back. "Write!"

And he had. He slept about three hours, woke up feeling as if he had slept ten, and wondering if he had dreamed the woman in the Rolls-Royce. But dream or no dream, he suddenly knew how to get around that problem in his story, and went to work.

Harry appeared a few hours later, a picnic basket in hand. "Miss Eleanor sends her regards, and provisions so that you need not interrupt your work."

"You can talk!" Bill exclaimed.

"When necessary," Harry said, and left.

Bill searched through the basket, and found an assortment of small sandwiches, a salad, a slice of chocolate cake and several choices of beverages. He also found an old-fashioned calling card:

Miss Eleanor Wingate

On the back she had inscribed her phone number. "Delicious," Bill said, holding it carefully, as if it might skip away, disappear as quickly as she had.

And so he went back to writing. Bill saw little of Ellie during the first few weeks which followed their ride through the hills, but he called her often. If he found himself staring uselessly at the place where the wall behind his computer screen met the ceiling, unsure of how to proceed, a brief chat with Ellie inspired him. They played a game with Hitchcock films and Woolrich stories.

"A jaguar," he would say.

"*Black Alibi*," she would answer. "A name scrawled on a window."

"Easy—*The Lady Vanishes*."

And his writer's block would vanish as well.

*   *   *

When Bill completed his manuscript, Harry brought him and the manuscript to her home for the first time. Bill, trying (and failing) not to be overawed by the elegance which surrounded him, handed her the box of pages. She caressed the corners of the box, looking for a moment as if she might cry. But she said nothing, and set it gently aside without opening it. She held out her hand, and he took it. She led him upstairs.

Later, waking in the big bed, he found her watching him. "Did you read it?"

"No," she said, tracing a finger along his collarbone. "I don't want there to be any mistake about why you're here. It's not because of what's in that manuscript box."

He savored the implications of that for a moment before insecurities besieged him. "Maybe you'd hate it anyway."

"I couldn't."

It was the last time they talked about the manuscript for three days. At the end of those three days, he mailed it to an agent, called his father to say he'd found other work, packed up his belongings and moved in with Ellie.

The agent called back, took him on as a client, and sold the book within a week. Bill was already at work on his second novel. The first one was a critically acclaimed but modest success. The second spent twenty-five weeks on the bestseller list. When Bill got his first royalty check, he asked Ellie to marry him.

She gently but firmly refused. She also refused after books three, four and five—all bestsellers.

Today, as he finished the chapter he was working on, he wondered if she would ever tell him why. Ellie could be very obstinate, he knew. If she didn't want to give him a straight answer, she would make up something so bizarre and absurd that he would know to stop asking.

"There was a clause in my parent's will," she said once. "If I marry before my fiftieth birthday, the house must be turned into an ostrich farm."

"And the courts accepted this?" he played along.

"Absolutely. The trust funds would go to ostriches and Mir would be very unhappy with you for putting an end to her healthy allowance."

"Your parents would have left Miriam a pauper?"

"She thinks she's a pauper on what I give her now."

"A pauper? On ten thousand dollars a month?"

"Pin money for Mir. We grew up rich, remember?"

"Hard to forget. Why not give it all to Miriam and live on my money instead?"

She frowned. "I'd be dependent on you."

"So what? I was dependent on you when I first lived here."

"For about four months. And you had your own money, you just didn't need any of it. Do you want to be married for more than four months?"

"Of course."

"So now you see why we can't be married at all."

He didn't, but he resigned himself to the situation. She probably would never tell him why she wouldn't marry him, or why she allowed Miriam, who often upset her, to come to the house on a regular basis to plead for more money.

*   *   *

"Where's Harry?" Miriam demanded when Bill answered the doorbell.

"On the phone," Bill explained as he took her coat. "He's placing ads for a cook and housekeeper."

"Not again," Miriam said.

"The last ones managed to stay on for about six weeks," Bill said easily.

Miriam turned her most charming smile upon him. She was gorgeous, Bill thought, not for the first time. A redhead with china blue eyes and a figure that didn't need all that custom tailoring to show it off. What was she, he wondered? A walking ice sculpture, perhaps? But he discarded that image. After all, sooner or later, ice melted.

"I don't know why you stay with her, Bill," Miriam purred, misreading his attention.

Bill heard a door open in a hallway above them.

"If you're here for a favor," he said in a low voice, "you're not being very kind to your benefactor."

Miriam stood frowning, waiting until she heard the door close again. Still, she whispered when she said, "Even *you* must admit that she drives the entire household to distraction."

"Yes," he said, thinking back to the night he met Ellie. "But distraction isn't always such a bad place to go."

"She's crazy," Miriam said scornfully. "And a liar!"

"She's neither. What brings you by this afternoon?" They were halfway up the stairs now, and although Bill thought Ellie was probably past being injured by Miriam's remarks, he didn't know how much longer his own patience would last.

Miriam pointed one perfectly-shaped red fingernail

at him. "How can you say she's not a liar? She once told you Harry was her father."

"She knew I wouldn't believe it. She never tells me any lie she thinks I might believe. Come on, she's waiting."

Bill had heard Ellie cross into one of the upstairs staging rooms. This meant, he knew, that she had staged some clues for him, placed objects about the room intended to remind him of specific Hitchcock movies. It was an extension of the old game they played, and one of the reasons that housekeepers didn't last long. The last one left after finding a mannequin, unclad except for Harry's cap, sitting in the bathtub. (*"The Trouble With Harry,"* Bill had said, earning praise from Ellie even as they tried to revive the fainting housekeeper.)

Ellie, knowing Miriam hated the game, always had one ready when her sister came to visit.

Wearing a pair of jeans with holes in the knees, Ellie was sitting cross-legged on top of large mahogany table, passing a needle and thread through colored miniature marshmallows to make a necklace. She smiled as she moved the needle through a green marshmallow.

"How much this time?" she asked without looking up.

"Ellie, darling! So good to see you."

Ellie glanced at Bill. "Too many Bette Davis movies." She chose a pink marshmallow next.

"What on earth are you doing? And why are you wearing those horrid clothes?"

"Shhh!" Ellie said, now reaching for a yellow marshmallow.

Bill was looking around the room. As usual in a game, there were many oddball objects and antiques in the room. The trick was to find the clues among the objects. "How many all together?"

"Three," Ellie answered.

"Oh! This stupid game. I might have known," Miriam grumbled.

He saw the toy windmill first.

"Foreign Correspondent," he said.

"One down, two to go," Ellie laughed. "How much money this time, Mir?"

"I didn't come here to ask for money," Miriam said, sitting down.

Bill looked over at her in surprise, then went back to the game.

Searching through the bric-a-brac that covered a low set of shelves, he soon found the next clue: three small plaster of Paris sculptures of hands and wrists. A man's hand and a woman's hand were handcuffed together; another male hand, missing the part of its little finger, stood next to the handcuffed set. *"The Thirty-Nine Steps."*

"Bravo, Bill. Of course you came here for money, Mir. You always do."

"Not this time."

"What then?" Ellie asked, watching as Bill picked up a music box from a small dressing table.

"I want to move back home."

Ellie stopped stringing marshmallows. Bill set the music box down.

Don't give in, Ellie, he prayed silently.

"No," Ellie said, and went back to work on her necklace. Bill's sigh of relief was audible.

"Ellie, please. I'm your sister."

"I'll buy you a place to live."

"I want to live here."

"Why?"

"It's in the will. I can live here if I want to."

Ellie looked up. "We had an agreement."

Miriam glanced nervously toward Bill, then said, "It's my home, too, you know. You've allowed a perfect stranger to live here. Well, I don't deserve any less."

"Why do you want to come back, Mir? You haven't lived here in years."

"I think it's time we grew closer as sisters, that's all."

Ellie only laughed at that. Bill was heartened by the laughter. Ellie was protective of Miriam, held a soft spot for her despite her abuses. But if that sister plea didn't get through to her, maybe there was a chance . . .

"Look, you've been living up here in grand style," Miriam said petulantly, "and I just want to enjoy a bit of it myself."

Bill saw Ellie's mood shifting, saw her glancing over at him. He felt awkwardness pulling ahead of his curiosity by a nose. He decided to leave this discussion to the sisters. It was Ellie's house, after all. She could do as she liked. He started to edge out of the room, but Ellie said, "This concerns you, too, Bill. Don't leave."

He wasn't put off by what others might have taken to be a commanding tone. In seven years, he had never heard the word "please" come out of her mouth. Although he thought of few things as certain when it came to Ellie, one certainty was that she rarely asked anything of others. Knowing this, he treated any request as if there were an implied "please."

"This isn't his house!" Miriam shouted.

"Lower your voice. He is my guest and welcomed here."

Bill turned away, forced himself to look again at the objects on the dressing table.

Ellie went on. "You spent all of your inheritance in less than two years, Mir. Grandfather knew you were like our parents."

Bill knew this part of the story. Their grandfather had raised the girls after their parents—wild, spoiled and reckless, according to Ellie—were killed in a car wreck. While Miriam received a large inheritance, Ellie's grandfather had left the house and most of his money to Ellie, thinking Miriam too much like his late daughter.

"Don't start speaking ill of the dead," Miriam protested to Ellie.

"All right, I won't. But the fact remains . . ."

"That you've made money and I've lost all of mine. Don't rub it in, Ellie. Now I've even lost the condo."

"I know."

"You know? Then you understand why I want to live here."

"Not really. But forget living here. I'll help you buy a home, free and clear. But this time, I'll keep the title so that you can't mortgage it endlessly."

"I want to live here. This is my home!"

"Fine. Then you won't get another dime from me."

Bill watched in the dressing table mirror as Miriam swallowed hard, then lifted her chin. "All right, if that's what you want to do. My bags are in the car. Harry can pick up the rest of my things—"

"No!" Ellie interrupted sharply, clenching her hands, smushing part of her marshmallow necklace. She shook her head, then said more calmly, "You won't badger that man. I swear you won't be allowed to live here if you do. I'll sell this place first."

"All right, all right. I won't cause trouble, Ellie. You'll see. I'll even bring my cook and housekeeper with me. That will save Harry a lot of work."

Bill was hardly paying attention by then. He was nettled. So nettled, he didn't offer to help Miriam with her bags as she left the room. He kept his back to Ellie, pretending to be caught up in the game again.

My guest. It was accurate enough, he supposed. Not "my lover." Not "my friend." Not "the man I want to spend my life with." My guest. He picked up the music box again.

"You've got a burr under your saddle, Bill. What is it?"

He ignored her for a moment, lifting the lid of music box. It played "The Merry Widow Waltz."

He heard Ellie sigh behind him. "I'm not happy about it, either," she said, "but there's nothing I can do. Perhaps having Miriam here won't be so bad."

He closed the lid of the music box. *"Shadow of a Doubt,"* he said, and schooled his features into a smile before turning toward her. "Thank you for all the effort, Ellie. It's always an amusing game."

She looked puzzled. He hadn't fooled her, of course. Belatedly he realized that she must have watched him in the mirror. But if she could be obstinate, well, by damn, so could he. He excused himself and left the room.

*   *   *

As he paid the tab in a bar that evening, Bill had to acknowledge that the slight had escalated into silent warfare, and much of it was probably his fault. He had not yet managed to tell Ellie how she had given offense. In one moment, it seemed of so little importance that he was ashamed of himself for thinking about it at all. In the next moment, it seemed to stand as a perfect symbol for everything that was wrong between them. There were several drinks between moments. But in the end, he had firmly resolved to talk to her, not to let one comment ruin all that they had shared until then.

Bill looked up to see a familiar figure coming toward him. Not the one he most wanted to see, but close enough. Harry had come to fetch him.

"Did she send you for me, Harry?" Bill asked, allowing Harry to lead him outside.

"No, sir."

"You came on your own?" he asked in surprise. Harry had never indicated approval of Bill, a lack Bill took to mean disapproval.

"No, sir," Harry replied, but Bill noticed that the old man actually seemed a little embarrassed to admit it. Harry gently guided him into the back seat of the Rolls.

Bill waited until Harry got into the car. He felt as if he might be sick, but he fought it off. "Why'd you come after me?" he persisted.

"Miss Miriam suggested it. She has many suggestions, sir."

Bill signaled him to wait, opened the door and spared the upholstery.

Harry drove him home, windows down. But even

over the long ride, Bill had sobered little. He made it into the house under his own steam, and began to climb the stairs. He swayed a bit as he reached for the bedroom doorknob, twisted it, and found it locked. He stared at it in his hand, as if somehow he were just doing it wrong, this simple act of opening a door.

Harry came in then, and quietly coming up the stairs, asked in a whisper if Bill might need some assistance. Bill was hanging on to the knob, staring dumbly at the door. Harry reached and tried the knob, then murmured, "It's locked, sir. Perhaps . . ." but his voice broke off as they heard another door open.

Miriam, clad in a nightgown that seemed to offer little difference from sleeping in the nude, smiled and called out, "Ellie left some things for you outside the bedroom off your office downstairs. I guess you're in the dog house tonight, Billy Boy."

"You seem happy to hear it," Bill said, trying to stand up straight. Having this greedy woman in the household would sorely try him. Harry stepped aside as Miriam came closer. Miriam tried to put an arm around Bill, giggling when he clumsily pushed her hand from his waist. She stepped back.

"Why do you two stay together?" she asked. "Ellie doesn't seem interested. I could see why you tried to win her over at first, but now—well, why bother? You've got plenty of money. Most women would consider you quite a catch."

"For your information," Bill said, his drunken state not obscuring her intentions, "I wouldn't make any money without your sister. If I leave her, I can't write. She's my Muse."

Whatever reply Miriam might have made was lost

when a loud crash sounded against the other side of the bedroom door.

"Ellie! Are you all right?" Bill called frantically.

"Go to hell!" came Ellie's voice from the other side.

Bill heard Miriam giggle behind him as she closed her bedroom door.

"Don't do this, sir."

Bill was so taken aback by Harry's plea that he stopped packing for a moment. But he shook his head and latched the suitcase.

"Sorry, Harry. I can take the silent treatment, and finding out that she threw a portrait of me against the door that night. I can even take the blame for starting this. But I can't stay here if she doesn't trust me."

Until that afternoon, Bill hadn't heard a word from Ellie in three days. After that first morning, when Harry brought Bill's clothes into the bedroom adjoining Bill's office, Bill hadn't tried to go back to the room he had shared with her. He had heard her move about in her office, just on the other side of the wall. Each day, she had gone from her room to her office and back again, speaking only to Miriam or Harry. Miriam, suddenly the solicitous sister, would take meals to Ellie in her room. Bill tried to ignore it, told himself her temper would cool, and he would be able to tell her just how much she meant to him, that she was much more to him than the means to an end. Until then, he would keep his distance.

But this morning she had ventured outside the house, asking Harry to take her for a ride. They had been gone for about an hour when Bill heard someone rustling papers in her office, and went to investigate. Miriam was bent over some documents on Ellie's desk, pen in hand.

"What are you doing?" he asked, startling her.

"None of your business."

He moved closer, and she snatched one of the pages off the desk and wadded it up in her hand.

"Why are you in Ellie's office?" he asked, glancing at a contract Ellie had signed, the document Miriam had been studying.

"I said, none of your business."

He reached out and grabbed the hand with the paper in it. She clawed at his face, struggling furiously, but he caught both of her wrists and squeezed until she let the paper drop. He bent to pick it up even as Miriam ran crying from the room.

He sat down at the desk, ignoring the sting of the scratches. The contract was nothing unusual, he noted, as he smoothed the paper out. Ellie's signature was on the scrap. But as he studied it closer, he realized it was *almost* Ellie's signature.

A tearful voice took his attention from the paper. "I caught him trying to forge your signature. I grabbed the paper he was practicing on and he attacked me!"

He looked up to see Ellie staring at him in disbelief.

"Ellie . . ." he protested, standing up.

"Did you do this to her?"

She held out Miriam's wrists. There were dark red marks on them.

"Yes, but Ellie . . ."

"I don't want to hear it!"

She led Miriam from the room, consoling her.

And so he left the house in the hills. He had no trouble finding a house to rent. He told himself he only rented one because he was too busy finishing his manuscript to do serious house-hunting. Never mind that he was finished before his deadline. While waiting for his editor's response, he began outlining another work, writing character sketches. He told himself this productivity was a sign that he was readjusting, living a new life.

But he knew that wasn't the truth. The truth was, he wrote because writing was all he had left. He felt closer to her when he wrote, even as he told himself he didn't miss her. But that was the biggest lie of all.

When his editor proclaimed the new manuscript Bill's best work, Bill didn't feel the sense of elation such praise might have once brought. Ellie wasn't his link to writing after all. It wasn't inspiration he missed; it was Ellie herself.

He found himself on Westwood Boulevard at three in the morning, staring at the place where the gas station had been. It was gone, transformed into a parking lot. But as he stared, a gold Rolls-Royce was pulled into the empty lot.

For a moment, his heart leapt. But then he saw that Harry was driving.

Alone.

It wasn't the first time he had seen Harry. Harry kept tabs on him, he knew. In the beginning, he thought that she might have asked Harry to do so, then realized that Harry only appeared on his day off. Harry seldom spoke to him, and never mentioned Ellie. But it seemed to Bill that Harry was looking older each time he encountered him.

"Evening, sir."

"Hello, Harry." And then, breaking a promise he had made to himself, he asked, "How is she?"

Harry seemed to perk up a bit. He studied Bill's face, then seemed to make up his mind about something. "She's not well, sir."

"Not well?"

"No, sir."

"Nothing serious, I hope?"

Harry was silent.

"Harry, did she put you up to this? Is she trying to get me to come back? Because I'm doing just fine on my own now."

Harry shook his head. "You disappoint me, sir." He stepped back to the car.

"Harry, wait."

Harry waited.

"Does she know you watch over me?"

"No, sir. But for some time now she has . . . I mean to say sir, that whatever has gone before, at present she may be too ill to contact you herself."

Bill frowned. "I don't like hearing that she's ill."

Harry stayed silent.

"I know she dislikes doctors. Has she been to a doctor about this illness?"

"Miss Miriam has supplied a doctor, sir. He often comes to the house to care for Miss Eleanor."

"Oh." He looked away from Harry's studying gaze for a moment. "Well, I don't suppose . . . that is, if Miriam has found a doctor who will make a house call, I don't suppose Ellie needs me for anything."

Harry hesitated, then said, "Permit me to say, sir, that I'm not certain Miss Eleanor has done well under this physician's care."

"Tell her that you saw me," Bill said. "Tell her that you saw me here. She'll know what that means. Tell her to—to let me know if she needs me."

Bill didn't sleep at all that night. If she were seriously ill . . .

He hesitated until late the next afternoon, then called the house. Miriam answered.

"Miriam, this is Bill."

"Bill the caterer? Terrific. About this evening . . ."

"No, no. Bill Gray. Let me talk to Ellie, please."

"Oh, that Bill." After a long pause, Miriam said, "She doesn't want to talk to you."

"Let me hear her say that herself."

"Listen, she has a new man in her life. One who doesn't cause so many problems. We're having a dinner party tonight and he's the guest of honor. So I really don't think you're someone she wants to talk to."

The line went dead.

A new man. He half-believed it. If the wrenching in his gut was any indication, he believed it more than half. But Harry said she was ill, seeing a doctor. Why would she throw a dinner party if she wasn't well? Why would Harry look for him if she was seeing someone else?

Not much later, he heard a car pull into his driveway. Bill looked out the window to see the Rolls. He hurried out the front door when he saw the look of worry on Harry's face.

"Is she all right?" Bill asked.

"Sir, I'm to give you this."

Harry pressed a key into Bill's palm.

"There is a dinner party tonight, sir. I believe the persons in attendance are interested in acquiring the house and surrounding properties."

"Ellie is selling the house?"

"No, sir. But there now exist documents which say Miss Miriam is given power of attorney over the sale of the house, due to her sister's ill health. And indeed, her sister is ill."

Bill looked down at the key.

"She said you could win the game, sir. Do you know what she means?"

"The game? The Hitchcock game. It must be *Notorious.*"

"The game is notorious, sir?"

"No, Harry. *Notorious* is a Hitchcock film. Claude Rains plays one of the leaders of a group of Nazi scientists living in Brazil. They're trying to build an atom bomb. Ingrid Bergman has married him, but as he discovers, she's an American spy working with Cary Grant."

"Does the key give you some clue about her health, sir?"

"No," Bill said absently, "but in a Hitchcock film, the story is always larger than the objects which become the focus of the suspense."

"I beg your pardon, sir?"

Bill continued to stare at the key, but answered easily. "The key is to a wine cellar, where an important secret is kept. But the film isn't really about spies and secrets. Cary Grant and Ingrid Bergman are in love, but misunderstandings and mistrust stand between them. It isn't until the end of the film, when he realizes that . . ." Bill suddenly looked up at Harry. "Harry, when you said she was ill . . . oh, no. Get me to the house at once! Drive like a bat out of hell!"

Harry complied. As they drove, Bill asked him questions that made Harry wonder if the young man had somehow spoken to Miss Eleanor, even though Miss Miriam had taken the phone out of Eleanor's room long ago. Bill asked about Miss Eleanor's symptoms, and every time Harry said, "Yes, sir. She's had terrible stomach cramps," or "Yes, sir, very dizzy," Bill seemed to grow more frantic.

"Keep the motor running," he said as they pulled into the drive. "I'll be out in a minute."

Bill burst through the front door, nearly knocking a startled maid off her feet. He could hear voices in the dining room, but he didn't bother with the dinner party in progress. He ran up the stairs.

"Sir!" The maid called. "You can't go up there!"

He ignored her.

His only moment of hesitation came as he stepped inside Ellie's bedroom and saw her for the first time in months. He had expected to find Ellie's bedroom door locked, but quickly realized why it wasn't.

She was too ill to run away.

He forced himself to move again, came quickly to her side. Her skin was jaundiced and she was so thin, almost skeletal, he thought, then pushed the thought away. Her hair, her beautiful hair, was dull in color and missing in patches. Her breathing was steady but rasping. He put his hands beneath her and lifted her frail body from the bed, keeping the blanket wrapped around her. He told himself that self-recrimination must wait.

Her big brown eyes were open now, watching him.

"Good to see you," she whispered.

"My God, Ellie." He tried to gather his wits. "How long has she been poisoning you?"

"Little at a time," she said, wincing as she spoke.

"Don't talk now, not if it hurts. Has it just been since I left?"

She nodded, the effort seeming to wear her out.

A month. A month of arsenic. "I'm not leaving again, Ellie. Except to take you with me."

She continued to watch him, but now the barest smile came to her lips.

He had started down the stairs when Miriam, dinner party in tow, entered the foyer.

"What are you doing?" Miriam screeched.

"I'm taking her to a hospital. To see a real doctor. You had better pray to God that I'm not too late."

Miriam tried to block his way. "She's too ill to move! You have no business . . ."

"Careful, Miriam," he said in a low voice. "She's awake and lucid. Shall we discuss this in front of your guests, or do you want to wait until after Harry describes your so-called doctor to the gents at the sheriff's office? Ellie's bloodwork will probably give them all they need to go after both of you."

Miriam paled, then stepped out of the way.

"What's going on here?" one of the guests demanded.

"My sister's . . ."

"*Fiancé*," Bill supplied, as he reached the front door. "Her fiancé is taking her to a hospital."

The group followed him toward the car. He wasn't watching them. He was watching Ellie. She moved her hand, covered his with it. Her skin was cool and paper dry. "You're safe now, Ellie," he told her.

"I'm coming with you!" Miriam said, hearing the guests murmuring behind her.

"No you aren't, miss," Harry said, helping Bill into the backseat.

"She's her sister!" one of the guests protested.

"Her sister will remain here with you," Bill said. "She wants to tell you about a Hitchcock film."

"What are you talking about?" another man asked.

"*Notorious,*" Bill said, closing the car door.

"You've won, sir, haven't you?" Harry said as they drove off.

"I've had help," Bill replied. "All along, I've had help."

Ellie squeezed his hand.

WHITE TRASH

*T*HE WOMAN DRESSED IN BLACK *ninja garb moved stealthily across the street, armed with a spray bottle of a popular herbicide purchased at her local hardware store. In the dim light of the streetlamp, she set the spray mechanism to "stream" and went to work. Quickly she moved the bottle in a graceful, sweeping motion. She left as furtively as she had arrived.*

Three weeks later, much to the horror of the jerks who lived across the street, a rather obscene directive appeared on their lawn, spelled out in dead grass letters. Alas for these evil neighbors, the Suburban Avenger had succeeded once again . . .

I looked up from my bowl of cornflakes and glanced across the street, wondering—just wondering, mind you—if I could get away with it.

In every nearly perfect suburban neighborhood, there is the family that makes it "nearly" instead of "perfect." In ours, it was the Nabbits. You could find the Nabbit house without a street number. I would sometimes use its distinctive features to guide other people to my own home. "We live across the street from the house with the pick-up truck parked on the lawn," I'd say. Or, "Look for the old mattress propped up against the side of the garage, then pull into the driveway directly opposite the box springs."

Sarah Cummings, who owned the pristine property to the right of the Nabbits, had warned us about these troublemakers from the day we moved into the neighborhood. "I call them the 'Dag Nabbits,'" she said. "Nola Nabbit is a tramp. You watch. If Napolean's army had been as big as the one that has marched through Nola's bedroom doors, they'd be speaking French in Moscow today. Daisy, the little girl, is okay. But the kid! He's a mess."

The kid was Ricky. Ricky Nabbit, I soon learned, was a frequent guest of the California Youth Authority. He had a seasonal habit of breaking into houses, shoplifting, and other purely selfish acts.

"As long as it's baseball season," Sarah told me, "We won't have any trouble. He's a baseball nut. But every winter"—here, Sarah shivered—"he robs somebody."

When Sarah heard that I would be working out of my home, she was elated. "Maybe you can help keep an eye on things," she said. Specifically, she meant Ricky Nabbit.

We had moved into our home in the spring of the year when Ricky turned fourteen. I would watch him walk home from baseball practice at the nearby park. Skinny, clean cut, and looking smartly athletic in his uniform, he wore a glove so often, I had visions of him eating with the mitt on his left hand.

Sometimes I would see Ricky sitting on the front porch, oiling his glove, while from inside the house, I heard his mother and her boyfriend shouting obscenities at one another at the top of their lungs. Even with the doors and windows closed, we could hear them. This was especially true during the months when Clyde Who Parks on the Front Lawn reigned over the household.

Clyde was, perhaps, no worse than his predecessors. No more a loudmouth lowlife than Bellamy the Belcher (whose wide-ranging eructative skills included saying the word "breast" as he burped) or Horace the Hornblower (who honked his car horn at all hours, as a mere introduction to rolling down his window and hollering "Nola! Get your ass out here!"). These were not their real names, of course, but my husband and I used this system to refer to them when lamenting our luck.

Nola stayed with Clyde for most of the season, but broke up with him just before the World Series with a world class drunken brawl in the middle of the street. Nola got a shiner, Clyde got the boot.

Our doorbell rang a few days later, and when I looked out through the peephole, I was surprised to see Daisy standing on our front porch. She had long blond hair and beautiful green eyes, but was shy and slightly overweight. She was carrying a big cardboard box full of canisters of candy.

She stammered out a good afternoon and asked if I would buy some candy for her church school fundraiser.

"Church school?" I asked.

She turned a deep red, and stepped back. If she had been a turtle, I would have been looking at nothing but a shell. I waited, tried to smile my encouragement. She swallowed hard and then explained that she attended a private school operated by a church. The church she named was a conservative Christian sect.

Even though her church school was part of a denomination other than our own, I bought a canister, telling myself that I was doing my bit for ecumenism and good neighborly relations.

I was leaving the house some hours later and saw her returning home, still carrying her box, looking weary and somewhat dejected. I noticed that the box was still nearly full.

"Daisy!" I called.

You would think I had fired a shot over her head. She halted, shrank back, and nearly dropped the box. As I crossed the street toward her, her eyes grew wide.

I stopped a few feet away from her. Out of striking distance. She relaxed a little. "I just remembered," I said, "that I need some gifts for some clients. The candy would be perfect. Could I buy more?"

She looked at me in complete puzzlement.

"Perhaps those ones you have with you have been spoken for?"

She shook her head. "N-n-no," she said, finally coming out of her daze. "No, ma'am, they aren't."

I bought the rest of the box, and took it home. She thanked me politely and stared after me as I crossed the street. By the time I had set the candy inside my foyer and returned to my car, she had disappeared inside her house.

"What the hell are you doing buying all this candy?" my husband asked that night. "I thought you were trying to lose weight."

"You're so gallant," I said. "Now, by my count, there's a missing canister. Are you going to share any of it?"

He grinned and went to retrieve his pirated treasure, then unwrapped the foil covering on a chocolate morsel and hand-fed it to me. "Mmmm," I said.

"I agree," he said. "But are we converting to a new religion?"

I explained what had happened with Daisy.

"You," he said, "are too easy."

"Gallant again."

A week later, Ricky came by and asked if he could wash our car. "Sure," I said, and paid him a dollar more than he'd asked, on the theory that honestly earned money might start to appeal to him. He washed our car every weekend until the rains started in November.

He was always charming and polite. My husband agreed that we were better off making a friend of this kid than an enemy. Sarah Cummings told me I'd live to regret my kindness.

With the November rains, the Nabbit's lawn grew taller; fast food containers littered their front yard. Their dog, a mangy Bassett hound that smelled as if it had never been bathed, continued to use neighbors' lawns as his outhouse. (If American factories had the output that dog did, we'd be the most productive country in the world.) Nola stayed up late and laughed louder than the music she played. When she left for work, the hound bayed all day.

The Suburban Avenger knew it was an old trick. She placed the paper bag filled with gathered dog droppings on the front porch, lit it on fire, rang the doorbell and ran. With glee, she watched Nola Nabbit stomp the fire out. You can use old tricks on some dogs, the Avenger mused . . .

The Cummingses put up a low wrought-iron fence and planted Italian cypress on the side that bordered the Nabbits'. The Fredericks, on the other side, did the same, but planted rose bushes. The Cummingses called the police whenever the music was played after ten o'clock. Nola started turning the radio off exactly at ten, and shouting "Good night, you old bitch!" toward the Cummings' house.

Around Thanksgiving, Mrs. Ogden, a seventy-year-old woman who lived next door to us, asked me to keep an eye on her house while she paid an overnight visit to her granddaughter. When she returned, she discovered that her home had been burgled; her jewelry, her stereo, a small television set and her secret stash of cash were gone. I felt guilty, even though Mrs. Ogden didn't blame me in the least. "You have to sleep sometime, honey," she said. "I wasn't hiring you as a guard. Who knows? Maybe I'll get some of it back. I etched my driver's license number on the stereo and T.V."

As it turned out, the thief was caught trying to fence Mrs. Ogden's stereo and later arrested, tried and convicted. The thief was Ricky Nabbit.

I didn't hear much about him for a couple of years. Sarah told me that he didn't get much of a sentence, partly because his father, who lived in a trailer park about five hundred miles north of us, had agreed to let Ricky live with him for a time.

About the time Ricky left, Nola got a new boyfriend. Doug seemed to be as rough a fellow as most of the others, but soon we all noticed a change. No loud fights or partying sounds late at night. The yard was cleaned up. The place still wasn't painted, the hound continued to leave its calling cards, and Nola drank less but still swore like a sailor. Still, on the whole, things seemed to improve. We couldn't even come up with a nickname for Doug.

"It's been fairly quiet," the neighbors would say to one another. They always looked at the Nabbit house when they said it.

Then Ricky came home.

He was over sixteen by that summer, and much taller. He had filled out, become stronger. He seemed less lively than he had been at fourteen, and there was a surliness in his expression that had not been there before.

At night, we began to hear Nola shouting. Doug left a week later. Daisy seemed quieter and paler. Of her, we only saw a girl carrying books to and from the house. And, as I did every year, I bought a case of her candy. I was getting better at giving it away before my husband and I ate more than a single can of it.

Ricky's friends started coming over to the Nabbit house to play ball. Ricky had been kicked out of the baseball league some time before (for stealing more than bases from the opposing team), but his love of the game remained. He practiced on the front lawn.

"Hey, batter, batter," I would hear them chant, day in, day out. They played with a light plastic ball, shouted "I got it," "Foul ball," and "No way am I out," "Steeee—riiiiike!" as well as certain other remarks that would have cost a Boy Scout his good sportsmanship badge. Ricky was not Boy Scout.

The shouting and the noise was annoying, yet we saw no reason to lodge a complaint. They were just kids, after all. And as long as he was playing baseball, Ricky could be seen by his nervous neighbors, none of whom had welcomed him back.

Ricky ignored all of us. He became industrious enough to mount a light on the garage roof, illuminating his small playing field for night games of catch. That this light also illuminated our bedroom was not something Ricky was thinking about. Ricky, we had discovered, didn't think about other people, except as a means to an end.

The Suburban Avenger had been waiting for this night. The Nabbits' car had been parked in front of her house, doors unlocked. She secured the frozen anchovy under the seat springs, driver's side. She might not be present when the discovery was made, still she would know that revenge had been, well, reeked . . .

It was a sunny Saturday afternoon in September when the hardball hit the bedroom window, shattering it. I was in another room, and rushed in to see large shards of glass on my husband's pillow, splinters of glass everywhere else. If the game of catch had taken place a few hours earlier, or later . . . I ran outside.

Two boys, Ricky and a kid he called Ted, stared up at the broken window. Although no one else played baseball anywhere near my home, I suspect they would have run away without owning up to the damage. But to Ricky's great misfortune, Sarah had been in her front yard when the baseball was thrown.

Nola came out of her house, too, ready to defend her chick against Sarah—until she saw the window.

"It's Ted's fault," Ricky said immediately. "He was supposed to catch it."

I reached down and picked up the ball, which had been prevented from going though the window by the screen.

"Hardball?" Nola shrieked. "What got into you, Ricky? Playing with a goddamned hardball!"

Ricky had no answer.

Looking nervously between Sarah and me, she grabbed on to her son's elbow and said, "This is going to come out of the money you earned at the swap meet, Ricky." I groaned inwardly, wondering which of my neighbors' stolen goods might be sold to pay for my window. "I think you owe this lady an apology," Nola went on. I got a grudging "Sorry," from Ricky and Ted.

She eyed the window. "I think I've got a piece of glass that might fit," she said. "Ricky can fix it."

"No thanks," I said, envisioning Ricky with an opportunity to case my house for a future burglary. "I'd rather have a professional glass company do it."

The glass company charged forty-five dollars to fix the window. That left us with the clean-up. I did that myself. I told Ricky he could pay me back in five-dollar increments over nine weeks. He smiled and said that would be fine.

When the first payment was due and no five dollar bill appeared, I interrupted the next baseball game. A complicated tale of woe that would have won applause from Scherazade was given to me, along with the information that Ted would be paying for the window, not Ricky.

"We'll have it tomorrow for sure," Ted said. Ricky just smiled.

My husband and I began arguing. I should have asked for all of the money from Nola on the day it happened, he said. I never should have made the agreement about the five dollars. I was too soft. I should have let him handle it. We were never going to see that forty-five dollars.

More days and more tales of woe, more smiles from Ricky and more arguments between my husband and me. Finally—after my husband refused to be budged from Nola's front doorstep, a payment was made. Twenty of the forty-five.

Sarah and I became better friends. It dawned on me that she had long sought an ally in her own battles with the Nabbits. "Don't let the Nabbits turn us into rabbits," she would proclaim.

At eleven P.M., the Suburban Avenger sought her secret weapon. The baseball game had just ended, but the lights were still glaring on the field. The Nabbits had driven off to the store to buy more beer. The Avenger took the ice cold water from the refrigerator and filled the trusty spray bottle. She knew she only had a few moments to act. She took her stance, steadied her weapon. Stream setting again. Squeezed the trigger. Her aim, perfected from practice on a certain Bassett hound, was true. As the icy water hit each hot light bulb, the bulbs went out with a satisfying pop and the Avenger returned to her hideout with time to spare . . .

The city changed to automated trash collection in October, and like other households, our four, individual, thirty-gallon trash cans were replaced with one large, wheeled monstrosity provided by the city. The rules were clearly stated. The attached lid on the new container must be closed when placed at the curb. No overloading. If you threw away more than fit in the trash can, you paid a charge for excess trash.

With two adults using a trash can designed to hold the trash of a family of five, we had no problems staying within the limits. But from the first week of the new program, there was trouble. I put the trash out, and went inside. Later, when I went out to place the recycling bin at the curb, I noticed our trash can, like the Nabbits', was overflowing. When I lifted the lid, I discovered that the Nabbits had placed several bags of their trash into our trash can.

I began to wait until Nola had left for work to put the trash out. Inconvenient, but effective. And it meant that I put the trash out every week, instead of sharing the chore with my husband.

My husband bewildered me by siding with Nola on this issue. He thought my outrage was wholly unjustified. "What if they're dumping something toxic into our trash can? Something illegal?" I asked.

"It's just trash," he said. Then, for good measure, added, "We'll never see that twenty-five dollars."

It was after he left for work that morning that my Suburan Avenger fantasies began. As the afternoon wore on, I was shocked at the avenues my own imagination would take in the name of righteous anger. I wanted to plant my fist in Ricky's smiling face.

In the next moment, I was ashamed of myself for thinking such a thing. Was this the result of watching westerns as a kid? Too much violence on T.V.? Was I reading too many mysteries?

I calmed down. The Suburban Avenger would be forced to stay in the realm of imagination. I needed to find a legal remedy. I went to the library and checked out a well-worn book on suing in small claims court, and began the process. I was finally becoming a true Californian. I was going to sue someone.

I realized that I had only heard the Nabbits' last name. Were there two t's or one? Two b's or one? I tried the phone directory. No Nola Nabbit listing.

The Suburban Avenger whispered in my ear.

I let my husband put the trash out.

After he left for work, but long before the garbage trucks arrived, I checked my trap. Sure enough, the trash can was bulging with added material. I felt nothing but smug satisfaction as I pulled a bag of Nabbit trash from the trash can, took it into my backyard and set it on a table I used for gardening.

My excitement built as I rummaged—wearing old clothes and a pair of rubber gloves—through the Nabbit bag. Few things can tell our secrets as thoroughly as our trash will. The courts had long ago ruled that once a person put their trash out at a curb, the expectation of privacy was gone. Trash was fair game. Even if Nola hadn't dumped the bag in my trash can, it would have been legal to search it. Still, I felt better knowing that she had walked the bag over to my side of the street. She should keep *her* trash out of *my* trash can, or be prepared to suffer the consequences.

It didn't take long to find an envelope addressed to Nola. It was marked "Please open immediately" and came from the electric company. It contained a past due notice. I didn't want to slog through the beer bottles, coffee grounds and cigarette butts that made up the next layer of the bag. I had what I needed. Feeling bad about not recycling the beer bottles, but knowing their presence in my recycling bin would be a dead giveaway, I hauled the Nabbit trash bag back out to the container at the curb.

I typed up the forms needed to begin the process of suing Nola, and filed them down at the courthouse. She bellowed her outrage in her typical fashion when the papers were served.

In December, our case went to trial. She dressed like a hooker for court and made a wholly inarticulate case for her defense. When the judge failed to accept her theory that Ted should be responsible for the damage, she shook her fist at him and insulted his antecedents, which undoubtedly did not help her in the least.

Not surprised that she lost the case, I was shocked when she actually paid the judgment. I cashed the check and presented the funds to my husband. "Twenty-five dollars, plus my court costs," I said. He wasn't nearly as pleased as I thought he'd be.

"Now we have to worry about them going to war with us," he said.

" 'Don't let the Nabbits turn us into rabbits!' " I quoted.

For all my bravado at that moment, I began to fear he was right. The next day, Ricky sat on his porch, staring toward our house with a blatantly hostile expression. I was afraid to leave the house, even for a few moments, worried that he might do some sort of damage while I was gone. My husband's predictions of war came to mind. I crossed the street to Sarah's house.

After she congratulated me on my victory in court, she agreed to keep an eye on my house while I took care of some errands. As I walked back to my driveway, I heard Ricky laughing mirthlessly behind me.

I finished my errands, then drove to a nearby department store. There I purchased various articles of dark clothing. Together, they created an ensemble which roughly matched the one I had imagined the Suburban Avenger donning for her escapades.

As I pulled back into the driveway, Ricky came back out onto his porch, to resume his stare-athon. I took the bags of clothing from my trunk and felt my confidence surge as I clutched them. I slammed the trunk and turned to return Ricky's stare. He went back into his house. Triumphant, I hid the clothing in the back of my closet. One never knew when a Suburban Avenger might be needed.

I later learned that Ricky was arrested that same evening, breaking into Sarah's house. He was going to be tried as an adult, and there was little doubt in anyone's mind that he would be convicted.

"Those two old prunes, they've been out to get my boy from the beginning!" Nola raged to other neighbors. She didn't find many sympathetic listeners, but her bad-mouthing was so non-stop, it began to grow irritating.

Not nearly as irritating, though, as her practice of turning on the light Ricky had mounted for baseball games. At two or three in the morning, our bedroom would suddenly be flooded with light. When I tried to talk to her about it, she flipped me the bird and slammed her front door in my face.

The next day, on my front lawn, I found a pile of dog

droppings so large, it could have been collected from a kennel. The war, it seemed was on. Thinking of her gesture at the door, I decided to buy a bottle of herbicide.

On the next trash day, my husband put the trash out. From my kitchen window, I could see that the lid was propped open. I walked out to the curb, and sure enough, there were extra bags of trash in our container. Consumed by curiosity, and ready to prepare for a little payback, I surreptitiously pulled the two Nabbit bags out and took them to the backyard.

Donning my trash-searching outfit again, I began carefully removing items from one of the bags. Most of the garbage was food waste that could go directly into a new bag. That done, I studied what remained, paying more attention to the contents this time. I began to know Nola Nabbit.

She smoked Winston filtered cigarettes and whatever she rolled up into ZigZag cigarette papers. She drank a variety of budget beers, and had polished off one bottle of cheap white table wine. She had been late on her mortgage payment this month. She drank a lot of coffee and her family ate a lot of fast food. She had been to see a podiatrist, and apparently hadn't paid him on time. She had been invited to a wedding. She had received a reminder card for Daisy's next dental appointment.

She had thrown away a pair of medium black stockings with a run in them, and replaced them with another pair of the same expensive brand. Apparently, a good pair of stockings were important to her. Objectively, I had to admit that Nola had nice legs. She knew it, too.

She had written notes while on the phone, mostly

first names, but on one sheet, a misspelled reminder: "Pay $30 by the 10th to Ricky's psichologist."

A list caught my eye. Stained with coffee grounds, I could still make out its title: "Ruls of the House." Beneath that,

1. Chors must be dun befor you play ball.
2. No going out at nite w/out teling me were you are going and who.
3. Crewfew is at ten.
4. *No lies.*
Braking of ruls will be delt with.

I stared at the list for some time, thinking of all the parents whose children become impossible strangers. Even Nola, poor example that she might be, had struggled with this problem.

My curiosity was stronger than my sympathy. I opened the second bag. It was from Daisy's room. Here was scratch paper with seventh grade math problems on it, and several false starts on a report on California Indians. There were notes from a Bible study class on Corinthians. (In her neat printing: "Now comes a time to put away childish things . . .") Hidden in some of the wadded up sheets of notebook paper were foil candy wrappers. I pictured a terrified Daisy sneaking chocolates from a hidden candy-sale canister, finding some solace in forbidden sweetness.

At the bottom of the bag was a letter:

Dear Cathy,
  Sorry we can't come to the wedding. There is big trouble with Ricky. Mom took money he

*had been saving and paid for a window he
broke. It made him mad, and you know Ricky.
He robbed our neighbor. He's done it before but
this time I think he will be in jail a long time. I
know what he did was wrong, but I will miss
him so much. He makes me laugh.*

*I guess I shouldn't be writing sad news to
someone who is getting married.*

The letter stopped here, and I imagined her suiting
action to word, discarding this letter and writing a
happier one. Living in that household, what could she
possibly write?

I sat there in the winter sun, staring at the letter for
a long time.

I gathered the Nabbits' trash together and put it in
a new bag. I took the bag out to the curb and shoved
it down into our container. After that day, my husband always took the trash out. I made room for
whatever the Nabbits brought our way.

The Suburban Avenger was laid to rest. I put away
childish things.

MEA CULPA

IT WAS GOING TO BE MY TURN NEXT, and I should have been thinking about my sins, but I never could concentrate on my own sins—big as they were—once Harvey started his confession. I tried not to listen, but Harvey was a loud-talker, and there was just no way that one wooden door was going to keep me from hearing him. There are lots of things I'm not good at anymore, but my hearing is pretty sharp. I wasn't trying to listen in on him, though. He was just talking loud. I tried praying, I tried humming "Ave Maria" to myself, but nothing worked. Maybe it was because Harvey was talking about wanting to divorce my mother.

It was only me and Father O'Brien and Harvey in the church then, anyway. Just like always. Harvey said he was embarrassed about me, on account of me being a cripple, and that's why he always waited until confessions were almost over. That way, none of his buddies on the parish council or in the Knights of Columbus would see him with me. But later, I figured it was because Harvey didn't want anybody to know he had sins.

Whatever the reason, on most Saturday nights, we'd get into his black Chrysler Imperial—a brand spanking new, soft-seated car, with big fins on the back, push-button automatic transmission and purple dashlights. We'd drive to church late and wait in the parking lot. When almost all the other cars were gone, he'd tell me to get out, to go on in and check on things.

I would get my crutches and go up the steps and struggle to get one of the big doors open and get myself inside the church. (That part was okay. Lots of other folks would try to do things for me, but Harvey let me do them on my own. I try to think of good things to say about Harvey. There aren't many, but that is one.)

I'd bless myself with holy water, then take a peek along the side aisle. Usually, only a few people were standing in line for confession by then. I'd go on up into the choir loft. I learned this way of going up the stairs real quietly. The stairs were old and wooden and creaked, but I figured out which ones groaned the loudest and where to step just right, so that I could do it without making much noise. I'd cross the choir loft and stand near one of the stained glass windows that faced the parking lot and wait to give Harvey the signal.

I always liked this time the best, the waiting time. It was dark up in the loft, and until the last people in line went into the confessional, I was in a secret world of my own. I could move closer to the railing and watch the faces of the people who waited in line. Sometimes, I'd time the people who had gone into the confessionals. If they were in there for a while, I would imagine what sins they were taking so long to tell. If they just went in and came out quick, I'd wonder if they were really good or just big liars.

Sometimes I would pray and do the kind of stuff you're supposed to do in a church. But I'm trying to tell the truth here, and the truth is that most often, my time up in that choir loft was spent thinking about Mary Theresa Mills. Her name was on the stained glass window I was supposed to signal from. It was a window of Jesus and the little children, and at the bottom it said it was "In memory of my beloved daughter, Mary Theresa Mills, 1902–1909." If the moon was bright, the light would come in through the window. It was so beautiful then, it always made me feel like I was in a holy place.

Sometimes I'd sit up there and think about her like a word problem in arithmetic: *Mary Theresa Mills died fifty years ago. She died when she was seven. If she had lived, how old would she be today, in 1959?* Answer: Fifty-seven, except if she hasn't had her birthday yet, so maybe fifty-six. (That kind of answer always gets me in trouble with my teacher, who would say it should just be fifty-seven. Period.)

I thought about her in other ways, too. I figured she must have been a good kid, not rotten like me. No one will ever make a window like that in my memory. It was kind of sad, thinking that someone good had died young like that, and for the past fifty years, there had been no Mary Theresa Mills.

There was a lamp near the Mary Theresa Mills window. The lamp was on top of the case where they kept the choir music, and that case was just below the window. When the last person went into the confessional, I'd turn the lamp on, and Harvey'd know he could come on in without seeing any of his friends. I'd wait until I saw him come in, then I'd turn out the lamp and head downstairs.

Once, I didn't wait, and I reached the bottom of the stairs when Harvey came into the church. A lady came down the aisle just then, and when she saw me she said, "Oh, you poor dear!" I really hate it when people act like that. She turned to Harvey, who was getting all red in the face and said, "Polio?"

I said, "No," just as Harvey said, "Yes." That just made him angrier. The lady looked confused, but Harvey was staring at me and not saying anything, so I just stared back. The lady said, "Oh dear!" and I guess that snapped Harvey out of it. He smiled real big and laughed this fake laugh of his and patted me on the head. Right then, I knew I was going to get it. Harvey only acts smiley like that when he has a certain kind of plan in mind. It fooled the lady, but it didn't fool me. Sure enough, as soon as she was out the door, I caught it from Harvey, right there in the church. He's no shrimp, and even open-handed, he packs a wallop.

Later, I listened, but he didn't confess the lie. He didn't confess smacking me, either, but Harvey told me a long time ago that nowhere in the Ten Commandments does it say, "Thou shalt not smack thy kid or thy wife." I wished it did, but then he'd probably just say that it didn't say anything about smacking thy stepkid. That's why, after that, I waited until Harvey had walked in and was on his way down the aisle before I came down the stairs.

So Harvey had been in the confessional for a little while before I made my way to stand outside of it. I could have gone into the other confessional, and I would, just as soon as I heard Harvey start the Act of Contrition—the last prayer a person says in confession. You can tell when someone's in a confessional because the kneeler has a gizmo on it that turns a light on over the door. When the person is finished, and gets up off the kneeler, the light goes out. But I knew Harvey's timing and I waited for that prayer instead, because since the accident, I can't kneel so good. And once I get down on my knees, I have a hard time getting up again. Father O'Brien once told me I didn't have to kneel, but it doesn't seem right to me, so now he waits for me to get situated.

Like I said, I was trying not to eavesdrop, but Harvey was going on and on about my mom, saying she was the reason he drank and swore and committed sins, and how he would be a better Catholic if there was just some way he could have the marriage annulled. I was getting angrier and angrier, and I knew that was a sin, too. I couldn't hear Father O'Brien's side of it, but it was obvious that Harvey wasn't getting the answer he wanted. Harvey started complaining about me, and that wasn't so bad, but then he got going about Mom again.

I was so mad, I almost forgot to hurry up and get into the confessional when he started the Act of Contrition. Once inside, I made myself calm down, and started my confession. It wasn't hard for me to feel truly sorry, for the first sin I confessed weighed down on me more than anything I have ever done.

"Bless me, Father, for I have sinned. I killed my father."

I heard a sigh from the other side of the screen.

"My son," Father O'Brien began, "have you ever confessed this sin before?"

"Yes, Father."

"And received absolution?"

"Yes, Father."

"And have you done the penance asked of you?"

"Yes, Father."

"You don't believe in the power of the sacrament of penance, of the forgiveness of sins?"

I didn't want to make him mad, but I had to tell him the truth. "If God has forgiven me, Father, why do I still feel so bad about it?"

"I don't think God ever blamed you in the first place," he said, but now he didn't sound frustrated, just kind of sad. "I think you've blamed yourself. The reason you feel bad isn't because God hasn't forgiven you. It's because you haven't forgiven yourself."

"But if I hadn't asked—"

"—for the Davy Crockett hat for your seventh birthday, he wouldn't have driven in the rain," Father O'Brien finished for me. "Yes, I know. He loved you, and he wanted to give you something that would bring you joy. You didn't kill your father by asking for a hat."

"It's not just that," I said.

"I know. You made him laugh."

I didn't say anything for a long time. I was seeing my dad, sitting next to me in the car three years ago, the day gray and wet, but me hardly noticing, because

I was so excited about that stupid cap. We were going somewhere together, just me and my dad, and that was exciting too. The radio was on, and there was something about Dwight D. Eisenhower on the news. I asked my dad why we didn't like Ike.

"We like him fine," my father said.

"Then why are we voting for Yodelai Stevenson?" I asked him.

See how dumb I was? I didn't even know that the man's name was Adlai. Called him Yodelai, like he was some guy singing in the Alps.

My dad started laughing. Hard. I started laughing, too, just because he's laughing so hard. So stupid, I don't even know what's so funny. But then suddenly, he's trying to stop the car and it's skidding, skidding, skidding and he's reaching over, he's putting his arm across my chest, trying to keep me from getting hurt. There was a loud, low noise—a bang—and a high, jingling sound—glass flying. I've tried, but I can't remember anything else that happened that day.

My father died. I ended up crippled. The car was totaled. Adlai Stevenson lost the election. My mom married Harvey. And just in case you're wondering, no, I never got that dumb cap, and I don't want one. Ever.

Father O'Brien was giving me my penance, so I stopped thinking about the accident. I made a good Act of Contrition and went to work on standing up again. I knew Harvey watched for the light to come on over the confessional door, used it as a signal that I would be coming out soon. I could hear his footsteps. He'd always go back to the car before I could manage to get myself out of the confessional.

On the drive home, Harvey was quiet. He didn't

lecture to me or brag on himself. When I was slow getting out of the car, he didn't yell at me or cuff my ear. That's not like him, and it worried me. He was thinking hard about something, and I had a creepy feeling that it couldn't be good.

The next day was a Sunday. Harvey and my mom went over to the parish hall after mass. There was a meeting about the money the parish needed to raise to make some repairs. I asked my mom if I could stay in the church for a while. Harvey was always happy to get rid of me, so he said okay, even though he wasn't the one I was asking. My mom just nodded.

The reason I wanted to stay behind was because in the announcements that Sunday, Father O'Brien had said something about the choir loft being closed the next week, so that the stairs could be fixed. I wanted to see the window before they closed the loft. I had never gone up there in the daylight, but this might be my only chance to visit it for a while. As I made my way up the stairs, out of habit I was quiet. I avoided the stairs which creaked and groaned the most. I guess that's why I scared the old lady that was sitting up there in the choir loft. At first, she scared me, too.

She was wearing a long, old-fashioned black dress and a big black hat with a black veil, which made her look spooky. She was thin and really, really old. She had lifted the veil away from her face, and I could see it was all wrinkled. She probably had bony hands, but she was wearing gloves, so that's just a guess.

I almost left, but then I saw the window. It made me stop breathing for a minute. Colors filled the choir loft, like a rainbow had decided to come inside for a while. The window itself was bright, and I could see details in the picture that I had never seen before. I started moving closer to it, kind of hypnotized. Before I knew it, I was standing near the old lady, and now I could see she had been crying. Even though she still looked ancient, she didn't seem so scary. I was going to ask her if she was okay, but before I could say anything, she said, "What are you doing here?"

Her voice was kind of snooty, so I almost said, "It's a free country," but being in church on a Sunday, I decided against it. "I like this window," I said.

"Do you?" she seemed surprised.

"Yes. It's the Mary Theresa Mills window. She died when she was little, a long time ago," I said. For some reason, I felt like I had to prove to this lady that I had a real reason to be up there, that I wasn't just some kid who had climbed up to the choir loft to hide or to throw spitballs down on the pews. I told her everything I had figured out about Mary Theresa Mills's age, including the birthday part. "So if she had lived, she'd be old now, like you."

The lady frowned a little.

"She was really good," I went on. "She was practically perfect. Her mother and father loved her so much, they paid a lot of money and put this window up here, so that no one would ever forget her."

The old lady started crying again. "She wasn't perfect," she said. "She was a little mischievous. But I did love her."

"You knew her?"

"I'm her mother," the lady said.

I sat down. I couldn't think of anything to say, even though I had a lot of questions about Mary Theresa. It just didn't seem right to ask them.

The lady reached into her purse and got a fancy handkerchief out. "She was killed in an automobile accident," she said. "It was my fault."

I guess I looked a little sick or something when she said that, because she asked me if I was all right.

"My dad died in a car accident."

She just tilted her head a little, and something seemed different about her eyes, the way she looked at me. She didn't say, "I'm so sorry," or any of the other things people say just to be saying something. And the look wasn't a pity look; she just studied me.

I rubbed my bad knee a little. I was pretty sure there was rain on the way, but I decided I wouldn't give her a weather report.

"Is there much pain?" she asked, watching me.

I shrugged. "I'm okay."

We sat there in silence for a time. I started doing some figuring in my head, and realized that I had been in my car accident at the same age her daughter died in one.

"Were you driving?" I asked.

"Pardon?"

"You said it was your fault she died. Were you driving?"

"No," she said. "Her father was driving." She hesitated, then added, "We were separated at the time. He asked if he could take her for a ride in the car. Cars were just coming into their own then, you know."

"You mean you rode horses?" I asked.

"Sometimes. Mostly I rode in a carriage or a buggy. My parents were well-to-do, and I was living with them at the time. I don't think they trusted automobiles much. Cars were becoming more and more popular, though. My husband bought one."

"I thought you were divorced."

"No, not divorced, separated. We were both Catholics. We weren't even legally separated. In fact, the day they died, I thought we might be reconciling."

"What's that?"

"Getting back together. I thought he had changed, you see. He stopped drinking, got a job, spoke to me sweetly. He pulled up in a shiny new motor car, and offered to take Mary Theresa for a ride. They never came back. He abducted her—kidnapped her, you might say. She was his daughter, there was no divorce, and nothing legally barring him from doing exactly what he did."

"How did the accident happen?"

"My husband tried to put a great distance between us by driving all night. He fell asleep at the wheel. The car went off the road and down an embankment. They were both killed instantly, I was told. I've always prayed that was true."

I didn't say anything. She was crying again. I pulled out a couple of tissues I had in my pocket and held them out to her, figuring that lace hankie was probably soaked already.

She thanked me and took one of them from me. After a minute, she said, "I should have known! I should have known that a leopard doesn't change his spots! I entrusted the safety of my child to a man whom I knew to be unworthy of that trust."

I started to tell her that it wasn't her fault, that she shouldn't blame herself, but before the words were out of my mouth, I knew I had no business saying anything like that to her. I knew how she was feeling. It bothered me to see her so upset. Without really thinking much about what I was doing, I started telling her about the day my father died.

Since I'm being completely honest here, I've got to tell you that I had to use that other tissue. She waited for me to blow my nose, then said, "Have you ever talked to your mother about how you feel?"

I shook my head. "She wanted me to, but since the accident—we aren't as close as we used to be, I guess. I think that's why she got together with Harvey. I think she got lonely."

About then, my mother came into the church, and called up to me. I told her I'd be right down. She said they'd be waiting in the car.

As I got up, the old lady put a hand on me. "Promise me that you will talk to your mother tonight."

"About what?"

"Anything. A boy should be able to talk to his mother about anything. Tell her what we talked about, if you like. I won't mind."

"Okay, I will," I said, "but who will you talk to when you start feeling bad about Mary Theresa?"

She didn't answer. She just looked sad again. Just before I left, I told her which steps to watch out for. I also told her to carry an umbrella if she went out that evening, because it was going to rain. I don't know if she took any of my good advice.

In the car, I got worried again. I was expecting Harvey to be mad because I kept them waiting. But he didn't say anything to me, and when he talked to my mom, he was sweet as pie. I don't talk when I'm in a car anymore, or I might have said something about that.

Harvey went out not long after we got home. My mother said we'd be eating Sunday dinner by ourselves, that Harvey had a business meeting he had to go to. I don't think she really believed he had a business meeting on a Sunday afternoon. I sure didn't believe it. My mom and I don't get to be by ourselves too much, though, so I was too happy about that to complain about Harvey.

My promise to Mary Theresa's mother was on my mind, so when my mother asked me what I was doing up there in the choir loft, I took it as a sign. I told her the whole story, about the window and Mary Theresa and even about the accident. It was the second time I had told it in one day, so it wasn't so rough on me, but I think it was hard on her. She didn't seem to mind, and I even let her hug me.

It rained that night, just like my knee said it would. My mom came in to check on me, saying she knew that the rain sometimes bothered me. I was feeling all right, though, and I told her I thought I would sleep fine. We smiled at each other, like we had a secret, a good secret. It was the first time in a few years that we had been happy at the same time.

I woke up when Harvey came home. When I heard him put the Imperial in the garage, I got out of bed and peeked from behind my bedroom door. I knew he had lied to my mom, and if he was drunk or started to get mean with her, I decided I was gonna bash him with one of my crutches.

He came in the front door. He was wet. I had to clamp my hand over my mouth to keep from laughing, because I realized that he had gone out without his umbrella. He looked silly. The rain and wind had messed up his hair, so that his long side—the side he tries to comb over his bald spot—was hanging straight down. He closed the front door really carefully, then he went into the bathroom near my bedroom, instead of the one off his room. At first I thought he was just sneaking in and trying not to wake up my mom, but he was in there a long time. When he came out, he was in his underwear. I almost busted a gut trying not to laugh. He tiptoed past me and went to bed. The clock was striking three.

I waited until I thought he might be asleep, then I went into the bathroom. There was water all over the place. He hadn't mopped up after himself, so I took a towel and dried the floor and counter. It was while I was drying the floor that I saw the book of matches. It had a red cover on it, and it came from a place called Topper's, an all-night restaurant down on South Street. I picked up the matchbook. A few of the matches had been used. The name "Mackie" was written on the inside, and just below that, "1417 A-3." I closed the cover and looked at the address for Topper's. 1400 South Street. I knew Harvey's handwriting well enough to know that he had written that name and address.

What was he doing with matches? Harvey didn't smoke. He hated smoke. I knew, because he made a big speech about it on the day he threw away my dad's pipes. I had gone into the trash and taken them back out. I put them in a little wooden box, the same one where I kept a photo of my dad. I never looked at the photo or the pipes, but I kept them anyway. I thought my mom might have found the place I hid them, but so far, she hadn't ratted on me.

I opened the laundry hamper. Harvey's wet clothes were in there. I reached in and pulled out his shirt. No lipstick stains, and even without lifting it close to my nose, I could tell it didn't have perfume on it. It could have used some. It smelled like smoke, a real strong kind of smoke. Not like a fire or anything, but stronger than a cigarette. A cigar, maybe. I had just put the shirt back in the hamper when the door flew open.

"What are you doing?" Harvey asked.

I should have said something like, "Ever heard of knocking?" or made some wisecrack, but I was too scared. I could feel the matchbook in my hand, hot as if I had lit all the matches in it at once.

Luckily, my mom woke up. "Harvey?" I heard her call. It sounded like she was standing in the hall.

"Oh, did I wake you up, sweetheart?" he said.

My jaw dropped open. Harvey never talked to her like that after they got married.

"What's wrong?" she asked.

"I was just checking on the boy," he said. He looked at me and asked, "Are you okay, son?"

Son. That made me sick to my stomach. I swallowed and said, "Just came in to get some aspirin."

"Your leg bothering you because of this rain?" he asked, like he cared.

"I'll be all right. Sorry I woke you up."

My mom was at the door then, so I said, "Okay if I close the door? Now that I'm up . . . well, you know . . ."

Harvey laughed his fake laugh and put an arm around my mom. He closed the door.

I pulled a paper cup out of the dispenser in the bathroom. I turned the cup over and scratched the street numbers for Mackie and Topper's, then put the matchbook back where I found it. By now, I was so scared I really did have to go, so I didn't have to fake that. I flushed the toilet, then washed my hands. Finally, I put a little water in the cup. I opened the door. I turned to pick up the cup, and once again thought to myself that one of the things that stinks about crutches is that they take up your hands. I was going to try to carry the cup in my teeth, since it wasn't very full, but my mom is great about seeing when I'm having trouble, so she said, "Would you like to have that cup of water on your night stand?"

I nodded.

Harvey watched us go into my bedroom. He went into the bathroom again. My mom started fussing over me, talking about maybe taking me to a new doctor. I tried to pay attention to what she was saying, but the whole time, I was worrying about what Harvey was thinking. Could he tell that I saw the matchbook? After a few minutes he came back out, and he had this smile on his face. I knew the matches wouldn't be on the floor now, that he had figured out where he had dropped them and that he had picked them up. He felt safe. I didn't. I drank the water and saved the bottom of the cup.

The next morning I got up early and went into the laundry room. Harvey's clothes were still in the bathroom, but I wasn't interested in them anyway. I put a load of his wash in the washing machine, checking his trouser pockets before I put them in. I made sixty cents just by collecting his change. I put it in my own pocket, right next to the waxy paper from the cup.

I had just started the washer when my mom and Harvey came into the kitchen. My mom got the percolator and the toaster going. Harvey glared at me while I straightened up the laundry room and put the soap away.

"You're gonna turn him into a pansy, lettin' him do little girl's work like that," he said to my mom when she brought him his coffee and toast.

"I like being able to help," I said, before she could answer.

We both waited for him to come over and cuff me one for arguing with him first thing in the morning, but he just grunted and stirred a bunch of sugar into his coffee. He always put about half the sugar bowl into his coffee. You'd think it would have made him sweeter.

That morning, it seemed like it did. Once he woke up a little more, he started talking to her like a guy in a movie talks to a girl just before he kisses her. I left the house as soon as I could.

Before I left, I told my mom that I might be late home from school. I told her that I might catch a matinee with some of the other kids. I never do anything with other kids, and she seemed excited when I told her that lie. I felt bad about lying, even if it made her happy.

All day, I was a terrible student. I just kept thinking about the matchbook and about Mary Theresa's father and Harvey and leopards that don't change their spots.

After school, I took the city bus downtown. I got off at South Street, right in front of Topper's.

The buildings are tall in that part of town. There

wasn't much sunlight, but up above the street, there were clotheslines between the buildings. The day was cloudy, so nobody had any clothes out, although I could have told them it wasn't going to rain that afternoon. Not that there was anything to rain on—nothing was growing there. The sidewalks and street were still damp, though, and not many people were around. I was a little nervous.

I thought about going into Topper's and asking if anybody knew a guy named Mackie, but decided that wouldn't be too smart. I started down the street. The next address was 1405, Linden's Tobacco Shop. I had already noticed that sometimes they skip numbers downtown. I stopped, thinking maybe that was where Harvey got the smoke on his clothes. Just then a man came out of the door and didn't close it behind him as he left the shop. As I stood in the doorway, a sweet, familiar smell came to me, and I felt an ache in my chest. It was pipe tobacco. It made me think of my father, and how he always smelled like tobacco and Old Spice After Shave. A sourpussed man came to the door, said "No minors," and shut it in my face. The shop's hours were painted on the door. It was closed on Sundays.

I moved down the sidewalk, reading signs, looking in windows. "Buzzy's Newsstand—Out of Town Papers," "South Street Sweets—Handmade Chocolates," "Moore's Hardware—Everything for Home and Garden," "Suds-O-Mat—Coin-Operated Laundry." Finally, I came to "The Coronet—Apartments to Let." The address was 1417 South Street. The building looked older than Mary Theresa's mother.

Inside, the Coronet was dark and smelled like a

mixture of old b.o. and cooked cabbage. There was a thin, worn carpet in the hallway. A-3 was the second apartment on the left-hand side. I put my ear to the door. It was quiet. I moved back from the door and was trying to decide what to do when a man came into the building. I turned and pretended to be waiting for someone to answer the door of A-4.

The man was carrying a paper sack and smoking a cigar. The cigar not only smelled better than the hallway, it smelled exactly like the smoke on Harvey's clothes. It had to be Mackie.

Mackie's face was an okay face, except that his nose looked like he had run into a wall and stayed there for a while. He was big, but he didn't look clumsy or dumb. I saw that the paper sack was from the hardware store. When he unlocked his door, I caught a glimpse of a shoulder holster. As he pulled the door open, he saw me watching him and gave me a mean look.

"Whaddaya want?" he said.

I swallowed hard and said, "I'm collecting donations for the Crippled Children's Society."

His eyes narrowed. "Oh yeah? Where's your little collection can?"

"I can't carry it and move around on the crutches," I said.

"Hmpf. You won't get anything there," he said, nodding toward the other apartment. "The place is empty."

"Oh. I guess I'll be going then."

I tried to move past him, but he pushed me hard against the wall, making me drop one of my crutches. "No hurry, is there?" he said. "Let's see if you're really a cripple."

That was easy. I dropped the other crutch, then reached down and pulled my right pant leg up. He did what anybody does when they see my bad leg. They stare at it, and not because it's beautiful.

I used this chance to look past him into his apartment. From what I could see of it, it was small and neat. There was a table with two things on it: a flat, rectangular box and the part of a shot they call a syringe. It didn't have a needle on it yet. You might think I'm showing off, but I knew it was called a syringe because I've spent a lot of time getting stuck by the full works, and sooner or later some nurse tells you more than you want to know about anything they do to you.

Mackie picked up my crutches. I was trying to see into the paper sack, but all I could make out was that it was some kind of can. When Mackie straightened up again, his neck and ears were turning red. Maybe that's what made me bold enough to say, "I lied."

His eyes narrowed again.

"I'm not collecting for Crippled Children. I was just trying to raise some movie money."

He started laughing. He reached in his pocket and pulled out a silver dollar. He dropped it into my shirt pocket. "Kid, you earned it," he said and went into his apartment.

I leaned against the wall for another minute, my heart thumping hard against that silver dollar. Then I left and made my way to the hardware store.

No other customers were in there. The old man behind the counter was reading a newspaper. I cleared my throat. "Excuse me, sir, but Mackie sent me over to pick up another can."

"Another one? You can tell Mackie he's got to come here himself." He looked up at me and then looked away really fast. I'm used to it. "Look," he said, talking into the newspaper, "I'm not selling weed killer to any kid, crippled or no. The stuff's poisonous." That's the way he said it: "crippled or no." Like I had come in there asking for special treatment.

I had too much on my mind to worry about it. I was thinking about why a guy who lived in a place like the Coronet would need weed killer. "What's weed killer got in it, anyway?" I asked.

He folded his newspaper down and looked at me like my brain was as lame as my leg. "Arsenic. Eat a little of that and you're a goner."

At home that night, I kept an eye on Harvey. I noticed that even though he was still laying it on thick with my mom, he was nervous. He kept watching the clock on the mantel. My mom was in the kitchen, making lunches, and he kept looking between the kitchen and the clock. When the phone rang at eight, he jumped up to answer it, yelling, "I got it." To the person on the phone, he said, "Just a sec." He turned to me and said, "Get ready for bed."

I thought of arguing, but changed my mind. I went into the hallway, and waited just out of sight. I hoped he'd talk as loud as he usually did.

He tried to speak softly, but I could still hear him.

"No, no, that's too soon. I have some arrangements to make." He paused, then said, "Saturday, then. Good."

That night, when my mom came in to say good night, I told her not to let Harvey fix her anything to eat, or take anything from him that came in a rectangular box. "He wants to poison you, Mom," I whispered.

She laughed and said, "That matinee must have been a detective movie. I was waiting for you to tell me about your afternoon. Did you have a good time?"

It wasn't easy, but I told her the truth. "I didn't go to a movie," I said.

"But I thought . . ."

"I went downtown. To South Street."

She looked more scared than when I told her that her husband wanted to poison her.

"Please don't tell Harvey!" I said.

"Don't tell Harvey what?" I heard a voice say. He was standing in my bedroom door.

"Oh, that he got a bad grade on a spelling test," my mom said. "But you wouldn't get angry with him over a little thing like that, would you, dear?"

"No, of course not, sweetheart," he said to her. He faked another laugh and walked off.

Although I don't think Harvey knew it, she hadn't meant it when she called him "dear." And she had lied to him for my sake. Just when I had decided that meant she believed me about the poison, she said, "You and I will have a serious talk very soon, young man. Good night." She kissed me, but I could tell she was mad.

That was a terrible week. Harvey was nervous, I was nervous, and my mom put me on restriction. I had to come straight home after school every day. I never got far enough in the story to tell her what happened when I went downtown; she just said that where Harvey went at night was his business, not mine, and that I should never lie to her again about where I was going.

We didn't say much to one another. On Friday night, when she came in to say good night, I couldn't even make myself say good night back. She stayed there at my bedside and said, "We were off to such a good start this week. I had hoped . . . well, that doesn't matter now. I know you're angry with me for putting you on restriction, but you gave me a scare. You're all I have now, and I couldn't bear to lose you."

"You're all I have, too," I said, "I don't mind the restriction. It's just that you don't believe anything I say."

"No, that's not it. It's just that I think Harvey is trying to be a better husband. Maybe Father O'Brien has talked to him, I don't know."

"A leopard doesn't change his spots," I said.

"Harvey's not a leopard."

"He's a snake."

She sighed again. She kept sitting there.

All of a sudden, I remembered that Harvey had mentioned Saturday, which was the next day, and I sat up. I hugged her hard. "Please believe me," I said. "Just this once."

She was startled at first, probably because that was two hugs in one week, which was two more than I'd given her since she married Harvey. She hugged back, and said, "You really are scared aren't you?"

I nodded against her shoulder.

"Okay. I won't let Harvey fix any meals for me or give me anything in a rectangular box. At least not until you get over this." She sounded like she thought it was kind of funny. "I hope it will be soon, though."

"Maybe as early as tomorrow," I whispered, but I don't think she heard me.

I hardly slept at all that night.

The next morning, Harvey left the house and didn't come back until just before dinner. He wasn't carrying anything with him when he came in the house, just went in and washed up. I watched every move he made, and he never went near any food.

"C'mon," he said to me after dinner, "let's go on down to the church."

A new thought hit me. What if the weed killer was for someone else? What if Harvey hired Mackie to shoot my mom? "I don't want to go," I said.

"No more back-talk out of you, buster. Let's go. Confessions will be over if we don't get down there."

I looked at my mom.

"Go on," she said. "I'll be fine."

As Harvey walked with me to the car, I kept trying to think up some way to stay home. I knew what Mackie looked like. I knew he carried his gun in a shoulder holster. I knew he liked silver dollars, because I had one of his in my pocket.

I looked up, because Harvey was saying something to me. He had opened the car door for me, which was more than he usually did. "Pardon?"

"I said, get yourself situated. I've got a surprise for your mother."

Before I could think of anything to say, he was

opening the back door and picking up a package. A rectangular package. As he walked past me, I saw there was a label on it. South Street Sweets.

My mother took it from him, smiling and thanking him. "You know I can't resist chocolates," she said.

"Have one now," he said.

I was about to yell out "No!" thinking she'd forgotten everything I said, but she looked at me over his shoulder, and something in her eyes made me keep my mouth shut.

Harvey followed her glance, but before he could yell at me, she said, "Oh Harvey, his knee must be bothering him. Be a dear and help him. I'm going to go right in and put my feet up and eat about a dozen of these." To me, she said, "Remember what we talked about last night. You be careful."

All the way to the church, Harvey was quiet. When we got there, he sent me in first, as usual.

"But the choir loft is closed," I said.

"It hasn't fallen apart in a week. They haven't even started work on it. Go on."

I went inside. He was right. Even though there was a velvet rope and a sign that said, "Closed," it didn't look like any work had started. I wanted to be near Mary Theresa's window anyway. But as I got near the top of the stairs, I noticed they sounded different beneath my crutches. Some of the ones that were usually quiet were groaning now.

I waited until almost everyone was gone. By the time I turned the lamp on, I had done more thinking. I figured Harvey wouldn't give up trying to kill my mom, even if I had wrecked his chocolate plan. He wanted the house and the money that came with my mom, but not her or her kid. I couldn't keep watching him all the time.

I turned the lamp on and waited for him to come into the church. As usual, he didn't even look toward me. He went into the confessional. I took one last look at the window and started to turn the lamp off, when I got an idea. I left the lamp on.

I knew the fourth step from the top was especially creaky. I went down to the sixth step from the top, then turned around. I held on to the rail, and then pressed one of my crutches down on the fourth step. It creaked. I leaned most of my weight on it. I felt it give. I stopped before it broke.

I went on down the stairs. I could hear Harvey, not talking about my mom this time, but not admitting he was hoping she was already dead. I went into the other confessional, but I didn't kneel down.

I heard Harvey finish up and step outside his confessional. Then I heard him take a couple of steps and stand outside my confessional door. For a minute, I was afraid he'd open the door and look inside. He didn't. He took a couple of steps away, and then stopped again. I waited. He walked toward the back of the church, and I could tell by the sound of his steps that he was mad. I knocked on the wall between me and Father O'Brien.

"All right if I don't kneel this time, Father?" I asked.

"Certainly, my son," he said.

"Bless me, Father, for I have sinned. I lied three times, I stole sixty cents and . . ."

I waited a moment.

"And?" the priest said.

There was a loud groaning sound, a yell, and a crash.

"And I just killed my stepfather."

He didn't die, he just broke both of his legs and knocked himself out. A policeman showed up, but not because Father O'Brien had told anyone my confession. Turned out my mother had called the police, showed them the candy and finally convinced them they had to hurry to the church and arrest her husband before he harmed her son.

The police talked to me and then went down to South Street and arrested Mackie. At the hospital, a detective went in with me to see Harvey when Harvey woke up. I got to offer Harvey some of the chocolates he had given my mom. Instead of taking any candy, he made another confession that night. Before we left, the detective asked him why he had gone up into the choir loft. He said I had left a light on up there. The detective asked me if that was true, and of course I said, "Yes."

The next time I was in church, I put Mackie's silver dollar in the donation box near the candles and lit three candles: one for my father, one for Mary Theresa Mills, and one for the guy who made up the rule that says priests can't rat on you.

After I lit the candles, I went home and took out my wooden box. I put my father's pipes on the mantel, next to his photo. My mom saw me staring at the photo and came over and stood next to me. Instead of thinking of him being off in heaven, a long way away, I imagined him being right there with us, looking back at us from that picture. I imagined him knowing that I had tried to save her from Harvey. I thought he would have liked that.

My mom reached out and touched one of the pipes very carefully. "It wasn't your fault," she said.

You know what? I believed her.

A FINE SET OF TEETH

I SAW FRANK DROP two cotton balls into the front pocket of his denim jacket and I made a face. "Those won't help, you know."

He smiled and said, "Better than nothing."

"Cotton is not effective ear protection."

He picked up his keys by way of ignoring me and said, "Are you ready?"

"You don't have to go with me," I offered again.

"I'm not letting my wife sit alone in a sleazy bar. No more arguments, all right?"

"If I were on a story—"

"You aren't. Let's go."

"Thanks for being such a good sport about it," I said, which made him laugh.

"Which apartment number?" Frank asked as we pulled up to the curb in front of Buzz Sullivan's apartment building. The building was about four stories high, probably built in the 1930s. I don't think it had felt a paintbrush along its walls within the last decade.

"Buzz didn't tell me," I answered. "He just said he lived on the fourth floor."

Frank sighed with long suffering, but I can ignore someone as easily as he can, and got out of the car.

As we made our way to the old stucco building's entry, we dodged half a dozen kids who were playing around with a worn soccer ball on the brown crab-grass lawn. The children were laughing and calling to one another in Spanish. A dried sparrow of a woman watched them from the front steps. She seemed wea-rier than Atlas.

Frank muttered at my back about checking mail-boxes for the first of the three flights of stairs, but soon followed in silence. Although Buzz had moved several times since I had last been to one of his apartments, I knew there would be no difficulty in locating the one that was his. We reached the fourth floor and Frank started to grouse, but soon the sound I had been wait-ing for came to my ears. Not just my ears: I heard the sound under my fingernails, beneath my toes and in places my mother asked me never to mention in mixed company. Three screeching notes strangled from the high end of the long neck of a Fender Stratocaster, a sound not unlike those a pig might make—if it was having its teeth pulled with a pair of pliers.

I turned to look at Frank Harriman and saw some-thing I rarely see on his face: fear. Raw fear.

I smiled. I would have said something comforting, but he wouldn't have heard me over the next few whammified notes whining from Buzz's guitar. A deaf man could have told you they were coming from apartment 4E. I waited until the sound subsided, asked, "Should we drop you off back at the house?" and watched my husband stalk over to the door of number 4E and rap on it with the kind of ferocious intensity one usually saves for rousing the occupants of burning buildings.

   Q: What's the difference between a dead trombone player and a dead snake in the middle of a road?
   A: The snake was on his way to a gig.

The door opened and a thin young man with a hairdo apparently inspired in color and shape by a sea urchin stood looking at Frank in open puzzlement. He swatted a few purple spikes away from his big blue eyes and finally saw me standing nearby. His face broke into an easy, charming smile.

"Irene!" He looked back at Frank. "Is this your cop?"

"No, Buzz," I said, "that's my husband."

Buzz looked sheepish. "Oh, sorry. I've told Irene I'm not like that, and here I am, acting just *exactly* like that."

"Like what?" Frank asked.

"I don't mind that you're a cop," Buzz said proudly.

"That's big of you," Frank said, "I was worried you wouldn't accept our help."

Buzz, who is missing a sarcasm detection gene, just grinned and held out a hand. "Not at all, man, not at all. It's really good of you to offer to take me to the gig. Guess Irene told you my car broke down. Come on in."

Buzz's purple hair was one of two splashes of color in his ensemble; his boots, pants and shirt were black, but a lime green guitar—still attached by a long cable to an amp—and matching strap stood out against this dark backdrop.

There was no question of finding a seat while we waited for Buzz to unhook his guitar and put it in a hard-shell case. The tiny apartment was nearly devoid of furniture. Two empty plastic milk crates and a couple of boards served as a long, low coffee table of sorts. Cluttered with the several abandoned coffee mugs and an empty bowl with a bent spoon in it, the table stood next to a small mattress heaped with twisted sheets and laundry. The mattress apparently served as both bed and couch.

There were two very elegant objects in the room, however—a pair of Irish harps. The sun was setting in the windows behind them, and in the last light of day, they stood with stately grace, their fine wooden scroll-work lovingly polished to a high sheen.

"You play these?" Frank asked him in astonishment.

Without looking up from the guitar, which he was carefully wiping down with a cloth, Buzz said, "Didn't you tell him, Irene?"

"I first met Buzz at an Irish music festival," I said. "He doesn't just play the harp."

"Other instruments, too?" Frank asked.

"Sure," Buzz said, looking back at us now. "I grew up in a musical family."

"That isn't what I meant," I said. "He doesn't just *play* it. He coaxes it to sing."

"Sure and you've an Irish silver tongue now, haven't ye, me beauty?" Buzz said with an exaggerated brogue.

"Prove my point, Buzz. Play something for us."

He shook his head. "Haven't touched them in months except to keep the dust off them," he said. "That's the past." He patted the guitar case. "This is the future." He laughed when he saw my look of disappointment. "My father feels the same way—but promise you won't stop speaking to me like he has."

"No, what you play is your choice."

"Glad to know at least one person thinks so. Shall we go?"

"Need help carrying your equipment?" Frank offered. I was relieved to see him warming up a little.

"Oh, no, I'm just taking my ax, man."

"Your ax?"

"My guitar. I never leave it at the club. My synthesizer, another amp and a bunch of other equipment are already at the club—I just leave those there. But not my Strat."

Q: How do you get a guitar player to turn down?
A: Put sheet music in front of him.

On the way to Club 99, Buzz talked to Frank about his early years of performing with the Sullivan family band, recalling the friendship his father shared with my late mentor, O'Connor.

"O'Connor told me to come to this music festival," I said. "There was a fifteen-year-old lad who could play the Irish harp better than anyone he'd ever met, and when he got to heaven, he expected no angel to play more sweetly."

"Oh, I did all right," he said shyly. "But my training wasn't formal. She tell you that she helped me get into school, Frank?"

"No—"

"It was your own hard work that got you into that program," I said.

"Naw, I couldn't have done it without you. You talked that friend into teaching me how to sight read." He turned to Frank. "Then she practically arm-wrestled one of the profs into giving me an audition."

Frank smiled. "She hasn't changed much."

"Sorry, Buzz," I said, "I thought it was what you wanted."

"It was!" Buzz protested. "And I never could have gone to college without your help."

"Nonsense. You got the grades on your own, and all the talent and practice time for the music was your own. But when your dad told me you dropped out at the beginning of this past semester, I just figured—"

"I loved school. I only left because I had this opportunity."

"What opportunity?" Frank asked.

"The band you're going to hear tonight," he said proudly.

I was puzzled. "It's still avant garde?"

"Yes."

"Hmm. I guess I never thought there was much money in avant garde."

"Not here in the U.S.—locally, Club Ninety-nine is about the only place we can play regularly, and they don't pay squat there. Our band is too outside for a lot of people."

"Outside?" I asked.

"Yeah, it means—different. In a good way. You

know, we push the envelope. Our music's very original, but for people who want the Top Forty, we're a tough listen. That's the trouble with the music scene here in the States. But Mack—our bass player—came up with this great plan to get us heard over in Europe. We made a CD a few months ago, and it's had a lot of airplay there. We just signed on for a big tour, and when it's over, we've got a steady gig set up in a club in Amsterdam."

"I had no idea all of this was happening for you, Buzz. Congrats."

"Thanks. I'm so glad you're finally going to get to hear us play—three weeks from now, we'll be in Paris. Who knows when you'll get a chance to hear us after that—Frank, it's been awhile since Irene heard me play and—oh!" He pointed to the right. "Here's the club. Park here at the curb. There's not really any room at the back."

He had pointed out a small, brown building that looked no different from any other neighborhood bar on the verge of ruin. A small marquee read, "Live Music. Wast Land. No Cover Charge Before 7 P.M."

"Wast Land?" Frank asked. "Is that your band?"

"The Waste Land. The 'e' is missing. And the word 'The.' "

"You named the band after the poem by T.S. Eliot?" Frank asked.

"You've read T.S. Eliot's poetry?" Buzz asked in unfeigned disbelief.

"Yeah. I think it made me a more dangerous man."

I rolled my eyes.

Buzz sat back against the seat and grinned. "Cool!"

Q: What band name on a marquee will always
   guarantee a crowd?
A: Free Beer

As we pushed open the padded vinyl door of Club
99, our nostrils were assailed by that special blended
fragrance—a combination of stale cigarette smoke,
old sweat, spilt beer and unmopped men's room—that
is the mark of the true dive. I was thinking of borrow-
ing Frank's cotton and sticking it in my nose.

Behind the bar, a thin old man with tattoo-covered
arms and a cigarette dangling from his mouth was
stocking the beer cooler, squinting as the cigarette's
smoke rose up into his own face. He nodded at Buzz,
stared a moment at Frank, then went back to his
work. We were ignored completely by the only other
occupant, a red-faced man in a business suit who was
gazing into a whiskey glass.

"I thought you said the band was meeting here at
seven," I said as we walked along the sticky floor
toward the stage. I glanced at my watch. Seven on the
dot.

"The others are always late," Buzz said. He set up
his guitar, then invited us into a small backstage room
that was a little less smelly than the rest of the bar. It
housed a dilapidated couch and a piano that bore the
scars of drink rings and cigarette burns. The walls of
the room were covered with a colorful mixture of
graffiti, band publicity photos and handbills.

"Is there a photo of your band up here?" Frank
asked.

"Naw. Most of those are pretty old. But I can show
you photos of the other members of the band. Here's

Mack and Joleen, when they were in Maggot." He pointed to two people in a photo of a quartet. Everyone wore the pouting rebel expression that's become a standard in band photos. The man Buzz pointed out was a bass player, about Buzz's age, with long, thick black hair. The woman, boyishly thin, also had long, thick black hair.

"That photo's about ten years old. Mack and Joleen were together then."

"Together?"

"Yeah. You know, lovers."

"They aren't now?"

"No, haven't been for years. But they get along fine."

Q: What's the difference between a drummer and a drum machine?

A: With a drum machine, you only have to punch in the information once.

"Over here's a photo of Gordon. He's a great drummer," Buzz said. "He hates this photo. He said the band sucked. Its name sure did."

He pointed to a photo of a band called "Unsanitary Conditions." Buzz was right—I didn't think too many club owners would be ready to put that on their marquees. The drummer, a lean but muscular man, wasn't wearing a shirt over his nearly hairless chest. He had also shaved all the hair from his head. He held his drumsticks tucked in crossed-arms. He was frowning. It didn't look like a fake frown.

Live, updated versions of two of the band members arrived a few minutes later. Gordon looked pretty much the same as he did in the "Unsanitary Conditions" photo. He was wearing a shirt, and he had short orange hair on his head, but the frown gave him away.

"Her royal-fucking-highness is late again, I see," he seethed, then upon realizing that Buzz wasn't alone, smiled and said politely, "Hi, I'm Gordon. Are you Buzz's folks?"

Frank snorted with laughter behind me.

"Oh man!" Buzz said in embarrassment. "These are my friends. They aren't *that* old!"

"Oh, sorry," Gordon said. "Buzz, did you listen to that tape I gave you?" He broke off as the door opened again.

Pre-empting a repeat of Gordon's mistake, Buzz quickly said, "Mack, these are my *friends*. Frank and Irene, this is Mack."

It was a good thing Buzz introduced us. Mack was now balding, and his remaining hair was very short, including a neatly-trimmed beard. I judged him to be in his mid-thirties, closer to our age than Buzz's, with Gordon somewhere in between the two.

"Hi, nice to meet you," he said, but seemed distracted as he looked around the small room.

"No," Gordon said, "Joleen isn't here yet. Shit, can you imagine what touring with her will be like?"

"Don't worry about it," Mack said placatingly. "She'll be very professional."

Gordon didn't look convinced.

"Uh, Buzz," Mack said, "the house is starting to fill up. Maybe you should find some seats for your friends."

I thought Mack was just trying to make the band's in-fighting more private, but when Buzz led us back out into the club, a transformation had taken place. Taped music was playing over the speakers, a recording of frenzied sax riffs that could barely be heard above people talking and laughing and drinking.

There was an audience now. The man in the business suit had left the bar, and the place was starting to fill up with a crowd that seemed mainly to be made up of young . . . as I sought a word for the beret-clad, goatee-wearing men and their mini-skirted female companions, Frank whispered, "Beatniks! And to think I gave away my bongo drums."

"Poetry and bongo drums?" I whispered back. "Did Kerouac make you want to run away from home?"

"As Buzz said, I'm not *that* old."

Buzz wanted us to sit near the stage, but I knew better. I muttered something about acoustics and we found a table along the back wall, next to the sound man. Buzz sat with us for a few minutes, and I was pleased to see that Frank was starting to genuinely like him.

Buzz might not be sarcastic, but he is Irish, and he was spinning out a tale about learning to play the uilleann pipes that had us weeping with laughter. Just then a woman walked on stage, shielded her eyes from the lights and said over one of the microphones, "Buzz! Get your ass up here now!"

Q: What's the difference between a singer and a terrorist?

A: You can negotiate with a terrorist.

The club fell silent and there was a small ripple of nervous laughter before conversation started up again. The sound man belatedly leaned over and turned off her mike. He shook his head, murmured, "*Maybe* I'll remember to turn that on again, bitch," and upped the volume on the house speakers. I could hear the saxophone recording more clearly now, but I was distracted by my anger toward the woman.

She was thin and dressed in a black outfit that was smaller than some of my socks. Her hair was short and spiky; I couldn't see her eyes, but her mouth was hard, her lips drawn tight in a painted ruby slash across her pale face.

"Joleen," Buzz said, as if the name explained everything. He quickly excused himself and hurried up to the stage as Joleen stepped back out of the lights. The other members of the band soon joined them on stage. If Buzz had been bothered by her tone, he didn't show it.

The group did a sound check, only briefly delayed while Joleen cussed out the sound man and proved she might not need a mike. The members of the band then left the stage with an argument in progress. Although I couldn't make out what they were saying, Gordon and Joleen were snapping at one another, the drummer looking ready to raise a couple of knots on her head. Mack was making "keep it quiet" motions with his hands, while Buzz seemed to be lost in his own thoughts, ignoring all of them.

"I think I'm going to need a drink," Frank said. "You want one?"

"Tell you what—I'll drive home. Have at it."

Frank spent some time talking to the bartender,

then came back with a couple of scotches. He downed the first one fairly quickly, and was taking his time with the second when the band came back on stage.

Q: How can you tell if a stage is level?
A: The bass player is drooling out of both sides of his mouth.

The sound man turned on his own mike and said, "Club Ninety-nine is pleased to welcome The Waste Land." There was a round of enthusiastic applause. Joleen held the mike up to her lips and said softly, "We're going to start off with a little something called 'Ankle Bone.' " Amid hoots and whistles of approval, the band began to play.

The music was rapid-fire and intricate, and quite obviously required great technical skill. Joleen's voice hit notes on an incredible range. There were no lyrics (unless they were in some language spoken off planet), but her wild mix of syllables and sounds was clearly not sloppy or accidental.

The rest of the band equaled her intensity. As Mack and Buzz played, their fingers flew along the frets; Gordon drummed to complex and changing time signatures. But at the end of the first song and Frank's second scotch, he leaned over and whispered, "Five bucks if you can hum any of that back to me."

He was right, of course, but out of loyalty to Buzz, I said, "They just aren't confined by the need to be melodic."

Frank gave an emperor's new clothes sort of snort and stood up. "I'm going to get another drink. I'll pay cab fare for all three of us if you want to join me."

Figuring it would hurt Buzz's feelings if we were both drunk by the end of his gig, I said, "No thanks."

Q: What do you call someone who hangs out with musicians?
A: A guitar player.

By the end of the set, I was seriously considering hurting Buzz's feelings. "Get outside!" one member of the audience yelled in encouragement to the band, and when the sound man muttered, "And stay there," I found myself in agreement. The crowd applauded wildly after every piece (I could no longer think of them as songs, nor remember which one was "Jar of Jam" and which was "Hangman's Slip Knot"), but long before the set ended, I had a headache that could drive nails.

Buzz grabbed a bottle of beer at the bar and came back to our table, smiling. Frank surprised me by offering the first compliment.

"You're one hell of a player, Buzz."

"Thanks, man."

They proceeded to go through an elaborate hand-shaking ritual that left me staring at my husband in wonder. I was spared any comment on music or male ceremonial greetings when Gordon grabbed the seat next to Buzz.

"Excuse us," Gordon said, turning his shoulders away from us and toward Buzz. "You never told me—did you listen to that tape?"

"Keep your voice down," Buzz said, glancing back toward the stage, where Joleen was apparently complaining about something to Mack. He turned back to

Gordon. "Yeah, I listened. Your friend's got great key-board chops."

"Yeah, and you have to admit, Susan's also got a better voice than Joleen's. Great bod, too."

Buzz glanced back at the stage. "Joleen's bod isn't so bad."

"No, just her attitude. Think of how much better off our band would be with Susan."

"But Joleen started this band—"

"And she's about to finish it, man. She rags on all of us all of the time. I'm getting tired of it. This band would be better off without her."

"But they're her songs."

"Hers and Mack's. He has as much right to them as she does."

Buzz frowned, toyed with his beer. "What does Mack say?"

Gordon shrugged. "I'm working on him. I know he was knocked out by Susan's tape. If you say you're up for making the change, I know he will be, too."

"I don't know . . ."

"Look, Buzz, I really love playing with you. Same with Mack. But I can't take much more of Joleen."

"But Europe . . ."

"Exactly. Think of spending ten weeks traveling with that bitch. You want to be in a car with her for more than ten minutes?"

I looked up and saw Joleen walking toward us with purpose in every angry stride. "Uh, Buzz—" I tried to warn, but she was already shouting toward our table.

"I know exactly what you're up to, asshole!"

Gordon and Buzz looked up guiltily, but in the

next moment it became clear that she was talking to the sound man. He didn't seem impressed by her fury.

"You're screwing around with the monitors, aren't you?"

The sound man just laughed.

Joleen stood between Frank and me and pointed at the sound man. "You won't be laughing long, mother—"

"Joleen," Buzz said, trying to intercede.

"Shut up, you little twerp! You don't know shit about music. If you did, you'd understand what this jerk is doing. *You* try singing while some clown is fooling around with your monitor, making it play back a half-step off."

The effect the sound man had created must have been maddening; the notes she heard back through the speaker at her feet on stage would be just slightly off the notes she sang into the mike. Still, I couldn't help but bristle at her comments to Buzz.

Instead of being angry with her, though, Buzz turned to the sound man and said, "Dude, that's a pretty awful thing to do to her. She's singing some really elaborate stuff, music that takes all kinds of concentration, and you're messing with her head."

The sound man broke eye contact with him, shrugged one shoulder.

"See?" Buzz said to Joleen. "He's sorry. I'm sure it won't happen next set." Before Joleen could protest, Buzz turned to us and asked, "How's it sounding out here?"

Picking up my cue, I said, "Wonderful. He's doing a great job for you guys."

"And what the hell would you know about it?" she asked.

"Joleen," Buzz said, "this is my friend from the paper."

She stopped mid-tantrum and looked at me with new interest. "A reviewer?"

"No," I admitted.

"Well, I was right, then. You don't know what you're talking about." She eyed Frank and said, "You or this cop."

"How did you know he's a cop?" Buzz asked, but before she could answer, Frank took hold of her wrist and turned it out, so that the inside of her arm was facing Buzz.

"Oh," he said, "junkies just seem to have a sixth sense about these things."

She pulled her arm away. "They're old tracks and you know it. I haven't used in years."

Frank shrugged. "If you say so. I really don't want to check out the places I'd have to look if I wanted to be sure."

She narrowed her eyes at him, but stomped away without another word.

"Shit," Gordon said. "You need anything else to convince you about what I said, Buzz?"

"She brought me into the band, man. It just doesn't seem right."

"If another guitar player came along, she'd do this to you in a minute," Gordon said. "You know she would."

Buzz sighed. "We've got three more nights here. Let's at least wait until we finish out this gig to make a decision." Gordon seemed ready to say more, but then excused himself and walked backstage.

The minute Gordon was out of earshot, Buzz turned to Frank. "Were they old tracks?"

"Yes."

"I feel stupid not noticing. Not that it matters. If they're old, I mean." His face turned red. "What I mean is, she can really sing."

I watched him for a moment, then said, "You like her."

"Yeah," Buzz said, and forced a laugh. "It's obviously not mutual." He looked toward the stage, then rubbed his hand over his chest, as if easing an ache. "Well, I better get ready for the next set."

Frank watched him walk off, then looked over at me. He pushed his drink aside, moved his chair closer to mine.

Q: What do you call a guitarist without a girl-friend?

A: Homeless.

Buzz seemed to recover his good humor by the time he was on stage. There was an air of anticipation in the audience now. It seemed that most of them had heard the band before, and were eagerly awaiting the beginning of this set.

As the band members took their places, I sat wondering what Buzz saw in Joleen. My question was soon answered, though not in words.

Buzz and Joleen stood at opposite ends of the stage, facing straight ahead, not so much as glancing at one another. She sang three notes, clear and sweet, and then Buzz began to sing with her, his voice blending perfectly with hers. It was a slow, melodic passage,

sung a cappella. The audience was absolutely silent—
even Frank sat forward and listened closely.

They sang with their eyes closed, as if they would
brook no interference from other senses. But they
were meeting, somewhere out in the smoky haze
above the room, above us all, touching one another
with nothing more than sound.

The song's pace began to quicken and quicken, the
voices dividing and yet echoing one another again and
again until at last their voices came together, holding
one note, letting it ring out over us, ending only as the
instruments joined in.

The crowd cheered, but the musicians were in a
world of their own. Buzz turned to Gordon and
Mack, all three of them smiling as they played increasingly difficult variations on a theme. I watched Joleen;
she was standing back now, letting the instrumental-
ists take center stage, her eyes still closed. But as Buzz
took a solo, I saw her smile to herself. It was the only
time she smiled all evening.

The song ended and the crowd came to its feet,
shouting in acclaim.

Q: Did you hear about the time the bass player
   locked his keys in the car?
A: It took two hours to get the drummer out.

Mack joined us during the second break between
sets. With Buzz's encouragement, he told us about the
years he studied at Berkeley, where he met Joleen, and
about some of the odd day jobs and strange gigs he
had taken while trying to make headway with his
music career—including once being hired by a

Washington socialite to play piano for her dog's birthday party.

We spent more time talking to Mack than to Buzz, whose attentions were taken by another guitar player, a young man who had stopped by to hear the band and now had questions about Buzz's "rig"—which Mack explained was not just equipment, but the ways in which the guitar had been modified, the set-up for the synthesizer, and all the other mechanical and electronic aspects of Buzz's playing.

"None of which will ever help that poor bastard play like Buzz does," he said. "Buzz has the gift."

"He feels lucky to be in this band," I said. "He has great respect for the other players."

Mack smiled. "He's a generous guy." As Joleen walked over to Buzz and handed him a beer, Mack added softly, "He's a little young yet, and I worry that maybe he has a few hard lessons to learn. Hope it won't discourage him."

"How do you two manage to work together?" I asked.

He didn't mistake my meaning. "You mean because of Joleen's temper? Or because we used to be together?"

"Both."

"As far as the temper goes, I'm used to her. Over the years we've played with a lot of different people; I've outlasted a lot of guys who just couldn't take her attitude. Great thing about Buzz is that he's not just talented, he's easy to get along with. He's able to just let her tantrums and insults roll off of him."

"And Gordon?" Frank asked.

"Oh, I don't think Gordon is going to put up with it

much longer. The musician's lot in life, I guess. Bands are hard to hold together. Talk to anybody who's played in them for more than a couple of years, he'll have more than a few stories about band fights and breakups."

"But from what Buzz tells us, you've worked hard to reach this point—the CD, the tour, the gig in the Netherlands—"

"Yeah, I'm hoping Joleen and Gordon will come to their senses and see that we can't let petty differences blow this chance. And I think they will." He paused, took a sip of beer. "You were also asking about how Joleen and I manage to work together after being in a relationship, right?"

I nodded.

"Well, she and I have always had something special. We write songs together. Musically, we're a good fit. When we were younger, when we first discovered that we could compose together, there was a sort of passion in the experience, and we just assumed that meant we'd be a good fit in every other way. But we weren't."

"Still," I said, "I'd think it would be painful to have to work with someone after a break-up."

He smiled. "I won't lie. At first, it was horrible. But what was happening musically was just too good to give up. The hurt was forgotten. Over the years, we each found other people to be with. And like I said, we have something special of our own, and we'll always have that."

He glanced at his watch. "Better get ready for the last set. You two want to come out to dinner with us afterwards?"

"Thanks for the invitation," Frank said, "but I'm wearing down. Irene, if you want to stay—"

I shook my head. "Thanks, but I'll have to take a raincheck, too, Mack."

"Sure, another time. I forget that other people aren't as wired after a gig as the band is. I'll check with Buzz—I can give him a lift home if he wants to join us."

I toyed with the idea of heading home early if Buzz should decide to go out to dinner with the band. But my mental rehearsal of the excuses I'd make on my way out the door was cut short when Buzz stopped by the table and said, "They asked me if I wanted to go to dinner with them, but they're just going to argue, so I'd rather go home after this last set. Is that okay?"

"Of course," I said, hoping my smile didn't look as phony as it felt.

Q: Why did God give drummers 10% more
    brains than horses?
A: So they wouldn't crap during the parade.

"What was the name of the first song in the second set?" Frank asked Buzz as we drove him home. He was being uncharacteristically quiet, staring out the car window. But at Frank's question, he smiled.

"It's called 'Draid Bhreá Fiacla.' That's Irish for 'a fine set of teeth.' "

"How romantic," I said.

"It is, really. Joleen rarely smiles, but once I said something that made her laugh, and she had this beautiful grin on her face after. When I saw it, I said, 'Well, look there! You've a fine set of teeth. I wonder why you hide them?' "

"Did she have an answer?"

He laughed. "In a way. She bit me. Not hard, just a playful little bite. So the next time I saw her, I gave her the song, and told her its name, and got to see the smile again."

"You wrote that song?" Frank asked.

"She worked on it some after I gave it to her, made it better. It belongs to both of us now, I suppose."

"Of all the ones we heard tonight, that one's easily my favorite," I said.

"Mine, too," Frank said.

"Joleen says it's too melodic," he said. "But I don't think she means it. She just doesn't want me to think too highly of myself."

Q: What's the difference between a viola and an onion?
A: Nobody cries when you chop up a viola.

"Well, thanks again for the ride," he said when we pulled up in front of his apartment.

"You have a way over to the club tomorrow night?" Frank asked. "I could give you a ride if you need one."

"Oh thanks, but the Chevette is supposed to be ready by late afternoon. I'm kind of glad it broke down. It was great to meet you, man."

"You, too. Stay in touch."

"I will. You take care, too, Irene."

After Buzz closed the car door, Frank said, "Let's wait until he's inside the building."

Having noticed the three young toughs standing not far down the sidewalk, I had already planned to wait. But Buzz waved to them, they waved back, and he made his way to the door without harm.

* * *

It was about three in the morning when we got to bed. When Buzz called at ten o'clock, we figured we had managed to have almost a full-night's sleep. Still, at first I was too drowsy to figure out what he was saying. Then again, fully awake I might not have understood the words that came between hard sobs. There were only a few of them.

"She's dead, Irene. My God, she's dead."

"Buzz? Who's dead?" I asked. Frank sat up in bed.

"Joleen."

"Joleen? Oh, Buzz . . ."

"She . . . she killed herself. Can you come over here? You and Frank?"

"Sure," I said. "We'll be right over."

By the time we got there, he was a little calmer. Not much, but enough to be able to tell us that Gordon had found her that morning, that she had hanged herself.

"It's his fault, the bastard!" He drew a hiccuping breath. "Last night, when they went out to dinner, he told Joleen he was quitting the band. Mack tried to talk him out of it, but I guess Gordon wouldn't give in."

"Gordon called you?"

"No, Mack. He told me she made some angry remark, said we'd just find a new drummer. Mack was upset, and said he didn't want to try to break in a new drummer in three weeks' time, that he was going to cancel the tour. He told her he was tired of her tantrums, tired of working for months with people only to have her run them off. It must have just crushed her—she worked so hard—"

I held him, let him cry, as Frank went into the kitchen. I could hear him opening cupboards. Finally he asked, "Any coffee, Buzz?"

Buzz straightened. "Just tea, sorry. I'll make it."

He regained some of his composure as he went through the ritual of making tea. As the water heated, he turned to Frank and asked, "The police will be there, won't they?"

"Yes. It's not my case, but I'll find out what I can for you. The detectives on the case will want to talk to you—"

"To me? Why?"

"Standard procedure. They'll talk to the people closest to her, try to get a picture of what was going on in her life."

"Do you think she—I mean, hanging, is it quick?"

"Yes, it's quick," Frank said firmly. I admired the authority in it, knowing that he was probably lying. Suicide by hanging is seldom an efficient matter—most victims slowly suffocate. But if Joleen's suffering hadn't been over quickly, at least some small part of Buzz's was.

"Thanks," Buzz said. "I thought you would know." He sighed and went back to working at making tea. I straightened the small living room, made it a little more tidy before Buzz brought the tea in and set it on the coffee table. We sat on the floor, although Buzz offered us the mattress-couch.

He took two or three sips from the cup, set it down, then went to stand by the window. The phone rang, but he didn't answer it. "Let the machine get it," he said in a strained voice. "I can't talk to anybody else right now."

The answering machine picked up on the fourth

ring. We heard Buzz's happy-go-lucky outgoing message, then the beep, then, "This is Parker's Garage. The part we were waiting for didn't come in, so the Chevette won't be ready today. Sorry about that."

"Aw, Christ, it only needed that!"

"Look, Buzz," I said, "if you need a ride anywhere, we'll take you."

"I've imposed enough on you. And after the last twenty-four hours, Frank has undoubtedly had his fill of Buzz Sullivan."

"No. Not at all," Frank said.

The phone rang again. This time he answered it.

"Hi Mack." He swallowed hard. "Not too good. You?" After a moment he said, "Already? . . . Yeah, all right."

He hung up and shook his head. "The club wants us to have our stuff out of there before tonight. They've already asked another band to play. Guess it's the guys who were going to start there when we went to Europe."

"You need a ride?" Frank asked.

"Yeah. I hate to ruin your weekend—"

"We're with a friend," I said. "It isn't ruined. What time do you need to be down there?"

"Soon as possible. He said the detectives want to talk to us down there. Club owner, too—he told Mack, 'I'm not too happy about any of this!'—like anybody is!"

Q: What's the difference between a bull and an orchestra?

A: An orchestra has the horns in the back and the ass in front.

We arrived before the others, and found the door locked. We walked around to the narrow alley, reaching the back door just as the owner pulled up—the bartender from the night before. He looked like he wanted to give Buzz a piece of his mind, but thought better of it when he took a look at Frank. Frank is six-four, but I don't think it's just his height that causes this kind of reaction among certain two-legged weasels. (I asked him about it once and he told me he got straight A's in intimidation at the police academy; I stopped trying to get a straight answer out of him after that.)

The owner grumbled under his breath as he unlocked the door and punched in the alarm code, then turned on the lights. I walked in behind him. I had only taken a couple of steps when I realized that Buzz was still outside; without being able to see him, I could hear him sobbing again. Frank stepped into the doorway, motioned me to go on in. I heard him talking in low, consoling tones to Buzz, heard Buzz talking to him.

I squelched an unattractive little flare up of jealousy I felt then; a moment's dismay that someone who had only known Buzz for a few hours was comforting him, when I had been his friend for several years. How stupid to insist that the provision of solace would be on the basis of seniority.

My anger at myself must have shown on my face in some fierce expression, because the owner said, "Look, I'm sorry. I just didn't get much sleep. This place don't close itself, and now at eleven o'clock, I've already had a busy morning. But I really am sorry about that kid out there. He's the nicest one of the

bunch. And I think he had eyes for the little spitfire."
He shook his head. "I never would have figured her
for the type to off herself, you know?"

"I didn't really know her," I said. "I just met her
last night."

"She had troubles," he said. "But she had always
been the type to get more mad than sad." He
shrugged. "I don't know. She was complicated—like
that music she sang."

He started moving around the club, taking chairs
off table tops. I helped him, unable to stand around
while he worked. In full light, the club seemed even
smaller and shabbier than it had in the dark.

Soon Buzz and Frank came in. Frank started helping Buzz to pack away his equipment. Within a few
moments other people arrived: the detectives, then
Mack and Gordon.

None of the band members seemed to be in great
shape. The detectives recognized Frank and pulled
him aside, then asked the owner if they could borrow
his office.

They asked to talk to Mack first. He went with
them. Gordon climbed the stage steps and began to
put away his cymbals.

Frank surreptitiously positioned himself between
Buzz and Gordon. They worked quietly for a while,
then Gordon said, "I'm sorry, Buzz. I—I never would
have said anything to her if I thought . . ."

"It's not your fault," Buzz said wearily, contradict-
ing his earlier outburst. He finished closing the last of
his cases and began helping Gordon.

Mack came out, and told the bar owner that the
detectives wanted to talk to him next. By then, most

of the equipment had been carried into the backstage room. All that was left was a single mike stand—Joleen's.

I walked onto the stage and stood where she had stood during "A Fine Set of Teeth." I thought of her voice, clear and sweet on those first notes, her smile as she listened to Buzz's solo. I looked out and wondered how she saw that small sea of adoring faces that must have been looking back at her; wondered if she had known of Buzz's loyalty to her; remembered the bite and figured she had. I thought of her giving the sound man hell; she had both bark and bite.

I saw Mack, standing at the bar, at about the same moment he saw me. He stared at me, making me wonder if I was causing him to see ghosts.

Feeling like an interloper, I stepped away from the empty mike stand, then paused. I had the nagging feeling that something about the stage wasn't right. When I figured out what it was, I called my husband over to my side.

"Tell your friends in the office not to let Mack leave," I whispered. "There's something he needs to explain."

"Are you going to tell me about it, or has being on this stage gone to your head?"

"Both. Where is Mack's equipment?" I asked.

Frank looked around, then smiled. "I'll be right back. And maybe you should try to stand close to Buzz. This will be hard on him." He took a step away, then turned back. "How did you know it was murder?" he whispered.

"I didn't. Not until just now. Ligature marks?"

He nodded.

I walked into the backstage room. Gordon sat on the couch. Buzz was sitting at the piano bench. I sat down next to Buzz and lifted the keyboard cover. "You play?" he asked.

"Sure." I tapped out the melody line of "Heart and Soul." "It's one of two pieces I can play," I said.

One corner of his mouth quirked up. "The other being 'Chopsticks'?"

"How did you know?"

"People just seem to know those two," he said, reminding me about the missing sarcasm gene.

"Come on," I said. "Play the other half."

"Half?" he said, filling in the chords.

"Okay, three-quarters."

Gordon laughed.

"Come on," Buzz said, "there's room for you, too."

"I'll pass," he said, "I don't even know 'Chopsticks.'"

We stopped when we heard Gordon shout, "What are you doing to Mack?"

We turned to see Mack being led out in handcuffs.

"They're arresting him," Frank said as they left. "For Joleen's murder."

"So tell me again how you figured this out," Buzz asked later, when we were back at his apartment. We were sitting on the floor, around the coffee table.

"Okay," I said. "We were the first ones at the club this morning, right?"

He nodded.

"You and Gordon both had equipment to pack up. Your equipment was still on the stage, because when you left Club Ninety-nine last night, you had every intention of coming back the next night. But one band member knew he wouldn't be back. He packed up his equipment and took it home last night."

"You figured that out just standing there?"

"I was thinking about that dirty trick the sound man pulled on her—making her hear her own voice a half-step off through the monitor. But the mike and monitor were gone. I knew you didn't pack them up, neither did Gordon. You had only worked on your part of the stage, or to help Gordon. So Mack must have taken Joleen's mike and monitor—but he hadn't been up on the stage this morning. I looked around and noticed his equipment was gone. It's not as elaborate as your rig, or Gordon's kit."

"And the marks you were talking about?" he asked Frank.

"You're sure you want to hear about this?"

"Yeah."

"There were two sets of marks on her neck—the one horizontal, across her neck—the other V-shaped, from her chin to behind her ear. The second marks would be typical of a suicide by hanging, but they were made by the rope sometime *after* she was killed. The first were the ones that marked the pull of the rope when someone stood behind her and strangled her."

He was silent for a long time, then asked. "Why?"

"He probably told her the truth at the restaurant," Frank said. "He had lost a lot of good players because of her attitude. Just as it looks like things have stabilized and The Waste Land's big break is coming along, she starts making trouble with Gordon."

"But she was the heart of the group! Her voice."

"Gordon was going to offer him a new singer," Frank reminded him.

"Susan?"

"I suppose he would have worked with Susan on the songs he had already written with Joleen, then taken Susan with the band to Europe."

Buzz frowned. "You're right. He had already given her a couple of them to learn. Susan sang them on the tape Gordon brought last night."

"Mack wanted to make sure he had sole rights to the songs."

"Oh, and then what?" Buzz asked angrily. "What did he think would happen down the road? Have you ever heard one of Mack's songs? Dull stuff. Technically passable, but nothing more. He just provided the wood. She set it on fire. With her dead, who would have provided that fire?"

"Now," I said, "I think you're getting closer."

They both stared at me.

"Buzz," I asked, "until you wrote 'A Fine Set of Teeth—' "

"You mean, 'Draid Bhreá Fiacla'?"

"Yes. Until then, had anyone other than Mack written a song with her?"

"No, but he didn't understand that either, did he?" he said, and looked away. "No, he couldn't."

I didn't contradict him, but I wondered if he was right. Perhaps Mack understood exactly what it meant, and perhaps Joleen, who had known Mack better than the others, also believed that the safest course was to hide any affection she felt for Buzz. I kept these thoughts to myself; bad enough to second-guess the dead, worse if the theory might bring further pain to the living.

When we were fairly sure he'd be all right, and had obtained promises from him that he'd call us whenever he needed us, we left Buzz's apartment.

We were in the stairwell of the old building when we heard it—the first few notes of 'Draid Bhreá Fiacla,' the notes a woman with a fine set of teeth used to sing with eyes closed.

The notes were being played on an Irish harp, and a young man's voice answered them.

TWO BITS

O N THE HOT JULY DAY on which he reached his majority, Andrew Masters came into a handsome fortune, yet at three o'clock that very afternoon he was focusing his attention on a twenty-five-cent piece. His contemplation of this infinitesimal portion of his wealth took place beneath a large, shady tree near Jefferson Road, just outside the western Pennsylvania town whose oil fields had made his father rich. His father had not owned the oil, but in his youth he had developed a special pump that oilmen needed. In the early 1870s, during the Pennsylvania oil boom that followed the war years, the oilmen had bought a great many pumps, bailers, cables and other equipment from Mr. Masters, so that his oil tool and supply company became one of the largest in the country. With a shrewd eye for a good investment, his riches increased.

His charming manners and unflagging industry

made him appealing to a handsome woman who came from an excellent and well-to-do family. Her family did not approve of the match; they were horrified when the young couple defied them by eloping. While Andrew's maternal grandparents had sworn never to allow his mother to inherit a cent, they had softened their hearts upon Andrew's birth—hence the fortune their first grandson now found at his disposal.

Yet it was upon twenty-five cents and not his several millions that young Andrew meditated now. He had spent the last few hours beneath the tree, knowing that he was not delaying any family festivities; there would be no cake or candles, no champagne or caviar. In the Masters family, this date had not been celebrated as Andrew's birthday since the day Andrew turned seven. For more than a dozen years, the first day of July had been commemorated only as "The Day We Lost Little Charlie."

Andrew himself thought of it in this way, and was as silent and stiff with remembered grief as were his parents. The manner in which his younger brother Charlie was taken from the family was destined to make this day infamous to all who remembered the events of fourteen years ago, and if there were fewer and fewer persons who recalled it, the Masterses would never be numbered among those who had forgotten.

On his seventh birthday, Andrew sat beneath this same old oak tree. In his mind's eye, he could even now clearly see Charlie, a cherub faced five-year-old, extending his small hand toward his brother and saying, "For your birthday, Andrew. I want you to have it."

In the hand was a small, unpainted wooden soldier, one whittled from a scrap of pine by Old Davey, the head groom of Papa's fine stable. Compared to the mechanical tin clown or the horsehair rocking horse up in their nursery, it was a poor sort of toy, but Andrew had coveted it. Still, he resisted temptation.

"Thank you, Charlie," he said. "But I can't take it away from you. Old Davey gave it to you."

Their conversation was interrupted by the rattle of an old buggy coming up the road. The horse was sturdy but unremarkable, while the buggy was out-and-out shabby, nothing like the smart surrey or the four-in-hand drag or any of the other fine carriages owned by the Masterses. This particular buggy was not unknown to the boys, for they had seen it only a week before. Andrew smiled, soon recognizing the two men in the buggy as those who had given them four peppermint sticks and a dozen pieces of taffy on that occasion. Mama did not approve of this sort of cheap candy, and the brothers had delighted in secretly consuming these confections not an hour before their supper.

"Hello, boys!" the driver called, pulling up. "Ain't ya lookin' fine today." Andrew could not return the compliment. The driver, who had told them his name was Jack, was a short man whose dark hair curled wildly around the edges of his cap. His bushy eyebrows put Andrew in mind of a caterpillar race. One of his eyeteeth was missing, and the remainder of his smile was tobacco stained. The man sitting next to him appeared to be a stretched out version of the driver, tall and thin, but with the same brows and fewer teeth. Jack introduced him as Phil. "Me and Phil is brothers, jest like you two. C'mon and join us, we're gonna buy us some fireworks!"

As Independence Day was only three days away, Charlie thought this would be a splendid adventure. Andrew hesitated. "I'll ask Mama," he said.

The men laughed. "Yer a mama's boy, ain't ya?" the thin one chided.

"Come on," Charlie urged him. "It will be a secret, just between us two!"

Andrew, who could only resist so much temptation in one day, gave in to this one. The men helped the boys up into the dusty conveyance, and crowded in after them. Andrew sat between the men, while Phil held Charlie awkwardly on his lap. They were hardly settled when Jack snapped the reins. The buggy lurched forward and they traveled at a quick pace down the road.

Andrew began to regret his decision almost immediately. The buggy was not well-sprung, and its jolting motion jarred his teeth. Phil and Jack, he thought, had not bathed in weeks. When they reached the road that would take them a short distance into town, Jack turned the wrong way. Andrew told him so, which brought a sharp look from Phil, but Jack merely explained that if they bought the fireworks in a place where his family was so well-known, someone would likely tell his father all about it. Imagining his father in an angry mood was enough to curtail further protest from Andrew.

The road smoothed a little, and Jack began to sing certain songs, those which he undoubtedly knew to be of a nature guaranteed to intrigue small, well-mannered boys, and Andrew and Charlie eagerly took up the task of learning the melodies and (most especially) the lyrics of these odes to bodily functions. They had never heard the like before, not even from Old Davey, whose sporadic bouts of cursing they had been thrilled to overhear on a few memorable occasions.

After a time, though, Andrew's enthusiasm waned and he began to look around him. He was unfamiliar with his surroundings, and began to worry that they had been gone too long. Phil, he noticed, was eyeing him in an unfriendly fashion.

Jack seemed to notice this, too, and said, "Nearly there, Phil. Don't git yerself huffed."

Phil grunted and sat back.

"Lookit here," Jack said, pointing ahead. "There's the little town we been lookin' for. Firecrackers'll be sold at a place jest on t'other side of town."

It was not much of a town, and Andrew thought he would be happy to be finished with their mission and on his way home again. To his surprise, though, Jack halted the buggy, pulling up across the street from a small store.

"Andy," Jack said, "Charlie here says it's yer birthday. Z'at true?"

Andrew nodded.

"Well, I think Mr. Andy here should get something special, then, don't you agree, Phil?"

"Sure," Phil said.

Jack reached into one of his pockets and produced a small coin purse, and from this, a quarter. He handed the coin to Andrew and said, "Go on, there's a store right over there. Spend it on anything you like. Two bits, jest for yerself."

One might think that a child raised among the luxuries of the Masters household might snub a mere twenty-five cents, but it was, in fact, the first coin that had ever been given to Andrew. Nothing so mundane as legal tender had ever before been allowed within his grasp: all purchases, all exchanges of money, were in the hands of his elders and their employees. Never before had he enjoyed anything that might be called his own money.

He glanced up from the coin to see a look of envy on his brother's face. He knew what he saw there well enough—from not long after the day Charlie was born, Andrew had often worn that look of envy. The fair-haired, sweet-tempered Charlie was more often in favor with his parents and the servants than was Andrew, who tended to be what Mama called "a willful child." This look of envy, coming from Charlie, was almost exclusively limited to those rare occasions when the boys were visited by their grandparents, the only people who looked upon Andrew with anything resembling favoritism. And now, staring at the shiny coin, Charlie was positively green.

For Andrew, the quarter's value grew.

"Go on," Jack was saying. "We'll wait here for you."

"I wanna go with you," Charlie cried as Jack helped Andrew down from the buggy.

"It's *my* birthday," Andrew said, turning his back on his brother, skipping his way to the store.

The store was of a type his parents would undoubtedly disdain. The windows were dusty, as were the tops of many of the jars and cans on the shelves. But to a boy of seven with two bits in his pocket, it was a palace of curiosities—buttons and ribbons, pencils and pipes, razors and soap—all received Andrew's study. He held his hands behind his back, not wanting to bring about the wrath of the palace's king, a sturdy balding man who stood behind the counter.

The proprietor, seeing the fine quality of the material and workmanship in Andrew's cap, shirt, knickerbockers and silver buckled shoes (few of his adult customers wore footwear as fine as the boy's), and noting the youth's quiet politeness, was himself all patience and kindness. Indeed, these were hard, lean years, and it would serve no purpose to turn away any customer. This boy's mother would be along soon, he thought, rubbing his hands together.

Andrew continued to stroll slowly through the narrow aisles. The air in the store was redolent with what he found to be an unusual mixture of scents: tobacco, leather, coffee, cheese, peppermint and vinegar. He saved for last an examination of the jars on the counter—horehound candy, licorice and all manner of other delights.

But each potential purchase was quickly dismissed as one other thought continued to occur to Andrew: taking home a piece of horehound candy or a peppermint would mean parting with his quarter. His lovely, shining quarter, with its full-figured Liberty seated in flowing robes, its eagle on the back. His hand closed tightly around it. No, it was *his* two bits.

It occurred to him that he need not spend his quarter in this store on this day, and the more he considered this idea, the better he liked it. The quarter itself was a prize, and if Charlie should nettle him, he would pull the shiny coin from his pocket and hold it before his younger brother. This thought of Charlie made him mindful of the fact that he had been in this store for quite some time now, and that Jack and Phil—especially Phil—might be angry with him for dawdling. He suddenly found himself uneasy over having left Charlie with only those two coarse men to keep him company. He bid the dismayed shopkeeper good day and left the store.

He was startled to find the street nearly empty and the sun much closer to the horizon. He controlled a growing panic only by telling himself that Charlie and the men had undoubtedly tired of waiting for him and had moved on to wherever the fireworks were being sold. He hurried down the street in the direction they had been traveling. After a few yards he began to run, but quickly reached the limits of the small town without seeing any sign of Charlie and the men.

Out of breath, he walked a little farther, feeling by turns angry and betrayed, then frightened for his brother, then worried and very alone. In this tumult of emotion his active imagination conjured up a variety of explanations for his situation:

—They had grown tired of waiting for him, bought the firecrackers and were now journeying back to Jefferson Road. (A vision that left him wondering why they hadn't called to him, or fetched him from the store.)

—Charlie had become ill, and the men had rushed him to a doctor's office. (Which led to a fruitless search among the few buildings of the small town.)

—The men had taken a different road back into town, had called at the store and learned that Andrew had already left, and were at this moment on the way home. (That this situation was his own fault, he was too ready to believe.)

—Charlie, angry over the gift of the quarter, had urged the men to trick Andrew, and they were at this moment laughing as they drank cool glasses of lemonade in the shade of the old oak. (Too unlike Charlie.)

Andrew, although cosseted and sheltered, was not a stupid child, and one last possibility took hold of his young mind. Perhaps the men had tricked both boys, and for reasons Andrew could not fathom, had stolen Charlie.

He felt hot tears fill his eyes, but dashed them away quickly. He wanted no harm to come to his brother, but he did not know what to do next. The thought of returning home without Charlie was unbearable.

He began to ask the few people he met on the street if they had seen Charlie or the men. Invariably, they had not. To his surprise, they were rude and brusque in their answers. These were hard people, he thought, nothing like the folk who surrounded him at home. The town and its few inhabitants suddenly seemed mean and low to him. He went back to the one place where he had been treated with courtesy.

The shopkeeper was less friendly this time, but politely told him that he knew nothing of anyone named Phil or Jack, had not seen a five-year-old boy named Charlie. When asked if he knew where firecrackers were sold, he proclaimed one could find them locally only in Andrew's hometown.

"Would you please take me there?" the boy asked.

"Take you there? I suppose I'm to close my shop and hire a rig?"

"My father would be willing to . . ." He stopped

before saying "pay you," because the phrase made him realize why the men might have stolen Charlie. His father would pay for Charlie's return—but Andrew, much cast down, certain he would be blamed for all that had gone wrong, wasn't sure his father would want his willful eldest son back at all.

"I'm sure your father would be willing to take you wherever you like," the store owner was saying, "but I can't leave my place of business."

"Please, sir, how far am I from Jefferson Road?"

"By the main road? About ten miles. Of course, as the crow flies, it's only about three."

"Which way does the crow fly?"

The man laughed. "Oh, westward over the oil fields, I suppose."

Andrew brightened a little at this. His father had taken him to the oil fields twice, most recently just two days ago. The oilmen knew his father. He might see someone there who would help him return home.

He thanked the proprietor and began walking toward the forest of wooden derricks he had seen on the way into town. When he reached them, he again became frightened. Although the paths between the derricks had the same sharp fragrance of oil-soaked wood and earth, there was no sign of the bustling activity he had seen at the other oil field, the one he had traveled to with his father. Here equipment was still and rusty with disuse, the drilling platforms damaged and empty. The wooden buildings attached to the derricks, which he knew to be called doghouses, were rickety and missing boards. Even the small offices and equipment shacks appeared to be abandoned. He remembered his father talking of wells that were dry, and wondered if this was an oil field full of such wells.

He told himself that he would sooner or later find other people, and walked toward the sun. Close up, the distance between the wells was greater, and the derricks seemed much taller. They loomed over him, silent giants which began to look identical.

His feet started to ache, and then to throb and burn, but still he walked toward the sun. That the distance he must travel to reach his home was nearly double the shopkeeper's estimate would not have mattered to him. He was thirsty and tired, but he continued to place one foot before the other, the sound of his steps a counterpoint to his troubled thoughts. He walked over hills whose shade was welcomed but confusing to his sense of direction. Coming to one rise, he at last saw the more familiar sight of an active field. He could not run, but began to shout for help as he drew closer and closer. One of the men who was climbing high on a distant derrick noticed him and pointed. Soon, two men rode horses to where he stood, swaying on his feet, exhausted more by his emotions than his exertions.

"Why, it's the Masters boy!" one of the men shouted, leaping down from his horse.

"Charlie," Andrew said, beginning to cry. "They stole Charlie."

At first, his parents rejoiced in his return. They had spent several hours alarmed by the discovery that their children were not playing under the tree and could not be located anywhere on the large property. They could not know that by the time the attic and stables had been searched, Jack had already given Andrew his quarter.

They wept over Andrew when the oil field boss brought him home, and had not remonstrated against him. But quickly their alarm returned; their fears for Charlie were expressed in recriminations hurled at his older brother, who should have known better than to get into a strange conveyance, who should have known better than to leave his brother for a quarter.

"Two bits!" Papa shouted. "Even Judas held out for forty pieces of silver!"

His mother intervened then, and separated them by taking Andrew to his room. But soon there were police to be answered, and not much later the detectives from Pinkerton's, and over time, endless others. Tough men, large men, ill-mannered men, always badgering him for descriptions and repetition of details, making unpleasant suggestions as to how it might have truly happened that Andrew was spared. Under this assault, details became confused in Andrew's mind, memories shifted, and to his father's fury, he could not name the town—or be certain of the roads, or how far he had traveled. Eventually the store he had visited was located, but as Andrew could have told anyone who might have listened, no one in that town had noticed Charlie and the two men.

A ransom note, postmarked from Pittsburgh, arrived three torturous days later. The letter, filled with misspellings, was eventually deciphered to be a demand for twenty thousand dollars, details of payment to be forthcoming. Papa declared himself ready to pay.

By now, newspapers were publishing stories of

"Little Charlie Masters," whose brother had abandoned him to kidnappers. This was, of course, not at all what the papers intended to convey, but it was how every story appeared to Andrew.

During this time Andrew slept and ate little, cried easily and was prone to nightmares of the worst sort. He could not help but notice that his parents no longer looked him in the eye, that the servants whispered. Had not Grandpapa arrived to protect him from his persecutors, and threatened to remove their one remaining son from their home, the Masterses might not have gone on as a family through the ordeal that awaited them.

The instructions never came. The explanation for the failure of the kidnappers to continue on their course was not uncovered until an enterprising Pinkerton's man compared descriptions of Jack and Phil with two robbers gunned down by police in Pittsburgh on the day the letter had been received. As he lay dying, one of the men—Jack, it seems—had said, "Never find Charlie now."

Questioning of the men's few known associates yielded nothing. The detectives advised the Masterses to assume their son was dead.

Never one to give up, Papa announced to the newspapers that he was offering forty thousand dollars— an astronomical sum, twice the amount demanded by the kidnappers—to anyone who returned his son Charlie to him. Other than renewed publicity and attention, nothing came of it.

Over the years following Charlie's kidnapping, Andrew learned to calmly accept his altered position in the family. His parents could not punish the kidnappers, so they punished the person they had come to view as an accomplice. They used the weapon of choice for persons of their breeding and social stature—civility. Andrew was accorded this, but little more. Charlie, by contrast, took on in memory saintly attributes he never had in life, became the perfect son denied to them. His room was enshrined, his toys left waiting for his return.

On Andrew's eleventh birthday, the one-hundred-fourth pretender (by Andrew's careful accounting) arrived at the Masters home. He was easily dismissed as yet another boy put forward by some schemer as "Little Charlie." There were always stories to go with these pretenders—of how the missing boy's "adoptive" parents had taken pity on some feverish waif who had then forgotten all of his previous life until just this moment—but Andrew could not bear to listen to another one. He asked Old Davey to saddle his favorite mare, then rode toward the town where Charlie had disappeared.

This time he did not venture into the town itself, where he had become a familiar and pitied sight, but turned off into the abandoned oil field. He rode slowly, and at times dismounted to take a closer look at some object. At last his search was, at least in one sense, rewarded. He spent another hour or two at the site, then rode home. That he was filthy and had ruined his clothes either escaped his parents' notice, or was (more likely) not thought to be worthy of their comment.

This he did not mind.

*   *   *

Now, as he stood beneath the oak on his twenty-first birthday, he put the quarter back in his pocket and removed a second object. It was a crudely whittled soldier, weather-beaten and oil-stained, found near an abandoned well.

The well was a disposal well, used to hold oil-contaminated water and sludge pumped from other wells. It was about sixteen inches in diameter; too narrow for an adult, perhaps too narrow even for a schoolboy, but not too narrow for the body of a small child. He had known that it would be useless to look down it for Charlie's remains; the well would be too deep.

Andrew had never been able to picture Phil and Jack planning to endure a child's company while waiting for ransom; if they had left Charlie with someone else while they robbed houses, that person would have long ago claimed his father's reward money. No genuine claimant had stepped forward.

Fourteen years had passed since Charlie disappeared, and the pretenders were growing fewer, but before the end of his father's life, Andrew's count of them would reach two hundred eighty-six. On this day, he did not yet know that number, but he did know what had happened to his brother. On this day, he simply rested in that knowledge, and took his revenge in his silence.

"Thank you for the birthday present, Charlie," he said, tucking away the second—and only other one— he had received since the day he turned seven.

A MAN OF MY STATURE

YOU ARE NO DOUBT surprised to receive word from me, my dear Augustus, but although I have been poorly served by my obedience to impulse, in this case I think it best to give in to my compulsion to communicate with you now. If I have already tried you beyond all patience and forbearance, you cannot be blamed, but I hope that your curiosity— upon receiving a letter from a man you believe to be dead—will be strong enough to lead you to continue.

I have written a letter to Emma, denying, of course, that I had anything at all to do with the death of Louis Fontesque, and telling her that she must not believe what will soon be said of her husband. I will leave that brief note to her here, to be found tomorrow in these rooms I have taken at the Linworth Hotel. But tonight, after darkness falls, I will venture from this establishment one last time; I will make the short jour-

ney to the letter box on the corner, not trusting the
desk clerk to mail this to you. He is an honest enough
lad, I'm sure, but after all, he now believes me to be
Fontesque, and when the hunt for Fontesque's killer
inevitably leads law enforcement officers here, the
young man's memory may prove too sharp by half. I
would not bring trouble to your door, Augustus.

I think it best to give you some explanation of
events. There are too many who, out of envy, would
be pleased to see a man of my stature in the community fall as far as I have—and in my absence, I fear
Emma will become the target of their ridicule. I will
have more to say on that score in a moment.

But first, old friend—I hope I may yet count you my
friend—let me offer a sincere apology to one who once
refused a very different opportunity. Because of your
refusal, you alone among my friends are safe from the
repercussions of my downfall. You alone never sup-
ported my notion of creating a new formula for syn-
thetic silk, you alone thought me bound for failure.

I was baffled by your reticence, having been so certain you would be eager to invest in Hardwick
Chemical and Supply's latest venture. I knew your
objections were not of a technical nature, for although
you have great business acumen, you are no chemist.
Of course I made no acknowledgment of your professional abilities to our friends, but I was rather quick to
point out (in my subtle way) your lack of scientific
expertise. I took pains not to be the one who belittled
you before them; still I planted seeds of doubt here
and there, and made the most of any other man's crit-
ical remark. For your wisdom, for your foresight—I
punished you.

I might now excuse myself by saying that my company had done well for its investors in the past, or that I desperately needed not only their cash but their faith, or that I was myself wounded by your criticism of my dreams. But even before the formula failed, I saw that I had wronged you, Gussie, and was never more burdened by regret than when I realized that I had done so.

In those early days I was heedless, and imperiled not only my own fortune, but those of my family and friends. But as I sit here in a small hotel in an unfamiliar city, possessed of little more than a stranger's traveling case and my own thoughts, I do not miss my standing in the community, or my wealth, or much of anything, save Emma and my friendship with you. And so it is to you, Gussie, that I entrust my final confidence.

What happened to me? I seized an opportunity, Augustus, and no serpent ever turned and bit a man more sharply.

My world began to fall apart a few days ago, when my shop foreman—have you met Higgins, Gussie? A good man, Higgins. Trusted me. Just as all one hundred of my employees trusted me.

Higgins came into my office that morning and told me that one batch of material had been sent through a partially completed section of the silk manufacturing line, to test the machinery. Rolling the brim of his cap in his hands, he muttered his concerns; there seemed to be some sort of problem with the process. "Maybe I just ain't seein' it as it oughta be, Mr. Hardwick," he said, "but a'fore we go any further, you'd best take a look."

I was not yet uneasy. Why should I have been? As I followed him out of the office, I could not help but feel a sense of pride. We walked through the older portion of the factory, where most of the workers were busy with our usual line of products. Men smiled and nodded, or called out greetings as I passed. Higgins was talking to me about the problem, which still had not seemed significant. We reached the new section, the place where several large crates of equipment stood unopened. Higgins was going on, blaming the suppliers, of course, certain the trouble was with the raw ingredients and not the product itself.

I listened to him with half an ear as I studied the machinery and the failed batch and—I saw it then, Gussie, though how I kept my face from betraying the horror I was feeling, I'll never know. The process—my process, useless. A small flaw I could not detect in the laboratory, now magnified on the floor of the factory—after so many thousands of dollars had been spent on the equipment.

Higgins was looking to me for an answer, as were a dozen or so of the men working near that section of the line. Looking at me, some with anxious hope, others with unwavering faith in my abilities. I kept my features schooled in what I prayed would pass for concentration on the problem.

"Well, Higgins," I said, "this will simply require a minor adjustment in the formulation. I expected that some little changes might be needed—no cause for alarm. You and your men have done a fine job here, it's nothing to do with you. Go on with installing the equipment, and I'll work on a new formula."

I heard audible sighs of relief. I told Higgins that I

had some business outside the office that morning, and left the building.

I walked aimlessly for several hours, thinking the darkest thoughts imaginable. The humiliation, the financial ruin—if it had only been me, and not so many others who would suffer, I might have borne it. And there was Emma to think of.

I am sure that if you place yourself in my shoes, you will understand how terrible it was to contemplate any suffering on Emma's part. If I am not mistaken, you have a special fondness for her, Augustus. I am not suggesting that you have ever behaved in any other than an exemplary fashion, my friend. On the contrary, you have been all that is polite and respectful. But I know your affections for her will let you see what others may not, and hope you will not blame me for contemplating the fact that I was worth more to Emma dead than alive.

This was not an original thought—any man with life insurance policies as large as mine will consider such a fact, even in better times. The investors had insisted upon this very reasonable precaution, and no one ever questioned my buying additional coverage to protect Emma should I meet with some accident and predecease her. I knew that even if I died by my own hand, the investors would be paid. But while the investors would receive a payment under nearly any circumstances, Emma would be denied the death benefit were I to commit suicide.

Perhaps, I thought, I could disappear at sea, in a boating accident. But would there be some lengthy delay in paying the benefit to Emma if my body were missing?

I had walked some distance by now, and I grew thirsty. Looking for some place to find refreshment, I began to take note of my surroundings. I was in a part of town not wholly familiar to me, a commercial district of some sort. I saw a fellow in neat attire step into a nearby bar. I took out my pocket watch, the one my grandfather gave to me, and saw that it was now just past noon.

As I entered the bar, I was pleased to note that the customers were not by any means loutish. Clean and decently dressed, they were neither as wealthy as those of our own set, nor common laborers. It was not a rowdy group; most were quietly talking to one another as they finished simple lunches of sandwiches and beer.

As I moved closer to the bar, one of the patrons standing at it turned to me and said, "Stopping in one last time before your journey, Fontesque?" He soon realized his mistake and quickly said, "Pardon me, sir. I mistook you for another."

"Well, I'll be—" the man next to him said, looking over his shoulder. "You can't be blamed, Bill."

"Don't put the gentleman to the blush, you two," the bartender said, perhaps wary of losing my custom. "What'll it be, sir?"

"Now, Garvey, admit he looks a bit like Fontesque," the second persisted.

"You've something of his build and coloring, sir," Garvey said, "but you're by no means his twin." Then nodding at the second man, he added, "I'm sure Jim here meant no offense."

"None taken," I said, feeling a desire to camouflage myself among these men. I would, for a few moments, pretend to be one of them, step out of the odious role of being Jenkin Hardwick of Hardwick Chemical and Supply. None of these men would look to me for advice or guidance, none of them had the least dependence upon me.

"Good of you, sir," Garvey was saying. "What's your pleasure then, sir?"

"Same as my eagle-eyed friends, here," I answered, smiling.

The one called Bill smiled back and said, "On me, Garvey."

I extended a hand and said, "Harry Jenson," as naturally as if that were the name my mother gave me.

Bill Nicolas and Jim Irving introduced themselves in turn, and we chatted amiably. Bill was an accountant, Jim, a purchasing agent for a manufacturing concern. I easily convinced them I was just returning from Seattle—which I had visited often enough to describe—and vaguely referred to an exporting business there. My appetite returned as I banished Jenkin Hardwick and became Harry Jenson, and Garvey brought me a beef sandwich. I had a nervous moment when Jim, admiring my suit, said that the job must pay well. I took refuge in smiling silence, and Bill, the more circumspect of the two, colored and quickly changed the subject.

My new friends left not long after, wishing Harry Jenson the best of luck, but saying they must get back to their offices. I nearly said that I must do the same, but caught myself in time. The place had emptied out, the lunch rush over, and I was swallowing the last of my beer when I looked up to see the very man I had been mistaken for enter the establishment.

It was an odd moment to be sure, Gussie. Garvey had told the truth when he said Fontesque was not my twin. Fontesque's eyebrows were a little heavier, his mouth a little larger. But he and I were of the same height, of the same build, and our other features were not altogether different. His nose was as straight as mine, his eyes as blue, his hair was the same dark brown—only cut a little shorter.

He was as shocked as I, or perhaps more so, because I had the benefit of a warning. Upon seeing me, he nearly dropped the drummer's case he was carrying. An idea which had begun to take seed in my mind caused me to linger; I wanted the opportunity to study Mr. Fontesque.

Garvey smoothed the way, saying, "Louis Fontesque, as I live and breathe! I was hoping you'd come in before Mr. Jenson left!"

Fontesque brusquely rejected the bartender's theory of our likely (if perhaps distant) relation to one another. He said he had no time for foolishness, giving the bartender some disgust of him. Garvey served his surly customer in a similar fashion, then was all politeness to me, filling my glass with his compliments before he withdrew to clear the tables at the back of the room.

Attempting conversation with my near look-alike, I remarked that I would not be surprised to learn that we were distant cousins, or some such. This was met by Mr. Fontesque with a shrug and a return to the contemplation of his suds. I was not daunted. Augustus, I ask you—how many would not see this fellow's entering that establishment at that moment as an opportunity unlikely to present itself again?

He was wholly uncommunicative until, seeing that he carried a drummer's case, I expanded on the tale I had told his fellows, and said I was the buyer for Hardwick Chemical and Supply, just back from a trip to Seattle. His attitude underwent an immediate change. He told me that he sold hardware especially designed for the mechanical needs of factories like Hardwick's—pulleys, cleats, slings, shims and such. I encouraged this line of talk. After some moments, he blushed to confess that he had once called at my company but was turned away.

"Why, I regret that I was not on hand to speak to you then!" I said in tones of outrage. "If you remember the name of the fellow who refused you, I'll see him reprimanded. Only a fool could fail to see the value of your merchandise to our company." At this Fontesque puffed up. While he agreed with me (at length) that the fellow who had turned him away was a fool, I schooled my features into an expression of grave consideration.

Recalling that when Bill had mistakenly greeted me as Fontesque, he had also mentioned something about a journey, I took a gamble. "Allow me to make it up to you, Mr. Fontesque," I said, in the tone of one hitting upon a grand idea. "You shall see Mr. Hardwick himself! Will you come by our offices in two days' time?"

Fontesque looked so immediately dejected, I nearly laughed. "No, sir. I regret I won't. I'm leaving for San Francisco on the morning train."

My relief was vast, but I dared not show it. I frowned as if in concentration. "Hmm. Mr. Hardwick is out of his office today, but will return this evening. I am scheduled to see him in his office at eight. I know it is rather late, but would you be prepared to come to his office at that time? I feel we have done you a wrong, and would not like you to leave town with such a poor impression of our company. I should very much like Mr. Hardwick to meet you."

"Hardwick himself?" he exclaimed.

"Yes. I wouldn't want others to know I had given you such special treatment, but if you are willing to be discreet about this invitation—"

He readily agreed to it, swearing that no one could keep a secret like Louis Fontesque.

I made one other stop before hurrying back to the factory. As I sat in the barber's chair, watching the beginnings of a transformation, I refined my plans. I ignored the sullen pouting of the barber. Over that good man's objections, I had instructed him to cut my hair in a style identical to Fontesque's; as I left, I assuaged his outraged sensibilities with a tip more handsome than my haircut.

The journey back to the factory was, I knew, a journey that would forever change my fate. I found my courage in this thought: while the task before me was distasteful, it was nothing in comparison to the image of Emma living in shame and deprivation.

At four o'clock, as usual, I called Higgins into my office and asked him to report on the day's work. He remarked upon my haircut, as I had hoped. He then proceeded in his customary fashion and gave the day's production figures without looking at notes. Higgins, I have long known, has a remarkable head for numbers.

I found myself thinking that if Higgins were better

educated, he might have achieved any position. Perhaps he would have been sitting where I did, owning a factory of his own. Or planning a murder.

My questions to him were nothing out of the ordinary, but I made a show of stacking the coins in my pocket on my desk as he spoke. I lined them up, six twenty-cent pieces, two dimes, two three-cent pieces, three two-cent pieces and a single, worn large cent piece. "One dollar and fifty-three cents," I announced, scooping them off the desk and returning them to my pocket. I pulled out my watch then, and said that I must send a message to Emma, telling her that I would be late. I told Higgins that I had thought about the silk process and was fairly sure that I had hit upon the answer to our problems. I would run some experiments in my laboratory that night.

Higgins asked if he might be of any assistance, or if there was anyone else who should be asked to stay and help me. I thanked him, but said no, it would not be necessary. There was nothing remarkable in this. My employees were used to my odd hours and solitary work in the laboratory.

In the hours between four and my appointment with Mr. Fontesque, there were many moments when I nearly abandoned my scheme. On several occasions, I thought of hurrying home to Emma, to see her one last time before I was forever parted from her. Nothing was more difficult than to contemplate leaving her without so much as a last word of good-bye. But I knew I could not hide from her the strong emotion I was feeling then, and all depended upon my remaining calm and presenting a picture of normality.

Just before eight o'clock, I went into the laboratory, and made my simple preparations. I could not bring myself to stay there, though, and began to walk around the building, making sure I was alone. The factory was empty, the machinery still. I recalled the pride I felt when I had walked through it earlier that same day. Would it die with me? Or would Higgins and the others contrive to keep it running? I thought the latter might be the case, and oddly, that made me all the more proud of the place. I turned my back on it and moved to wait in the reception area.

When Fontesque arrived, I had calmed myself. I took his coat and hung it on a hall tree near the front door. I told him that Mr. Hardwick was working in the laboratory. "He's about to conduct a rather fascinating experiment," I said, and offered to take him there. As we walked, I expressed my hope that Mr. Fontesque had not been forced to travel far from his hotel for this appointment.

"No," he said, "I'm staying at the Charles."

When I said I did not know of it, he happily supplied its location. Good of him.

I opened the door to the laboratory, and stood slightly behind it as he walked in. The display of beakers and glass tubing enthralled him long enough for me to reach for the short, thick board I had left behind the door, to raise it, and—forcing myself not to shut my eyes as I did so—to deliver the blow which killed him instantly.

I felt for his heartbeat to be sure I had not merely stunned him. There was none. Perhaps this is why there was very little bleeding.

I exchanged the entire contents of his pockets for

my own, even sacrificing my watch. I picked up his drummer's case. I carried it to the front door, setting it near the coat, and walked back to the laboratory. I moved the body to the place where I might have stood working, taking care not to let his heels drag on the floor. I went into my office, to my private safe, used the combination known only to me, and took most of the petty cash I keep on hand there, leaving some cash behind to avoid suspicion should the police break the safe open at some later date. I then had with me enough money to sustain me in a modest way for a few weeks.

I returned to the laboratory, started the fire and hurried out, putting on Fontesque's coat and hat, carrying his large and battered drummer's case.

The lamplighter had already passed through the streets by the time I began to make my way toward Fontesque's hotel. I hurried along the cobblestones, trying to turn my thoughts from the destruction of all I had built. I could not look back, Augustus, not even as I heard the cries of alarm when I was several streets away. No scent of acrid smoke reached me; only Fontesque's scent. It was the scent of his cologne and his tobacco and his sweat, his very body, some part of his skin left to line the coat, an obscene lining made to fit over my own skin. I was uncomfortable in it.

I pulled the hat low and averted my face as I passed into the hotel. It was a modest but clean establishment. The room key I found in his pocket was stamped with the number 114, and I used it to open that door.

I had not taken a liking to Fontesque, but I was struck forcibly with a sense of the monstrousness of my crime as I stood in his room. The detritus of his daily life—a lonely life, it seemed—moved me more powerfully to a sense of shame than had his lifeless body. Scattered about the desk and dresser were various small wooden and metal objects, small tools and pulleys and gears, the items by which he earned his living.

His living. The irony was not lost on me.

On the bed were a few more of the objects, and an open leather satchel with a stained handle. It contained a pair of dark stockings, one with a hole in the toe; a set of garters; a nightshirt; two cotton handkerchiefs; undergarments; a pair of black suspenders; two neatly folded shirts; a pair of trousers and two small wooden objects not unlike the others on the bed. Near the washstand was a dampened and crumpled towel, a bottle of hair oil, a simple shaving cup and brush, a rubber comb (I could not help but miss my ivory comb and its silver case), a small bottle of inexpensive cologne and a little leather kit. The kit held a razor and strop, and a pair of scissors.

There were a few sheets of paper on the desk, among them a carbon copy of a list of his company's wares. He had evidently puzzled over some sums, for one page held crossed out numbers and columns of figures; eventually I saw that he was trying to work out his commission on an order.

Knowing I would not sleep that night—I had no desire to lie where he had lain—I began to study the list of objects, and opened up the drummer's case. The case was much neater, being partitioned off into numbered slots. I began matching the objects to descriptions on the list of wares, and was able to place almost every item strewn about the room back into the case. In this way I occupied the worst hours, those when I most clearly realized what I had done, what I had lost. I concentrated on these objects instead of my sins.

In the end I had replaced everything but the two wooden objects I had found in his satchel. These were stained and worn, and were, I decided, most likely some sort of shim that had been returned by a customer, or which was no longer in use.

I looked with pride at the case. I did not recognize all of the various implements, but this was of little concern to me. I had already decided that I would not take up Mr. Fontesque's business. Sooner or later I might meet someone who knew him well enough to reveal me as an impostor.

Still, it would be best if Mr. Fontesque was thought to be alive, at least until I was safely out of town.

There was no trouble on that score. I changed into his clothes, packed my own with his belongings, and waited until the last moment before leaving the room to settle his account. The desk clerk was more concerned with the faces on the crisp bills than that of a departing guest, and so I escaped undue notice. I did not want to be recognized while waiting at the station, so I timed my appearance on the platform just as the seven o'clock train pulled in with a loud whistle and a squeal of brakes, bellowing cinder-filled smoke from its stack. As the noise of its arrival subsided, I heard a paperboy calling out a headline: "Hardwick Factory Fire Kills Owner!" I kept my head lowered, purchased a paper and tucked it beneath my arm.

I boarded the train, praying that no one who knew me or Fontesque would be riding in the coach cars. The train was not crowded, and I set the cases on the seat next to me to discourage unwanted company. Oh, for a private car as I was used to! But no one molested me.

That no man greeted me as Fontesque could not surprise me. He had been a surly man, and of no importance to our community. I, on the other hand, felt sure that I might be recognized at any moment, even in Fontesque's sorry raiment. Imagine my feelings, then, when I opened the newspaper to hide my face behind it and was greeted with what was meant to be my own likeness on the front page!

It was, to be sure, a rather poor engraving copied from an old photograph. (You remember the one in the small wooden frame which stood above the mantle in the library? Perhaps you would be so kind as to discover if some Johnny Lightfingers from the *Clarion* stole it from my home?) As I calmed myself, I decided that the too thin lips and enlarged nose in this depiction would be of help; perhaps I would benefit from the artist's lack of attention to detail.

I am sure you saw the headline:

J. HARDWICK KILLED IN FIRE

Aside from my growing dislike of the engraving itself, the two articles on the front page were all I could want them to be. I studied the article on the fire first. Although the pumping crew had arrived in time to douse the fire before much damage was done to the factory itself, the laboratory was destroyed. The fire was thought to have been the result of some experiment gone awry. The body found within the laboratory was burned nearly beyond recognition. (More thoroughly than I had hoped.) My coat had been found in the undamaged entry, still hanging on the hall tree. On the body, an object believed to be my watch was also found. But the prime piece of identifying evidence was supplied by Higgins, who indeed remembered that I had counted out $1.53—exactly the amount of heat-damaged coins found on the deceased.

Blessing Higgins, I moved to the other article; a touching tribute to my achievements that nearly had me weeping over the loss of myself.

And so I went on to San Francisco, and booked a room at this establishment, the Linworth Hotel, which is neither mean nor luxurious. For the better part of two days, I slept, exhausted by events and emotions.

Last night I went out to obtain a simple dinner, and as I made my way back to the hotel, I purchased a newspaper. This I took to my room, and feeling much alone, began to read.

The article which prompted this letter to you was on page ten.

The story of a fire in a northern city might not have been worthy of the attention of the San Francisco paper, but in this case, there were large insurance premiums which might have been paid upon Jenkin Hardwick's death. Might have been paid, except for one curious problem—the body of Mr. Jenkin Hardwick was two inches shorter than it should be.

Two inches shorter? But Fontesque had stood next

to me in that saloon, walked next to me, and always at my exact height! Our boots, though of a different quality, did not differ in the size of their heels. What had gone wrong?

I frantically searched my mind for some explanation, and found myself staring at Hardwick's satchel. I opened it and spilled the contents onto the bed.

The two strange wooden objects clattered together like castanets. They were easily identified now: lifts. The damnable man wore lifts in his shoes!

To be undone by something so small as a vain man's attempt to hide his lack of stature is more than I can bear at this point, Augustus. Sooner or later, even a man like Fontesque will be missed, and when accusations of fraud are raised and his likeness to me is recalled by the patrons of that saloon, the truth will be known. Emma's nature will not allow her to lie to the police; neither is there any wiliness in her—I cannot hope she will think to mislead them by saying that I, too, wore lifts.

And Augustus, although others may not believe it, Emma was at the heart of this, as she owns my own heart. Please, I beg of you, do all you can to shield her from what is to come.

I, for my part, will have made better use of my knowledge of chemistry by the time you receive this. In my room, an effective potion awaits me, a strong poison—one which will not allow me to fall short of my current goal.

Farewell, Gussie, from the world's biggest fool.

MISCALCULATION

"ALL SET?" Ada asked. "Of course you are. There isn't a Girl Scout in the world who took 'be prepared' as seriously as you did, Sarah."

"From the size of that trunk I saw poor Mr. Parsons carrying out of here, I'd say you're the one who's over-prepared," Sarah Milington replied. "Really, Grandmother, we're only staying on the *Queen Mary* overnight."

"I'm sure you're right," her adoptive grandmother said, embracing her as she reached her. "And it's likely I still haven't brought half of what I really need. You're the one who's best at details. If you would come to live with me again—"

"Grandmother . . ." Sarah warned.

"Never mind, I won't pester you about that now. I think a trunk makes it seem so much more like a real cruise—Oh, here's Robert," she said, seeming so pleased that Sarah had to tamp down an annoying little flair of jealousy. More irritating, she was fairly sure Robert Parsons had noted her discomposure.

Although he was always polite to her, Sarah had yet to feel completely at ease around Parsons. Some of this unease was undoubtedly due to her grandmother's delight in surrounding both Parsons's background and his position in her household with an air of intrigue, but Sarah knew this was only part of why she felt self-conscious when Parsons was near.

For all his own quietness, his presence in this house caused of a great deal of talk. He was the inspiration for plenty of local gossip—gossip that undoubtedly pleased Ada Milington. Robert Parsons—goodlooking, broad-shouldered and not more than thirty years old, had been part of Ada's household for nearly a year now.

At first, Sarah had believed that the rest of the staff, all much older than Parsons and notoriously protective of her grandmother, would rebel at his presence. In this she was mistaken. Parsons, she now reflected—recalling that he had just carried the largest trunk she had ever seen out to the van—was undoubtedly a godsend to the aging servants. He seemed more than willing to do heavy lifting and to take on any task, no matter how arduous. And, she was forced to admit, he gave every sign of being sincerely devoted to her grandmother.

Sarah knew she had no real personal complaint to make of him. Long accustomed to her grandmother's love of outrageous behavior, she decided that it was not her place to interfere. Ada had survived four husbands, and if she now wanted to have a fling with a man almost fifty years her junior, Sarah would not be the one to object.

Ada turned to the rest of the staff, which had gathered in the entry. "We're off on our cruise!" she announced grandly, waving a kiss at them. Amid tossed confetti and their boisterous cheers of "Bon voyage," and "Many happy returns!" she took Parsons's arm and allowed him to lead the way to the van.

He hadn't loaded the luggage very efficiently, Sarah thought with a frown, seeing that he had strapped the huge trunk to the long rack on the van's roof. By simply removing a seat, he could have fit it inside. The wind resistance would have been lower, and she would have obtained better gas mileage. She was considering this problem when Parsons, after gently helping Ada into the front passenger seat, surprised Sarah by opening the sliding door to the side of the van and seating himself in the back.

No wonder he had left the seat in place! She felt herself blush at the thought of her grandmother marching up the *Queen Mary*'s gangplank with this virile-looking male in tow. And if Robert Parsons was sharing a room with Ada—but then, she quickly reminded herself, that was none of her business.

Ada's smile told her that her grandmother was waiting for a challenge, but Sarah merely started the van and began the drive to Long Beach.

She couldn't help but feel herself an injured party, though. She had wanted to talk privately to her grandmother, perhaps even to confide in her about the dream she had had last night—a recurring, claustrophobic dream from her childhood, of being locked in a closet. That was certainly not possible now. She could picture Robert Parsons's amusement over that.

"A little ridiculous to have Bella and the others throwing confetti," she said aloud. "It isn't really a cruise, after all."

"I'm pretending it is," Ada answered. "It's the closest I can come to a cruise. You know I get seasick."

"I know nothing of the sort. You've been on real cruises."

"And got sick on the last one. Never again. I do love the ocean, I just don't want to be feeling it pitch and roll as I blow out my candles. So this will be my cruise—perhaps my last one."

"It's not a cruise," Sarah repeated obstinately.

"Technically, no."

She might have left it at that, but when she glanced at the rearview mirror, she saw that Parsons was smiling. Smugly, she thought.

"Technically, it isn't even a ship," she added.

"No?" Ada said, turning to wink back at him.

Sarah felt her fingers tighten on the steering wheel. "No. It's officially classified as a building now, not a ship. It's permanently moored at that pier. It doesn't move. It doesn't go anywhere."

"You don't say," Ada replied.

"It's afloat," Robert said. "It moves with the tide."

Sarah fell silent.

After a moment, Ada said wistfully, "I saw her sail once, long ago. Back in the days when she did sail, when she was definitely a ship."

"You saw your first husband off to war," Robert said.

He sounded bitter, Sarah thought. Was he jealous of Ada's previous husbands? It seemed absurd. Perhaps it was only this first husband, she thought.

Elliot. She was fairly sure he had been the first. Or was it Arthur?

Sarah knew little about any of Ada's husbands. Ada was someone who lived, by and large, in the present day, seldom discussing her past. And by the time Sarah had come to live with Ada, the last of Ada's four spouses had been dead for more than twenty years.

Sarah tried to remember the little she had been told. There had been an Elliot, an Arthur, a Charles, and finally John Milington, Sr.—the father of the man who had adopted Sarah. Yes, that was the order. She remembered that Ada had married the first one when she was eighteen, and that he had died in World War II.

Bella had once let it slip that Ada had a son from that marriage, a son who so disliked Ada's third husband, mother and son had become estranged. Sarah frowned. Or was it a son by the second husband who disliked the third? Sarah could not remember. She couldn't even recall Ada's eldest boy's name. She did recall Bella's warning never to mention this son to Ada. Not wanting to cause Ada pain, or to make trouble for the old housekeeper, Sarah had kept her silence.

She glanced at Ada, and saw that her grandmother was frowning. It was then that another implication of Robert's remark came home to her.

"If you said good-bye to your first husband that day, he must have sailed on the *Queen Mary* when she was used as a troop ship, during the war."

Ada nodded. "I never saw him again."

"But being on the ship again—won't it be sad for you?"

Ada smiled and shook her head. "No, Sarah dear. Not at all. I was never actually aboard the ship, of course. We said good-bye at the dock. And the ship doesn't even look the same on the outside now. She was painted a dull gray then, and her portholes were blackened. She was called 'the *Grey Ghost*' during the war."

"I read about that period of the ship's history," Sarah said. "The *Queen Mary* was able to cross the Atlantic in four or five days, which made her the fastest ship on the sea—capable of outrunning German submarines, if need be. She was even faster than German torpedoes." She paused, frowned and added, "Faster than the ones used at the beginning of the war. There was a bounty on her. Hitler promised he would give a quarter of a million dollars and Germany's highest honors to the submarine captain who sank her."

"My, you have read up on her," Robert Parsons said.

Sarah responded as she always did under stress. She turned to numbers. "Yes. The ship made a great contribution to the Allied efforts. During the war, the *Queen Mary* carried over seven hundred-and-sixty-five thousand military personnel over half a million nautical miles."

She saw that Parsons was smiling again, until Ada said, "One of those three-quarters of a million was mine."

"Yes, of course," Sarah said. "I'm sorry."

Robert reached forward and took Ada's hand.

Ada, never one to brood, soon changed the subject. She began to recite the guest list for the party. Sarah stayed silent, only half-attending as local dignitaries and old friends were named. While a woman of Ada's wealth and influence would never have trouble finding guests for her parties, it was her reputation for holding lively, out of the ordinary celebrations which made her invitations much sought after.

At last the *Queen Mary* came into sight. Sarah, seeing the long, sleek giant before her, its trio of mammoth red stacks cuffed in black towering above them, quickly realized that all the reading she had done about this historic vessel could never do it justice.

"A building?" she heard Robert Parsons ask.

"No," Sarah said quietly. "A ship, a beautiful, beautiful ship."

"Nothing like her in the world," he agreed. "Wait until you're aboard."

"You've been on the *Queen Mary* before?" she asked, surprised.

"A few times," he said, but Ada began directing her to the hotel entrance before Sarah could ask more.

As they were welcomed by the staff at the registration desk, Sarah's eyes roved over the Art Deco lines of the ship's interior, the etched glass and shining brass, the rich exotic woods that surrounded her—crafted into curving, sumptuous, smooth surfaces and marquetry unlike any she had ever seen.

She was recalled from her admiration by Ada's voice. "The small bag to Mr. Parsons's suite, please. The trunk and the rest of this group to mine, all except those two very serviceable but dowdy bags, which I'm sorry to say, belong to my granddaughter."

Sarah followed mutely as they were shown to their

rooms, noting that like Ada, Robert was staying in one of the royalty suites. Each suite, Sarah knew, featured a large sitting area separated from a spacious bedroom, a private bath and an additional small bedroom with a single twin bed in it—servant's quarters. In the ship's glory years, the luxurious suites had been occupied by the wealthiest of first class passengers, who paid the equivalent of an average Englishman's annual wages for round-trip passage—a large sum, even with the servant's fare and all meals included.

Robert's suite was near Ada's, but not adjoining it. Having braced herself for the likelihood that Ada would make the most of such a romantic setting, Sarah was surprised by this arrangement. He had been given a room that certainly placed his status well above that of hired help, but an adjoining room would have made assignations much easier.

Ada had offered a suite to Sarah, but Sarah had opted for one of the staterooms. Not as grand as the suites, it was nevertheless spacious, and like the suites, had many original furnishings in it. Sarah opened the two thick portholes, which provided a view of the Long Beach shoreline and downtown skyline. Taking a deep breath of cool air, she soon put aside her questions about her grandmother and Parsons. She spent the next half hour exploring her own luxurious room.

Soon her toiletries had been neatly arranged, her clothes hung in one of the closets, and nearly every other item she had carried with her stowed in an orderly fashion. She was just deciding where she would place a pair of books she had brought—about the history of the ship—when the phone rang.

"Sarah? Be a dear and run along to the Observation Bar, will you?" Ada said. "I told Robert I would meet him there, but now I've learned that Captain Dolman will be here any moment."

"Captain Dolman? Is he the ship's captain?" Sarah asked.

"No, no, an old friend. An army captain, retired for years. Now be a dear and don't make Robert wait there alone—some young wench might look at his handsome face decide to lead him astray. A man like that, drinking alone in the bar—the consequences are not to be thought of."

"I don't—"

"Think you can find it? Of course you can. It's near the bow of the ship, on the Promenade Deck. Thank you, dear, it's such a relief to know I can depend upon you."

Sarah bore this with her usual good grace. She climbed the stairs to the Promenade Deck and moved quickly through the ship's shopping gallery to the cocktail lounge. Stepping into the curving, multi-level room, she saw before her a row of tall windows with a view of the main deck and bow, and the harbor beyond; nearer, in the room itself, a nickel-colored railing made up of a mixture of creatures real and mythological. She turned; above the mirrors behind the bar, she saw a painting that, up until now, she had only seen in black-and-white photographs of this room. For several long moments, she forgot all about looking for Robert Parsons.

The painting stretched across the length of the bar, and depicted a street scene. More than two dozen figures were caught in motion. They were people from all walks of life, dancing hand-in-hand: sailors, bakers and men in top hats cavorted with stout matrons, elegantly clad ladies and women in everyday dress. All were laughing as they circled round and round in celebration. Pennants fluttered above them; one of the revelers had lost her footing, but this was forever that moment before the others would notice.

"Makes you want to join them, doesn't it?" a voice said from just behind her right ear.

Startled, Sarah turned and found herself nearly nose-to-nose with Parsons. "No, Mr. Parsons—"

"Robert—"

"No, Mr. Parsons," she said, taking a step away from him. "It doesn't. They're all about to stumble over the one who has fallen."

He looked up at the mural and smiled. "They'll help her to her feet and carry on with the dance."

"At best, they'll step over her and continue without her."

He shook his head, but said nothing.

"The banners carry the insignia of St. George," she said quickly, fixing her eyes on the painting.

"In honor of King George the Fifth's twenty-fifth year as king," Parsons said, "which is being celebrated by the dancers. The work was painted by A. R. Thomson—and is called 'Royal Jubilee Week, 1935.'"

She turned scarlet.

"Oh, now you're angry with me. I've spoiled your fun. Let me buy you a glass of wine."

"I don't—"

"You can toss it in my face if you like. I'll present myself as a target."

"No, no I'm sorry. It's a bad habit of mine, spouting off facts and figures nobody cares to hear."

"But you're wrong—I'm very interested in what you have to say, Miss Milington."

"Please, let's go back to Sarah and Robert."

He smiled. "All right." He motioned to a doorway. "I'm sitting outside, but if you find it too chilly there for you—"

"No, I prefer it," she said truthfully.

She was seated at his table, shielded from the afternoon breeze by a row of Plexiglas panels. Belatedly, she remembered to deliver her message.

"It was kind of you to walk all the way here to tell me," he said, "but Ada is so seldom on time, I don't think I would have worried."

"I think she sent me as your chaperone," she admitted.

He laughed. "No, no, I doubt that. Tell me, have you had a chance to see much of the ship yet?"

"No, I've only just unpacked."

"Hmm. Then you must let me show you some of the more interesting sights—"

"I'm not sure—"

"You aren't afraid of me, are you?" he asked. "I promise you won't come to any harm."

Not unaware that this was the longest conversation she had ever had with him, she said, "Oh, no, I'm not afraid. It's just that Grandmother may not like me to dominate so much of your time."

"Trust me, she'll be delighted. Besides," he added quietly, "she'll have other demands to make of me later."

Again Sarah felt herself blush.

"You misunderstand—" he began.

"It isn't any of my business," Sarah said quickly,

relieved to see Ada approaching, accompanied by two elderly gentlemen, one on each arm. The men seemed to be doing their level best to keep up with her. Sarah, acquainted with most of Ada's friends, did not know either of these men. But as they drew closer, she thought one of them did seem familiar.

Ada came to their table with long strides, flamboyantly garbed in a hot pink and turquoise jogging suit, wearing a white turban. How does she manage, Sarah wondered, to wear such silly outfits and still look great?

"Sarah!" Ada called out, "Meet the congressman!"

"Oh, not yet, not yet!" the taller of the two men exclaimed. "A mere state senator at the moment, but with your grandmother's generous help, I may trade Sacramento for Washington, D.C." He extended a hand. "Archer Hastings, my dear, at your service."

"A pleasure to meet you, Senator," Sarah said, now realizing why he seemed familiar. She was sure she had seen him on the evening news once or twice. He wasn't the senator for their district, but Ada had many political friends, not all them her own representatives.

When Ada introduced the second man, Gerald Dolman, the retired army captain turned crimson and nodded in Sarah's direction, but did not meet her eyes. He was a thin man with a prominent Adam's apple. It bobbed as he swallowed nervously. She wondered why he was so flustered over meeting her, but soon decided he was merely shy—he would not, in fact, look directly at any of the others, and the blush which had stolen over his neck and face remained throughout the time he sat with them.

Archer Hastings had no such reticence. He gave the

others a quick biography of himself, a sort of resume from the time he was a paperboy in the 1930's. He spoke at length about his enlistment in the army, his service (mostly behind a desk) during World War II. By the time he was telling them about his return to California and his establishment of an accounting firm, the drinks had arrived. *What a pompous ass,* Sarah thought, but Hastings was only warming up.

"Have you had a chance to tour the ship?" Ada was asking him.

"Yes, yes. Wonderful! Wonderful place for this lovely lady to celebrate her birthday," he said to the others. "I'm certainly looking forward to that party tonight. The Grand Salon. Used to be the first class dining room. Largest single public room ever built on a ship. You could fit all three of Christopher Columbus's ships in there and still have space left over. Have you seen it yet, Sarah? No? Oh, you must see it. Probably won't let you in while they're getting ready for the big to-do, but"—he winked conspiratorially—"you have friends in high places. Then of course, you will see it tonight, won't you? Yes, a grand ship."

Captain Dolman was making quick progress through his drink as Hastings went on.

"A symbol of triumph over the Great Depression, that's what it was to the British," the politician said.

"Yes," Robert Parsons said, "she was a symbol of hope."

For reasons Sarah could not understand, this caused Captain Dolman and Ada to look at him sharply. But Hastings was oblivious.

"I've always liked the British," he was saying.

"Don't you like them? Sure. Like to do things on a grand scale—just like you, Ada. Say, did you know that if you measure from the *Queen Mary*'s keel to the top of her forward funnel, this ship is one hundred and eighty feet tall? That makes her eighteen feet taller than Niagara Falls! Now, that's something, but her length is spectacular. If you could stand this ship on end, it would be taller than the Washington Monument. Taller than the Eiffel Tower, too. In fact, the Empire State Building would only be two hundred feet taller."

"Two hundred and thirty feet," Sarah said without thinking.

Parsons smiled, Ada laughed, and Captain Dolman nervously rattled the ice in his glass, which he was studying intently. Archer Hastings seemed taken aback until he noticed Ada's reaction, then burst into hearty guffaws. Sarah felt her own cheeks turning red, and wondered if her complexion now matched Captain Dolman's.

"I warned you, Archer," Ada said. "She's a wonder with numbers. As addicted to facts and figures as you are."

"Really?" Hastings seemed unable to resist the challenge of testing this claim. "I suppose you know about the anchors?"

Sarah hesitated, but seeing Ada's expectant look, answered, "There are two eighteen-foot long anchors, each weighs sixteen tons. The anchor chains are each nine hundred and ninety feet long. Each link of an anchor chain weighs two hundred and twenty-four pounds."

"Very good, very good," he acknowledged,

although Sarah thought he did not seem to be truly pleased. "Your grandmother told me you had an excellent head for figures. Numbers have always been a specialty of mine. Making good use of them, not just dithering around with some theoretical nonsense. Of course, one can't expect a young lady to have an appreciation of statistics; rare enough to find one who has any kind of brain for mathematics in the first place. No wonder your grandmother is so proud of—"

Sarah fixed him with a narrow glare, but it was Robert who interrupted, saying, "Mrs. Milington is proud of her granddaughter for a great many reasons, of course. Her abilities with mathematics and statistics are just one source of that pride."

Hastings seemed to finally become aware Ada was looking at him in a way that seemed to indicate that subtraction—from the amount he was hoping to receive from her for his campaign—seemed the most likely piece of arithmetic to be going on in her mind.

"Oh, Sarah, I apologize," he said quickly. "I behave just like a crotchety old man on some occasions. You are clearly an exceptional young lady! I am astounded at your knowledge of the ship."

"I haven't seen much of it," she confessed in some confusion, still amazed at Robert's defense of her, and uncomfortable with all the praise Hastings had heaped upon her.

"But she's read a great deal," Robert said.

"Ask her anything about it!" Ada said.

Sarah noticed a particular gleam in his eye as he said, "All right. What type of fuel did the *Queen Mary* burn?"

"Bunker C oil," she answered promptly. "The ship averaged thirteen feet to the gallon."

Ada gave a crow of laughter.

"Thirteen miles to the gallon?" Hastings asked.

"No, sir. Feet, not miles."

Hastings, skeptical a moment before, now became fascinated by Sarah's love of data and would not be side-tracked from his game. He asked for statistic after statistic, and Sarah answered accurately every time.

She could not help but feel a glow of pride, and her original appraisal of Hastings mellowed considerably. But just as she was saying that there were over six miles of carpet on the ship, she happened to glance at Robert Parsons. He was frowning at Hastings, and his fists were clenched on the table.

I'm boring him, Sarah thought, all the pleasure suddenly going out of the game. Her voice trailed off, and she stared down at her hands, too humiliated to continue. Robert was obviously wishing that Hastings would stop encouraging her. She probably hadn't amused anyone other than Hastings and her grandmother; Robert and Captain Dolman, she was sure, were wishing Ada had left her at home. She had been an obnoxious, unbridled know-it-all.

She was about to apologize when she heard Robert say, "I have an extra pass for the next guided tour, Sarah. Would you care to go on it?"

She had not thought she could be more deeply mortified, but she was wrong. So he wanted to send her off on a ship's tour, as if she were a child not ready to share the company of adults. Well, and why not? She had just behaved as if she were the kid in the class who waves his hand and shouts, "Me! Me! Call on me!"

"Thank you," she managed to say.

"Yes," her grandmother agreed, "an excellent notion."

So even Ada was defecting, she thought, as Robert, ever the gentleman, stood and helped her from her chair. She was a little surprised when he continued at her side, but she said nothing. She crossed the bar and took the exit to her left, and still he followed. As they passed two of the larger shops along the passageway, he said, "These were once the first class passengers' library and drawing room. Winston Churchill was given use of the drawing room when he was aboard the ship during World War II. He and other leaders finalized plans for the invasion of Normandy while on this ship, probably in that room."

Sarah glanced into the rather barren souvenir shop that now occupied the space.

"Don't worry," he said, reading her thoughts. "Not all of her dignity has been lost."

"Where does the tour begin?"

"The port side of this deck," he said.

"I'm sure I can find it," she said.

"Undoubtedly. But I'm going with you."

"But you've been before . . ."

"Yes," he said, "but much of the ship can only be seen on the tour. You don't mind if I join you?"

"Of course not."

The tour (she couldn't prevent herself from counting the group—eighteen sightseers, including the two of them) was led by a retired naval officer. Parsons stayed at her side, but did not touch or crowd her. She soon relaxed and began to thoroughly enjoy the tour itself, fascinated by the grandeur and history of the ship.

When the tour group reached the cabin class swimming pool, she heard a woman say, "I've heard that it's haunted."

Sarah looked around the room of beige and blue-green terra-cotta tiles, the etched wire-and-glass image of an ancient sailing ship behind her, the glimmering mother-of-pearl ceiling above, the empty, sloping bottom of the pool itself. There were no windows or portholes, but the room was large enough to prevent her from feeling claustrophobic. Nothing about any of it struck her as particularly scary, nothing sent a chill down her back. But when she turned to make a joke to Robert about ghosts who had turned green from chlorine, she saw that he was pale, and had a strange, intense look on his face.

The guide was making light of the woman's remark. "Do you mean the woman in the mini-skirt or the one in the bathing suit? I'd settle for a glimpse of either one."

"There's more than one ghost?" the woman asked.

"Oh yes, the ship has long been reported to be haunted," the guide said lightly. "If you believe in such reports, this ship is loaded with ghosts. Myself, if I see one, I hope it's one of the young ladies who rove in here."

The group laughed and began to move after the guide as he went on with the tour. Robert, however, remained motionless, and continued to stare into the pool.

"Robert?" Sarah asked. "Are you feeling ill?"

When he seemed not to hear her, she touched his sleeve. "Robert?"

He turned to her with a start. "Oh—I'm sorry, we've fallen behind. We'd better catch up with the others." They were not far from the group, though, and once they reached it Sarah asked again if he was feeling ill.

"No," he said, "I'm fine now, thank you."

She did not believe him, and glanced back at him several times as they made their way to the next area, along a catwalk over one of the cavernous boiler rooms. He was still pale.

By the time the formal tour was finished, though, he seemed himself again, and Sarah happily allowed him to accompany her to the other shipboard exhibits. He seemed to enjoy her enthusiasm as she was able to see the anchor chains and lifeboats and all the other parts of the ship she had read about. She lost her self-consciousness over her study of the ship's statistics and decided her knowledge gave her a better appreciation of what she was seeing now.

Not that her appreciation was limited to the ship's physical power. There was nostalgia, pure and simple, to be relished. She lingered over photos of Winston Churchill, Queen Elizabeth, Clark Gable, Marlene Dietrich, the Duke and Duchess of Windsor, Spencer Tracy, and other famous passengers. She tried to take in every detail of the displays of passenger accommodations and dining rooms.

Robert, cheerful through most of their exploration of the ship, grew solemn when they reached the wartime exhibits on the Sun Deck. The subject matter deserved solemnity, Sarah thought. His mood, however, seemed to remain grim even after they left the exhibit. She felt much more at ease with him by then, which gave her the courage to ask him what was troubling him.

He hesitated, then said, "Did you see how the soldiers were forced to live aboard this ship?"

Sarah, recalling the photos of thousands of soldiers crammed together on the decks of the ship, shuddered. "Yes, it was very crowded—"

"Crowded? You like numbers. The ship was designed to carry about two thousand passengers. On one of its wartime voyages, it carried over sixteen thousand men."

"It carried sixteen thousand, six hundred-and-eighty-three," Sarah said. "The largest number of people ever to sail on any ship—a record that still stands."

"Sarah, think of what that meant to each of those sixteen thousand!"

She had seen some of this in the exhibit, of course. Tiers of standee berths—narrow metal frames with a single piece of canvas stretched over them—six and seven bunks high, each only eighteen inches apart. The men slept in three shifts; the beds were never empty. Soldiers were given colored badges to be worn at all times; the badges corresponded with a section of the ship where the soldiers were required to stay throughout the voyage.

But for Sarah, who had struggled for years with a fear of confined spaces, thinking about what it actually meant to each soldier was nearly unbearable to her. Suddenly, she felt dizzy, unable to breathe.

In the next moment she heard Robert Parsons saying, "My God, I'm so sorry! I forgot! Let's go outside, onto the Sun Deck."

She raised no objections, and found herself feeling a mixture of relief that she was once again in the open air and acute embarrassment that her grandmother had apparently informed Robert Parsons about her problem.

When he tried to apologize again, she said, "I do believe you're much more upset about this than I am. I'll be all right."

"When did it start?" he asked.

"My claustrophobia? Didn't Grandmother tell you that, too?"

"No. She's never said anything about it. I've noticed it before—at her dinner parties. Too many people in the room and you have to go outside. On nights when it's too cold to be outdoors in an evening gown, you step out for a breath of fresh air."

She was quiet for a moment, not sure what to make of his observation of her. Then she said, "I don't know why this memory has been so persistent, but when I was about four, at the orphanage, I was once punished for something by being shut up in a closet. I don't remember what I had done wrong, or even who put me in the closet. I just remember the darkness, the sensation of being confined, the smell of the coats and mothballs. I was terrified. I remember counting, singing a song about numbers to stay calm."

He put an arm around her shoulders, gave her a brief hug. But he seemed to know not to hold on to her—not when she was feeling so close to the memory of that closet. He let her be. As she felt herself grow calmer, she ventured a question of her own. "I've been thinking—the way you responded to the wartime exhibit—do you have problems with claustrophobia, too?"

He shook his head. "No, I don't."

"But it was personal for you somehow, wasn't it? You're too young to have fought in anything other than the Gulf War—"

"My grandfather went to war on this ship."

"Oh! You have something in common with Grandmother then."

He smiled slightly. "Yes. Ada and I have a great deal in common."

Not wanting to pursue that subject, she said, "So your grandfather told you about traveling on this ship?"

"No," Parsons said, looking out over the railing, toward the sea. "He died before I was born. Even before my father was born. My grandfather died aboard the ship."

"Aboard the ship?" she repeated, stunned.

"Yes. He was a young soldier, newly married. His wife was pregnant with their first child, although he didn't know that when he left for war. He was, by all accounts, a bright and talented man with a sense of humor; he used to draw cartoon sketches of his fellow soldiers and mail them home to my grandmother. He went off to war, not willingly parted from her, but willing to fight for his country." He paused, then added bitterly, "He was murdered before he had a chance to reach his first battle."

"Murdered?!"

"Yes."

Sarah's own thoughts raced. It was not difficult to see that under the crowded wartime conditions aboard the ship, tempers might easily flare. She suddenly knew without a doubt that his grandfather had been killed near the swimming pool; this, she was sure, accounted for Robert's reaction when they were in that area of the ship.

"I'm sorry, Robert," she said. "What a terrible blow for your grandmother."

"She didn't learn exactly what happened until many years later. She thought he had been killed in action."

"Was the killer punished?"

"No. He got away with it. Listen, I shouldn't be talking to you about this," he said. "You're here for a pleasant occasion and Ada would tan my hide if she knew I was—"

"Ada doesn't entirely rule my life," Sarah said. "I'm glad you told me. Does she know about your grandfather?"

"Oh, yes."

"And she still insisted on bringing you here!"

"Sarah, as I've told you, I've been here before." He smiled. "And not just to lay my family ghosts to rest. I'll admit that was why I made my first visit, but I found I couldn't dislike this ship—she's not to blame for what happened to my grandfather. I suppose I fell in love with her style and elegance. She was built for pleasure—a thing of beauty, not death and destruction. And she's a survivor. Of all the great luxury liners built before the war, the *Queen Mary* is the only survivor."

They resumed their tour of ship. He had saved the art gallery, one of his favorite rooms on the ship, for last. As they left it, he said, "Ask Ada to tell you what sort of relationship I share with her."

"Why don't you tell me instead?"

"I promised her I would leave that to her."

They soon reached the stateroom. As he was about to leave her at her door, he paused and said, "Something was troubling you this morning."

Her eyes widened.

He shrugged. "I saw it. In your face, I suppose. Your eyes."

"It was just—just something silly," she said. "Just a dream."

"A nightmare?"

"I dreamed of that closet—the one at the orphanage."

"You're all right now?"

"Yes. I'll be fine."

He started to walk off, then turned and said, "Thank you for taking the tour with me."

"My pleasure," she said softly.

When she had finished dressing for the party, Sarah knocked on her grandmother's door. Ada opened it herself, beckoning Sarah in as she returned to her dressing table. To Sarah's surprise, Ada was nearly ready, and she was attired not in one of her wild ensembles, but in a very simple but elegant black dress.

"Are you feeling all right?" Sarah asked.

Ada gave a shout of laughter. "It's best not to let everyone become too sure of what I'll do next. Do you like it?"

"You look fantastic." She gave her a kiss. "Happy birthday, Grandmother."

"Thank you, my dear. How was your afternoon with Robert?"

"Very pleasant. He said I should ask you about your relationship with him."

She raised an eyebrow. "He did, did he?"

"Yes. Now don't tease or put me off, Grandmother."

Ada smiled into the mirror as she fastened an earring. "Do you like him?"

"Grandmother!"

"I'll tell you this much. He's not my employee." She grinned wickedly, then added, "And he's not my lover. Oh, don't try to look innocent, I know what's being said. But he's not. I have no romantic interest in him—none whatsoever."

"But you seem so close—"

"We are very close. But that has nothing to do with the price of eggs, so get off your pretty duff and pursue the man." She turned and gave Sarah a quick kiss. "You were very sweet not to offer your old granny any competition for that young fox."

"Grandmother!"

"You're attracted to him, Sarah. Have been from the day you met him."

"What utter nonsense."

"Is it?"

Sarah opened her mouth to protest, closed it again.

Ada laughed and turned back to the mirror. "I thought so. Well, my dear, you have my blessing."

The birthday party was wildly successful. Sarah, returning from one of her frequent strolls on one of the upper decks, saw Ada dancing an energetic fox trot with Captain Dolman—who was an excellent dancer, but still seemed very nervous. Ada, she noticed, had spent a great deal of time with Captain Dolman. Although Sarah had been dreading another encounter with Senator Hastings, she had not seen him since the first hour of the party, when he had been talking to Robert. Surprised that he would pass up an opportunity to work a crowd this wealthy and influential, she was, nevertheless, pleased that she had been spared another round of quizzing.

She hadn't seen much of Robert, either. She had danced with him once, but he had seemed so preoccupied that she had difficulty holding a conversation with him.

"I'm terrible company tonight," he said as the dance ended. "May we try this again, another evening? Just the two of us?"

Telling him she would consider that a promise, she resolved not to make a nuisance of herself to him.

Now, several hours later, she strolled near Ada's table. Although the invitations had said, "No gifts," a few of Ada's friends had ignored these instructions. When her grandmother returned from the dance floor, Sarah offered to take the packages to her room.

"Thank you, Sarah!" she said, "How very thoughtful of you." She gave Sarah the key to the room and turned to accept an offer to waltz with one of her other guests. Captain Dolman offered to help Sarah, but as there were only five boxes to be carried, she politely declined his assistance.

As she came down the stairs, her arms full, she was surprised to see Robert leaving his suite, his face set in a forbidding frown. He did not see her, however, and quickly moved off in the opposite direction, toward the elevator. She nearly called to him, to ask what was troubling him, but decided not to delay him, as he was so apparently in a hurry.

She managed to open the door to Ada's suite, only to discover that she had entered through the servant's door, rather than the main door, which opened into the sitting area. This part of the suite—this small room, and beyond it the bathroom and large bedroom, were closed off from the sitting room, and except for the light from the hallway behind her, it was in darkness. Sarah tried to reach for the old-fashioned light switch, but couldn't manage it with her arms full of boxes and holding the key. She decided to lay the boxes on the twin bed. But as she stepped inside, the door closed behind her with a loud click. The small room was plunged into nearly total darkness. Panicking, blindly rushing back to the door, Sarah whirled and stumbled over something. The boxes went tumbling from her arms as she fell, and she heard the flutter of papers, felt them raining down on her. She scrambled to her knees, ran her hands wildly over the wall, and found the switch.

For a moment, she could only catch her breath and wait for her heartbeat to slow. Gradually, she noticed that she had knocked over an old leather briefcase. It had opened, and its contents had spilled across the room.

Gathering the gifts first, she was relieved to see that none of them were damaged. She placed them on the bed. She then went to work on collecting the scattered papers.

Most seemed to be old letters bearing three-cent

postage stamps. Among them, she saw an old photograph; the smiling young soldier in it looked familiar to her, she thought, picking it up. The back of the photo bore an inscription in a neat masculine hand. "Give me a kiss goodnight, Ada—I'll return every one with interest when I come back home to you! Love, Elliot."

Her grandmother, Sarah realized, had brought a photo of her first husband taken on this ship, where she had last seen him. Moved by this, she carefully returned the photo to the briefcase. But it was as she gathered the scattered envelopes that she received a shock. The letters, postmarked during 1942, were addressed to Mrs. Elliot Parsons.

Parsons. Elliot Parsons.

Robert was related to Ada. He was her grandson. She knew it as surely as she knew anything. Her mind reeled. Robert was Sarah's cousin—her adopted cousin, at any rate. And all this time—all this time!— Ada had made a guessing game out of her grandson's identity. Why?

Mechanically, Sarah began putting the letters away. She came across one other item, a drawing. A cartoon. The subject of the cartoon had aged, but he was easily recognized. The Adam's apple was exaggerated of course, and so was the blush. "Capt. Dolman, our fearless leader," was scrawled at the bottom of one corner of the drawing.

The room seemed to be closing in on her and she stood up and made her way into the sitting room. She turned the light on, and moving to the portholes, opened one, and took a deep breath of the cold air. She sat down in a nearby chair. She was glancing at the carpet, noting a pair of parallel lines on it. Wheel marks from a dolly or handcart, she thought to herself, just as she heard a key sliding into the lock.

She braced herself for a confrontation with Ada, but it was not Ada who opened the door. Robert Parsons stood before her.

"Sarah? Are you all right?"

"I'm fine."

"Ada's worried about you," he said, closing the door behind him, crossing the room to sit near her. "She's been waiting for you to bring her key back. Are you sure you're okay?" he asked, glancing at the open porthole.

"I'm fine, cousin."

He stiffened. "She told you—and apparently didn't do a very good job of it."

"No, I found out quite by accident. By being clumsy. I knocked over a briefcase full of letters from your grandfather. I didn't mean to snoop, but . . . well, I didn't read the letters."

"Sarah, I've never wanted to hide anything from you. Ada insisted, and I let her talk me into it. I never should have gone along with it."

"Why? Why didn't she want me to know?"

He hesitated, then said, "For two reasons. The first is that she didn't want you to get hurt. She was afraid—after the way the Milingtons treated you—she didn't want you to feel as if I were more important to her than you are. I'm not Sarah—honest to God, I'm not."

When she didn't reply, he said, "You've been her granddaughter for years. If you don't want to share her, I'll understand."

"Oh, it's not that!" she said. "It's just—just a lot to take in."

"Yes, it's a lot for me to take in, too, and I've had a year to get used to the idea. She didn't even know I existed. I managed to track her down when I was trying to learn more about what happened to my grandfather—to Elliot Parsons. Ada and my father were estranged."

"Because of his stepfather? Ada's next husband?"

"Yes. So you know about that?"

"Not much."

"When my dad died, I wanted to learn more about his side of the family, and meet this grandmother of mine. I also wanted to know more about my grandfather. At first, I just wanted to find out if my father's story was true, that his father had died aboard the *Queen Mary*, while on the passage to Europe. I learned much more. And I told Ada what I had learned."

"About his murder?"

"Yes."

"What's the second reason she didn't want to tell me?"

But before he could answer, there was a knock at the door of the suite. "Robert? Sarah?" they heard Ada's voice call.

Robert opened the door to admit Ada and Captain Dolman.

"Here's your key, Grandmother," Sarah said.

Ada studied her as she took the key, then rounded on Robert. "You told her!"

"No," Sarah said, and explained how she had learned that Robert was Ada's grandson. "And he is just about to tell me the second reason you didn't want me to know about it."

"Nonsense!" she said firmly. "Now, although the party was wonderful, I'm completely exhausted, so all of you will please leave my room. All except Sarah."

"Ada—" Robert began.

"Now," she said, giving him a look that would have sent an emperor running. It was more than enough for Captain Dolman. For several long minutes, it seemed that Robert would refuse to obey.

"I'll be all right," Sarah said. His frustration evident, Robert finally followed Dolman's lead.

But in the meantime, Sarah had given some thoughts to the events of the day, and when the door closed behind Robert, she asked, "Where is Senator Hastings?"

"How should I know?"

"You know. Why did you invite him?"

"He practically invited himself."

"I don't believe that. He's not running in your congressional district; he's not your state senator. And he is certainly not the type of person you would back in either race."

"Whom I invite to my own birthday party—"

"A party on a ship where, according to Robert, your first husband was murdered—"

"Robert will have to learn to keep quiet. Although I daresay you might receive more of his confidences than anyone else would."

"I should hope so. I'm his cousin."

"He doesn't think of you in that way, Sarah. I can guarantee you that much. And that is not to say that he doesn't want to be related to you."

Blushing, Sarah said, "Don't try to change the subject, you wily old woman."

Ada smiled, but didn't reply.

"You invited two men I've never heard you mention before, and you were with both of them before the festivities began. One of them disappeared not long after the party started. The other man hasn't been three feet from your side all night; you have a funny little caricature of him drawn by your late husband."

"What you think you're getting at, I'm sure I don't know," Ada said.

"I think you were getting at something—or rather, someone tonight, Grandmother. Maybe it's too late for justice—legal justice. But you've arranged for revenge, haven't you?"

Ada said nothing. She moved to the porthole, looked out at the harbor.

"Grandmother, you can trust me. I—I may not be family, but I love you as much as—"

"Don't talk nonsense!" Ada said, her voice quavering. "Of course you're my family. I don't want you to come to any harm, don't you see? And you wouldn't like this particular brand of revenge."

Sarah took a deep breath, and said, "Have you murdered a state senator, Grandmother?"

Ada turned to look at her. "You think I'm capable of that?"

"No," Sarah answered.

"Thank God for that, at least."

"Well, if you haven't killed him—" She looked around the room, an idea suddenly occurring to her. Horrified, she said, "Grandmother—the trunk! You've locked him in the trunk!"

"Yes," Ada said.

"Where is it? Where's the trunk?"

"Sarah—"

"It's in Robert's room, isn't it? That's why Robert had the other key to your room—you didn't give it to him, he already had it." Her eyes went back to the carpet. "The wheel marks—that's what made them. Oh, Grandmother! It isn't right."

"Where are you going?" Ada asked in alarm, as Sarah hurried toward the door.

Sarah didn't answer.

She could hear the phone in his room ringing, even before she got to the door. It was quiet on the ship now; most of the guests had turned in for the night.

When he answered the door, she said, "I don't care what Grandmother said to you just now—"

"Come inside," he said, glancing up and down the passageway.

Once the door was closed behind her, he said, "She only wants to protect you, Sarah. I'm in too deep now, but you don't have to be involved. It would be better if—"

"Remember that painting?" she interrupted. "The one of the dancers, in the Observation Bar?"

He nodded.

"I don't want to be an outsider, Robert. We're all in this together. Please, Robert—"

"All right," he said, "but Sarah—"

She heard a muffled thumping sound, and pushed past Robert into the bedroom.

The trunk lay near the foot of the bed. She heard the thumping sound again. Her face pale, she turned to Robert and said, "Let him out!"

"In a moment, when your Grandmother and Captain Dolman arrive."

But images from her own nightmares surrounded her, and when she heard the thumping again, she turned to Robert with such a look of horror on her face that he relented, and began unfastening the trunk's latches.

As he lifted the lid, she saw that Hastings was bound and gagged. His face bore an expression that quickly passed from relief to anger.

"Wait in the other room," Robert said. "I'll bring him out."

A few moments later, an irate Archer Hastings was led to a chair in the sitting room.

"You're out of that box thanks to Sarah," Robert said. "But if you raise a ruckus of any kind, you'll go right back into it."

Sarah saw the fear in Hastings's eyes.

"The trunk is custom made, isn't it?" she said to Robert. "It's built to be the same size as a soldier's berth on the ship."

"Yes."

There was a knock at the door, and in another moment, Ada and Dolman had joined them.

Hastings glared angrily at Ada.

"You'd like to see me arrested, wouldn't you?" Ada said to him.

He nodded vigorously.

"The feeling is mutual." She turned to her grand-daughter. "Do you know how Elliot died?"

Sarah shook her head.

"Tell me, Sarah, was the *Queen Mary* air conditioned?"

"Not all of it—not until later years, after the war."

"And before the war?"

"Not on all decks. It wasn't necessary. The ship was built for travel on the North Atlantic. The electric fireplaces in the first class cabins—"

"Never mind the fireplaces," Ada said. "You just made an important point. The ship was built for North Atlantic crossings."

"You knew that, didn't you, Mr. Hastings?" Robert said.

Hastings made an angry sound behind the gag.

"Oh, pardon me. I'll remove the gag, but I'll expect you to keep your voice at a conversational level. If you don't—" He nodded toward Captain Dolman, who held a gun aimed at Hastings. "I'm afraid Captain Dolman, who is an excellent shot, will be allowed to fulfill his fondest wish."

"Now see here," Hastings said as the gag was removed, "I've heard for years about Ada Milington's crazy parties, but this is too much! Let me go now, and we can forget this ever happened."

"As you've forgotten what happened to those men you murdered?" Ada asked.

"I don't know what you're talking about!"

"Sarah," Ada said. "How many standee berths were placed in the cabin class swimming pool?"

"One hundred and ten," she answered promptly. "Was that where Elliot was assigned while on the ship?"

"Yes," Dolman answered. "My unit was sent to that hellhole."

"It was crowded for everybody!" Hastings said. "There was a war on, remember? We needed to get troops to Europe and the Pacific."

"And that was your responsibility," Robert said.

"Yes, of course it was. I made this ship ten times more efficient for the transporting of troops."

"The numbers got bigger and bigger, thanks to you."

"That's right. That's why you didn't grow up speaking German or Japanese, sonny boy."

"I fought against them," Dolman said, "but they were the enemy then, and the war was on. But you weren't supposed to be our enemy, Hastings. Troops weren't supposed to die because of you."

"You're insane! All of you! I worked at a desk job! I didn't kill anybody. Sarah—" he pleaded, turning to the one person who seemed inclined to show him mercy.

But Sarah had been thinking about the questions that had been asked so far. "The ship has no portholes in the pool area," she said, frowning. "The room is completely enclosed. During the war, the pool was drained, but that would mean that the temporary berths were positioned . . ." She looked at Robert.

"Yes, you've guessed it."

"Directly above one of the boilers," she finished, staring at Hastings now.

"We crossed the damned Equator in a ship built to go from Southampton to New York," Dolman said. "The tropics, Hastings. Do you know what it's like to watch men dying of the heat? Suffocating to death? No fresh air, just the stench of people getting sick and sweating and some of them dying. Temperatures over a hundred and ten degrees—and that's on the upper decks. Down where we were, it was a damned oven, Hastings. I say we put you in that trunk and we heat it up until you feel your blood boiling. You should have had to watch men like young Elliot Parsons die. I had to, Hastings, and I'll never forget it!"

"There was no way I could have known—" Hastings pleaded. "We were just trying to do our best to fight the war."

"Until now," Dolman said, "I didn't know who made the decisions about how we were going to be loaded in there. There wasn't any escape for us then, and there shouldn't be any for you now."

"You aren't going to kill me! Not for something that happened so long ago! Not for a simple miscalculation!"

"What do you want from him?" Sarah asked.

"Withdraw from the Congressional race," Ada said.

"What?"

"And resign from office," Robert added.

"You'll never get away with this!"

"People get away with things like this all the time. You've been getting away with murder for over fifty years."

"It wasn't murder, I tell you! We didn't know."

Sarah frowned. "But you must have known."

"What?"

"The voyage Elliot Parsons sailed on—it wasn't the first voyage to cross the Equator." She looked at Hastings. "You didn't miscalculate. You accepted the fact that some men might die on the voyage."

There was a long silence, broken only when Robert said, "Bravo, Sarah."

"We can prove all of this, Hastings," Ada said. "Retire as a State Senator, or lose an election in shame."

"Do you think anyone is going to care about what happened then?"

"Put him in the trunk again!" Dolman said. "He'll have just as much room to move around as we did. Let's see him win an election from there."

"No—no! I won't run for office. I swear I won't. Just let me out of here!"

"Don't trust him!" Dolman said.

"There's another alternative," Robert said, opening a drawer in a built-in desk.

"What?" Hastings asked, apprehensively.

Robert didn't answer right away, but when he turned around, he held a syringe.

"What's in there?" Hastings asked.

"Oh, you'll just have to trust me," Robert said, "maybe it will give you a fever—something that will make your blood boil, as Captain Dolman says—or maybe it will just help you to sleep."

When State Senator Archer Hastings awakened, he was hot, unbearably hot, and thirsty. He was still on the ship, he realized hazily. The damned ship. And, he realized with alarm, he was not in his bed, but in an enclosed space—the trunk. He pushed against the lid—it flew open.

Shaking, he crawled out of it, onto the bed. He was still hot, miserably hot, and the terror of the trunk would not leave him.

He reached for the phone next to his bed, and said thickly, "Help. Send a doctor in to help me. I'm ill."

Not much later, a doctor did arrive. He stepped into the room and said, "Are you chilled?"

"Chilled? Are you mad? I'm burning up!"

"So am I," the physician said, and turned down the thermostat. "Open the portholes and you'll be fine."

"Those damned people!" Hastings exclaimed.

"Which people?" the doctor said, in the tone of one who has encountered a lunatic.

"Mrs. Ada Milington—is she still aboard?"

"Oh no. I'm the last of Ada's party still on the ship. She said you'd had a bit too much to drink last night and asked me to make sure you got off the ship all right. She was in a rush."

"I'll bet she was."

"She asked me to give you a message. She said for you to remember that you have an open invitation to a pool party."

Hastings frowned. "Where's she off to? I need to talk to her."

"Oh, I believe she's well on her way to Glacier Bay by now—one of the Alaskan cruise lines. She said something about her grandchildren getting married at sea. Quite eccentric, Ada," the doctor mused, as he was taking his leave. "Yes eccentric—but I'd take her seriously, if I were you, sir." He paused before closing the door. "Shall I ask the hotel to send someone to help you with that trunk?"

"No! I don't want the damned thing."

The doctor shrugged and left.

Hastings brooded for a moment, considered the odds of convincing anyone that he had been kidnapped by Ada Milington. He would retire, he decided. There was a sense of relief that came with that decision.

All the same, he continued to feel confined. He

hurried to a porthole, opened it and took a deep breath.

For Archer Hastings, it offered no comfort.

AUTHOR'S NOTE

Although Archer Hastings and all other characters in this story are entirely fictional, the *Queen Mary* statistics in this story are real. Under the control of Allied military personnel, the ship made an enormous contribution to the war effort. However, conditions were extremely crowded, and soldiers did die during voyages into the tropics—most often in the cabin class pool area above the boilers. This story is dedicated to memory of those young men.

AN UNSUSPECTED
CONDITION
OF THE HEART

NOW AND AGAIN YOU may call me a rattlepate and tell me I don't know what's
o'clock, Charles, but even you will account
me a man who can handle the ribbons. And a dashed
good thing it is that I am able to drive to an inch—or
I'd have bowled your cousin Harry over right there in
the middle of the road. I daresay running him over is
no less than he deserved, for he'd overturned as beautiful a phaeton as I'd ever seen, which was a thing as
nearly as bad as wearing that floral waistcoat of his in
public—upon my oath, Charles, even the horses took
exception to it.

"Oh, thank heaven," he cried, even before I'd settled the grays, "it's dear old Rossiter!"

Two days earlier, the fellow had all but given me
the cut direct at Lady Fanshawe's rout, and here he
was, addressing me as if I were an angel come down
the road just to save him.

"Dallingham!" I replied. "What on earth has happened? I trust you've taken no hurt?"

"Nothing that signifies," he said, dabbing at a little cut above his left brow. "But I am in the devil's own hurry and here this phaeton has lost a wheel and broken an axle!"

"Let me take you up, then," I said. "Will your groom be able to manage those bays?"

"Yes, yes," he said, already climbing up next to me. "I'd just instructed him to take them back to that inn we passed—five miles back or so, and to see about repairs. May I trouble you take me there? I must see if they've something I can hire—"

"Nonsense, Dallingham, can't imagine they'd have so much as a horsecart to hire. I'm on my way to Ollington—to see my Aunt Lavinia. I'll take you along as far that, and if you need—"

"Ollington! Why, I'm to dine at Bingsley Hall this evening, and—"

"Bingsley Hall?" I said. "Well, that is on my way. No trouble at all."

"My thanks, Rossiter!"

The grays were restive, and I put them to. A moment later, he said, "Perhaps you can save me from disgrace."

I doubted there was any possibility of such a thing, but I said, "Oh?" (Just like that, you know—"Oh?" I believe I raised a brow, but I can't swear to it.)

"Have you met Lord and Lady Bingsley?" he asked.

"Never had the pleasure. They do not go about much in society. I believe my aunt has some acquaintance with them."

"Damned recluses, the pair of them."

"I beg your pardon? Did you not just say you were invited to dine there?"

He smiled. "Oh no, I'm to stay there a fortnight!"

"A fortnight! With the Bingsleys!"

"Well, yes, as it turns out, we're related!"

"You are related to Miss Bannister's aunt and uncle?"

He laughed. "Wish me happy, Rossiter! I'm newly married!"

"Married!" I could not hide my shock.

"Yes, as of yesterday. And in future you must refer to Miss Bannister as Lady Dallingham. We were married by special license. She's gone on to Bingsley to—er, prepare my welcome."

Charles, I own I was left speechless. The grays took advantage of my lack of concentration, and a rather difficult moment passed before both my horses and my composure were back in hand.

"Well, then," I said, rather bravely, really, "I do wish you happy. Miss—er, Lady Dallingham is a lovely young woman."

"Oh, I suppose the chit's well enough," he said, "but there can be no doubt that her fortune's mighty handsome."

As you can imagine, this blunt speech left me appalled. Of course, all the world knew that Dallingham was hanging out for an heiress, and that he had followed in his father's footsteps—meaning that his gaming had finally destroyed whatever portion of the family fortune the old man had not already lost at faro and dicing.

I know you'll not take offense at my putting it so

baldly, Charles—after all, neither your cousin Dallingham nor his father could be ranked among your favorites, and your father was estranged from his late brother for many years. I recall that Dallingham applied to your esteemed parent for assistance with his debts on more than one occasion, and that your father—quite rightly—showed him the door.

Of course, even as I took him up that night, I knew that Dallingham was not without friends. He could make himself charming when need be. I will own that Dallingham's handsome face made him agreeable to the ladies, but most matchmaking mamas steered their chicks clear of him, knowing he hadn't a feather to fly with, and that his reputation as a rake was not unearned.

I fear Miss Bannister was easy prey to such a man. She is an orphan. Her guardian was a half-brother who gave little thought to her; he gave her over to the care of her aunt and uncle, Lord and Lady Bingsley— Lord Bingsley also serving as the trustee of the large fortune that will come to her a few years hence.

But the Bingsleys, as I have said, do not go about much, and have not been seen in Town for some years. When Miss Bannister was old enough to make her come-out, therefore, her half-brother arranged that she would spend the season with her godmother, a most foolish woman, who could by no means be accounted a suitable chaperone.

I soon had it from Dallingham that her half-brother— undoubtedly misled by Dallingham's charm—had granted his consent to this hasty wedding.

"You think it unseemly, high stickler that you are!" Dallingham accused me now.

"I? A high stickler?" I said. "Oh no. One only wonders, what brought about a need for such haste?"

"Tradesmen and others," he replied, quite honestly.

"Forgive me if I speak of matters which do not closely concern me, Dallingham," I said, "but you find me all curiosity. Miss Bannister's godmother has bandied it about that Miss Bannister does not come into her fortune upon marriage. She must reach the age of twenty."

"Ah, and you wonder that I could wait so long? The expectation, my dear. The tradesmen foresee a day in the not-so-distant future when I shall be a very wealthy man. They are willing to forestall pressing me until that day. In fact, they are quite willing to extend my credit."

We turned to idle chitchat for a time, during which he let fall that the lovely phaeton he had so recently overturned was yours—I am so sorry, Charles!

I changed horses at Merriton, and we were well on our way again when he said, "Sorry to have cut you out where the Bannister was concerned old boy. But I daresay my need was the more pressing. From all I hear, Rossiter, you're as rich as Golden Ball."

"No such thing," I said coolly.

He chuckled. "No need to cut up stiff with me," he said. "You've had your eye on her, haven't you?"

"My dear Dallingham," I said, "she is your wife. It would be most improper in me to respond to such a comment."

In truth, Charles, she had come to my notice. However, unlike most women—who are drawn to me by my fortune and rank—she had no need of either. This being the case, I was sure I held no attraction to

Miss Bannister. While I don't suppose a *great* many children have been frightened by my visage, or told by their nursemaids that I shall come to steal them if they don't mind their manners, I've not Dallingham's handsome face.

I did not blame the ladies of the *ton* for being taken in by him, for I too readily remembered one beauty who flattered me into believing that all mirrors lie, and 'twas a heady experience. That was long after I'd had my town bronze, so what chance does a chit fresh from the schoolroom have against the influence of a handsome face?

By the time we arrived at Bingsley Hall, my spirits were quite low. These were by no means lifted when Dallingham, at the moment we passed the gatekeeper's lodge, announced with a covetous eye, "She's to inherit all this, too, you know! Bingsley dotes on her."

I had every intention of leaving at the first possible moment, but Lord Bingsley would not hear of it. For my part, I could not help but like the old fellow and his lady, who proffered every kindness imaginable— the upshot of this being my acquiescence to the Bingsleys' insistence that I stay the night. My relative was not expecting me at any certain date, and so I agreed to break my journey with them.

"Good man! For we've something of a celebration this night, haven't we?" Lord Bingsley said, clapping Dallingham on the back.

Dallingham, who had apparently already met Lord Bingsley, seemed relieved not to be met by an outraged relative when introduced to his wife's aunt. Lady Bingsley, if not quite as effusive as her husband, was nonetheless all that a hostess should be.

For her part, the former Miss Bannister seemed, as always, becomingly shy in the company of gentlemen, and to my own relief, was not at all demonstrative with her new spouse.

In fact, dear Charles, the two of them seldom looked at each other. Dallingham was eyeing the thick carpets, the beautiful vases, and charming chandelier with the air of a man who is calculating the price each might fetch at auction. One would have thought him a solicitor's clerk, practicing the art of taking inventory of the Bingsleys' estate. He made little effort to hide his happy contemplation of taking possession of their goods upon their demise. He divided his time between this and the depletion of Lord Bingsley's cellars.

Watching him, I found myself seething, until I felt a gentle hand on my sleeve. "My dear Lord Rossiter," the new Lady Dallingham said softly, "how glad I am that you have come."

She moved away rather quickly, and spoke to her aunt, all the while blushing.

I did not suppose for a moment that Dallingham, a man whose name has been linked with two actresses and any number of fair Cyprians, thought her very lovely. She tended to plumpness, a little. Her face was not that of a classic beauty, and no one would mistake her for a diamond of the first water. But there are other gems than diamonds, my dear Charles, and I found much in her that was admirable and becoming.

I wanted to ask if something was troubling her, if there was any way in which I might be of service, but I had no opportunity for private speech with her that evening—which was, I tell you plainly, easily one of the strangest nights of my life.

We were beset by real difficulties at table that evening. Dallingham wasn't paying the least attention to me or his wife; he was admiring the silver and china, repeatedly congratulating Lord Bingsley on his fine cellars, making gratifying comments to Lady Bingsley on the excellence of the soup *á la reine,* and remarking on the beauty of the epergne at the center of the table. (It depicted tigers chasing one another round about—not to my taste, frankly—don't like to dine with figures of things that would just as soon dine on me.)

But just as the second course—a haunch of venison, saddle of lamb, boiled capon, and spring chicken—was served, Lady Bingsley said in a ringing voice, "Pistols at dawn!"

Dallingham and I exchanged looks of some consternation, even as Lord Bingsley calmly replied, "You'll never do me in that way, my dear."

"I know a good deal about pistols," her ladyship replied. "Don't I, Amelia?"

"Yes, Aunt," the former Miss Bannister replied.

"Yes, yes," said his lordship, "but for all that you know about them, you are an execrable shot." He continued to apply himself to the venison, even as her ladyship appeared to apply herself to the problem of shooting him. Dallingham, so far from being dismayed, seemed on the verge of losing any semblance of gravity still left to him, while his new wife calmly continued to take small bites of the lamb.

Within a few moments, his lordship looked up from his plate and said, "Arrow through the heart. While you sleep."

"I must say—" I began weakly.

"Nonsense!" said her ladyship firmly.

"It is not nonsense!" protested my host. "I'm a demmed sight better with the bow and arrow than you are with pistols. I'll creep into your room through that old priest's hole."

"Now, there you're out!" said her ladyship. "The priest's hole is in Lord Dallingham's room—the exit, in any case."

At this, Dallingham, who had been drinking steadily from the moment of our arrival, was overcome with mirth.

"I find nothing amusing . . ." I tried again.

"By Jupiter!" his lordship said, "You're right! Hmm. In that case, it shall have to be something more subtle. Perhaps when you go riding—"

"Please!" I said. "Your lordship, your ladyship . . . I beg pardon . . . not my place, really . . . but I can't possibly face the next course if there is to be nothing but this talk of murder!"

There was a moment of profound silence before his lordship said, "Not face the next course? Rubbish! There's to be lark pudding!"

And so the exchange of murder plots continued. I would have made good on my threat to excuse myself from the table, lark pudding or no, had not the former Miss Bannister looked at me so beseechingly, I forgot all else.

By the time the ladies retired to the drawing room and Lord Bingsley offered his excellent port, though, I had heard our hosts exchange no fewer than twenty threats of foul play, and had decided to leave this odd household by first light, beseeching looks or no. Miss Bannister had married a bounder, but it was his place to take her away from such humbuggery, not mine.

But Dallingham was extremely well to live by then, as the saying goes—or at least, in too much of a drunken stupor to converse. Other than expending the effort required to continue to drink, he seemed to be using whatever powers of concentration remained to him to prevent himself from falling face first into the table linen he so admired.

Sitting there over port, blowing a cloud with his lordship, I sought an excuse for an early departure. But as if reading my mind, his lordship said, "Must forgive us, Rossiter. Her ladyship and I are not much in company, as you must know. You are outraged, as any good man would be." He paused, and looking at Dallingham, said in a low voice, "Unlike yon jack-anapes! Were I twenty years younger, I'd darken his daylights! But here . . . well, we keep the ladies waiting. I only mean to ask you—nay, beg you—and I'm not a man who often begs!—beg you to see your way clear to remain with us another day or two."

"My dear Lord Bingsley—" I began, but in what was becoming a habit in him, he interrupted.

"For Amelia's sake!" he whispered, then added, in a normal speaking voice, "You'll grow used to our havey-cavey ways, I'm sure."

I bowed to a man who—as I was to learn—was a masterful persuader.

Two stout footmen carried the jug-bitten Lord Dallingham to his chambers that night. That his wife slept apart from him did not surprise me in the least—I only hoped that she had locked the door against him.

He did not appear at breakfast, when Lord Bingsley asked if I would be so good as to accompany his niece, who wished to ride her mare about the estate. "Going to miss Bingsley Hall, she tells me. By God, Bingsley Hall shall miss her!"

"Perhaps Lord Dallingham would like to join us," I suggested.

"Daresay he would," Lord Bingsley said, "if he hadn't eaten Hull cheese! My valet informs me he shot the cat! Too blind to find the basin like a decent fellow, damn him. Wonder if he'll be so fond of that carpet now!"

"I—I believe I shall find Miss—Lady Dallingham," I said, feeling a bit queasy myself.

He offered to accompany me to the stables. We delayed some moments on the steps to exchange pleasantries with Lady Bingsley, who was to call upon an ailing tenant that morning. His lordship, determining that there was some slight chill in the air, begged her to wait while her maid should fetch a shawl, and once this item was retrieved, solicitously placed it about his lady's shoulders. He handed her up into the carriage, and her little dog as well, and then a large hamper of food for the tenant's family, and, after receiving assurances from the coachman that he would not drive too fast over the country lanes, stood watching the carriage as it pulled away.

At the stables, he saw to it that I was very handsomely mounted on a fine gelding. I assisted his niece—who wore a delightful blue velvet riding habit—with her mare, and in the company of a groom who stayed some distance behind us, we rode out.

Lord Bingsley's lands were in good heart, and if I had been Dallingham, no doubt I would have been estimating their yields. But my mind was wholly taken up with the thought that I had forever lost the opportunity to ask the woman beside me to become Lady Rossiter.

"How do you fare this morning, Lady Dallingham?" I asked, trying to accept that fact.

"Oh, please do not address me by that hateful name!"

"Hateful? But—"

"May I count you my friend, sir?"

"Most certainly! If there is any service I may render—"

"I am afraid, Lord Rossiter, that I have been duped."

"By me?" I asked, aghast.

"Oh, no, Lord Rossiter! Never by you!"

"I don't understand, Lady . . . er, beg pardon, but I don't know quite how one should address—"

"Amelia," she said. "I should like it above all things if you would call me Amelia."

"Very well, Amelia, and you shall please call me Christopher—no, dash it! Call me Kit."

"Do your friends call you Kit?"

"Yes."

"Well, then, *Kit,*" she said—and by the saints and angels, Charles, she could have asked for the world from that moment on. She didn't.

"I am so sorry that a man of your sensibilities was forced to . . . to accustom himself to the odd behavior of my aunt and uncle," she said. "They mean well, but—"

"Mean well! Talking of poison and setting traps with old armor or contriving to make a fellow walk beneath loose roof tiles!"

"Oh, Kit, no! They are trying to get me to show a little—I believe Uncle calls it 'rumgumption.' "

"I beg pardon?" I said, all at sea.

"Oh, I know I shouldn't use cant—"

"No, no, I mean—I don't mind it—the cant, I mean—but what the blazes have you to do with their plans to do one another a mischief?"

"One another? Oh no, Kit—"

"Discussing—over the syllabub, mind you—how they're going to put a period to the other's existence!"

"But that is not what they are about, Kit! I am sure . . . that is, I begin to wonder . . . well, the thing of it is, perhaps I should murder Harry!"

"What!"

"Oh, yes. It's the only way out of this tangle I'm in."

"My dear Amelia! Surely—"

"You see," she said, exhibiting an inherited tendency to stop a fellow from saying what he ought to say, "Peter—he's my half-brother, you know—Peter told me that Harry had some—some rather displeasing information about my dear aunt, and that Harry would make it public, if I didn't marry him straight away. Only now I find out that my aunt doesn't care a fig about any of it, that it was some old scandal from long ago, and Uncle Bingsley called me a goosecap, and said that Peter and Harry had arranged it all between them, because according to my parents' will, a certain sum of money came to Peter on my marriage, which is why he wanted me to have a London season in the first place, which I wouldn't have cared for at all, because really it's quite exhausting and gives one the headache, except that it afforded me the chance to—to meet a few admirable persons, although he— they—seemed to take little interest in me, for which they can hardly be blamed, and so—and so I married Harry."

I was much struck by this speech, once I had sorted it out, and said, "The dastards! When I think what Dallingham and your half-brother have conspired to do! Why—why, I shall thrash the two of them! This is positively gothic!"

"Oh, no, Kit, do not! I have made a great mistake, and I've been a sad featherbrain, as my uncle says—"

"But surely the marriage can be set aside!"

She turned very red.

"Beg pardon!" I murmured, a little crimson myself. "Don't know what possessed me to—"

"No, no! It is just—I was so very foolish! But to have a man with Lord Dallingham's looks and address tell me that only his desperate love for me drove him to such measures to bring me to the altar—well, I realize now that he was merely ensuring that our marriage could not be annulled. As for my giving into such nonsense—it is all vanity, I'm afraid. My head was turned. 'Perhaps he cares for me after all!' I thought. So silly of me. My aunt says it comes of reading too many novels. But she's mistaken, of course. It is because am a plain woman, and—"

"Never say so again!" I protested.

She was silent for a time, then said, "You are kind. Perhaps you cannot know what it is like to be flattered in that way."

"Oh yes, I can," I said.

"You? Oh, it isn't possible."

I laughed. "My dear, I have learned it was not only possible but probable, as it must be for every unmarried person of fortune."

She made no reply.

After a moment, I asked, "How came you to bring him here?"

"My uncle had come to Town, because Peter had sent word to him that he was owed money—on the event of my being wed. I had thought Uncle would be in a rage, but he was all that was civil, and merely told Dallingham that perhaps he should like to come to Bingsley Hall for a fortnight, and saying that one day all his own wealth and property would come to me, so Harry may as well become acquainted with the place."

"And Dallingham couldn't wait."

"No." She sighed. "But I won't cry craven—I shall contrive to live with Lord Dallingham. I only wanted you to know—well, I was so surprised to see you with him, and so grateful. It has done my nerves a deal of good to know you are at hand, although undoubtedly you've found this visit quite dreadful!"

That evening, Charles, as we sat down to dine, I found my attitude toward murderous speech had undergone a sea change. I listened to my lord's and ladyship's schemes with rapt attention. And when Lady Bingsley was so good as to teach me the names and properties of certain plants in the nearby woods, I was an apt pupil.

Now, none of this has any bearing, of course, on the sudden death of Lord Dallingham. He died, as was ascertained by the magistrate, of an apoplexy brought on by an unsuspected condition of the heart. He had been drinking steadily throughout his visit to Bingsley

Hall—Dallingham, not the magistrate, I mean—and an empty bottle of very fine port was found near his bed. This life of dissipation, the magistrate believes, led to the gentleman's untimely demise.

Like other gentlemen of the law in centuries before him, the magistrate did not observe the exit to the priest's hole. It is a very small hiding place indeed—as I discovered by viewing it from the entrance, which was in my own chambers.

Amelia puts off her black gloves in another week, when you may expect an announcement of our betrothal in the *Times*.

One other thing I must mention, though, Charles. More than once—rattlepate that I am—it has occurred to me that now that the late Lord Dallingham has passed on to his reward without an heir, you are in line for the title. It has also occurred to me that you had never before allowed the late Harry the use of so much as one of your tenant's wheelbarrows, let alone your own new phaeton. I say, old friend—thank goodness you weren't in it when that wheel came loose!

However, should you ever feel the urge to loan another phaeton to someone, Amelia's half-brother may be glad to make use of your generosity.

How very good to be able to confide in you, my dear, dear Charles!

Your most Obedient & etc.
—Kit

THE MAN IN
THE CIVIL SUIT

I HAVE A BONE TO PICK with the Museum of Natural
History. Yes, the very museum in which the peerless
Professor Pythagoras Peabody so recently met his
sad, if rather spectacular, demise. I understand they are
still working on restoring the mastodon. But my griev-
ance does not pertain to prehistoric pachyderms.

If the administrators of said museum are quoted
accurately in the newspapers, they have behaved in a
rather unseemly manner in regard to the late Peabody.
How speedily they pointed out that he was on the
premises in violation of a restraining order! How
hastily they added that he had similar orders placed
upon him by a number of institutions, including the
art museum, the zoo, and Ye Olde Medieval
Restaurant & Go-Cart Track! When asked if he was
the man named in the civil suit they filed three days
ago, how rapidly the administrators proclaimed that
Professor Peabody was no professor at all!

Oh, how quickly they forget! They behave as if the Case of the Carillean Carbuncle never occurred. A balanced account of recent events must be given, and as one who knew the man in the civil suit better than any other—save, perhaps, his sister Persephone—I have taken on the burden of seeing justice done where Pythagoras Peabody is concerned.

Although Pythag, as his closest friends—well, as I called him, because frankly, few others could tolerate his particular style of genius at close range—although Pythag never taught at a university or other institution, it is widely known that the affectionate name "Professor Peabody" was bestowed upon him by a grateful police force at the close of the Case of the Carillean Carbuncle, or as Pythag liked to call it, 300. (Some of you may need assistance understanding why—I certainly did. Pythag explained that the first letters of Case, Carillean, and Carbuncle are C's. Three C's, taken together, form a Roman numeral. I'm certain I need not hint you on from there, but I will say this was typical of his cleverness!)

Need I remind the museum administrators of the details of 300? This most unusual garnet was on display in their own Gems and Mineralogy Department when it was stolen by a heartless villain. True, the museum guards were in pursuit long before the ten-year-old boy left the grounds, and after several hours of chasing him through the halls, exhibits, and displays—including a dinosaur diorama, the planetarium, and the newly opened "Arctic and Antarctica: Poles Apart" exhibit—while conducting what amounted to an elaborate game of hide-and-seek, they caught their thief.

Unfortunately, the Carillean Carbuncle was no longer on his person, and he refused to give any clue as to its location. This was, apparently, a way of continuing the jollification he had enjoyed with these fellows. Not amused, the museum called the police. The boy called in his own reinforcements, and his parents, in the time-honored tradition of raisers of rogues, defended their son unequivocally and threatened all sorts of nastiness if he were not released immediately. The boy went home, and the Carillean Carbuncle remained missing.

Enter Peabody. Actually, he had already entered. It was Pythag's habit to be the first guest to walk through the museum doors in the morning, and the last to leave at closing. He made himself at home in the Natural History Museum, just as he once had in the art museum, and in the zoo. (The trouble at Ye Olde Medieval Restaurant & Go-Cart Track occurred before we were acquainted, but Pythag once hinted that it had something to do with giving the waiters' lances to the young drivers and encouraging them to "joust.")

I have said I will give a fair accounting, and I will. Pythag was a man who knew no boundaries. His was a genius, he often reminded me, that could not be confined to the paths that others were pleased to follow. I know some stiff-rumped bureaucrats will not agree, but if he were here to defend himself, Pythag would undoubtedly say, "If you don't want a gentleman born with an enviable amount of curiosity to climb into an elephants' compound, for goodness sakes, rely on more than a waist-high fence and a silly excuse for a moat to keep him out."

Likewise, he would tell you that if your art museum docent becomes rattled when a gentleman with a carrying voice follows along with a second group of unsuspecting art lovers, telling them a thing or two the docent failed to mention to his own group, well then, the docent stands in need of better training. Pythag enjoyed himself immensely on these "tour" occasions, tapping on glass cases and reading aloud from wall plaques to begin his speeches.

He soon varied from the information in these written guides, however. He often told visitors that when X-rayed, the canvases beneath the museum's most famous oil paintings were shown to be covered with little blue numbers, a number one being a red, two a blue, and so forth. This, he claimed, was how the museum's restoration department could make a perfect match when repairing a damaged work of art. He also claimed to be such an expert as to be able to see the numbers with his naked eye, which, he said, "Has quite spoiled most of these for me."

The art museum director, Pythag declared, would soon be under arrest for the murder of Elvis—the director's supposed motive for the killing being to increase the value of his secret, private collection of velvet portraits of The King. (I understand the We Tip Hotline, tiring of Pythag's relentless pursuit of this idea, blocked calls from the Peabody home number.)

I'll wager a tour with Pythag was much more interesting, if less enlightening, than one taken with the regular docents. The art museum, however, was unwilling to offer this alternative. It seemed a little harsh to tell him that he, and not the director, risked arrest if he returned. As Persephone argued when she came to fetch him home, how could anyone in his right mind fault a person for being *creative* in an *art* museum?

Please don't bother to mention Pythag's exile from the Museum of Transportation. Pythag would tell you that a velvet rope may be seen by a man with panache (and if he could have withstood one more p in his moniker, panache would have been Pythag's middle name) as less a barrier than an invitation to step over it and into the past. He went into the past by way of an eighteenth-century carriage, as it happened, and ever seeking the most realistic experience possible, Pythag had to bounce in it a bit. "I promise you," Pythag told the irate curator, "the King of Spain bounced when *he* rode in the dratted thing."

Perhaps you have already seen from these examples that Pythag was the perfect man to consult on the matter of the missing carbuncle. Who was more qualified to determine what a clever boy, let loose in a museum, might do? Indeed, I readily admit that for all his genius, Pythag's enthusiasm sometimes led him into rather childish behavior. I concede that he was subject to bouts of stubbornness over silly things, bouts that made him not much more than a child himself at times.

On the very afternoon the carbuncle was stolen, for example, he *insisted* on staring into the penguins' eyes in the Antarctic exhibit, convinced that each penguin retained on his retina a memory of its last moments. If he could catch the reflection of this last recollection, he decided, he could experience the thing itself—it would be, he said, "Bird's eye déjà vu." This was one of those times when, were I not courting Persephone, I would have been tempted to leave the exhibit without him. Nothing I said would convince him that memory resides in the brain rather than the eye. He utterly rejected my claim that these were not the penguins' actual eyes, but glass reproductions, and rebuked me loudly and in horrified accents for suggesting such a thing.

But as Persephone was most appreciative of my willingness to watch over her brother and accompany him to public venues, I did my best to overlook his occasionally irritating behaviors. Persephone, brilliant and far less given to acting on impulse than her brother, told me that restraining orders were a small price for Pythag's genius, but she'd just as soon not be asked to pay any larger prices for it.

Thus I made an effort to distract him from the penguins by mentioning his beloved mastodon. (Pythag had a fondness for all things the names of which begin with the letter "p." His attachment to the mastodon puzzled me, and I wondered if he was taking on the letter "m" as well, until I noticed that he constantly referred to it as the "proboscidean mammal.") Pretending to be struck by a sudden inspiration, I muttered something to the effect of, "an elephant's ancestors might also 'never forget,' " then asked Pythag if he thought there might be some memory retained in the eye socket of the mastodon. The ruse worked, and soon we were off to the Prehistoric Hall.

Here he was again distracted, this time by the sight of several policemen carefully searching for the carbuncle. Pythag managed, in his inimitable way, to quickly convince a detective that he was an official at the museum. He induced the fellow to follow him to the planetarium—not a bad notion, for the young thief had most certainly visited this facility during his flight.

The carbuncle being ruby in color, Pythag's theory was based on meteorology. "Red sky at night is a young rogue's delight!" he shouted as we ran after him. He believed the boy might have been planning to alter the color of the light in the planetarium projector. With the help of the policeman, he hastily disassembled the rather costly mechanism, but alas, it was not the hiding place.

At my suggestion that they both might want to quickly take themselves as far away from the results of their work as possible, Pythag made one of his lightening-like leaps of logic, and announced that "Polaris was beckoning." We sped back to the polar exhibits.

Here Pythag had another brainstorm, saying that there was something not quite right about the Eskimos, and delved his hand into an Inuit mannequin's hide game bag. In triumph, Pythag removed the carbuncle.

On that day, you will remember, he was the museum's darling. Pythag's new policeman friend, perhaps distracting his fellows from the disassembled projector, extolled Pythag's genius in solving the mystery of the missing gem, and proclaimed him "Professor Peabody," by which address the world would know him during the brief remaining span of his lifetime.

Not many days later, tragedy struck. Having dissuaded him from climbing atop the mastodon skeleton's back, and seeing that he was again entranced by the penguins, I felt that it was reasonably safe for me to answer the call of nature at the Natural History Museum. But when I returned from the gents, Pythag was nowhere to be found.

I heard a commotion at the entrance to the exhibit, and rushed toward it, certain he would be at the center of any disturbance. But this hubbub was caused by the bright lights and cameras of a cable television crew from the Museum Channel. The crew was taping another fascinating episode of "Naturally, at the Natural." This particular segment focused on a visit by the museum's newest patron, Mrs. Ethylene Farthington. Mrs. Farthington was possessed of all the right extremes, as far as the museum was concerned: extremely elderly, extremely wealthy, and extremely generous. Add to this the fact that she did not choose to meddle in the specifics of how her donations would be spent, and you see why the director of the museum thought her to be perfection itself.

Her progress through the polar exhibits was regally (if not dodderingly) slow, but none dared complain. For reasons that do not concern us or any other right-thinking person, Mrs. Farthington was fond of places made of ice, and her sponsorship of this exhibit was but the beginning of the largesse she was to bestow on the museum. That day, she was on her way to sign papers which would finalize her gift of a staggering sum to the museum. She would also sign a new will, supplanting the one that currently left the remainder of her enormous estate to her pet tortoise, and establishing in its stead a bequest for the museum. Apparently, there had been a falling out with the tortoise.

So taken was I by the sight of the frail Mrs. Farthington gazing at the faux-glaciers, I nearly forgot to continue my search for Pythag. If I had not chanced to glance at the opposite display, where I saw a familiar face among the penguins, I might not have known where to look for him. The face was not Pythag's, although the clothes were those of the man who now asked me to address him as "Professor." No, the face was that of an Inuit mannequin. How careless of Pythag! Everyone knows Inuits and penguins do not belong in the same display!

I did not for a moment imagine that Pythag was cavorting about the museum in the all-together. He had decided, undoubtedly, to expand upon his experience with the hide bag, and bedeck himself in the clothing and gear of the Inuit.

I was a little frightened to realize that I knew his mind so well, even if gratified to see that there was one rather unusual member of the Inuit family represented in the display. I had no difficulty in discerning which of the still figures was Pythag, and had I never met him before that day, I doubt I would have failed to notice the one apple which seemed to have fallen rather far from the Inuit family tree. There are, undoubtedly, few blond Inuits. Besides, none of the other mannequins blinked.

Otherwise, he was remarkably doll-like, clad in all his furs, and I was unable to fight a terribly strong urge to enjoy a few moments of seeing Pythag forced to be still and silent. How many times since that day have I told myself that had I foregone this bit of pleasure, disaster might have been avoided!

When I turned to see if anyone was watching

before bidding him to hurry away, I was vexed to espy Mrs. Farthington and entourage approaching the display. There was nothing for it now but to wait until the group had passed on to the next display. But as if taking a page from her tortoise's book, Mrs. Farthington was not to be hurried, and stood transfixed, perhaps on some subconscious level perceiving what Pythag had perceived so recently—that something was not quite right about the Eskimos.

Pythag was masterful. Even under this prolonged scrutiny, he—as the saying goes—kept his cool. Or would have, were it not for the television lights. The heat they generated would have made puddles of the exhibit if any of the ice and snow had been real. Instead, it made a puddle of Pythag. He began to perspire profusely.

I do believe he still might have carried it off, had not Mrs. Farthington chanced to look at him just when he felt forced to lift a finger to swipe a ticklish drop of moisture from the end of his nose.

Mrs. Farthington, startled to see a mannequin move, clutched at her bosom and fell down dead on the spot.

The tortoise inherited.

When his friends in the police department refused to pursue a criminal case against him, Pythagoras Peabody was sued by the museum.

Persephone was not pleased with me.

This last was uppermost in my mind when I strolled alone through the museum the day after the civil suit was announced, and my own suit of Persephone rejected. Had I not loved her so dearly, I might have been a little angry with Perse. Her brother was a confounded nuisance, but she blamed me for his present troubles. I should have kept a closer watch, she told me. Had *she* deigned to accompany him on his daily outings? No. Monday was the worst day of the week, as far as she was concerned. That was the day her lunatic brother stayed home. I decided to give her a little time with him, to remind her of my usefulness to her.

One would think I would have gone elsewhere, now that I had the chance to go where I pleased, but there was something comfortable about following routine at a time when my life was so topsy-turvy. So I returned to the museum.

Standing before the great mastodon, I sighed. It had been Pythag's ambition to ride the colossus. Could it be done? To give the devil his due, that was the thing about going to a place like this with Pythag—he managed, somehow, to always add a bit of excitement. I mean, one really doesn't think of a museum as a place where the unexpected might happen at any moment. Unless one visited it with Pythag.

Why should Pythag have all the fun? I overcame the hand-railing with ease.

It was not so easy to make the climb aboard the skeleton, but I managed it. I enjoyed the view from its back only briefly—let me tell you, there is no comfortable seating astride the spine of a mastodon. Knowing that Pythag would be nettled that I had achieved this summit before him, I decided that I would leave some little proof of my visit. I made a rather precarious search of my pockets and found a piece of string. Tied in a bow about a knot of wires along the spine, it did very nicely.

The skeleton swayed a bit as I got down, and the only witness, a child, was soon asking his mother if he might go for a ride, too—but in a stern, Pythag-inspired voice, I informed her that I was an official of the museum, repairing the damage done by the last little boy who climbed the mastodon, a boy whose parents could be contacted at the poor house, where they were working off payments. Although we haven't had a poor house in this city in a century, she seemed to understand the larger implications, and they quickly left the museum.

As anticipated, Persephone called the next day.

"Take him," she pleaded. "Take him anywhere, and I'll take you back."

"Persephone," I said sternly.

"I know, and I apologize, dearest. I will marry you, just as we planned, only we must wait until this suit is settled. I won't have a penny to my name, I'm afraid, but the three of us will manage somehow, won't we?"

"Three of us?"

"Well, I can't leave poor Pythagoras to fend for himself now, can I?"

And so once again, I found myself in the Museum of Natural History with Pythag at my side. He had donned a disguise—a false mustache and a dark wig. A costume not quite so warm as the Inuit garb, but no less suited to its wearer.

He began teasing me about my recent setback with Persephone. If he was an expert at devising trouble-some frolics, Pythag's meanness also derived benefit from his ingenuity. When he told me that Perse would never marry me, that she had only said she would so that I would continue to take him to the museum, I felt a little downcast. When he averred that she would keep putting me off, always coming up with some new excuse, I found his Pythagorean theorem all too believable.

I had experienced such taunting before, though, and I rebuffed his attempts to hurt and annoy me by remaining calm. Outwardly, in any case. The result was that he became more agitated, more determined to upset me. At one point, he said that she would never marry me because I was dull, and lacked imagination and daring.

"Really?" I said, lifting my nose a little higher. "As it happens, *Professor*, I have done something you haven't dared to do."

His disbelief was patent.

"I've climbed the mastodon," I told him.

"Rubbish," he said.

"Conquered the proboscidean peak."

"Balderdash!"

"Not at all. There's a little piece of string, tied in a bow on his back to prove it."

It was enough to do the trick. He climbed, and it seemed to me the skeleton swayed more than it had the day before. As I watched him, and saw him come closer to my little marker, it became apparent to me that I had tied the string at a most fragile juncture of supporting wires.

It was a wonder, really, that I hadn't been killed.

The thought came to me as simply as that. One minute, Pythag was astride the spine, asking me to bring him a piece of string, so that he might tie his own knot. I imagined spending the rest of my days nearly as tied to him as I would be to his sister. All my life, protecting treasures of one sort or another from a man who thought rules were only for other people, never himself.

"You must bring my own string back to me," I said. "That is how it's done."

And that was how it was done.

I was horrified by the result, and remain so. Mastodon skeletons are, after all, devilishly hard to come by. Persephone is convinced that the experts there are actually enjoying the challenge of reassembling the great beast.

The museum, no matter what it may say to the papers, is considering dropping its civil suit, hoping to extract a promise from Persephone not to pursue a wrongful death action against them. We are mulling it over.

I say *we*, because Pythagoras was mistaken, as it turns out. His sister will marry me. I confessed all to her, of course. Persephone merely asked me what took me so long to see what needed to be done.

Persephone and I are indeed well-suited.

THE HAUNTING
OF CARRICK HOLLOW

I REACHED THE END OF THE DRIVE and pulled the
buggy to a halt, looking back at the old house, the
modest structure where I had been born. At
another time, I might have spent these moments in
fond remembrance of my childhood on Arden Farm,
recalling the games and mischief I entered into with
my brothers and sisters, and the wise and gentle care
of my loving parents. But other, less pleasant memories had been forged since those happier days, and
now my concerns for the welfare of my one surviving
brother kept all other thoughts from me.

Noah stood on the porch, solemn-faced, looking
forlorn as he watched me go. It troubled me to see him
there; Noah had never concerned himself overmuch
with formal leave-takings—only a year ago, he would
have all but pushed me out the door, anxious to return
to his work in the apple orchards.

Upon our father's death six months ago, Noah had

inherited Arden Farm. From childhood, we had all of us known that Noah would one day own this land, and the house upon it. The eldest sons of generation upon generation of Ardens before him had worked in these same orchards. In our childhood, I had been the one whose future seemed uncertain—no one was sure what useful purpose such a bookish boy could serve. Now Noah spoke of leaving Arden Farm, of moving far away from the village of Carrick Hollow.

At one time, this notion would have been nearly unthinkable. Noah had always seemed to me a steadfast man who did not waver under any burden, as sturdy as the apple trees he tended. But then, as children, we never could have imagined the weight that would come to rest on him—indeed, on everyone who lived in our simple New England village.

I pulled my cloak closer about me, and told myself I should not dwell on such matters. I turned my thoughts to my work. When I first returned to Carrick Hollow after medical school, I wondered if my neighbors would be inclined to think of me as little Johnny Arden, Amos Arden's studious fourth son, rather than Dr. John Arden, their new physician—but my fears of being treated as a schoolboy were soon allayed. I attributed their readiness to seek my care to the fact that the nearest alternative, Dr. Ashford, an elderly doctor who lived some thirty miles away, was less and less inclined to make the journey to Carrick Hollow since I had set up my practice there.

Now, driving down the lane, I considered the patients I would visit tomorrow morning. Horace Smith, who had injured his hand while mending a wagon wheel, would be the first. Next I'd call on old

Mrs. Compstead, to see if the medicine I had given her for her palsy had been effective.

A distant clanging and clattering interrupted these reveries. The sounds steadily grew louder as I neared a bend in the road, until my gentle and usually well-mannered horse decided he would take exception to this rumbling hubbub. He shied just as the source of this commotion came trundling into view—an unwieldy peddler's wagon, swaying down the rough lane, pulled by a lanky, weary mule.

My horse seemed to take even greater exception to this plodding, ill-favored cousin in harness. The peddler swore and pulled up sharply. I have never claimed to be a masterful handler of the reins, and it took all my limited skill to maneuver my small rig to the side of the narrow lane, which I managed to do just in time to avoid a collision. The mule halted and heaved a sigh. And there, once my horse had regained his dignity, we found ourselves at an impasse.

This was obviously not, by the peddler's reckoning, any sort of calamity. After profuse apologies, but making no effort to budge his wagon—which now blocked my progress completely—he chatted amiably for some minutes on matters of little consequence. He then ventured to offer to me—a gentleman he was so sorry to have inconvenienced—several of his wares at especially reduced prices. "Far lower," he assured me, "than any you could find by mail order catalogue. If you will only consider the additional savings in shipping costs, and how readily you might obtain the goods you need! Consider, too—you may inspect any item before purchase! You will find only the finest quality workmanship in the items I offer, sir! And you must own that buying from one with whom you are acquainted must be seen to be superior to purchasing by catalogue!"

"Pardon me," I said, a little loftily, hoping to stem any further flow of conversation, "but we are not at all acquainted. Now if you would be so good as to—"

"But we are acquainted!" he said, with a clever look in his eye. "You are Dr. John Arden."

I was only momentarily at a loss. Sitting at my side, in plain view, was my medical bag. Any local he had visited might have told him that the village physician, Dr. John Arden, had urged them not to buy patent medicines or to be taken in by the claims of those who peddled tonics.

"Forgive me, Mr."—I squinted to read the fading paint on the side of his wagon—"Mr. Otis Merriweather, but I cannot agree that knowing each other's names truly acquaints us."

He grinned and shook his head. "As near as, sir, as near as! You've been away to study, and were not here on the occasion of my last visit to Carrick Hollow. You are young Johnny Arden, son of Mr. Amos Arden, an apple farmer whom I am on my way to see."

"Perhaps I can spare you some trouble, then," I said coolly. "My father has been dead some months now."

He was immediately crestfallen. "I'm sorry to hear it, sir. Very sorry to hear it indeed." I was ready to believe that his remorse was over the loss of further business, but then he added, "Mr. Arden was a quiet man, never said much, and little though I knew him, he struck me as a sorrowing one. But he was proud of you, boy—and I regret to hear of your loss."

I murmured a polite reply, but lowered my eyes in shame over my uncharitable thoughts of Mr. Merriweather.

"And Mr. Winston gone now, too," he said.

My head came up sharply, but the peddler was thoughtfully gazing off in the direction of the Winston farm and did not see the effect this short speech had on me.

"Do you know what has become of him?" Mr. Merriweather asked. "I'll own I was not fond of him, but he gave me a good deal of custom. It seems so strange—"

"Not at all strange," I said firmly. "These are difficult times for apple growers—for farmers of any kind. Have you not seen many abandoned orchards in Carrick Hollow? Indeed, we aren't the only district to suffer—you travel throughout the countryside in Rhode Island, and you must see empty farms everywhere. Scores of men have left their family lands and moved to cities, to try their luck there."

"Aye, I've seen them," he said, "but—but upon my oath, something's different here in Carrick Hollow! The people here are skittish—jumping at shadows!" He laughed a little nervously, and shook his head. "Old Winston often told me that this place was haunted by . . . well, he called them *vampires*."

"Winston spoke to you of vampires?" I asked, raising my chin a little.

He shifted a bit on the wagon seat. "I wouldn't expect a man of science to believe in such superstitious nonsense, of course! But old Winston used to prose on about it, you see, until my hair fairly stood up on end!"

"Mr. Winston was always a convincing storyteller."

"Yes—but nonsense, pure nonsense!" He paused, and added, "Isn't it?"

"I never used to believe in such things," I said.

"And now?"

"And now, perhaps I do."

Merriweather's eyes widened. He laughed again, and said, "Oh, I see! You pay me back for guessing your name!"

I smiled.

"Here, now!" he said, "I've left you standing here in the lane, taking up your time with this idle talk—Otis Merriweather's all balderdash, you'll be thinking." He cast a quick, uneasy look at the sky. "Growing dark, too. Hadn't realized it had grown so late. I hoped to be in the next town by now, and I'm sure you've patients to attend to. Good day, to you, Doctor!"

With a snap of his reins, he set the mule into motion. Soon the clattering, jangling wagon was traveling down the lane at a pace that made me realize I had underestimated the homely mule.

My own vehicle's pace was much more sedate. I wondered how much faster the peddler would have driven if he had known how much I knew of vampires. I had long made it my business to make a study of the subject. I knew that tales of vampires had been whispered here and there in New England for more than a hundred years, just as they had been told in Egypt, Greece, Polynesia and a dozen other places. The New England vampire has little in common with those which caused such panic in Turkish Serbia and Hungary in the last century—no fanged creature attacks unwitting strangers here. No, our Rhode Island vampires have always more closely resembled ghosts—spirits of the dead who leave their tombs in the night, to visit their nearest and dearest as they dream. Our vampires are believed by some to cause the disease of consumption—it is they, we are told, who drain the blood of living victims into their own hearts, and who thereby cause their victims' rapid decline. The Ardens were never among the believers of such superstitions, never held with any talk of vampires. Indeed, how clearly I remembered a winter's night five years ago, when I assured my youngest brother there wasn't any such thing.

"Mr. Winston said that Mother will come for me," Nathan said. "Will she, Johnny?"

"Pay no attention to him," I said, smoothing his fair hair from his damp forehead. His eyes were bright, and his cheeks ruddy, but he was far too frail for a six-year-old boy. His cough was growing worse. He needed his sleep, but Winston's talk of vampires had frightened him. I tried to keep my anger at our neighbor's thoughtlessness from my voice. "Mother loved you, and would never harm you, you know that, Nate. And she's up in heaven, with all the angels. You must not worry so. Just try to get well."

"But Mr. Winston said—"

"Mr. Winston is a mean-spirited old busy-body," I said with some exasperation. "He only means to frighten you, Nate."

Nathan said nothing, but frowned, as if making a decision. After a while he took hold of my hand. "I'm glad you've come home, Johnny," he whispered. "I know you wish you were away at school—"

"No, Sprout, I could not wish to be anywhere else if you need me."

He smiled at the nickname. "You'll stay with me tonight, won't you?"

"Of course I'll stay with you," I said, and reached into one of my pockets. "And see here—I'm armed—look what I've brought with me!"

"The slingshot I made for you!"

"Yes, and I've gathered a few stones for ammunition," I said, winking at him. "So you're safe now. Only get some sleep, Sprout. I'll stay right here."

He slept soundly. Noah came in to spell me, even though I protested I would be fine. "I know," he whispered, "but please go downstairs to see to Father, Johnny. Try to talk him into getting some sleep."

Downstairs, my father stood near a window, looking out into the moonlit night. I thought he looked more haggard than I had ever seen him. The previous year had taken a great toll on him, and when Nathan fell ill early in 1892, Father could barely take care of himself, let alone a small boy with consumption. So I came home from the private school for which my godfather had so generously paid my tuition; my instructors had been understanding—my family, they knew, had suffered greatly of late. Even though this was not the first occasion upon which I had been called home, my marks were high and I was well ahead of most of my classmates in my studies; the headmaster assured me that I would be allowed to return.

I found my father greatly changed—indeed, Arden Farm itself seemed changed. Winter was the time he usually pruned the trees, but now as I stood next to him at the window, I saw the sucker branches reaching sharply into the winter sky, casting strange shadows everywhere.

"Half my orchard has been felled," he remarked, and I knew he was not talking of the trees, but of the toll consumption had taken on his family. "First Rebecca, then Robert and Daniel. Last month, your mother—dearest Sarah! I've said prayers and made my peace with the Lord. And still he wants more. Is this my God?"

"Noah and I are healthy," I replied, trying to keep his spirits up. "And Julia is with her husband in Peacedale. She's well."

From the other room, we heard the sound of Nathan's cough. "Now my youngest!" my father said.

"Noah and I will care for Nathan. He'll get better."

But neither of us could easily hope that Nathan would recover. Too many times in the past year, consumption had robbed us of those we loved. Ten-year-old Rebecca's cough started early in 1891, and her illness progressed slowly at first. She rallied in the spring, and we thought all would be well. But in August, the cough came back. She was soon coughing up blood—we knew she would not live long after the blood started. By the end of the month, she was dead.

Robert and Daniel, my older brothers, took ill the week before Rebecca's funeral. Mother wrote to me less often, her time taken up with care of them. When she did write, her letters were filled with news of neighbors who had also taken ill, or of the advice given to her by Dr. Ashford. "He tells me to give to them fresh air, to keep them clean, to change their clothes often," she wrote. "I confess to you, dear John, that I am quite worn down—each day, I take them outdoors, read to them, and try to keep their spirits up. This is the most difficult of all my duties.

They miss Rebecca, and they know their own symptoms are identical to hers. Still, I will do all I can to keep my boys alive. God keep you safe, John!"

But despite all her efforts, by October, I came home again—for Robert's funeral. And thus I was there, three days later, when Daniel told us he had dreamt of Rebecca and Robert.

"They were here, sitting on my bed. They weren't sick. They said I had helped them to get better." Two days later, he passed away during the night.

I returned to school, but Mother's letters grew fewer still. I thought it was grief that kept her from writing, but when I came home for the Christmas holidays, I immediately realized that the cause was otherwise—the wracking cough of consumption was no longer an unfamiliar sound to any of us.

"Why did you not tell me?" I asked my father.

"She did not want us to take you from your school," he said. "She has come to believe you will be safer there than here."

I hurried to her bedside. She looked so thin and weak.

"John, you are home!" she whispered to me as I sat beside her. "Rebecca, Daniel, and Robert are with the Lord. I'll be with them soon. They are good children. They'll not bother me. I have not dreamt of them. They won't come and take me."

"What does she mean?" I asked my father, when she fell asleep again.

"Winston!" he said angrily. "He's all about the village, telling everyone that the consumption is caused by vampires."

"Vampires!"

"Yes. He tells his tales to any who will hear him.

Gets the most ignorant of them to believe that the spirits of the dead consume the living, and thus the living are weakened!"

"But surely no one believes such things!"

"In the absence of any cure, do you blame them for grasping at any explanation offered to them? Grief and fear will lead men to strange ways, Johnny, and Winston can persuade like the devil himself!"

"Yes, he was ever one to seek attention," I agreed.

"He has gained a great deal of it during this crisis," my father said. "And the rituals he has driven some of the more superstitious ones to perform! It sickens me!" He shivered in disgust.

Mother died two nights after Christmas, as Father held her, singing hymns to her. The next day, he dressed her in her favorite dress and sent word to the undertaker. The stonecarver had already completed her headstone, and her burial place had long been chosen.

Noah wrote to me of Nathan's illness in late January of 1892, and I hurried home again. That first night back, as I studied my father's face, etched in grief, I saw that my mother's death had wounded him even more deeply than I had imagined. I had never doubted their love or devotion to one another, but I had not before realized how much of his strength must have come from her. If this great man could be made so weak, what would become of us? I suddenly felt as small and frightened as a boy of Nathan's age.

"Papa!" I said, placing a hand on his shoulder.

He looked at me and smiled a little. "It is some time since you called me 'Papa.' "

"You—you need your sleep," I said. "Won't you go up to bed?"

The smile faded. "So empty, that room . . ." he murmured.

"Please, it's so late and you seem so tired—"

"I cannot—I will not be able to sleep there."

Understanding dawned. "Then I'll make a place up for you here, near the fire. But you must sleep. Please. Nathan and Noah need you. I need you."

And so he consented, but when I left him to go back to Nathan, he was staring into the fire.

The next morning, my father gently shook me awake. I sat up stiffly in the chair next to the bed where Nathan still slept. I could hear our dogs barking. Father gestured for me to step into the hallway.

"Winston is on his way up the drive! I've asked Noah to delay him all he can. But I must tell you this— make sure Nathan hears nothing of his foolish talk."

I started to tell him that Nathan's head was already full of Winston's foolish talk, but he had hurried off.

I stood near the window of Nathan's room, straining to hear the conversation that was taking place below. Winston was a large man, whose new derby, well-made coat and fine boots signaled his prosperity, but could not improve his rough features. As my father approached, Winston's pock-marked cheeks were flushed. He eyed the dogs warily, until Noah called them to heel.

"Will you not ask me in, neighbor?" Winston asked, fingering his heavy gold watch chain.

"My youngest is ill," my father said firmly. "I would not have you disturb him."

My father's lack of hospitality did not delay Winston from his mission. He took a deep breath, and said in loud voice, "I fear for my community, for my neighbors and their families! I know you're scared for what remains of yours, too. I can see it in your eyes, Arden. Rebecca took the boys, then they took Sarah. Now, Sarah's taking Nathan. John and Noah will follow, and you'll be last. Julia may be far away enough to be safe, but there is no certainty of that."

"My family's safety is my own concern, Winston."

"Your obligation is greater than you perceive, Arden!" Winston shot back. "The vampires look beyond your family! Lavinia Gardner has the consumption."

"Isaac's wife is ill?" my father asked, dismayed.

"Yes. And she's dreamt of your wife! There's only one way to stop this—the ritual must be performed! It has worked for Robinson, and others as well. This is a warning, Arden! If you're afraid to do what is necessary, I'll do it myself!"

"You'll go nowhere near the graves of my beloved!" Father shouted. "I know of your ritual, Winston. I've spoken with Robinson. He's not the same man—he's alive, but he looks for all the world as if he believes himself damned."

"Nonsense!" Winston blustered. "What's more important, Arden? Maintaining your own selfish prejudices, or the survival of Carrick Hollow? Our eldest sons and daughters are fleeing—they've taken factory jobs in Providence and Fall River."

"There are many reasons they leave. You have no wife or children, Winston. Allow me to take care of my own."

"A fine job you're doing of it! Half of them dead!"

Noah stepped forward, his fists clenched. I could not make out what he said to Winston.

"Noah," my father said, "it's all right. Try though he

may, Mr. Winston can not harm me with his words."

"Think of your neighbors, Arden!" Winston said. "Think of Isaac if you won't think of your own sons!" He turned on his heel and strode quickly down the lane, dried leaves swirling in his wake.

"Johnny?" I heard a small voice say.

I turned from the window to see Nathan watching me. "So you're awake, Mr. Sleepyhead!"

"I heard Mr. Winston yelling at Papa."

"Yes, and had I known you were awake, I would have opened the window and used this fine slingshot to knock old Thunderpuss's fancy derby right off his silly head."

Nathan smiled and said, "I should have liked to have seen you do it," and went back to sleep.

The thaw broke the day Lavinia Gardner died. Isaac Gardner came to visit us two weeks later. Noah stayed with Nathan as I sat with Father, watching Isaac wring his hands.

"You know what I think of Winston," he began. "And I would not come to trouble you, Amos, except—except that, before she died, Lavinia called Sarah's name several times."

"Our wives were good friends," my father said.

Isaac shook his head. "That's not what I mean, Amos. I mean, called her name as if she were within speaking distance. I'd tell her, 'Sarah's dead,' and she'd say, 'No, Sarah Arden is rattling me again. She comes at night and shakes me and the cough starts up.' "

My father sat in stunned silence.

"Your wife was very ill—" I began gently.

"Yes, John," Isaac said, "and I told myself that she was right out of her head, although of course

Neighbor Winston had a good deal to say otherwise, and he's caught my daughter's ear. Even before Jane took ill, she was asking me if maybe we should pay attention to what Winston had to say."

"The news of Jane's illness only reached us yesterday," my father said. "I was sorry to hear of it, Isaac. I had always hoped that she and Noah—well, I can only offer my prayers for her recovery."

"She's all I have left in the world, Amos," Isaac said. "As hard on you as it has been, losing so many—well, I don't know what I'll do if Jane suffers like her mother did." He paused, then said, "But I'm here, Amos, because I want you to know what things have come to—and God forgive me, but I need your help. Jane no longer doubts that Winston's right."

"What?"

"Yes. Just last night, she told me, 'Mother will take me just like Sarah Arden took her.' And she pleaded with me, Amos—'Mr. Winston knows the way to stop this. You can't let me die!' "

My father was silent.

"I told her," Isaac said, his voice breaking, "I told her, 'Jane, think of it! Think what you ask me to do! Your mother—let her rest in peace!' And she said, 'But father, she's not resting in peace now. She can only rest forever with your help.' "

"Good God, Isaac!"

"I don't believe in it, not for a minute, Amos. But *she* does. And what's worse, now more than half the village does, too! Winston's got them all stirred up. What they say of you, I'll not repeat."

"I'd as soon you didn't!" Father said, casting a glance at me.

"I've gone to Pastor Williams. He doesn't promote the ritual, but he doesn't oppose it, either. He's only human, and Winston holds some sway with him, too."

"With his coffers, you mean. I hear Winston's most recent donation makes up what is needed for the new roof on the church."

"Amos!"

"Yes, yes, I'm ashamed of making such a remark. Forgive me, Isaac." He sighed and said, "What do you need from me?"

"Help me to do it."

"The ritual?" my father asked, horrified.

"Amos, you're my best friend in all the world, else I wouldn't ask it. But I need someone there—someone who hasn't lost his mind in all this vampire madness. Otherwise, God knows what is to become of me! I need your strength!"

His strength is failing! I wanted to protest, but my father was already agreeing to help his old friend.

Father would not let us go with him on the day the ritual was performed. When he came home, his pallor frightened me. I gave him soup and warm bread, but he did not eat. He would not speak of what happened, but late that night, I heard him weeping.

Jane Gardner died two days later.

If we had thought this would put an end to Winston's cause, we were mistaken. A town meeting was held the next week. I sat next to Father, near the front of the room, when Winston presented his case. Father had told Noah that Winston could not hurt him with his words, but how wrong he had been!

"The future of our community is at risk!" Winston declared, fingering his gold watch chain. "Many of our dearest friends and family members have died from consumption. We've taken action against the vampires, with one notable exception." He stared hard at my father. "Those in the Arden family!"

There was a low murmur, a mixture of protest and agreement.

Winston held his hands out flat, making a calming motion. "Now," he said silkily, "I have great sympathy for my neighbor, Amos Arden. The death of his wife and three children is a terrible loss for him. But in consumption, the living are food for the dead, and we must think of the living! The graves must be opened, and the bodies examined! If none of their hearts is found to hold blood, we may all be at peace, knowing that none are vampires. But if there is a vampire coming to us from the Arden graves, the ritual must be performed! This is our only recourse." The room fell silent. No one rose to speak, but many heads nodded in agreement.

Father stood slowly, grasping the chair beside me. "The thought of disturbing the peace of my wife and children sickens me. I do not believe in this superstition, but I see no other way." He glanced toward Winston, then said, "If I refuse, I have no doubt that some other will take the task upon himself. He takes a great deal upon himself, but the thought of his hands on my wife's remains—" He broke off, and I saw that he was trembling, not in fear, but in anger. He looked around the room, but many of our neighbors would not meet his gaze. "I will agree to the ritual," he said at last, "but no one else will touch my wife."

The exhumation was set for two days hence, and

under other circumstances, would have occupied all my thoughts. Instead, all my energies were taken up with the care of Nathan, whose condition suddenly worsened. He bore it bravely, worrying more about his father than himself. "Papa is troubled," he said, and pleaded again and again with me to tell him what had so disturbed our parent.

On the night before the exhumation, I told my father that Nathan's condition terrified me. "He needs a doctor! He has night sweats now, and the coughing is ceaseless. He has so little strength and—"

"I know, John. I know."

I was silent.

"With all that has befallen us," my father said, "I'm sorry, John, I cannot afford to bring Ashford here again, even if he would come."

"What do you mean, 'if he would come'? Of course he would!"

My father shook his head. "I have not wanted to tell you this, son, but—the last time Dr. Ashford saw him, three weeks ago, he told me Nathan's case is hopeless. Your brother is dying."

I had known it, of course, without being told, but still it was a blow. Childishly, I struck back. "So you resort to Winston's witchcraft!"

He looked into my eyes and said, "Do you think I would hesitate for a moment to save any of your lives by any means I could? By God, I'd offer my own life if it would save his!"

"Papa—I'm sorry! I just can't understand why you've agreed to this ritual. It didn't work for Jane Gardner. I've heard of other unsuccessful cases—"

"I don't do this because I believe it will cure consumption. But it is a cure for mistrust. A bitter remedy, but a necessary one."

"I don't understand."

"You will go back to school soon, and perhaps you will never return to Carrick Hollow. No, don't protest—whether you do or not, Noah and I will continue to live here. We who live in the countryside depend upon our friends and neighbors. My neighbors are depending on me now, to do something which they have come to believe will keep them safe and well. No matter how repulsive I find it, John, I must do this to keep their trust."

That night, my sleep was fitful. Nathan's cough was horrible, and nothing I did could bring him any relief. My brief dreams were filled with images of decaying flesh and bones, of coffins unearthed, of Winston's thick hands reaching into my mother's grave.

The morning broke bright and warm, unusual for an early spring day in New England. We had agreed that Noah would stay with Nathan; a suggestion that he met with both relief and some guilt. But my father knew that Noah's anger toward Winston had already nearly led to blows, and asked him to stay home.

A group of ten men, including poor Isaac Gardner, gathered in the village. Winston tried to lead the way to the cemetery, but Isaac shouldered him aside, and let my father go ahead of them. I saw my father hesitate. I took his hand, and together we walked to the familiar section of the churchyard, the one I knew so well from that winter of funerals. As we stood at the foot of the four newest Arden graves, Winston's voice interrupted my silent prayers.

"Dig up all four coffins," he directed.

"All four!" my father protested.

"We must be certain!" Winston said. "We'll place them under that tree. Once they are all exhumed, we'll open them one at a time. Start with the children."

Father, Isaac, and I stood away from the group. At a nod from Winston, their picks and shovels struck the earth. They began to dig, never looking up at us. My father swayed a little on his feet, and Isaac moved nearer, placing a firm hand on his shoulder. Together we stood listening to the rhythm of the digging, the downward scrape and lift, the thudding fall of the soil as they attacked my sister's grave. Soon, the top of Rebecca's coffin was struck. How small that coffin looked! The earth was moved from around its sides, and ropes were placed under the ends. The coffin was lifted from the grave and placed under a nearby tree. In two more hours, two other coffins were taken from the earth—the larger coffins of my brothers, Robert, who had been but eighteen, and Daniel, a year younger—the age I was now. As each coffin was brought up, my prayers became more urgent and the fact of the exhumations more real.

The group moved to Mother's grave. Again, shovels broke into the soil. The digging slowed now—the first frenzy long past, the men grew tired. At last, they pulled her coffin from the earth and set it with the others, beneath the tree. I moved toward it, and placed my hand on the lid of her box. I felt the cool, damp wood, and the small indentations made by each nail. I broke out in a cold sweat, and my hand shook. I turned when I heard the creak of the nails being pried from the other coffins.

Father's hand gently touched my arm. I moved away.

When they had finished loosening all the nails on the top of each of the coffins, Winston directed the men to remove the lid of Rebecca's. With horror, I gazed at the unrecognizable form that—had it not been for her dress and the color of her hair—I would not have known as my sister. This child's face, impish and smiling not so very long ago, was now nothing more than a skull, covered with sunken, leathery skin; her small, white hands now nothing more than thin bones covered with dark, dried sinew. My throat constricted—I could not swallow, could not breathe. Rebecca! Little Rebecca! My memories of her could not be reconciled with what I saw. I had taught her how to write her name, I thought wildly—I had heard her laughter. This could not be my sister . . .

Winston was studying her. I wanted to claw his filthy eyes out.

"No," he said, and the lid was quickly replaced.

He said the same thing when he gazed upon the remains of my brothers, who also appeared mummified, their dry skin stretched tight over their bony frames.

I tried hard to control my emotions, but this was increasingly difficult. By the time we reached my mother's coffin, only my desire to deny Winston any glimpse of weakness kept me on my feet.

They slid the coffin lid off the edge of the box. Father and I looked down at Mother's face. She looked peaceful, remarkably like the day we buried her, despite the three cold months that had passed. Her nails and hair appeared longer, and in places, her skin had turned reddish.

"Ahh," Winston said, moving closer. "As I suspected. But we must examine the heart to be certain."

"You'll not touch her!" my father cried.

Winston smiled, and turned to the others. "Light the fire."

"By God, Winston—"

"Oh, indeed, I'll not touch your vampire wife. You must be the one." He handed my father a long knife.

My father stared at it.

"Get on with it, man!" Winston ordered.

"John," my father said, anguished, "leave us. Go home. It was wrong of me to bring you here—"

"I'll not leave you, Father."

He shook his head, but turned back to the open coffin. He set the knife aside, and with trembling fingers, tenderly moved her burial gown down from her neck. I heard him sob, then saw him lift the knife. He cut a gash in her chest.

"The heart, the heart!" Winston said eagerly.

Father's face seemed to turn to stone—cold and gray. He pried the wound open, then took the knife and cut away her heart. Bloody fluid ran from the wound onto her dress.

"You see! She's the one, she's the vampire!"

As from a distance, I heard the other men gasp, and saw their quick gestures—signs against evil.

"Put it in the fire, Arden!" Winston directed.

"No!" I said weakly, but Father walked toward the blaze. He let the heart drop from his fingers; the fire hissed and sparked as it fell into the center of the flames.

Father walked back to mother's coffin, placed the lid on it, and began to hammer it shut. I picked up one of the other hammers—tears blinding me, I worked at his side. Without speaking, several men did the same for the other coffins. Each coffin was slowly lowered back into its grave, and in silence we began to cover them again—but Father buried mother's coffin alone, refusing the others' help with a steely look in his eyes.

I saw Winston warming his hands over the fire. He caught me looking at him and smiled. "You should thank me. I've saved your life this day, John."

Before the others could stop me, I slammed my fist into his jaw.

My father led me away from them, and with Isaac we made our way back home. All the way down the lane, I could not help but be troubled over what I had seen, and wondered at it. That my mother could be a vampire, I did not for a moment believe. I knew there must be a rational, scientific explanation for the blood that had been in my mother's heart. I swore to myself that I would study anatomy and medicine—yes, and vampires, too—and learn all I could about consumption and its causes.

When we returned to the house, Noah held Nathan's body in his arms.

My medical schooling was the best in New England. The Boston area had many fine schools, and Springhaven University was among them. Springhaven was the choice of my godfather, as it was his alma mater, and he was a respected alumnus and benefactor.

Medical school was not easy for me. The work itself was not difficult, though much harder than my earlier schooling, to be sure. I took to the reading, lectures, and discussions with great interest, but it was the hustle and bustle of Boston that caused me discomfort. The size of the city, its noises and smells, always left me ill at ease. Although I loved the work, I was homesick.

Early on, I learned that there had been nothing unusual about the appearance of my mother's body, given the conditions of her burial—the coldness of the ground, the brief length of time she had been buried. The heart is a pump, my anatomy instructor said, and at death, blood and other fluids often settle there and in the chest cavity after the heart ceases beating.

My professors called consumption by another name—tuberculosis, or TB. Tuberculosis was not an enigma to these men of science. Over forty years before my brother's death, sanitariums were being established in Europe, and TB patients were living longer lives. But of all the discoveries that had been made about the disease, perhaps the most exciting had come in 1882, when Robert Koch identified its true cause—*Mycobacterium tuberculosis*. Koch's discovery proved that TB was transmitted from a consumptive to a healthy person through bacteria contained in the consumptive's cough—not by vampires.

Although saddened that my knowledge had come too late to save my family, I had no difficulty accepting these new discoveries. But educating the public, whether the poor of Boston or the farmers of Carrick Hollow, was a challenge. I determined to practice medicine in Carrick Hollow upon graduation, to do my best to counter the superstitious remedies that offered no real hope to its inhabitants.

I visited one of my chief correspondents and supporters soon after my return—old Dr. Ashford received me gladly, and we talked at length about the medical histories of families in the area and exchanged information on the latest medical supplies and pharmaceuticals. We also discussed my schooling and how much medical education had changed since he had taken the title "doctor."

"The War of the Rebellion was where I learned medicine," he said. "We learned on our feet, not from the books. I haven't had much of a head for the science of it—just tried to do what worked." He paused, then added, "Remember, John, that folks here are quite independent, even when it comes to medicine. They take care of their own problems, using the same remedies their grandparents used. It's hard to fight their traditions."

"I suspect that will be the hardest part of my job," I replied. "I have confidence that I can do some good here, if my neighbors will only accept me."

"You've always had both the mind and the manner for medicine," he said. "You'll do well in Carrick Hollow. It's time they had a doctor as fine as yourself."

As it happened, the residents of the village took me in with open arms, proud of my accomplishments, and glad to have a physician so nearby. Several of them helped me to convert a building formerly used by a lawyer into a small clinic, which had the advantage of living quarters on the upper story.

I had the good fortune to be of some help to my first patients, and soon others were ready to follow my medical advice and help me to establish my practice. I fell easily into life in Carrick Hollow, surrounded by the sense of community I so missed in Boston.

Only one problem continued to trouble me—my father's state of mind.

Father had never fully recovered from the deaths in our family, especially not from the loss of my mother. Noah had been greatly relieved when I told him that I meant to set up my practice in the village. "Perhaps you will be able to cheer him," he said. "He has not been the same since—since the day Nathan died."

But although he was always kind to me in those months, my father never smiled, and seldom spoke. His sleep was often disturbed by nightmares, and if not for our constant coaxing, he would not have eaten enough to keep his strength up. He worked hard, but the joy he had once taken in his labors was gone. There was a lost look in his eyes, and the smallest happiness seemed beyond his reach. It was as if, on that long ago day at the cemetery, his own heart had fallen on those flames, and turned to ashes with my mother's.

His lifelessness was a condition found in others in Carrick Hollow— in Isaac Gardner, in Mr. Robinson, and in others who had performed Winston's brutal ritual. Bitterly I reflected that nothing in my medical training would cure these men. I vowed that no one in Carrick Hollow would ever be forced to endure that ritual again.

Soon after I had opened my office, I was given an opportunity to make good on that vow. I was visited by Jacob Wilcox, a middle-aged man just returned to Carrick Hollow from factory work in Fall River. His rumbling cough was a tell-tale sign of tuberculosis, but my examination revealed that the disease was in its early stages.

I recommended the best hope for his recovery—the strict regimens of a sanitarium. I suggested one in the Adirondack Mountains, which had the advantages of being close to Rhode Island and less costly than those in the western United States. He thanked me, took the information, and went on his way.

A few days later, at my father's request, I visited the farm. Coming down the drive, hearing the welcoming bark of our old dogs, I felt what had become a customary mixture of sadness and deep comfort in returning to my childhood home. Noah and my father came out to help me stable the horse, and my brother and I spoke of inconsequential things. I could not help but notice that Father seemed agitated, and Noah wary.

My father did not broach the subject that concerned him until we had finished eating our simple meal—a meal he had barely touched. He put a log on the fire, then turned to me and said, "I'm told that you saw a patient with consumption today."

"Yes," I answered hesitantly. I had not previously told him of my devotion to the study of consumption, and I was concerned that he would be touched on the raw by any mention of it.

He frowned. "I talked to young Wilcox after you saw him. What is this treatment you prescribed? Why do you send him to the mountains?"

"In hope of curing his consumption," I said.

"Curing! Is it possible?"

"Sometimes, yes." I began to tell him of the benefits the TB patient might find in life in a sanitarium—exposure to a healthful climate, enforced rest, fresh air, proper care and good nutrition. "And of course, the sanitarium separates those who have this contagion from any who might be vulnerable to it, so the disease is less likely to be spread to others."

"You have especially concerned yourself with the study of—you call it 'TB?' "

"Yes."

His questions became more persistent, and soon I was talking to him of Brehmer, Villemin, Koch and all the others whose discoveries had brought us to our present understanding of the disease. My father listened with rapt attention, but I saw that he became more and more uneasy as I spoke. Soon, however, I recognized that he was dismayed not by what I had learned about TB, but by his own previous ignorance.

"Dr. Ashford did not know of this!" he said. "Your mother, the children—their consumption was a death sentence! I should have sought another physician, a younger man, such as yourself. If we had known of these sanitariums—"

"It still might not have helped—sanitariums only give consumptives a *chance* to recover. Some people survive, others arrive only to die a few weeks later."

"But Nathan—your mother, Robert and Daniel— all of them, even Rebecca—they might have lived had we sent Rebecca away?"

"I don't know. There were so many others in Carrick Hollow who were ill that winter. Perhaps they would have caught TB from Mrs. Gardner, or Jane, or another. We cannot always cure this disease, Papa. I can't say for certain who would live and who would die. For all that men in my profession have learned, life and death are still in God's hands."

He was silent.

"We cannot change the past, Papa. I only hope to save others from the horror our family experienced. In truth, my most difficult battle is not against the disease, but rather the ignorance—the sort of ignorance which allows men like Winston to convince others that the afflicted are beset by vampires. As long as he spouts his nonsense, others will die, because he will have his neighbors believing that spiritual mumbo-jumbo—and not infection—are at the root of the disease."

"You are too kind, John," he said slowly. "You fail to mention the truly damned. Men like your father, who will be persuaded that barbaric rituals must be performed on the bodies of their dead—"

"Papa, you never believed him. You had other reasons. Do not torture yourself so!"

"There is no escape from it."

"Then try to find some peace where I have—in helping the living. That is how my mother's memory is best served—the sooner we educate our neighbors in the truth of this matter, the less influence men of Winston's stripe will have over them."

I was gratified, the next day, to see that he seemed to have dedicated himself to this cause, and that he was to some degree transformed by his devotion to it. Whenever I happened to glance out my office window, I saw my father talking in an animated fashion to any who would hear him. He was a respected member of the community, and had no shortage of listeners. Isaac Gardner was with him, and he, too, seemed to have taken up the banner. By the early afternoon, Mr. Robinson had stopped into my office to ask if what my father said was true—that vampires had nothing to do with consumption, that some people were being cured of it in sanitariums. I verified that it was so, and watched his eyes cloud with tears. "Then what

Winston told me to do to Louisa's body—the ritual—that was all for naught?"

"I'm afraid so," I said gently.

He swore rather violently regarding Mr. Winston, then begged my pardon, and left. I watched him walk across the street to join the growing crowd that had gathered around my parent. I smiled. My father, Isaac Gardner and Mr. Robinson would all do a better job of convincing the others than I ever could.

I was vaguely aware that the crowd was moving off down the street, but I was soon caught up in the care of a young patient who had fallen from a tree, and forgot all about vampires and consumption. I set his broken arm, and sent him and his grateful mother on their way. I had just finished straightening my examination room when the door to my office burst open, and my father, Noah, Isaac Gardner, Robinson and a great many others came crowding into the room. They carried between them a man whose face was so battered and clothing so bloodied that I would not have recognized him were it not for a memorable piece of ostentation he was never without—a heavy gold watch chain.

"Winston!"

The others looked at me, their eyes full of fear.

"Lay him on the table!" I ordered.

It took only the briefest examination to realize that he was beyond any help I could offer. He was already growing cold. "He's dead."

I thought I heard sighs of relief, and I turned to face them. They all stood silently, hats in hand.

"Who did this?" I asked.

No one answered, and all lowered their eyes.

"Who did this?" I asked again.

"Vampires," I heard someone whisper, but I was never to know who spoke the word. No matter what I asked, no matter how I pleaded to be told the truth, they remained resolutely silent. Winston's blood was on all of them; there was no way to distinguish a single killer from among the group. I went to my basin, to wash his blood from my own hands. The thought arrested me. These were neighbors, friends—my father, my brother. I knew what had driven them to this—I knew. Had I not lived in Carrick Hollow almost all my life?

"What shall we do with him?" one of them asked.

I dried my hands and said, in a voice of complete calm, "I believe it is said that for the good of the community, one who is made into a vampire must be cremated."

I could show you the place in the woods where it was done, where the earth has not yet healed over the burning. Nature works to reclaim it, though, as nature ever works to reclaim us all.

I would like to tell you that the last vampire of Carrick Hollow had been laid to rest there, and that we now live in peace. But it is not so.

Not long after Winston's death, people who had lived in our village all their lives began to leave it. Farms were abandoned. We would tell strangers that it was the economy—and in truth, some left because it was easier to make a living in the cities. But that would not explain the mistrust the inhabitants sometimes seem to feel toward one another, or the guilty look one might surprise in the faces of those who hastily travel past Winston's farm.

I thought the peddler was unlikely to return. He had seen something that frightened him, though he might not know enough to put a name to the emptiness in a young doctor's eyes. I knew it for what it was, for I had seen it in my father and Isaac and Mr. Robinson and so many others—Carrick Hollow is a haunted place, haunted by the living as well as the dead.

Oh yes, I believe in vampires—though not the sort of bogeyman imagined by fanatics like the late and unlamented Winston.

But if vampires are the animated dead, dead who walk upon the earth—restless, hungry, and longing to be alive again—then I could never deny their existence. You see, I know so very many of them.

Indeed, I am one.

AUTHOR'S NOTE

While Carrick Hollow and its inhabitants are entirely fictional, some New Englanders were ascribing the cause of consumption (tuberculosis) to vampires late into the 19th century; newspaper accounts and other evidence indicate rituals such as the one described here occurred at least as late as the 1890's in rural Rhode Island.

THE ABBEY GHOSTS

I DID NOT MEET the Eighth Earl of Rolingbroke until he was twelve years old. I was in some measure compensated for the lack of our acquaintance during those first dozen years of his life, not only by the deep friendship my stepbrother and I formed over the years we did have together, but also because I was occasionally allowed to spend time with him after his death.

His death had come unexpectedly, and before he attained his thirtieth year. That first evening after his funeral, I sat before the fire in the Abbey library, weary and yet certain that my grief for him would not allow me to sleep. Not many hours earlier, my late stepbrother had been laid to rest in the family crypt. Lucien's body had been placed next to that of his wife—who had died five years before, shortly after giving birth to Charles, their only child.

Lucien's orphaned son was much on my mind. I

had looked in on Charles just before ten o'clock. The day's events had been exhausting for him as well, and he slept, though his young face seemed sad even in repose.

I poured another glass of port as the mantel clock struck eleven. I had dismissed the servants for the evening, not able to bear their solicitude, nor their misery. They had loved Lucien as much as I, and the strain of this terrible day was telling on us all. I chose to spend the last few hours of it alone, thinking of Lucien and the years we had shared as brothers. How I would miss him!

I clearly recalled our first meeting.

Lucien's father married my widowed mother, and my mother and I came to live at the Abbey. I had met the Seventh Earl of Rolingbroke, my new stepfather, on only two previous occasions—brief interviews which had put me quite in awe of that forceful man. I entered his home believing I was quite without a champion—my mother, for all her beauty and good-heartedness, was a timid soul, far more likely to suffer a fit of the vapors than to defend me.

The Abbey itself was daunting—a rambling structure, larger by far than the small estate where I had been raised, and very much older. I fully expected that a boy of my size might be lost within it, and even if his newly remarried mother should take the trouble to look for him, she might never discover which winding staircase or long gallery held his remains.

Not the least of my anxieties concerned my new stepbrother. I expected resentment from Lucien, then twelve, and two years my senior. My first impression of him led me to believe that he was a cool and distant fellow. As we entered the Abbey, he stood back from the others, regarding me lazily from his greater height. I was afraid, and trying not to show it—but I must have failed, for his father muttered something about "Master Quakeboots."

Lucien's expression changed then, and he welcomed me by bowing and murmuring for my ears only, "Lord Shivershanks, at your service." I choked back a laugh, received his rare but charming smile in return, and like any recipient of that smile, knew all would be right with the world.

Lucien soon became both friend and brother, offering wise-beyond-his-years guidance and his seldom bestowed affection. He taught me how to get on well with my stepfather, protected me against a bully or two, and allowed me to accompany him in every lark imaginable. He taught me the ways and traditions of the Abbey. He also taught me how to find several secret passages within it, and told me stories of its past, thrilling me with tales of ghostly, headless monks haunting the north (and only remaining) tower, of hidden treasures and ancient curses.

"And we must not forget the Christmas Curse," he whispered to me one chilly evening in late November— when, as usual, he had made use of a priest's hole to come into my room and visit long after the servants believed him to be abed.

"Can there be such a thing?" I asked.

"Oh yes," he said, with one of his mischievous smiles. "You, my dear Edward, have not had the felicity of meeting my Aunt and Uncle Bane and their pack of hellborn brats—Henry, William, and Fanny. Utter thatchgallows."

"Thatchgallows!" I laughed.

"Shhh! Yes. Born to be hanged, every man Jack of them—and Fanny, too. We shall have to prepare for their arrival. They'll try to harass you, of course, But don't worry. Every time one of them behaves odiously, you are to remind yourself that soon we will be handing them a reckoning."

He was not mistaken. Lord and Lady Bane brought their three interesting offspring to the Abbey not two weeks later. The servants had prepared for their visit by carefully removing the most treasured and fragile objects of the household from sight. From the moment they passed through the imposing entrance of the Abbey, our home was turned upside down. Henry and William, true to Lucien's prediction, made it their business to make me suffer. Henry was my own age, William a year younger, but they were both taller and stronger than I. All three children favored their father, Lord Alfred Bane, who was both brother-in-law and cousin to the earl. Lord Bane was a red-haired man whose countenance could easily be brought to match it in color. His softest whisper was nothing less than a shout—and he seldom whispered.

His sons were equally loud, and seemed never to stand still for a moment. They contrived to poke, pinch, trip, and jostle me at every opportunity. By the end of their second day among us, I was quite bruised, but did not doubt for a moment that Lucien would come to my aid. In his quiet way, he often did so, surprisingly able to control them as no one else seemed able—giving a quelling look to Henry or William that always made them back off until they chanced to find me apart from him.

When those opportunities arose, any feeble attempt on my part to defend myself caused them to set up a caterwauling that served as a siren call to Lady Sophia Bane. This fond mother relished coming to their aid, and invariably boxed my ears as she rang a peal over my head. On these occasions, my own mother, who knew better than any general how to retreat in good order, would announce that she felt a spasm coming on, and—clutching her vinaigrette to her bosom—excuse herself from the battleground.

Lady Bane complained constantly, perceiving faults everywhere: The food was not to her liking. The servants were never to be found when needed. The room in which she sat was too chilly—when the fires were made larger, she was too warm, and protested that the chimneys smoked. The rooms into which they had been installed were uncomfortable for this reason or that.

"Not what we are accustomed to at Bane House!" was a refrain we soon wearied of hearing.

When she declared that their rooms were inconveniently located, my stepfather raised his brows. "But my dear Sophia! They are the very rooms you insisted upon after refusing the ones you had last year, when you thought I was trying to banish you to a far wing of the Abbey."

It made no difference. Lucien later told me that his father and aunt had been raised separately—the earl spent most of his childhood at the Abbey, with Lucien's grandfather. Lucien's grandmother—who disliked life in the country nearly as much as she disliked her husband—lived in Town, with her daughter, Sophia.

I was grateful for these insights. However, Fanny constantly spied on Lucien and me, so we had little opportunity for private speech such as this. After several months of being almost constantly in his company, being unable to share confidences with Lucien made me experience a loneliness that surprised me. But then one evening, just as I was feeling quite sure this would be my most miserable Christmas ever, Lucien winked and smiled at me.

We had been engaged in playing Jackstraws, but Fanny's governess, who had been overseeing our activities that evening, called the proceedings to a halt—perceiving, I suppose, that this was not the sort of game the Banes could play without violence. As she moved across the room to put the game away, Lucien turned to me and said, "Do you suppose the ghost will walk tonight?"

"What ghost?" the Banes said loudly and in unison.

"The Headless Abbot, of course," he replied.

Fanny's eyes grew round.

"What nonsense is this?" asked the governess, but with an air of interest.

"Long, long ago," Lucien said, casting his spell over us, "a castle was built here—its ruins form part of the north tower. But the castle itself was built over ruins—ruins of an even older abbey, which is how our home came to be named.

"In the days when the Abbey was truly an abbey, a war broke out between two powerful lords. One winter's night, not long before Christmas, the abbey came under attack, which was a shocking thing, because this was then considered a holy place, with relics and the like. Knights in armor rode their horses into the chapel, where the abbot was leading the evening prayer, and the captain of these rogues took out his broadsword and *swoosh!*" He made a slicing motion with his hand.

All three Banes and the governess gasped—and I believe I did, too, for though I had heard this tale before, never had Lucien related it in such a dramatic manner.

"Yes," Lucien said darkly, "he beheaded the holy man where he stood, and his knights murdered all the other monks—defenseless men at their prayers."

This earned another gasp.

"But why would they do such a thing!" the governess said.

Lucien seemed to hesitate to answer, his manner that of one who was deciding whether or not he should impart a great secret. "The attackers," he finally said, "had heard a legend, a tale of a treasure kept in the abbey. It probably wasn't true, for although they examined every cupboard and cabinet, and pulled at loose stones and tiles, and looked in every room and hall for its hiding place, they could not find the treasure." He paused, then said, "The powerful lord to whom the knight had sworn his loyalty sent a messenger to the captain, saying that he needed his warriors, and so they must make all haste to the battlefield. The greedy captain pretended to have an illness, and sent all but a small number of knights to join their lord in battle, while he remained to continue his search at the abbey."

He lowered his voice. "But during the night, on the very first evening this small company stayed in the abbey, the men who stood guard were startled to see a strange sight—a man, wearing a monk's robes, his face hidden by its cowl, seemed to appear out of nowhere. Unlike the brown-robed monks they had slaughtered so mercilessly, this one was dressed all in white, save a splash of red on his chest. 'Who goes there?' cried one of the knights. The figure in white halted, and lowered his cowl. With horror, the knights saw that the apparition *had no head.*"

"The abbot!" William said breathlessly.

"Yes," Lucien said. "The guards screamed in terror, awakening the others. The knights were frightened, but their captain tried to brazen it out. 'Show us your treasure!' he shouted. And the abbott began to lead the way. The captain called to his five bravest men, and they followed the monk into a secret passage. The others were too frightened to go near him, and waited."

Again, Lucien paused.

"Yes, yes! Then what happened?" Henry insisted.

Lucien smiled. "They were never seen again!"

There was a suitably awed silence, then William said, "But the treasure! What happened to the treasure?"

"It was never found. Accidents befell any who tried to discover it—especially those who ventured near the old sanctuary. Eventually, this land was given to one of our ancestors. He had the portion of the Abbey that had been the sanctuary sealed off, and built his castle over it. But the local people will tell you that the Headless Abbot still walks on winter nights. Some say they've heard the sound of hoofbeats coming from the part of the Abbey which lies nearest the sanctuary— the ghostly horses of the accursed knights."

"Which part of this old pile is that?" Henry asked, trying for nonchalance.

Lucien appeared to reflect, then answered, "Why, I believe it is very near to your rooms."

All Henry's bravado disappeared. "Mother!" he screamed, running from the room. Fanny burst into tears and soon followed him. William hurriedly escaped on her heels.

"My word!" the governess said, rather pale, although perhaps she feared her employer's displeasure more than headless monks, for she hastened after her charges.

"My compliments," said Lucien calmly. "You appeared suitably frightened. If you continue to play your part so well, my dear Edward, I believe we can have them on their way by first light."

I decided not to admit that I was genuinely frightened, but I think he knew in any case, for the delightful prospect of the Bane's departure made me smile, and when he saw it, he said, "That's the barber! They've been beastly nuisances to me, but worse to you, poor boy." He looked closely at my face, which had served as a target for Henry's fists a little earlier in the day. "Daresay you'll have a mouse under your right eye. Was it Henry who tried to darken your daylights?"

I nodded, fairly certain that Henry had indeed given me a black eye.

"Nasty fellow, Henry. I'll have to think of some special treat for him. But never mind that—you've got more bottom than the lot of them. Game as a pebble, you are!"

Such praise, delivered for the most part in cant expressions he had learned from one of the grooms, delighted me so much, he had to remind me to appear to be frightened.

"We must be prepared, for my father will be demanding an explanation of us soon, I'm sure."

The thought of being called before the earl was enough to restore my pallor.

"Excellent," Lucien said, his smile broadening when Fibbens appeared at the door.

"If your lordship and Master Edward would be so good as to come with me?" the young footman said, his face revealing nothing. "Your lordship's father asks that you join the other members of the family in the drawing room."

"To receive a rare trimming from my Aunt Sophia?" Lucien asked.

There was the slightest twitch at the corner of Fibbens's mouth before he answered, "I'm sure I could not say, your lordship."

As we approached the drawing room, Lucien whispered to me, "It is absolutely essential, dear Edward, that you stand as close to my father as possible."

These were daunting instructions indeed. Summoning all my courage, I did as he asked, making my way to the earl's side even as Lady Bane began to deliver herself of what promised to be a lengthy speech on the lack of manners of certain members of the younger generation. Henry, William, and Fanny, hardly exemplars of etiquette, eyed us with smug satisfaction.

"Never mind that, Sophia!" Lord Bane interrupted, loud enough to cause my mother to shrink back against the cushions of the sofa she occupied, but silencing—however briefly—his own wife.

No sooner had I taken up my position near the earl's chair than he stood, picking up a decanter and walking toward Lord Bane, as though none of the havoc in the room was actually taking place. I looked to Lucien, who subtly signaled me to stay where I was.

"Lucien," the earl said quietly, as he finished refilling Lord Bane's glass, "I don't suppose you would mind troubling yourself to give me a brief summary of the events of this evening? I am particularly interested in those which caused your cousins to fly to their mama and hold to her skirts."

Lord Bane laughed at this, even as his wife protested. As my stepfather walked back toward me, he paused, and seemed to study me for a moment before refilling his own glass and returning the decanter to the drinks tray. "Edward," he said, in the gentlest voice I had yet heard him use, "come stand here with me by the fire. My sister tells me all our chimneys smoke, but I fear I'll need to feel some warmth while Lucien recites his chilling tale."

So we moved nearer the fireplace, with its holly-draped mantel. The warmth of the fire felt good, and so did some nearly imperceptible change in my stepfather's manner toward me. Lucien began his tale, but the earl kept his eyes on me.

"As you have so often told us, Aunt Sophia," Lucien said, "you are a woman who is accustomed to finer treatment than we may afford you here at the Abbey, in part because you consider London your home, and were not often here as a child. That being so, I do not imagine the tale of the Headless Abbot has come to your ears."

"I should say not!"

Lucien turned to his father. "I thought it only fair to warn my dear cousins about him, sir."

"Your dear cousins," the earl repeated. "Just so."

Lucien again recounted the legend, this telling no less unnerving than the previous one. My mother had recourse to her vinaigrette no fewer than five times, but was an avid listener.

"Poppycock!" Lord Bane declared. "Fairy tales."

"I used to think so," Lucien said. "But if it's just a fairy tale, there ought to be a good earl in it. But there isn't, you see."

"A good earl?" his father asked, looking sharply at him.

"Yes, Father. The abbey should have been protected by a good man, someone who cared about the defenseless men who lived there. He would not have let the ruffians who descended on the abbey have their way."

"Perhaps he was otherwise occupied," the earl said.

Lucien shrugged. "Perhaps he did not see his duty."

The earl raised a brow. "Perhaps he was taking a switch to the backside of his impertinent son."

Lucien gave a little bow. "I trust in your wisdom, sir. You must have the right of it."

"Doing it much too brown, Lucien!" the earl said, but there was a twinkle in his eye, which did not abate, even as his sister upbraided him for using such terms.

"And why you talk of earls, which has nothing to do with the case, I'm sure I don't know!" Lady Bane protested. "You seem to forget, dear brother, that Lucien has frightened poor Fanny and her brothers half to death!"

"I beg your pardon, Aunt Sophia," Lucien said, when she paused to draw breath, "if I've caused you or my cousins any fright. But I do think the experience of seeing the ghost or hearing the hoofbeats is much less frightening if one is *prepared*. Imagine the shock one might feel, if he were to see a bloodstained, headless apparition floating outside his window at midnight, if he *didn't* know the legend."

"Nonsense!" Lady Bane declared. "We've spent Christmas here these past three years and more. Why have we never heard this legend before now?"

"If I may offer an explanation, Aunt Sophia?" Lucien said. "There is only one section of the Abbey which is haunted—beneath the chambers you occupy. No one is ever disturbed in any other part of the house, so we did not wish to frighten you with the tale. But since you wished to have the rooms nearest the north tower—"

"Oh! So this is my fault is it? Well, I'll tell you why we are just now hearing of your ghost, my good fellow! Because some who've never been here before this year have invented tales. Outsiders!" She rounded on me, pointing. "It's you!"

She received a chorus of approval from her offspring. I quailed before them, but then I felt the earl's large hand on my shoulder. I winced a bit as he touched a bruise, and his hand shifted slightly. At that moment, I became aware that the room had fallen silent. Everyone was looking at the earl, whose face was a mask of cold fury.

"Are you assuming that my wife's son has no place in our family?" he asked, icily. "I assure you, Sophia, he is not an outsider here. Lucien thinks of Edward as his brother, and I think of him as my son. Indeed, there are blood relations I would much liefer disown—and may."

I could hardly believe my own ears, which were soon assaulted.

"No offense meant!" Lord Bane shouted.

He had spoken loudly enough, I was sure, to startle the villagers (including the deaf vicar) from their beds, several miles away. The earl, however, appeared not to have heard him. "Perhaps, Sophia, you would find Christmas in Town more to your liking."

"La!" she said nervously, "how you do take one up! Bane is right—I meant no offense. Lucien's lurid tale has quite overset me!"

With that, she snapped at her children, telling them it was long past time for them to be abed, remonstrated with the governess for not having seen to it, and said, "Bane!" in a commanding tone that had her husband soon bidding all a good night.

"You, too, should be in bed, Edward," my mother said.

"Time we all were," my stepfather said. "Go on up, if you like, my dear. I'd like a brief word with the boys before I retire for the evening."

As soon as she had left, the earl turned to Lucien, and said in a lazy voice, "I trust we have yet to see Act III of your little drama?" Despite his tone, I could see the amusement in his eyes, and for the first time, I perceived a likeness between the earl and his son that went beyond Lucien's physical resemblance to his father.

"Tomorrow evening, sir. Tonight would be too soon. They are Banes, and being such, need time to think."

"You frighten me—far more than your telling of the legend did—though I credit you with an admirable performance."

Lucien bowed again, and said, "I had an excellent teacher."

The earl gave a sudden shout of laughter, then said, "Impossible boy!"

"Again, sir—"

"No, don't say I taught you to be such an impudent hellion, for I'll swear I did not!"

"Then I shall say nothing, sir—except—except—thank you, sir!"

The earl raised a hand in protest. " 'Tis the other way 'round, I believe." He turned back to me and gently lifted my chin. "I see I have been remiss in your education, Edward. Or perhaps—yes—Lucien, you must teach your brother to be handy with his fives." He paused, then added, "Lady Rolingbroke need not be apprised of it."

"Thank you, sir!" I said.

"Oh, I demand a high price! If you fail to rid me of the Banes, you and that makebait Lucien will be served gruel for Christmas dinner—by whatever headless monk I can find to take it to the dungeon!"

We were destined to eat a sumptuous feast. Before Lucien and I sought our beds, he enlisted my aid in creating a few hoofbeats along the secret passages near each of the Bane's bedchambers. Henry had awakened to feel a ghostly presence in the form of a room that was suddenly terribly cold, not knowing that Lucien had merely left the entrance to one of the draftiest passages open for a time.

We left it at that. The next morning, of course, we denied hearing anything like hoofbeats. When Henry swore he had felt the ghost, and not even the other members of his family related similar tales, Lucien grew thoughtful, saying, "I wonder why he would single you out?"

This made Henry go very pale, and ask again if no one else had felt a bit chilly last night.

No one had, of course. The earl went so far as to say he had rarely slept so well.

Lady Bane was perhaps made suspicious by this remark, for she gave her husband a speaking look and asked him to accompany her into the village. Henry was rather quiet that day, if a little jumpy. William, owing to the increased watchfulness of several footmen and others, did not have any chances to harm me that morning. He later confided to us that Lord and Lady Bane had found the villagers ready to repeat all the salient points of the legend, and in many cases to enlarge upon it. After hearing something of this at luncheon, the earl strode up to Lucien and me as we were on our way to the stables. "Lucien, dear boy, I take it I am going to be generous to my tenants this Boxing Day?"

"Extremely, sir," his unrepentant child replied. "But it should interest you to know that Aunt Sophia's dresser has told Bogsley that she doesn't expect the Banes to remain in this, er, 'accursed place' another night."

"Don't tell me you've enlisted my staid butler in these schemes? I would think it beneath Bogsley's dignity."

Lucien seemed to ponder before answering, "Perhaps, Father, it would be best not to inquire too closely on some matters."

"Good God!" the earl declared, and walked away, seeming shaken.

The following night, I helped again with hoofbeats, and later to make howling sounds as Lucien—and Fibbens—contrived to swing a headless "apparition" past their windows. Bogsley had recommended the village seamstress who made the monk. Each of the Banes caught no more than a fleeting glimpse of this phantom, but judging from the pandemonium which broke loose, this glimpse was more effective than a full night's haunting. The Banes, looking haggard, were on the road back to London before noon, swearing never to return to the Abbey.

The earl declared it the most delightful Christmas gift his son had ever bestowed upon him, causing my mother a great deal of puzzlement.

As we grew older, I learned how rare a gift I had found in Lucien's affection for me, and saw how infrequently he troubled himself to form friendships. He nevertheless grew into a man who was invited everywhere— and while his fortune, breeding, and rank might have guaranteed that to him in any case, there was a vast difference between the welcome Lucien was given by leading members of the *haut ton* and that afforded to others. That I benefited from my connection to him is without doubt, and was a fact decried by Lord Henry Bane, Mr. William Bane, Miss Fanny Bane, and the Dowager Lady Sophia Bane, who made no less imposing a widow than a wife. Lucien's aunt might complain all she liked about "persons who were no blood relation" enjoying "privileges above their station," but she found few who paid heed to her.

Our parents died together in a carriage accident when Lucien was but twenty-two. He succeeded to his father's dignities, and two years later, married well. His wife was a young beauty with a handsome dowry, although his own wealth precluded anyone from imagining him a fortune hunter. Lucien, unlike so many of our order, married for love.

I was myself by no means penniless, having come into an inheritance through my mother's family. Not long after Lucien wed, feeling restless, I used some of my own fortune to buy colors, and left for the Peninsular War, to see what I could do to hamper Boney's efforts in Portugal and Spain. Lucien and I exchanged letters, and although the mail was not always reliable, his correspondence made my soldier's life easier to bear. Some made me long to be home, of course. Of all of these, the most heart-rending was the one in which he told me of both the death of his wife and of the birth of his son.

It was not his way to be effusive—neither in grief nor in joy—but in this letter he wrote a litany of all the small pleasures he would miss—hearing the soft rustle of her skirts as she entered the library while he read, watching her blush at an endearment, listening to her sing softly to herself as she walked through the Abbey gardens, unaware that he was near—and I came to a new understanding of how deeply he had cared for her. Beyond that one letter, he never wrote to me again of her, though even over the great distance between us, I could sense Lucien's sadness.

But gradually, over the next two years, I began to

see that he had found a new source of joy, as well. Letter after letter described the latest news of Charles Edward Rolingbroke, my nephew and godson. Lucien clearly doted on his heir. I saved these letters, as I had every letter before, reading them again and again.

I next saw Lucien when he approached my bed in a dismal London hospital. He looked for me there after Ciudad Rodrigo. He had seen my name among the lists of wounded and used his influence to discover what had become of me. I heard someone say, "Captain, you've a visitor." I opened my eyes, and there stood Lucien, looking ridiculously worried. Delirious with fever, nevertheless I recognized him—at least for a few moments, when he seemed to me some last vision granted to me before dying. I was too weak even to speak to him, and remember nothing more than smiling foolishly at him. Neither do I remember being moved from that place, and taken to Rolingbroke House, his fashionable London residence. The quality of my care was improved immeasurably, and eventually, the fever subsided.

When at last I no longer burned alive with it, I was still weak and somewhat confused about my change of circumstance. I knew I was in Lucien's home, and fell asleep not long after a recollection came to me of Lucien arguing with a doctor, refusing to allow me to be bled. This was confirmed by the doctor when I awoke the next morning. He chuckled. "No, wouldn't let me bleed you, and offered to—how did he put it now? Oh yes, he promised to draw my own claret if I caused you to lose one more drop of yours. Well, my fine captain, I'd as soon fight Boney himself than try to cross swords with the earl." My wounds, he told me, would leave me with a few scars and a permanent limp. "But only two days ago, I tried to convince his lordship that your funeral service should be arranged, so you are in far better case than expected."

Not much later, Lucien himself came into my room, under strict orders not to make his visit a long one. I told him I did not want to burden him with the care of a lame stepbrother who was weak as a cat and not of as much use.

"I shall fetch that doctor back here," Lucien said, "and demand a return of his fee. He distinctly told me you were no longer delirious, but here you are, speaking utter nonsense!"

"Lucien—"

"No, wait! Tell me you aren't feverish, for I'm only allowed a short visit, and I shall be driven mad by your nephew if he isn't allowed to at last lay eyes on his Uncle Edward."

"He's here?" I asked.

But that question was answered by the entrance of a small boy, who, over his nurse's protests, opened the door and ran toward his father. He was the spit and image of Lucien.

"Papa!"

"Your lordship," the flustered nurse said, "I beg your pardon! I'll take him right out again."

"Oh, no, madam!" Lucien exclaimed in mock horror. "Leave him with me. My brother has seen enough warfare as it is."

She left us, and no sooner had the door closed than Charles's questions began.

Did I feel better? Yes.

Had I hurt my head? Yes, that was why I wore a bandage.

Had I hurt my leg, then, too? Yes.

Did a Frenchy hurt me? Yes.

He offered to send his father to hurt the Frenchy in return. I thanked him, but said I would prefer we all just stayed home together for a time, for I had missed my brother, and would like to become acquainted with his son.

Why was my skin so brown? A soldier spends a great deal of time in the sun.

"That will do, Master Pokenose," Lucien said, causing his son to giggle. Obediently, though, Charles ceased asking questions. He sat quietly while Lucien discussed plans for removing to the countryside. Quite against my will, I began to fall asleep. Charles brought this to his father's attention, which brought a rich laugh from Lucien. "Indeed, youngster, you are right. We'll let him rest for now."

I murmured an apology, stirring awake as I felt a small hand take my own.

"Papa says you're a great gun and we must help you to get better."

"My recovery is assured, then," I said, "but it is your papa who is the great gun."

Over the next three years, I would come to believe more and more in the truth of that statement. Fibbens was made my valet, a job that for some months involved the added duties of attending an invalid. I came to value him greatly. As my physical strength returned, though, it was Lucien and his son who would not allow me to retreat from the world.

Charles's energetic encouragement and Lucien's refusal to permit me to mope over my injuries kept me from falling into a fit of the dismals. Before long, I seldom thought so much of what I could not do, as what I could. Charles continued to delight me—I could not have been more attached to him if he had been my own boy.

On the night following Lucien's funeral, recalling my brother's life, I wondered how I would be able to comfort Charles over the days to come, when the numbness I felt now would undoubtedly wear off.

When Lucien's horse, Fine Lad, had returned riderless to the stable just three days earlier, a large group of men searched frantically for him—servants, tenants, and neighbors. It was I who found Lucien. I had followed a route he often took through the woods when he rode for pleasure and discovered his motionless form along this path. He lay pale and bleeding beneath a shady tree—a thick, broken, bloodstained branch beside him. I did my best to staunch the wound on his head, and to keep him warm, even as I shouted for help.

All along the way back to the Abbey, the men who helped me carry him on a litter, and then to place him in a wagon, recounted several of the strange riding accidents of which they had heard. It was their way, I realized later, of trying to make sense of what seemed impossible—that Lucien, an excellent horseman, would be so careless while riding among low-lying branches. I had the broken branch with me, though, to prove it, as much to myself as anyone. And I would show it to Lucien, and ask him what the devil he was about.

A fractured skull, the doctor said. Lucien never regained consciousness.

I knew the sort of blind rage that is the consort of our worst grief. I thought of burning the branch that had struck him. I thought of taking an ax to the tree, felling that which had felled him. I thought of shooting the horse.

I did none of these. Perhaps it was the horse's name that cleared my mind: Fine Lad.

Charles needed me.

That single thought cooled my rage.

Lucien's will made me Charles's guardian and trustee. I knew he did not merely want me to keep Charles's fortune safe, to simply be certain that he was sent to the best schools. I was to teach him what the Abbey meant to his family, what it meant to be the Earl of Rolingbroke, what he owed to his name, and owed to the memory of two good men who had held the same long list of titles before him. I had no fear that Charles would fail to be a credit to them—he was already so much his father's son.

That evening, sitting before the fire, remembering Lucien, I knew that I would protect my young godson with my life. As the clock struck midnight, I vowed that I would do my damnedest to keep Lucien alive in his memory.

I had no sooner made this vow than the library door flew opened, startling me. Charles, pale and tearful, ran toward me, frantically calling my name. I opened my arms to him, taking him up on my lap, and waving away the small army of concerned servants whose grasps he had eluded.

As the door to the library closed again, I tried to soothe him. "What's wrong, nipperkin?" I asked, thinking I already knew the answer.

"Papa's alive again," Charles sobbed.

"What?" I said, thinking I must have misheard him.

"Papa's alive. But he was dead, and now he scares me."

Was this some strange manifestation of a child's grief, I wondered? "What do you mean, Charles?"

The boy shivered. "I mean, I saw him. His ghost."

I sought an explanation. "You were sleeping—"

"It was not a dream!" he insisted, with a familiar obstinacy.

I hesitated, then asked, "Charles, have you been speaking to the Banes?" The odious family was here—the dowager, Henry, William, and Fanny. The Banes had insisted on sleeping in a different wing than the one they had last occupied, although Henry now pooh-poohed the ghost story, saying it was undoubtedly one of Lucien's larks.

They had arrived, clearly, not so much for the funeral as for the reading of the will, and to say they were angry with its terms is to vastly understate the matter. Had William not intervened, the dowager, it seemed, would have been carried off on the spot by an apoplexy. "It is of no use, Mama," he said. "You should have known how it would be."

The dowager continued to bemoan her faithless nephew's lack of consideration for his own family, but not quite so intensely. Nevertheless, there was enough ill-concealed venom among the Banes to recall to me my first encounter with them, and I made sure Charles was never left alone with them.

"No," Charles said now. "I don't like them."

"You are a wise young man."

"Then why don't you believe me?"

"Did I say I did not believe you? Kindly refrain from making assumptions."

"What are those?"

"Er—don't believe you know something until you're sure you do know it."

He frowned as he puzzled this out, but he had stopped crying.

"Do you know, Charles—the more I think about this, the more I'm sure there is nothing to be frightened of here. Your father loved you very much, and would never harm you."

"Yes," he said, slowly. "And I have a great many things I should like to say to him, that I have been thinking of these past few days. But one can't help but be frightened of ghosts, even good ghosts."

"No one can blame you for feeling frightened. I'm glad you came to me. I promise I will protect you, Charles. Your father asked that of me, and I gave him my word that I would."

He sat quietly with me for a time, lost in his own thoughts. He was past the age when he wanted to be carried or held, which gave me some idea of how terrified he was now. I was sure he had merely dreamed of Lucien, but I knew he did not believe this to be the case.

"Do you think he was trying to tell me something?" Charles asked.

"Perhaps he was," I said.

"What?"

I reached for a packet of fragile papers lying on the

small table next to us. "Let's see if we can guess. When I was fighting in the Peninsula, and your father and I were far away from one another, he wrote these letters to me. Would you like me to read them to you?"

He nodded, and I chose one of the letters Lucien had written about him. He was pleased and laughed at Lucien's comical descriptions of him as an infant, then asked me to read another. So we continued, until he suddenly said, "I smell smoke."

"You *have* been listening to your Aunt Sophia."

But before he could protest, I heard the shouts of the servants, and cries of "Fire!"

"We must help them put it out!" Charles said, jumping up from the chair.

I knew the same impulse, but what came quickly to mind were a series of drills that Lucien had insisted upon. I had always had the role of finding Charles in whatever room he might be in, and taking him to safety. I used to argue with Lucien, saying that a man with a pronounced limp was hardly the most suitable person to be saving his heir, but he remained stubborn on this point. Remembering my vow of hardly more than an hour before, I grabbed Charles's hand before he was out of reach. "Your lordship," I said sternly, using the form of address which he knew to be a command to be on his best behavior. "You must not run toward the fire. You must allow me to keep you safe— just as we practiced. Come now."

I saw the briefest mulish cast to his face before he relented, and allowed me to lead him out of the library. Fibbens, his face blackened with soot, was rushing down the stairs. "Oh, thank goodness!" he cried in relief. "Forgive me, Captain—we feared the young master had returned to bed! His chambers are on fire!"

"My room!" the young master wailed.

"He will tell you more when we are all safely outside," I said, more shaken by Fibbens's announcement than I cared to admit. "What of the staff and the other guests?" I asked, as we made our way.

"Everyone accounted for, sir. The fire has not spread beyond the young master's chambers. If you do not mind, I'd like to assure the others that his lordship is safe—"

"Yes, of course."

"Thank you, sir. Those who are not attempting to put out the fire should be downstairs shortly."

At the front steps, it occurred to me that we were without cloaks, and Charles was without shoes. A fault in our drills, which had taken place in summertime. There had been little snowfall of late, but it was cold. I placed my coat around Charles's small shoulders—much to his delight—and lifted him into my arms.

Soon the Banes began to join us on the front drive. Aunt Sophia was wrapped in what I recognized to be William's many-caped driving coat. She'd not had time to put on her wig, and looked a positive fright. Fanny seemed to have borrowed boots from one of her brothers, but no coat—she shivered in a rather unbecoming nightgown. Henry appeared before us still fully dressed, but rather well-to-live, as the saying goes—from his unsteady walk, I suspected he had made substantial inroads on the Abbey's wine cellars. William, too, was dressed, although from his mother's criticisms, it was clear that he had remained in the building longer than she believed safe.

"And look! Your new coat from Weston—ruined!"

The expensive coat of blue superfine was indeed smudged. "Unlike some others I could name," he sneered, looking reproachfully at Henry, "I attempted to make sure the old pile didn't burn down around my family's ears!"

Henry waved a vague hand of disinterest and stared toward the building. Smoke had stopped billowing from the window of Charles's room. I prayed that meant the fire was under control.

"Here, Fanny," William said, taking off the coat. "You wear it. You look as if you're likely to freeze to death."

But Fanny, after bestowing a grateful smile on him, proved to be her mother's daughter. "Ugh!" she said, wrinkling her nose. "It smells of smoke."

William rolled his eyes.

"*I* do not know why I allowed you to talk me into staying at this accursed place!" his mother said to him.

"I talked you into it! That's a loud one!"

"Do not use that horrid cant with me, my young man! I won't have it!"

I realized that Charles was providing an interested audience to this by-play. Still holding him, I walked a bit apart from them.

Bogsley and Fibbens appeared, bearing cloaks and blankets. Fibbens attended the Banes, while the elderly butler approached us.

"Bogsley, please tell me what has happened!" Charles said.

"I am pleased to say, your lordship, that the fire is out, and little damage done. Your dear father had made preparations, you know, and the staff responded in a way that would make him proud, if I do say so myself."

"The next time I see him, I shall tell him how well you did," Charles said.

Bogsley, that most self-controlled of all God's creatures, did not blink an eye, but I heard the slightest catch in his voice as he answered, "Thank you, your lordship. I pray that will not be for some time yet."

"One never knows," Charles said.

Worried over the effect these words seemed to have on the butler, I quickly said, "You've given us good tidings indeed, Bogsley. I trust none of the staff took any hurt?"

"None whatsoever, sir."

"Please thank everyone for saving our home," Charles said, then turned to me. "Perhaps Cook could give a jam tart to each of them."

"Yes, or whatever other treat might be managed," I said, pleased with his show of manners, but hard-pressed to maintain my gravity.

"Your lordship is very kind," Bogsley said.

"Thank you so much for the cloak, Bogsley," I said. "I do not think his lordship intends to return my coat."

At this Charles laughed, and we made our way indoors.

Only the promise of a jam tart convinced Charles to spend a few moments with Fibbens, while I inspected the damage. The hallway reeked of smoke, but the flames had been confined to one portion of Charles's room.

"I'm afraid his lordship won't be able to sleep in here this evening, sir," Bogsley said.

"You remain the champion of understatement, Bogsley." Charles's bed had been reduced to ashes.

"Thank you, sir. It would seem that a candle or lamp was left burning on his night stand, and ignited the bed curtains."

"Except that being something of a little lion, his lordship does not suffer a fear of the dark, as some children do. He *prefers* a dark room, and has never required any sort candle or lamp to be lit in his room. And in fact, he closes his bed curtains about him, to keep out the light."

"Yes, sir."

"I looked in on his lordship earlier this evening. He was sound asleep. There was no candle burning in here at that time. I brought one in with me, and used it to see my way out. Has anyone else been in here this evening?"

"Until we were engaged in extinguishing the fire, no sir. I should say, no member of the *staff* entered this room since his lordship called for you, Captain Edward. But by that time, his lordship was rather determined to find you on his own."

"And the Banes?"

"I'm afraid I couldn't say, sir—not just at this moment."

I knew he would discreetly question the Banes's servants. After a moment's silence, I said, "I will speak plainly to you, Bogsley. I am concerned for his lordship's safety."

"Understandably so, sir."

"I will do my best to resolve this matter as soon as possible. In the meantime—"

"You may rely on me, sir—indeed, on all of us."

"For which I'm grateful. Please have a truckle-bed placed in my room until we can make other arrangements. I need not add that I would prefer we do not alarm his lordship with our concern."

I thanked him again and fetched my nephew from the kitchen, where he was, as usual, being cosseted past redemption.

Charles, pleased that we would be sharing a room, nevertheless protested my plan to place him in my bed, while I slept on the truckle-bed.

"But Charles," I said, "there are no bed-curtains on the truckle-bed, and as you can see, there is a great deal of moonlight tonight."

He had no argument against this and thanked me politely before allowing me to tuck him in. "But keep the curtains open just a bit, if you please. Then I shall know you are here, keeping me safe." So much, I thought, for hiding our concern.

I lay awake on the truckle-bed, listening to his breathing settle into the rhythms of sleep. My feet suddenly felt a little cold, and then I heard a voice whisper, "Well done, Master Quakeboots."

I sat bolt upright. By the light of the moon I could make him out, a faint but definite image of my dead brother, sitting at the foot of my bed.

My heart pounding, I opened my mouth to let out a cry, but I was frozen with fright.

"Please don't," he said. "I frightened Charles so badly early this evening, I don't think I can forgive myself if I do so again. I cannot tell you how awful it is, Edward, to become a specter of horror to those you love. It nearly puts me in sympathy with Aunt Sophia, parading about without her wig."

I felt a giddy sensation, but stopped myself short of laughing aloud. "By God, it *is* you!" I whispered.

"Lord Shivershanks, at your service." He gave his familiar little bow.

"Oh, Lucien, how I've missed you already! How shall we contrive to get along without you? Whatever possessed you to ride so carelessly?"

He gave me a look as cold as the winter night. "My dear Edward, do not be a sapskull! Would I have endangered my life—to say nothing of the future of that precious boy sleeping next to you? Carelessly toss away my days with him? When have you ever known me to take foolish chances since his arrival?"

"Exactly my thoughts, Lucien, truly—"

"Yes, I heard you say so not long before I—well, I haven't completely departed now, have I?"

"How good it is to be able to speak to you again! But—is it terrible for you?"

"Not in the least—well, no, that isn't true. There are things that one longs for, and can never have in this state, so one certainly feels a desire to—to get on with it, shall we say? As much as I am loath to leave you—and I promise you, I did my best to stay—now I feel something like a traveler who has harnessed his horses, placed his trunks on the coach, and climbed within—but sits in his own drive."

"Not—not unsure of his destination!"

He laughed, and said, "Hardly gratifying that you have doubts! But you may be at ease on that score. I'm quite curious about the place, but my departure has been delayed. I gather I have some unfinished business here, and it isn't difficult to see what it is. First, we must find my murderer, for that person is threatening my son's life, now that I am—supposedly—out of the way."

"Your murderer!" I said blankly.

"My dear Edward, have you not been attending?"

"The branch—"

"Was off the tree before it struck my head."

"But I saw the place on the tree where the branch had broken off. It was not cut clean, as it would have been if cut off the tree with an ax."

"I'm not saying my murderer was stupid. I'm only saying that the branch was already broken off the tree before it was applied—with some force—to my head."

"Then how—"

"I'm not sure of all the particulars, but I'll tell you what I do know. Examine Fine Lad, if you would, please—why are you looking so pale? You aren't going to faint on me, are you?"

"The horse—I almost had him shot."

He studied me for a moment, then said, "If I could have found a way to leave you without grief, Edward, I would have."

I could not speak.

"I take it the poor creature has not been sent to his equine reward?"

"No, I decided that I needed to think of Charles, and not of killing horses or felling trees."

"Dependable Edward. I could not have left Charles in better hands. Still, what impressive vengeance you planned on my behalf! I'm touched, truly. Now—let us channel that determination toward saving my son."

"Yes. Tell me more about what happened to you—and your horse."

"I was about to slow him, knowing we were coming up to that tree, when something slowed him for me—rather abruptly. Without the least warning, Fine Lad—who is quite sure-footed—stumbled hard near that tree. I flew from his back, landing flat on my face, the wind knocked out of me—disgraceful, but please note that I was still holding fast to the reins. I slowly raised myself to my hands and knees—a bit unsteadily—when suddenly a cloaked figure stepped out and knocked me senseless with that blasted branch. Hurt like the very devil—briefly."

"A cloaked figure?"

"I'm afraid he was off to one side—the better to swing that branch, I suppose. All I saw were a pair of men's boots—rather expensive Hessians, if I'm any judge—and the front of a large, black cloak. I was struck down before I saw a face, but I'd lay odds my attacker was wearing a mask."

I considered this, and said, "Can you travel from the Abbey grounds?"

"I'm not sure. I can move within the Abbey, and at least as far as where you were standing tonight. I'm rather new at this," he added apologetically.

"Were you in Charles's room when the fire started?"

"No, although—it's the strangest thing, Edward. I was merely looking in on him, watching him sleep, when I felt this urgent need to appear to him, even though I knew it would scare him—as if it were so vital to awaken him, I could not remain hidden."

"It was vital," I said. "Had he not come to me in the library, he might have perished in that bed."

"And Henry Bane would have become the Earl of Rolingbroke."

"Yes. But it was William whose coat smelled of smoke and showed signs of being singed."

"Hmm. How disappointing. William has actually spoken kindly to me once or twice in the past few years. But then, he needed to borrow money." He sighed. "He's not immediately in line for the title, but I suppose if two Rolingbrokes could be disposed of, Henry might have a short tenure as well."

"Who are you talking to?" a child's voice asked.

I looked in some dismay at Charles, peering at me sleepily from the bed. I glanced toward Lucien, but he had disappeared.

"Myself, Charles."

"That's a loud one," he said, yawning.

"I beg your pardon?" I said, and thought I heard a ghostly chuckle near my ear.

But Charles had fallen asleep again, and though I whispered Lucien's name, he did not reappear that night.

Charles was still sleeping peacefully when I bestirred myself just before dawn the next morning. I awakened Fibbens, who gladly kept watch over him while I went to the stables. I went down the row of stalls until I came to that of Lucien's favorite, Fine Lad. An old groom was with the big dark bay, applying fomentations to its legs.

"I'm afraid he'll be scarred, sir," the old man said, showing me the horizontal cuts which neatly crossed the front of Fine Lad's forelegs. "But he should be right as rain otherwise."

"Those wounds—could they have led to the late earl's injuries?"

"I wondered about it, sir, and thought p'haps he'd been tripped up, like. But then there was that branch, so I figgered our Fine Lad here hurt himself on the way home."

"Tell me—what do you mean, tripped up?"

"It's an old bad 'un's trick, sir—they puts a rope across the road."

"But the earl would have seen such a rope."

"Beggin' your pardon, but no, sir. The way it works is, Mr. Thief finds a place near a tree, like, and ties th' rope around its trunk. Then he lays the rope across th' road, and covers it with leaves, so it's hidden. Along comes a fine gentleman like our lordship, and Mr. Thief waits until he's near abreast of 'im, and yanks hard as hell—beggin' your pardon—he pulls it tight, see, and the horse can't stop nor mebbe even knows what's hit 'im, and while all's confusion, he coshes th' fine gentleman—if he ain't already knocked in the cradle by the fall. Then he robs him, and that's that."

"How do you know of this 'tripping up'? Has this ever happened near here before?"

"Oh, not near here, sir. But I rememory it did happen to the earl's—beggin' your pardon—the late earl's uncle."

"Lord Alfred Bane?"

"Yes, sir. 'Is lordship's groom told me of it. Said that when 'is lordship were a young man, he was served just such a nasty trick, and took an awful blow to the side of 'is brainbox—and that's how he went deef in one ear, which is why 'is lordship was forever shouting. I used to hate it when that man came near our horses—his late lordship, I mean, no disrespect intended—but y'see, ours t'weren't used to all that shoutin' and carryin' on. So his groom tells me what happen'd t'him, and tells me that the robbers got to look no how anyways, 'cause Lord Bane hadn't more 'n a few shillings on 'im, whilst they were caught and hanged, which is what they deserv'd."

I rode my own horse back to the place in the woods where I had found Lucien. I searched for a likely place for an ambush, and found it just a few feet away. I did not find a rope, but one tree bore a mark on its trunk, a line that might have been made by a thin rope being pulled taut—and within the bark near that line, I found strands of bristly fiber, as from a cord or rope.

I searched on the side of the path directly opposite, as I might have searched for signs of an enemy's camp during the war. My search was rewarded—I discovered a spot with a good view of the path, where sticks and leaves had been crushed. It was a place near a fallen log where fragments of brown shell told me that someone had eaten walnuts while they waited for the sound of an approaching rider, a place where someone's boots had made marks in the soft, damp earth.

I spent a little time also in studying the tree which had supposedly caused Lucien's injury, and the place where the branch had broken off. I rode my horse slowly down the path, halting in front of the tree, which allowed me an even better view of the point of breakage.

Back at the Abbey, I again examined the branch. I

spoke to Bogsley and two other servants before I went to my room and changed out of my riding clothes—which had become somewhat soiled during my explorations. I cleaned up in time to join Charles for breakfast. By then, most of the family was in the breakfast room. Lady Bane—wearing a purple turban—declared that the previous evening's disturbance had quite ruined her appetite.

I thought Charles might make some remark about this, as her plate was quite full, but he seemed lost in his own thoughts, not even responding to her lecture about young children never being allowed to dine with their elders at Bane House. At one point, he looked up and smiled and winked at me, just as his father might have done. But before I could respond with more than an answering smile, my attention was drawn back to Lady Bane, who asked why I was smiling, and if I thought fires in the middle of the night were amusing.

"Mother!" William said desperately, "Your breakfast grows cold. Do try to eat something."

She ignored him. She had other complaints to make, and ended her lengthy list of criticisms by saying, "We are leaving immediately after breakfast, Edward, and I cannot tell you what a relief it will be!"

"I'm sure it defies description," I said.

She eyed me in an unfriendly manner, but was distracted when William said, "I am staying—if it will not be an imposition, Edward?"

"Staying!" Lady Bane thundered. "Why?"

"To better acquaint myself with my cousin," he said.

"Edward is not your cousin!"

"I meant Cousin Charles," William said, then added, "And Edward, too, of course."

Henry, who entered the room at just that moment, said, "An excellent notion, William! I believe I will join you."

William seemed displeased, but said nothing. There was no opportunity for him to speak. Lady Bane found their plans extremely objectionable. The matter was decided when Fanny said, "I'll leave with you, Mother."

It was decided because Lady Bane, ever contrary, said, "No, I'll not have it said that I was backward in any attention due to my family. We'll all stay."

Into the awkward silence which met this decision came Charles's voice. "I wish to discuss a private matter with Uncle Edward," he said, then frowning, added, "If you will excuse us, please?"

He stood, then took my hand, and led me to the library. He closed the doors, then said, "All right, Papa!"

"Excellent, youngster!" Lucien said. "My son, as you can see, Edward, is a stout-hearted fellow."

"I've known that for some time now," I said.

"He whispered to me during breakfast!" Charles said gleefully. "He was with me while you were out riding this morning."

"And Fibbens?"

"I believe he has recovered from his initial shock," my brother said. "I've asked him to break it gently to Bogsley."

" 'Zooks, Lucien! Is this wise?"

"I'd prefer they knew, rather than to come across me, er—accidentally. Fibbens will be here shortly to take Charles through one of the passages to the servants' quarters. Charles will be my ambassador."

"That means I'm going to tell them *I'm* not scared of Papa, so then they won't be either. I'm helping."

"Yes," I said, "you are."

As soon as Fibbens—amazingly at home with members of the spirit world, it seemed to me—had led Charles from the room, I told Lucien what I had learned. He listened thoughtfully.

"I took another look at the branch this morning," I said. "I realized that the bloodstains were on a section of the branch that you could not have struck with your head while riding. The bloodstains were on a part of the branch that was too close to the trunk of the tree—close to where it broke off from the trunk."

"A part of the branch much thicker, I suppose, than the section I would have struck if I *had* ridden into it."

"Yes. The Banes undoubtedly heard the story of their father's encounter with ruffians many times. And of the persons currently staying or working at the Abbey, only the Banes and their personal servants would not know that Charles prefers his chambers to be darkened."

"It could be one of the Banes's servants, I suppose," Lucien said, and I did not miss the note of hopefulness in his voice.

"No servant would gain from your death, Lucien. I do not like the idea of scandal in the family any more than you do, but Charles is very young, and by the time he is in society, this will be long forgotten."

Lucien gave a bitter laugh. "Murder is unlikely to pass so quickly from even the *haut ton*'s collection of shallow minds. But for now, our first thoughts must be for Charles's safety."

"Yes."

"So it is a Bane," he said. "I do not believe it was Lady Bane—she would have made sure her wig was on."

I laughed. "Nor can I picture her waiting patiently in the woods, or wearing Hessians."

"All well and good. But now what?"

"I'm not certain which of the three 'thatchgallows,' as you once called them, it is."

"Surely not Fanny?"

"I would have ruled her out, until you told me of the boots. She was wearing a pair of them last night—and William and Henry were each already wearing their own. She's strong. And remember how she used to spy on us?"

"Yes. But what would she have to gain?"

"I don't know. Does she bear you any grudge?"

"Nothing to signify." He couldn't exactly blush, but he was obviously embarrassed.

I raised a brow. "She had a *tendre* for you?"

"She believed we ought to marry. It was certainly not out of affection—it was a stupid idea placed in her head by her pushing mama. Aunt Sophia also tried to persuade my father that I should marry Fanny, but he was opposed—said he had seen at least three bad results of a marriage of first cousins. Alfred Bane was their first cousin, you will remember. Aunt Sophia was quite insulted, and nothing was said for years, but shortly after he died—let us say I told them I would respect my father's wishes on the matter. When I became a widower, I almost thought Fanny would raise the subject again, but I think the notion of being stepmama to Charles put an end to her pursuit. Now—

let's look at Henry and William, then. William's coat reeked of smoke."

"According to Fibbens, William did attempt to help put out the fire. But since he was not trained in one of your drills, he was more a nuisance than a help, and Bogsley—in his inimitable Bogsley way, persuaded him to leave before he caused harm. Still—how did he find out about the fire so much sooner than the others?"

"And Henry?"

"Supposedly drunk."

"Supposedly?"

"Oh, several bottles of your finest port are missing."

"Charles's port! But you sound as if you doubt he drank them."

"I'm not sure. I find myself wondering where the empty bottles are, and why, at breakfast this morning, he did not appear to be suffering any ill-effects of such a binge."

"A veteran drinker might be able to manage both the bottles and the morning."

"True. And since I have long avoided the Banes, I have no idea if our cousin is a souse or abstemious."

"Which leaves us where we started."

"Do you know, this morning I found myself thinking like a soldier for the first time in a long time."

"Meaning?"

"We must use strategy, Lucien. And I believe we would do well to take the offensive, rather than wait for the murderous Bane to make another attempt on Charles's life."

"Ah!" he said, smiling. "You want to set a trap."

"Yes. We will each have a role—including Charles.

Do you suppose, dear Lucien, that you could play the part of a headless monk?"

Charles proved to be his father's equal as an actor. He staged a perfect tantrum, with Fibbens providing able support, just outside the morning room, where Henry had settled into a chair before the fire to read a newspaper. Lucien told us that was how he was occupied just before Act I, Scene I. Five minutes or so later, a child's voice was heard in the hallway just outside the morning room door.

"There's no such thing as ghosts!" Charles said angrily.

"Perhaps not, your lordship, but the north tower is dangerous. Your father meant to undertake repairs but—"

"*I'm* not afraid. It's *my* treasure!"

"Not so loud, please, your lordship!" Fibbens said, knowing perfectly well that Henry Bane was undoubtedly pressing his ear to the door.

"Uncle Edward knows how to find it." Charles declared. "We're going treasure hunting!"

"Not with a houseful of guests, your lordship. It would be—er, impolite."

That was my cue. "Charles, Charles! Are you talking that treasure nonsense again?" I asked. After a brief pause, I said, "Fibbens, I believe I will need my heavier cloak—and his lordship will need his own as well."

"Yes, sir," Fibbens said, and treading heavily, left the hallway.

"Charles, what have I told you about the treasure?"

"That we will find it tonight, because you promised Papa you would show me where it is."

"Yes. And what else?"

"Not to tell the Banes. But Fibbens isn't the Banes."

"Fibbens is entirely trustworthy, but you never know who might be listening. So please don't discuss it with anyone else. Now, here's Fibbens with our cloaks. Have you your gloves? Excellent. Let's go for our walk."

Two slight variations on this performance were given—once for the benefit of Fanny and once for William.

Only Lady Bane seemed to enjoy a normal appetite at dinner that evening. Charles kept looking conspiratorially at me, which required no real acting.

Lucien's role was proving the most difficult. To our dismay, he could not move objects, and any attempt to dress him in something other than the riding clothes he had been wearing on the day of his accident met with utter failure. Bogsley had unearthed the old headless abbot—the one the village seamstress had manufactured for that long ago Christmas haunting. It was losing its stuffing and looked a little aged, but we only needed the robe itself. However, when Lucien tried to put it on, it simply fell to the ground.

Making the best of what he could do, he practiced materializing, and soon had the knack of partial materialization. "I do so hate the prospect of being dead from the neck up," he said, when he had managed to appear before us without a head. Charles, who had been rather thrilled with our story of swinging the "headless monk" past the Banes's windows, asked the housekeeper if it might be possible to repair it. She stuffed a few pillows into the old costume, and our headless abbot had yet another round of life. Before falling asleep, Charles enjoyed playing with this large, if rather gruesome doll.

"Boys is all alike," was the housekeeper's assessment, with a nod toward Lucien and me.

At ten o'clock that evening, I awakened Charles from his brief slumbers. Bundled up in warm clothing, we carried shielded lanterns as we went through one of the secret passages to the north tower. The tower was built into the rise on which the Abbey stood. Perhaps at one time, it had indeed towered over the castle that had been here, but very little of the castle remained. Now the only apparent entrance to the tower was near the top of it—the tower was more akin to a well than a tower—more of it was reached by descending a staircase than by climbing. It was dank, musty smelling, and of no practical use.

I knew of no Rolingbroke who would dream of tearing it down.

After the treasure story had been spread about, Fibbens, several footmen, and other servants had taken turns keeping an eye on the Banes. None of them had yet been seen at the only tower entrance—the only entrance they would know of. In addition to it, there were two means of reaching the tower by secret passage. The one we were in ended on a sturdy, wide, stone platform, about halfway up (or down, as it seemed) the tower. Above us, a relatively new wooden staircase led to the tower entrance, off one of the Abbey hallways. Below us, at the foot of a crumbling stone staircase, was the other. As boys, Lucien and I had explored it, half-hoping, half-dreading we'd encounter the Headless Abbot. We found damp stones and little else.

Charles and I waited in relative comfort, hidden from view, our lantern shielded. We soon knew who the first of our arrivals would most likely be—Lucien came to report that within a few minutes of one another, Henry and Fanny had each softly knocked at the door to my room, and peered inside. They had then hurried back to their own rooms.

But it was William who opened the door at the top of the stairs, carrying a candle. He had opened the door and was halfway down the stairs when the door opened a second time. He turned to see Fanny.

"What on earth are you doing here?" he asked her.

"I might ask the same of you."

"I'm looking for Henry. Do you know where he is?"

"I haven't the vaguest. Where are Edward and the brat?"

In the darkness of our hiding place, I laid a finger to Charles's lips. He nodded his understanding.

"How should I know?"

"I should have known it was all a Banbury tale," she said.

"What are you talking about?"

"Don't try to gammon me, dear brother. You're here looking for the treasure, too!"

"I'm not worried about any treasure—"

"Not worried about any treasure! That's a loud one! You who've been punting on River Tick for I don't know how long!"

"If Mama could hear you using such terms—"

"Mama is sound asleep. Go on, deny that you're one step ahead of the bailiff."

"All right, I deny it. I'm not in debt. I've come about—thanks to Cousin Lucien."

"What!"

"I never told you or Henry, but it's true. He helped me, Fanny."

"Why you?"

"Because he cared about the family, you bacon-brain! Wasn't just the money—he talked to me. Made me think, I tell you. So if anyone is planning any further mischief around here, they'll have to come through me. I was too late for Lucien, and last night, I was sure I was too late to help Charles. But this time I've caught you, and I tell you I won't allow it!

"Help Charles? Mischief? What on earth are you talking about?"

"My horse is in the stall next to Fine Lad. I think you know what that means."

"That he's eating his head off at his lordship's expense."

"Fanny!"

She eyed him malevolently. "Enough of your nonsense, William. Let me by. Edward and the brat will be down here any minute—probably working their way through the secret passage now."

"Secret passage!" William said. "What secret passage?"

"The place is full of them. Don't you remember me telling you that when we were here that last Christmas?"

William frowned. "No."

"Well, maybe I told Henry, then. Which is of no importance in any case! Move off this staircase before I have to shove you off!"

"Touch me, and I'll tell Mama that nothing pleases

her spinster daughter so much as to dress up like a man and ride astride!"

"Oh! You won't be alive to tell her! They'll be burying you next to Lucien!"

"*Now!*" I heard Lucien say, and I pulled the shield off the lantern.

The sudden light caught the attention of the two Banes. But it was Lucien who caused William to give out a blood-curdling scream.

Charles clung to me, apparently more frightened by the scream than anything that had gone before.

"Lord Almighty!" Fanny said. "You frightened the life right out of me. What's gotten into you! You'll bring the whole house down on us!"

William, the color gone from his face, pointed a shaking hand toward Lucien.

"What?" Fanny said. "Speak up, now!"

"The Headless Abbot."

"Headless Abbot! I don't see any Headless Abbot! It's just a light coming from one of those passages I told you about."

"Don't you see him?" William cried. "In riding clothes!"

"Are you back to giving me trouble over that? What's it to you if I find men's clothes more sensible for riding?"

Lucien tried moving closer to her. But while William swayed on his feet, Fanny was oblivious to him.

"William?" she said. "Are you feeling quite the thing?"

In frustration, Lucien materialized completely.

"Lucien!" William said, and fainted. Unfortunately, he was still on the stairs when this happened. Lucien tried to make a grab for him, but William fell right through him, tumbling down to the ledge.

Now Fanny screamed, but she obviously still could not see my brother.

"Fibbens, please take his lordship to safety," I said, over Charles's protests. "Ask Bogsley to bring some men with a litter to me." And picking up a lantern, I limped out as quickly as I could to the landing, where William lay in a heap.

"Edward!" Fanny called, hurrying down the stairs and straight through Lucien without so much as a blink, "Oh, help him, Edward!"

She stood nervously watching me. William made a groaning sound, and opened his eyes. "Edward?" he said dazedly. "Was it you all along?"

He then caught sight of Lucien standing behind me, though, and fainted once again.

I did my best to make him more comfortable. "Help will be here soon, Fanny," I said.

"He's broken his arm," Lucien said, "but I don't think he has any more serious injuries. Why do you suppose he could see me, but she can't?"

"I don't understand it," I said.

Fanny, thinking I spoke to her, said, "Well! I understand it! It's all because of Lucien's stupid story about the monk. He thought he saw the ghost. Just your lantern light, I daresay."

We heard a sound then, a faint cracking noise from below.

Fanny's face grew pale. "The abbot!" she said weakly.

"Henry," I called, "are you down there in the dark eating walnuts?"

A long laugh echoed up the tower.

"Henry!" Fanny exclaimed.

"Get help," I said to Lucien.

"I'll stay here, thank you," Fanny replied. "Besides, you said help is already on the way."

"Oh it is, dear Fanny, it is!" Henry said, lighting a lantern. He started up the stone stairs. "Where's Charles?"

Lucien made a wild banshee sound, and swooped toward Henry. Nothing.

"Never mind the brat," Fanny said impatiently. "Here's your brother broken to bits!"

"I wouldn't trouble yourself too much over William, Fanny." Henry said. "He discovered my little plan, so I think it's best if the next accident concerning an earl has something to do with trying to save my brother. Edward and Charles make a valiant, combined effort. Alas, it will be unsuccessful."

"Will no one talk sense to me?" Fanny asked.

"Your brother Henry wants to be an earl," I said. "So he murdered Lucien—right, Lucien?"

"Right."

But Henry laughed and said, "Don't tell me you think you can try that ghost business on me at this age, Edward! Now where's that treasure? I warn you, I'm armed."

"You'll never own the Abbey's treasure," I said. "The Abbey's treasure then, as it is now, was in the good men who have lived here—Lucien, and his father, and Charles."

"Henry," Fanny said, "tell me you didn't harm Lucien!"

"Lucien? Oh, not just Lucien. Don't forget his

father and his ninnyhammer of a stepmother—you didn't think that carriage overturned by chance?" I heard the sound of rock falling, and Henry said, "When I am earl, I shall have these steps repaired."

"You'll never be earl!" Lucien vowed.

I heard a commotion in the passageway. Fibbens's voice was calling desperately, "Your lordship, no!"

Suddenly a white, headless figure with a blood-stained cassock came barreling onto the landing. Fanny, who did not see me grab hold of the small boy who carried it, let out the fourth scream to assault my ears in nearly as many minutes.

Lucien grabbed the pillow ghost, and went flying off the landing. Literally. Previously unable to support it, this time—perhaps somehow strengthened by his need to protect Charles—he was able to make the Headless Abbot billow impressively, and to aim it directly at Henry Bane. Henry fired his pistol at it, but the stuffed costume came at him inexorably, and knocked him from the stone stairs. His fall was harder than William's, and fatal.

I called to Lucien, but he had disappeared.

Two weeks later, William, recovered enough to be moved, left with his sister and the much quieter dowager for Bane House. They wanted to be home in time for Christmas, which was drawing near. William and his sister were getting along fairly well by then—as we all were—and none of us told the dowager about her daughter's clothing preferences. Although a scandal of a far more serious nature had been avoided, both Henry's duplicity and his death had left Lady Bane shaken.

But even with the Banes gone and the immediate crisis over, I was feeling dismal, as was Charles. One night he came to the library at midnight, upset—not because he saw a ghost, but because it had been so long since he had seen one. I tried to explain his father's traveling coach analogy, but Charles wanted that coach to return. "At least for visits," he said tearfully.

I took out the packet of letters again, and read to him—this time, the letter Lucien had written to me on the death of his wife.

"I used to be able to picture her so clearly after she was gone," a familiar voice said. "To feel her watching over Charles and me, sharing our joys. Do you know, I believe I now know why Fanny and Henry couldn't see me, but you who've loved me can?"

"Papa!" Charles cried out.

"Yes, my boy, I'm back—for a visit."

Gradually, over the years, we saw less and less of him. By the time Charles had grown into a man, it was no longer necessary to trouble Lucien to be our ghost. By then, we knew how to recall his spirit in other ways— through fond remembrance, and the knowledge that we can never be truly parted from those we love.

And that, I've come to believe, is the true spirit of Christmas.

DEVOTION

J ORDY!" Ralph Kendall bellowed.

When homicide detective Frank Harriman arrived, Kendall had been watching the Cartoon Network—a *Bugs Bunny* episode. Kendall had opened the door with a smile. The minute Frank explained why he was there, though, Kendall had grown serious, and turned the set off.

The man was broad-shouldered and tall, only an inch or so shorter than Frank's own six-four. He was wearing a white T-shirt and shorts that barely met over his middle. His face and arms were sunburned, and his blond hair was thinning. His eyes were blue and—before Frank had told him of his neighbor's death—full of laughter.

"Jordy!" he called again. "You get down here right now, you hear me?"

An upstairs bedroom door opened—no more than

a crack. "Coming!" a young man called down in an exasperated voice, then shut the door again.

"Teenagers," his father said on a sigh. "He was out all night, didn't get home until God knows when—you have any children, Detective Harriman?"

Frank Harriman shook his head. "No, Mr. Kendall, I don't. About the Toller boy—"

"Poor kid. I guess Lexie's an orphan now, isn't he?" Kendall said.

Harriman thought he would feel relieved if that turned out to be the worst of eight-year-old Lexington Toller's troubles.

"Maybe for the best, though," Kendall said, before Frank could reply. "I never did like Victor Toller," he said now. "I can't say I'll miss him. Guy was a jerk. Still, murder . . . I mean, you think he was robbed or something?"

"We're not certain, but we don't think so."

"So some maniac is running around in my neighborhood?"

"That's unlikely. There was no sign of forced entry."

"Well, Toller, he was a specialist at pissing people off, so who knows. I sure hope nothing has happened to Lexie, though. He's a cute little kid. Real quiet. Shy. Can't ever get two words out of him at a time. I guess the aunt will get Lexie after all—say, wait a minute! Did you check with her?"

"He isn't with Sarah Crane," Frank said. "We've checked."

Kendall frowned, then turned toward the stairs. "Jordy!" he called again.

"When you said Ms. Crane would 'get Lexie after all,' " Frank asked, "what did you mean?"

"Oh, she's been trying to get custody of the kid for about a year now. Lexie's mother has been dead for four years or so, and I guess she was on the outs with her folks—they didn't like Toller. Sarah told us she didn't even know her sister had died, and that it took her a while to track down Toller and the kid."

"It seems you know her fairly well?"

"Sure, because Gabe—my youngest boy—and Lexie are friends. My wife is always trying to fatten that kid up, too. I keep telling her he's stronger than he looks—you ought to see him play ball with Jordy and Gabe. Mary doesn't listen to me though—Lex comes over to see Gabe, and she fixes him lunch or a snack."

"So you've met his aunt—"

"Oh, gosh, I let myself get blown off course there, didn't I? Yes, we know her. One day, Sarah comes over to pick him up, and we all get to talking. Nice woman. And I tell you, even though it took her a while to locate him, there isn't anything she wouldn't do for that boy."

"She sees a lot of him?"

"Well, at first, yes. Toller liked the idea of someone taking the kid off his hands for a few hours. But then she started talking about having Lexie live with her, and the two of them have been—had been—at war ever since. And I can't say I blame Toller for being mad at her. Jordan's mother died when he was just two, and if my first wife's sister ever tried to take him away from me—well, he's an adult now, isn't he?"

"Yes. About Ms. Crane—"

Kendall was not to be hurried, though. "Mary, my wife—she's my second wife. Gabe is my son by this marriage, but long before he came along, Mary loved Jordy like he was her own. Even adopted him. And I think having a little brother like Gabe makes Jordan more patient with younger kids. But that wasn't what you asked about, was it?"

"Even though Toller was angry with her," Frank asked, "did Ms. Crane still visit Lex?"

"Oh, yes. I thought I saw her over there last night."

From interviews with other neighbors, Frank already knew that Sarah Crane had visited Toller the previous evening, and that she had argued loudly with her brother-in-law. But he asked, "About what time was that?"

"Oh, I guess it was about six-thirty that she came by. It was getting dark, and I went out to call Gabe in. She was already there, helping Lex carry his bat and glove." He frowned for a moment.

"What's wrong?"

"Oh—just trying to make sure I had that time right. But that's right. About six-thirty."

"Gabe is Lex's age?"

"Yes, they're in the same class at school. Not that you'd know it if they were standing side-by-side. Lex is kind of shrimpy, you know? Gabe's taller. I wish he was here. Mary will be bringing him home from his Little League game in about an hour or so, if you can wait."

Wondering if he had been going house-to-house when a trip to the local ballpark would have done the trick, he asked, "Is Lex on the Little League team?"

"Hell, no. Toller doesn't let that poor kid do anything!" Kendall said in disgust. "And he loves baseball. Toller tends to—uh, take naps in the late afternoon. Works early in the morning, gets off about two, and—well, not to mince words, he drinks. There. I've said it. So if Toller tied one on, which was more often than not, Lex would sneak out and play street ball with the other kids. Wasn't so hot at it at first, but Jordan talked them into letting the kid play, and he's darned good at it now. Got a home run last night, Gabe said."

"I'll probably still be in the area when your wife gets back, so if you don't mind—"

He heard the creak of stairs and looked up to see a tall young man coming toward them. Jordan Kendall had just turned eighteen, according to the neighbors, but Frank thought he looked older. He wore jeans and a tank top, and was barefoot. He was a younger, more handsome version of his father. He had dark circles under his blue eyes, but those eyes were watchful. He rubbed a hand over his short-cropped hair.

"Welcome to the land of the living, Sleeping Beauty," Kendall said to him, then turned to Frank. "Detective Harriman, this is Jordan."

"Detective?" Jordan's eyes widened. "What's going on?"

"We're trying to locate one of your neighbors, Lexington Toller. Can you tell me when you last saw him?"

He shrugged. "Lex? Last night, I guess. Is he in trouble?"

"His dad has been murdered, Jordy," Mr. Kendall said.

"Murdered?" He looked to Frank. "Someone murdered Mr. Toller?"

"Yes. We're investigating that, but at the moment

our first concern is for Lexington. What time was it that you saw him?"

"I don't remember—evening, I think. Maybe six or seven o'clock, something like that. I waved to him when he was going into his house. His aunt was over there."

Frank asked him a few questions about what the younger boy had been wearing, if he had seen anyone else at the house, when he had last talked to Lex. His answers fit those he had heard from others: Lex Toller had been wearing jeans and a white T-shirt, his aunt had been at the house, and he had last spoken to him when they had been playing softball in the street. Jordan had been the umpire for a game played by the younger kids.

"Do you have any idea where he might go if he was scared?" Frank asked.

"No. I mean, you might ask my brother. He hangs out with him. To me, he's just a little pest—you know, always tagging along."

"Jordan!" Mr. Kendall said, frowning. "Lexie—"

"He's okay, but he's Gabe's friend. You should ask Gabe."

"Thanks, I will. Can you name any of his other friends?"

Jordan shrugged. "He's kind of shy. Ask Gabe." He looked to his father. "Can I go now? I have a bunch of stuff I gotta do."

Kendall looked to Frank. "Sure," Frank said.

Frank watched the teenager speculatively as he hurried out of the house. He turned back to Kendall. "Did you know Mr. Toller's wife?"

"Oh, gosh, that's been what—three, four years ago

now? Barely knew her then—just to nod to. Skinny blonde. Didn't come out of the house much. Guess she was sick most the time." Kendall shifted on his feet, then said, "I'm sorry about Jordy being so—abrupt, I guess you'd call it. Teenagers, you know, sometimes they're scared and don't want to show it. I know he didn't seem upset, but—"

"Oh, no need to apologize. People take that kind of news in different ways. I think Jordan was upset." He wasn't sure it was about Toller, but he kept that to himself.

Kendall smiled. "Well, yes. I'm glad you understand."

Ben Sheridan heard a tapping sound on the driver's side window of his pickup truck, just a few inches away from his head. His neighbor's fake fingernails, drumming on the glass. For a moment he was tempted to pretend that he didn't hear it. With luck, he'd kill her as he backed out, and get a reduced sentence based on the testimony of his other neighbors. He could claim the camper shell blocked his view, or that the dogs distracted him . . .

Tap-tap-tap. What the hell were those fingernails made of—iron?

He sighed and rolled down the window. She grinned and leaned in, folding her arms over the sill, thrusting her breasts toward him. Despite the fact that the mid-September weather was a little too cool for it, she was wearing her usual ensemble, a skimpy black swimsuit top and pair of tight faded denim shorts that barely covered her ass. It was probably an appealing outfit the first time she wore something like it forty or fifty years ago. She was still slender, but Ben figured she must have spent most of those decades in the sun, because as far as he was concerned, these days she just looked like beef jerky in a bikini.

"I'm in a real hurry, Alice," he said brusquely, leaning away from her. "Mind stepping back from the truck?"

"Hello, Professor!" she said, as if he hadn't spoken. She flipped her straight, shoulder-length hair—with a slight green tinge from the chlorine in her pool—away from her face and looked back at the bloodhound and the German Shepherd. "Hi, Bingle! Hi, Bool! Going on a search?" He knew where her own searching eyes would look next, and felt himself tense. Someone unaware of her particular proclivities might have mistaken the direction of her gaze. But Ben knew she wasn't staring at his crotch. She was staring at his lower left leg.

He was grateful that he had jeans on today, not because they hid the prosthesis he wore, but because he knew that Alice was hoping to catch a glimpse of the point where his left leg had been amputated below the knee.

"Ben, why don't you come over for a swim?" she said, still not looking at his face.

"Alice!" he shouted.

She blinked and shook her head, as if he had awakened her from a trance.

"I have to leave right now," he gritted out. "Immediately. I'm in a hurry."

"Okay. Well, come on by later." She took one step back.

He wasn't going to waste this chance. He put the

truck in reverse, glanced behind him and backed out. He drove off, not looking in the rearview mirror until he was sure he was too far away for her to run after him. She stood motionless in his driveway.

He noticed Bingle watching him from his crate. The dark, longhaired shepherd (shepherd and some other breed—no one was quite certain of the mix) was cocking his head to one side.

"I don't know what to do about her, either, Bingle," Ben said.

Bingle—whose first of three owners had named him *Bocazo*, Spanish for "big mouth,"—began to answer at length with a series of sounds that Ben was convinced were an attempt to imitate human vocal tones.

Bool thumped his tail against his own crate. The bloodhound was an amiable fellow, not half as bright as Bingle, but nevertheless excellent at his work. Together, there were few search situations they couldn't cover.

That was thanks to David, he knew. Ben had taken over the handling and training of the dogs after his close friend and colleague, David Niles, had been murdered by the same man who had left Ben an amputee. Ben was adjusting to life with a prosthesis— he had returned to work, was active, was in a great relationship with a woman who also trained search dogs. But David's death still haunted him.

No day passed without a reminder of him. The dogs were the strongest reminder, of course. David had survived a childhood of physical abuse—in part, he had told Ben, because the aunt who raised him after his abusive father's death had interested David in training dogs. David used his knowledge of dog training and anthropology for volunteer search and rescue work, and for cadaver dog work—to search for the missing, or their remains.

Ben never started a search without thinking of David, and of all the work David had put into these dogs, all the affection he had given them. Ben didn't believe he had David's capacity for forgiveness, but continuing David's work was important to him, a way of saying David's work had mattered. And despite the inherent stress in trying to find missing persons before they came to harm, Ben found he enjoyed the search and rescue work.

He glanced at the directions Frank Harriman had given him and forced himself to concentrate on the job at hand. Frank Harriman and his wife—Irene Kelly—were among Ben's closest friends. Frank had called a few minutes ago to ask Ben if he would bring his search dogs to a neighborhood about seven miles from Ben's home.

"We've got a homicide, a male in his late thirties," Frank had said. "Turns out he was a widower, raising a kid on his own. We're just starting to work here, but we can't locate the boy. There are some indications that he might have been taken from the home, maybe even injured. We want to find him as soon as possible, of course, and I thought you might be able to help out."

"You said his name is Alex?" Ben asked, studying the boy's photograph.

"No," Frank said. "Lexington. Neighbors call him Lex or Lexie. Think you'll be able to help us out here?"

"Hope so," Ben said absently, not looking up from the photo. A skinny kid with straight blonde hair, a crooked smile, and dark circles beneath his blue eyes looked back at him. "You have anything more recent? In this photo, he looks as if he's younger than eight—five or so, maybe."

Frank shrugged. "Neighbors say he looks like that one, that he's small for his age. You know how it is with searches for kids—they change quickly, but the parents don't take as many photos once the kids are school age. And it doesn't look as if Toller was exactly staying on top of things here, does it?"

Ben looked toward the body of Victor Toller, which lay face down on the living room carpet, in a north-south position, so that his head was not far from the front door. Toller was a little over six feet tall, big-boned, with thick arms and broad shoulders. And a skull that had taken several crushing blows during a struggle that had left its mark on the living room.

Ben noticed a shotgun propped near the front door. "I take it the gun hasn't been fired?"

"No, not recently. It's loaded, though. Neighbors say that was always there."

"Christ, with a kid that young in the house?"

"He wasn't anybody's idea of Mr. Responsible, it seems."

Ben glanced around the room. He doubted it had been orderly even before Toller met his fate. It reeked of booze and cigarette smoke, mixed with the rancid scent of cold greasy food. Empty bottles could be found on almost every flat surface. A quick glance at their labels showed that Toller's tastes seemed to have varied from vodka to beer and cheap red wine.

Crumpled paper wrappers, plastic foam hamburger boxes, and other scattered "to go" containers made up a monument to meals purchased at drive-up windows. A chair not far from the body had been knocked over. There were bloodstains on it.

There were bloodstains consistent with Toller's head injury, apparently delivered by the heavy fireplace poker being photographed by an evidence technician. Ben could see blood and hair on it. He glanced across the room, and saw the rest of the set of tools near the fireplace. There were no ashes in the fireplace.

Ben said, "You think his attacker probably dropped him where he stood?"

The evidence technician looked up, first at Ben, and then at Frank.

"It's all right," Frank said to the technician. "He's authorized to be here. This is Dr. Ben Sheridan. He's a forensic anthropologist, but he's also a search dog handler. He's going to help us look for the boy. Ben, this is Mark Collier, one of our crime scene specialists."

Collier nodded. "Good to meet you. Look up on the ceiling and this nearest wall—judging from the spatter patterns, someone swung hard, connected, then stood over him here and made sure he was a goner. You should show him the boy's room, Frank. Dr. Sheridan, if I can be of help, let me know."

"Who found the body?"

"Toller has a hunting buddy who came by for him about five this morning. Got a little worried when he saw the car here but didn't get an answer, so he looked in the window and saw this."

Frank carefully led Ben down a hallway—both of them doing their best not to disturb another technician, who was trying to raise prints from the hall door. "Note that there are no visible bloodstains leading away from the body or on the hall carpet up to this point," Frank said, as they reached a bedroom door. "So, my guess is the same as yours—Toller didn't get up again after he received that blow. But what worries me is that there are some bloodstains in the boy's bedroom, and some blood drops leading from here."

Ben saw crime lab markers near a few blood spots on the hall floor. He bent closer, and saw that they were slightly elongated, as if whoever was bleeding was moving. He looked toward the end of the hall, where sunlight came in through the barred window of a door. "That leads to the backyard?"

"Yes."

"Why the bars? Is there some treasure in the kid's room?"

"Far from it. Take a look," Frank said, gesturing to a doorway to the left. "At first glance, I wondered if this room was some sort of guest room. Didn't seem lived in. Especially not by a boy. Toller had a gun collection in his own room. I suspect that's what the bars were for."

When he looked in Lex's room, Ben agreed—it didn't look like a child's room at all. No toys were visible, just a few school books, aligned with the corner of a small desk. No posters or pennants on the walls. No radio, no CD player. No computer or electronic games. Not so much as a teddy bear. Another crime lab worker was photographing the two exceptions to the orderliness—the shattered glass of a picture frame and bloodstains on the pillow of the otherwise neatly made twin bed. Some of the shards of glass from the frame were bloodstained, too. In the photo, a thin, dark-haired woman held Lex in an affectionate hug. "Is this the boy's mother?" Ben asked.

"I don't think so. Neighbors say the mother was blonde, and died about four years ago. When I described the woman in the photo, they told me she's probably his aunt—his mother's sister. She was over here last night, and two of the neighbors heard loud arguing."

"You've tried to reach her?"

"Pete just talked with her."

"So does your partner think the boy could be with her?"

"She says no, but Pete's still not sure about that. With the blood you see here—you can understand why I'd like to have Bingle and Bool go through the place."

"Yes. I'll start with Bool. Is there a laundry hamper here?"

There were socks and underwear in the hamper, along with a pair of pajamas. "Anybody else touch these clothes today?"

Frank asked Collier, who said, yes, there was a pre-liminary look through the hamper—the outfit the kid was last seen wearing was not with the other laundry, so they were assuming he was still in his jeans and T-shirt.

"Why don't you pre-scent the dog with that bloody pillowcase?" Collier asked.

"Because I don't know that the blood is the child's."

"Oh."

"Maybe the bathroom—"

"Looked like somebody had washed up in there," Collier said. "Towels were a little damp. May have bandaged a wound—there were fragments of gauze in the wastebasket."

Ben raised a brow and turned to Frank. "Toothbrush or fireplace poker—you want the child or the suspect?"

"Both, but the boy is our first concern."

"Toothbrush it is, then," he said, and went into the bathroom. He used gloves to take the child-sized toothbrush from its holder and placed it in a plastic bag. They walked out to the shady spot where another officer—a dog lover who had worked with Ben on previous cases—was keeping an eye on the crated dogs.

Bingle greeted him with a little song of anticipation, perhaps already smelling Toller's body. Like Bool, Bingle was trained in cadaver work, and probably thought this would be an easy day's work. But it was big, drooling, sweet-natured Bool he'd work with first today.

Frank held the toothbrush bag while Ben put on a daypack with water and other basic supplies for the search. He clipped a small two-way radio on his belt, gave the other one to Frank, and put Bool in his working harness. The harness was necessary for any control over Bool—and for the safety of both Ben and the dog. Once on the trail, the big bloodhound would become oblivious to everything but the scent—he'd walk out into traffic if he was trailing someone who had stepped into the street. David had once told Ben of a time when Bool had been following the trail of a lost hiker, and had gone halfway over a cliffside before David managed to haul him back—the hiker, it turned out, had fallen to his death at the same spot several hours earlier.

Ben wasn't very optimistic about what they'd find in this type of search environment today—concrete and asphalt wouldn't hold the scent the way a more natural environment would. But Bool had surprised him before.

"Since we've got blood drops in the hallway leading toward the back door," he said, "let's start on the back porch."

Frank had done search work with Ben in the past, and knew that his role would be that of "second man." Ben would be focused on the dog, while Frank followed at a short distance to ensure Ben's safety. He'd keep a clear view of the search terrain, call for back up if needed, and take control of the dog if Ben was hurt. With luck, he'd also have the role of helping Lex Toller once he was found. If a suspect was with Lex, Frank would be the one to apprehend him.

When they reached the Tollers' back porch, Ben took the plastic bag from Frank and removed the toothbrush. Making sure the dog had his nose directly over the bristles, Ben said, "Find 'em, Bool!"

With Bool, this pre-scenting—giving the dog a "sample" of Lex's scent to work with—was essential. The dog put his nose to the porch and immediately caught a trail, almost pulling Ben off his feet as he headed to the side of the house. From there, he quickly found a small opening and was ready to burrow under the porch before Ben called him back and praised him.

A burly uniformed officer who had been watching hem with some curiosity said, "He's not under there. That's one of the first places we looked."

"You looked under the house?"

"Yes, sir. Figured if he was scared, that's where he might hide. I didn't crawl, but I used a flashlight—"

"Let's take another look," Frank said.

"Hold Bool," Ben said. "I'm in jeans, you're in a suit. Let me crawl."

"There's no one under there," the officer said again.

Frank said, "Maybe you should be the one to crawl."

"I'll go," Ben said again, to the officer's relief. "I took up anthropology knowing I'd get to play in the dirt." He took a flashlight from his pack and got down on his stomach.

When the leg of his jeans pulled up enough to reveal his Flex Foot prosthesis, he heard the cop say, "Oh, Jesus, fella, here—let me do it. I didn't know you were a cripple."

Ben looked up at Frank with a look of mock horror. "I'm a cripple? When did that happen?"

Ignoring the officer's flustered attempts to explain himself, Ben put his head through the opening, which looked just wide enough for his shoulders. Bool whimpered, wanting to follow.

Ben didn't immediately go further. He could see that someone else had already crawled there.

"He might not be in here now," Ben called to Frank, "but he's been here. The dirt's soft under here, and I can see hand and footprints. Not big enough to be a man's."

They seemed small even for an eight-year-old, he thought. He tried to avoid the boy's path. The prints seemed to be both coming and going, but he wasn't sure. There were also stains in the dirt that might be blood. Brushing aside thick cobwebs that hung from the joists, he made slow but steady progress. Finally, beneath the front of the house, the trail came to a halt. There was a hollowed out place, a small burrow roughly a yard long and eighteen inches deep. He pointed the flashlight into it and drew in a breath.

"Frank," he said, using the radio. "He's not here now, but I think he has been. And I've found his toys. Come around to the foundation vent at the front of the house. You can see it through there."

Frank brought Bool back to his crate before heading to the side of the house. He then crouched down and looked into the vent, which was missing its cover—assuming that one might have once been on it. Ben's flashlight illuminated the hollowed out space in the dirt. In addition to a red lunch pail and Thermos, he saw a neatly arranged collection of toys and other playthings—miniature cars, a bag of plastic toy soldiers, a flashlight, a grass-stained baseball, a toy periscope, a mirror, a magnifying glass, and two model airplanes that had seen better days.

Frank looked into Ben's face and saw the question that was on his own mind reflected there: what kind of life had this child lived here, if he hid with his toys beneath the house?

"A periscope, flashlight, mirror, and this—" Ben said. He held up an index card that someone had laminated in plastic. A handwritten cheat sheet for Morse ode. "Everything a secret agent—or a kid hiding from his dad—needs."

Frank looked at the houses across the street. Several could be seen from the crawl space vent, including the Kendalls'.

His cell phone rang. He saw his partner's number on the display. "Pete? What's up?"

"Anonymous call just came in saying the kid is alive and well in the woods near Lake Arrowhead. Location was fairly specific, but I thought you might want to know. San Bernardino Sheriff's Department is already on the way up there."

"A call." Frank rubbed his hand over his forehead, thinking about what Pete had just said. "This hasn't been out on any media yet, right?"

"Right. No public information release yet."

"Any trace on the call?"

"Payphone near a convenience market. We've got someone on the way there now, but I'm sure she's long gone."

"She?"

"Caller was female, sounded young."

"The aunt?"

"Not unless she can be two places at once. I was talking to her again when the call came in."

"But it was local? Not from Arrowhead?"

"No, from here in Las Piernas. Makes me worry about the kid, though. It gets damn cold up there at night. Maybe Ben could go up there with the dogs. What do you think?"

He looked back at the Kendall house, thought of Ralph Kendall saying that Jordy had been "out all night."

"Frank?" Pete asked.

"I'll talk to Ben. Meantime, do me a favor and try to find out if Jordy Kendall has a girlfriend."

When Frank, Ben, and the dogs arrived at the search area in the mountains, the Sheriff's Department already had a command post set up, and searchers out, but without any luck. Ben had worked on searches in the area before, and introduced Frank to Greg Fischer, the deputy in charge.

"Ben," Fischer said, looking at his filthy jeans and shirt, "you fall down or something?"

"No, but I take my weekly bath on Sunday, so this only has to last another day."

Frank asked, "Any property near here owned by a family named Kendall?"

"I'll check," Fischer said. Ten minutes later, he told them, "Down the road, about half a mile." He gave Frank the address. "You want to tell me why you want to know?"

"Just a hunch. Connection with the boy's family. Come along if you like."

"I need to coordinate from here, but give me a call if you think you're on to anything. Think we might need a warrant?"

"I don't know. We'll call you if it looks that way."

At the Kendall property, Ben harnessed Bool again. Before long, the dog had picked up a trail. It seemed to lead from the house to the driveway, and down the road a short distance, but the dog lost it after that.

Ben praised him and brought him back to the truck. "Might have been in a vehicle. Bool can some- times track a scent of someone traveling in a vehicle,

ut conditions don't seem to be the best for him
ere."

"He's given us a good start," Frank said. "I called
ischer, and he said to keep him posted. He might pull
ome of his guys over this way to help out."

"Let's give Bingle a try."

Half a mile in the opposite direction from the Sheriff's
earch area, Bingle, who worked off lead, began bark-
ng, and rushed back to Ben.

"He's found him!" Ben said, and praised Bingle in
Spanish, the language he used to give the dog commands, then encouraged him to "refind." The dog
bounded ahead a little, looked back at Ben and
arked.

"He's alive, right?" Frank said, knowing that
ingle was trained to howl when he found a dead
ody, to bark for a live find.

"Yes, but who knows what kind of shape he's in,"
en said, hurrying after the dog, who was impatiently
arking again. He continued in this way for several
ards.

When Ben first saw Lex Toller, the boy was holding
ghtly to Bingle's neck. Once again, Ben thought there
must have been some mistake. Bingle was a big dog,
nd weighed more than many children of that age, but
is child was too small for eight, surely.

Lex was bundled up in a down jacket and a knit
ap—both looked new. Beneath the jacket Ben could
ee a light sweater. He had a pair of soft long pants
n—the type made for hiking in cold weather. The
ocks and shoes he wore looked new as well. There
vas a sleeping bag at his feet, and a supply of energy

bars and water—and a teddy bear. There was a gauze bandage on his chin, a smaller bandage on his hand. There was a bruise on his forehead. He looked at Ben with a mixture of curiosity and apprehension.

"¡Muy bien, Bingle! ¡Qué inteligente eres!" Ben said.

Bingle showed his pleasure at the praise, but stayed with the boy, and seemed willing to let the boy hug him as long as he liked. Not something most dogs enjoyed, but no one would ever convince Ben that Bingle and Bool were like most dogs. Bingle was nuzzling the boy now, then lifted his ears and wagged his tail.

A moment later Ben heard what Bingle had heard first—Frank coming up behind him. He heard Frank stop a few feet away.

"Hi, Lex," Ben said easily. "I'm Ben. That's Bingle. And this is my friend Frank. We've been looking for you."

For a moment, he didn't think the boy would reply, but his brows suddenly pulled together and he asked, "What did you say his name is?"

Ben knew he wasn't asking about the detective. "Bingle."

"Hi Bingle!" he said to the dog, and giggled as he got a kiss on the ear. "Is he a Spanish Shepherd?"

"Mostly German Shepherd," Ben said, moving a little closer. "He understands Spanish and English."

"Good dog, Bingle!" Lex said.

Bingle returned this salutation with another kiss.

"Are you hurt?" Ben asked.

Lex shook his head.

Ben heard Frank making the radio call to Greg Fischer.

"You're sure you're okay?" Ben asked Lex. "I see some bandages."

The boy's hand came up to touch his chin, and his eyes clouded a little. "I want Aunt Sarah."

"Your aunt? Okay. Let us make sure you aren't hurt, and I think we can take you to her."

He shook his head.

"Why not?"

"I have to wait here for the police. I can't leave with anyone else."

"I'm a police officer," Frank said, and held out his badge for Lex to see. "Did Jordy ask you to wait for the police?"

His eyes widened, but he said, "No." He looked away, and petted Bingle. "I want Aunt Sarah," he said again.

They got no other information from him. If they asked him any questions, he said, "I want Aunt Sarah." If he said anything else, it was a question about Bingle—or Bool, once he had been introduced to the bloodhound. He had a nearly endless supply of questions about them.

"Why do these dogs work so hard for you?" he asked Ben at one point.

"We're friends."

"It seems like more than friends," he said. "Like— I don't know what. But more."

"Yes, I guess it is," Ben said. "Devotion."

He thought again of David, and decided he would have liked this day's work.

Greg Fischer guided them to a nearby hospital. A doctor examined Lex, and said that other than the cuts and a few bruises, he was fine. "Not even dehydrated," he said. "And if that kid spent the night outdoors, I'm a monkey's uncle."

"What about the cuts?"

"Those bother me, but they look more like they came from something with a sharp edge—broken glass would be my first guess. And they've already started to heal. Someone rinsed them out and put antibacterial ointment on them."

"And the bruises?"

"Harder to know. He tells me he fell. The newest ones do look like that—consistent with a fall against a piece of furniture. He's got older ones on his back, those look to me like someone hit him with a belt."

While Lex was getting back in the truck, Frank pulled Ben aside. "I know it's been a long day, and you and the dogs deserve to go home and rest. But there's one more thing I'd like to have you check out. You can go home and change, feed them, whatever you need to do, but I think Bool can help us put this together."

Ben listened to his request, thought of Alice in her bikini, and said, "I've got dog food with me. I don't need to go home."

When Frank brought Lex into the Las Piernas Police Department headquarters, Pete and Sarah Crane were waiting for them. Lex's aunt gathered the boy into her arms and held him close to her as she wept with relief. "Oh, Lex, I'm so glad you're safe. Oh, honey, I've been so worried about you."

After a moment, Frank said, "Ms. Crane, we know you're anxious to get home, but we have some questions for both you and Lex, so we'll need to ask you to stay here for a little while longer."

"After all he's been through?" she asked indignantly.

"We're not exactly sure what he has been through, ma'am. Perhaps you'll have better luck than I did persuading him to answer our questions."

She seemed ready to rebel, but then asked, "Have you told him yet?"

He shook his head.

"Lex, do you know what happened to your father?"

He didn't answer.

"Lex, I'm sorry. Your daddy—your daddy is dead."

"I know. Can I live with you now?"

She looked worriedly at Frank.

"Lex, were you there when he died?" he asked. "You aren't in trouble. We just want to know what happened."

He frowned, then said, "I want to go home with Aunt Sarah."

Frank sighed.

"Please Detective Harriman," Sarah Crane said. "I promise we won't leave town or—please, let me take him home. He's been through so much!"

The phone on Frank's desk rang. He answered it while Pete made another try to get Lex to talk about anything other than dogs and where he wanted to live. It was Ben.

"Any luck?" Frank asked.

"Yes. I gave Bool the command to 'find 'em' as he sniffed the ground near the foundation vent. I thought that would be kind of a long shot. He was in and around the house, including the bathroom and the place where the body was earlier in the day. Then he headed across the street."

"To Jordan Kendall's house?"

"To his pick-up truck."

"Let me speak to the officer who's with you. I want that kid down here for questioning, but I want to make sure we handle this right."

"Before you talk to him, I should let you know something else. Bool found this scent near the stand that holds the other fireplace tools. The lab has the poker now, but I'd say whoever was in that pickup truck has been near that stand."

"Thanks, Ben."

Ben was happy to be on his way home with the dogs. His girlfriend, Anna, was already there waiting for him with her own dogs. She had called his cell phone, just to see how his day had gone. He had talked about the successes of the day, but she must have heard something in his voice, because she offered to come over.

"I'll even cook dinner."

"That'd be great," he said. "Besides, Alice won't go near my place if your car is in the driveway."

"Oh yeah, you need me tonight," she said, laughing. "Don't worry. I promise I'm able to defend a grown man with two big dogs from Alice and her sinking cantaloupes."

He laughed and told her he'd see her soon.

Maybe by the end of the night, he wouldn't be thinking so much about small boys who kept treasures under houses.

* * *

Ralph Kendall was undoubtedly pacing in the room next to them, Frank thought. He had willingly brought Jordan with him to the LPPD Headquarters, and Frank was glad that he had not yet had to place Jordan under arrest—the rules changed with custody. But the Kendalls had come here voluntarily. He separated them, telling Kendall that for legal reasons, they needed to talk to witnesses separately. That much was true. He was under no legal obligation to be truthful when questioning witnesses. At eighteen, Jordan Kendall could be questioned out of the presence of his father.

"Jordan, we know you were inside the Toller house," Frank began.

Jordan stared at his folded hands and said nothing.

"And Lex was found not far from your family's cabin. He's told us you brought him there." A lie, but it didn't seem to concern Jordan.

"We record all 9-1-1 calls," Frank said, and for the first time, saw that he had Jordan's attention. "Your girlfriend—" Frank consulted his notes. "Monica? Her voice is on the tape, giving directions to find Lex that were a little mixed up. That could have led to his death, of course, but we were lucky. We found him anyway."

He watched the young man shift in his seat.

"We have witnesses that saw her make the call, so she's good for an accessory to kidnapping charge, and we can probably make her an accessory to Toller's murder while we're at it."

He turned pale.

"Didn't think about that when you involved her, did you?"

"She had no idea what I was asking her to call about," he said.

"She can tell that to the jury, of course. Maybe they'll believe her when she says that if someone asks her to call the police and tell them where to find a little boy in the woods, she thinks nothing of it."

He put his head in his hands. "Don't do anything to Monica. I'm the one you want. For everything. I killed Toller. I took Lex to the mountains. All of it." He looked up at Frank in defiance, and said, "And I'm proud of it! I'd do it again."

Frank waited, then said, "Tell me what happened."

"You see those cuts on Lex's face and hand? You know how he got them? His old man smashed a photograph of Lex and his Aunt Sarah into his face. That big man, smashing glass into that little kid's face! Lex put a hand up to defend himself, but that just meant his hand got cut, too."

"Had Toller ever hit his son before?"

Jordan looked away. "I don't know. I think he did, but Lexie would never tell me. One time I told him I'd beat the crap out of his dad if his dad ever hurt him, and he said I'd better not, because his dad would shoot me. Even if he didn't beat him, he hurt him in other ways. His dad picked on him, he always said mean things to him. Didn't even feed him. Toller was a drunken son of a bitch who could go on a binge and forget he had a kid. Lex ate more food from our kitchen than he did from that one over there. You see his room? His dad wouldn't let him have toys."

"I saw his hiding place. There were toys there."

Jordan shook his head. "I gave those to him. I felt sorry for him. So did my mom. We gave him Gabe's hand-me-downs so he'd have something to wear. He's so small, Gabe's clothes from kindergarten fit him when he's in third grade."

"So your parents thought he was abused, too?"

"They called a social worker on him once. She made Toller clean up the house, and after about three months, that was that. Everything went back to the way it was. My parents said Lex would have been taken away if anything really bad had been going on. Shows what they know. That was before Sarah found Lex." He looked pleadingly at Frank. "They'll let her take him won't they? They won't put him in a home, or anything like that, will they?"

"She'll probably be able to keep him."

He sighed. "Then it's worth it." But Frank thought he looked scared.

"Did Lex call you to come over after he was hurt?"

Jordan nodded. "Not call, really. Just after Lex went in from the baseball game, his aunt came over. We knew his dad was pissed off at Sarah. We all heard them arguing. Heard him yelling that Lex would never live with her as long as he had anything to say about it. When he was in a mood like that, Mr. Toller was a real asshole. Lex almost always hides under the house when his dad is drunk and awake. So, I was kind of watching out for a signal. Sure enough, he sent one. You saw the mirror?"

"And the Morse code."

"Yeah, well, he knew I'd be watching for word from him. So, when I got over there, and Lex crawled out, he was scared—and he'd been hurt. He was cut and bleeding. It pissed me off. So I went in the house, and told Toller he was a big old asshole and to quit picking on Lex. We fought."

"Where?"

"In the living room. Near the door. He went for this gun of his that he keeps by the door, and I grabbed the poker and whacked him with it as hard as I could. I—I kept hitting him." He swallowed hard. "I guess I went a little crazy. But once I knew he was dead, I cleaned up Lex and got him out of there."

"He was willing to go with you after seeing you kill his father?"

"He was still outside. I made sure he didn't even see his dad. I took him over to my truck and told him to wait in it. I went into my house and took some winter clothes Gabe hardly ever wore, and a teddy bear he never played with, and gave them to Lex. I brought him up to the cabin. I stayed with him overnight, and early this morning, I set him up where I thought he'd be easy to find. Then I came home. If you hadn't found him soon, I was going to go back up there to make sure he was okay."

Frank thought this through, then had Jordan go over it again several times.

Pete knocked, stuck his head in the door. "Frank, can I borrow you for a minute?"

When Frank stepped out and closed the door, Pete said, "Look, I've been listening in the other room, and so has the lieutenant. Congratulations on the confession, but hasn't your day been long enough? You've got more than enough to hold him."

"Something's not right. He's in an argument with Toller, Toller is within reach of a gun, and this kid manages to cross a trash-filled room and reach a fireplace poker, grab it, cross the room again and bash Toller's head in before Toller notices any of this, or turns around?"

"Kid was young and fast."

"Pete—"

"Ah, all right. So Toller wasn't going for the gun."

"You saw where the body was."

Pete sighed. "Well, somebody hit him with that poker before he got to the door, that's for damned sure."

"I wonder. Call the coroner's office and see if we can get somebody to take a look at Toller tonight. I want to make sure the poker is the weapon."

"Want to make sure—you saw the hair and blood!"

"If you call right away, we might be able to get a preliminary tonight."

"Miracles. He wants miracles," Pete said, but went to make the call.

While he waited for the coroner's report, he asked Jordan more questions, ones that seemed to make him more uneasy than recounting the details of the actual murder.

"Where are the clothes you were wearing when you killed him?"

He hesitated, then said, "I threw them away."

"Where?"

"I don't remember."

"Your house? The cabin?"

"I don't remember."

"What about the clothes Lex was wearing?"

"I threw them away, too."

"Why?"

"He had bled on them, when his father cut his chin."

"Where were you when you changed your clothes?"

"I don't know!"

"You know what I think, Jordan? I don't think you did kill Toller."

Jordan looked panicked. "Yes, I did! You gotta believe me."

"I don't."

"Why would I lie about that? Why would anybody lie about that?"

"To protect someone they care about."

"I'm not saying anything more to you. Weren't you supposed to read me my rights or something?"

"You aren't under arrest."

"I'm not under arrest? I confessed to murder and I'm not under arrest? What the hell kind of police department is this? I can't remember where I dropped off my dirty laundry, and you're going to let me go free?"

Pete returned, and motioned Frank out of the room again.

"Good call, Frank. Coroner says the poker wasn't the murder weapon. Something bigger hit him first. He was already dead. What do you think this kid's game is?"

"Is Sarah Crane still here?"

"Yes, and not happy about it."

"Bring her and Lex down here."

"Lex?" Jordan said. "Don't tell them anything."

"Jordan, what is going on here?" Sarah asked.

Jordan just shook his head.

"Lex, Jordan is really a great friend, isn't he?" Frank said.

Lex nodded.

"He's in big trouble right now. And I only know ne person who can help him."

"Lex, I'm not even under arrest."

Frank stayed silent.

"Lex, do you know something about your father's eath?" Sarah asked.

Lex nodded.

"Lex, no!" Jordan said.

"You butt in again," Frank said to him, "And I'll ave you locked up."

Lex's eyes grew round. "Don't hurt him!"

"It's okay," Jordan said quickly. "He's not going to urt me. Nobody's going to hurt anybody. Not any-nore."

Lex looked from Jordan to Frank.

Frank said, "He wants me to arrest him, Lex. But I on't want to."

"Jordan?" Sarah asked. "What's going on?"

"Jordan won't give you a straight answer," Frank aid. "His intentions are good, and he's trying to be a ood friend to Lex. Lex has needed his protection, nd I think Jordan would do just about anything for im. But he isn't thinking about how hard it will be on Gabe and his father and his stepmother if he goes to ail."

"Jordan, you said nothing bad would happen to ou!" Lex said.

Jordan leaned his elbows on the table, and covered is face with his hands, but didn't answer.

"Aunt Sarah visited me," Lex said quickly, as if n a rush to set things straight. "I was bragging to er, because I'd just hit a home run. But my dad heard us talking, and he looked out the window. He saw us walking before I could hide my baseball things."

"Under the house?" Frank asked.

Lex nodded.

"Victor grew angry with me because I bought Lex a baseball bat," Sarah said. "A baseball bat—can you believe it? But Victor said Lex couldn't have anything he didn't give him, and he never gave the poor child a thing."

"He said I was bad. He said I wasn't good enough to have toys," Lex said.

"That's the sort of thing he often said to Lex," Sarah said. "Victor and I argued about that, and a number of other subjects before I left last night."

"He was drunk," Lex said.

"Another thing that happened a lot," Sarah put in.

"He said I could never live with her. He said I couldn't play baseball any more, or go over to Gabe's house, or talk to Jordan. I figured it was just talk, but then he wrecked my picture."

Frank crouched down so that he was eye-level with the boy. "Your father hit you on the face with the picture of you and your aunt, didn't he Lex? That's how you got the cuts?"

Lex nodded. "It—it made me really mad. I had been mad before, but this time, I don't know, I just couldn't take it. I told him I was going to tell on him. I told him I was going to tell Jordan, because Jordan said that if he ever hurt me again, he was going to kick my dad's ass. And he would have, too!"

Jordan looked up at him. "Lexie—don't say anything more."

Lex shook his head. "I don't care if they put me in jail."

"No one's going to put you in jail," Sarah said, but she looked uncertainly at Frank.

"He said he'd teach Jordan not to put ideas in my head," Lex went on. "He said he was going to kill him. I tried to grab on to him, to stop him. I said, 'Pick on someone your own size!' He pushed me down, and I hit my head. But I fell down near my baseball bat. He was laughing, and making fun of me. You know, saying 'Pick on someone your own size!' over and over. So I picked up the baseball bat and I got up on top of the chair, because then I was his own size, and I told him to stop. He thought that was real funny. He said, 'Soon as I take care of your friend, I'm going to make you stand on that chair while I whip you.' He turned around and was starting to reach for that shotgun, and so—so I swung the bat and hit him. Hard."

Tears started rolling down his face, and he brushed them away. "He didn't move. I hated him. But I didn't mean to kill him. I just didn't want him to hurt Jordan."

"And Jordan came over and tried to help you?"

"He tried to make it look like he did it—with the poker. He hid the bat, because it had my fingerprints on it. Jordan always tries to help me. No matter what I do wrong, he's good to me. When nobody else liked me, Jordan was my friend. He liked me even before Gabe. He stuck up for me. He taught me baseball." He moved over to Jordan and said, "That came in handy, don't you think?"

Jordan put an arm around his shoulders. "Lex, you say the damnedest things."

Lex hugged him tightly.

*   *   *

The long evening grew longer, but by the end of it, Lex
was released into Sarah Crane's custody, and Jordan
went home with Ralph Kendall. After many discussions with attorneys and district attorneys, no charges
were brought against anyone involved in the case.
Sarah had already started taking Lex to see a
counselor—more, she said, to help Lex get over eight
years of hell than one night of finally escaping it.
Neighbors, teachers, and friends wrote letters to the
district attorney on both Lex's and Jordan's behalf.

"Look out, Jordan!" Lex shouted, but his warning
came too late—as Frank watched, Bingle intercepted
the baseball throw and slyly lured the other players
into a game of chase.

Due to public pressure, the D.A. decided quickly
not to pursue a case against Lex. But Jordan was an
adult, and baseball season was starting up again by
the time the D.A. told Jordan that he had finally
decided that no charges would be brought against
him.

On the day they got the news, Jordan agreed to
meet Frank and Ben at Sarah Crane's house. Ben
brought the dogs along, too. Lex took Jordan's good
news as if expected, but the presence of the dogs drew
a response of unbridled enthusiasm. Frank thought he
saw changes that went beyond the fact that his cheeks
were no longer hollow, that the dark circles beneath
his blue eyes were almost gone. That look of apprehension around adult men—always excepting Jordan—
wasn't completely gone, but there was a little more
confidence in the way he moved.

Ben saw it, too, and again thought of David. aybe with the help of Sarah and his friends, Lex ould be okay. Maybe someday Lex would find mething in life that would mean as much to him as arch and rescue work had meant to David.

When he had worn down from playing with the gs, Lex sat down beside them.

Ben said, "I hear you gave a lot of help to Jordan. ot people to write letters, things like that."

"I had to. With me and Jordan—he's my friend, but s more than friendship. It's—what was that word u said, about the dogs? I don't think people have it often, but they should."

Ben frowned in concentration, but Frank remem-red it first.

"Devotion."